Captain Bacawly

and the
Breakaway Bandits

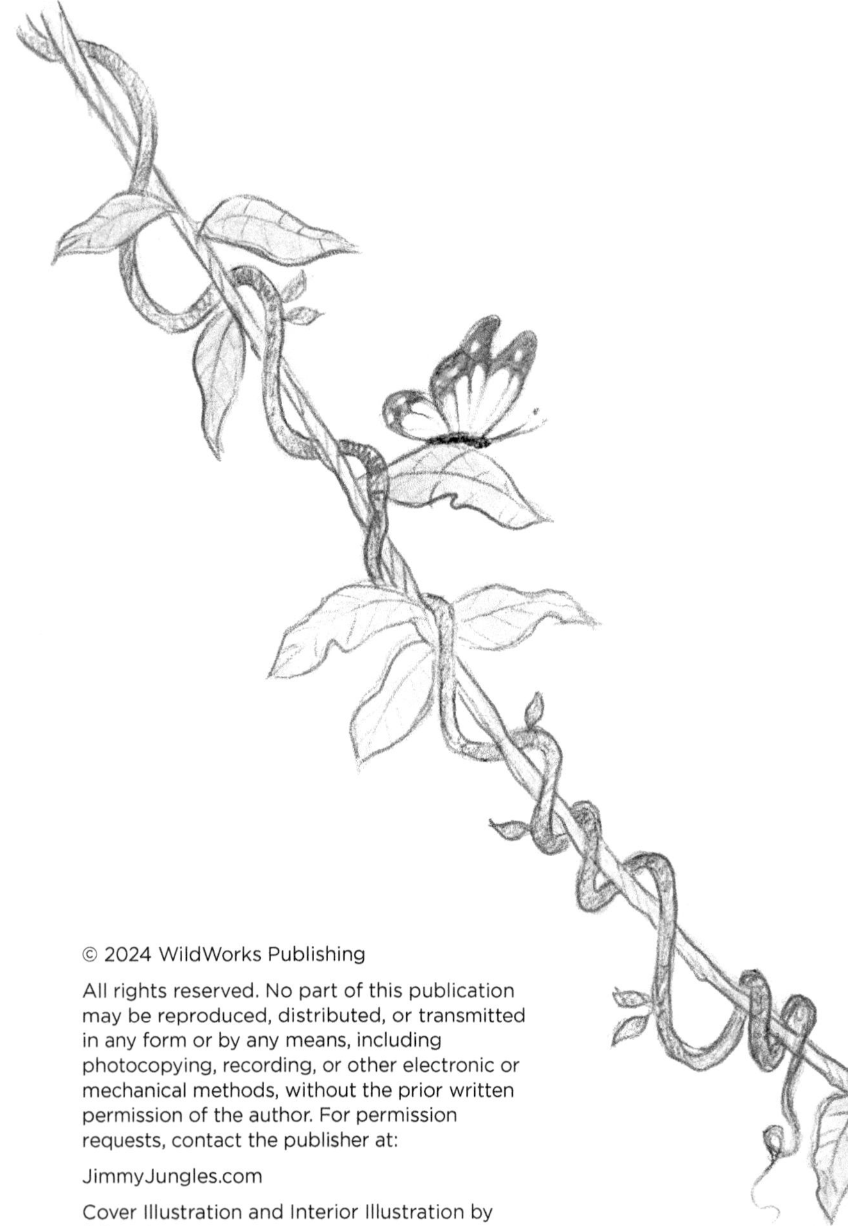

JimmyJungles.com

Cover Illustration and Interior Illustration by Oliver Itson

Interior design by AnnetteWoodGraphics.com

Printed in the United States

ISBN: 979-8-9906813-0-9

Dedicated to all who are lost,
all who struggle, and yet still
dare to dream so big.
—Jimmy

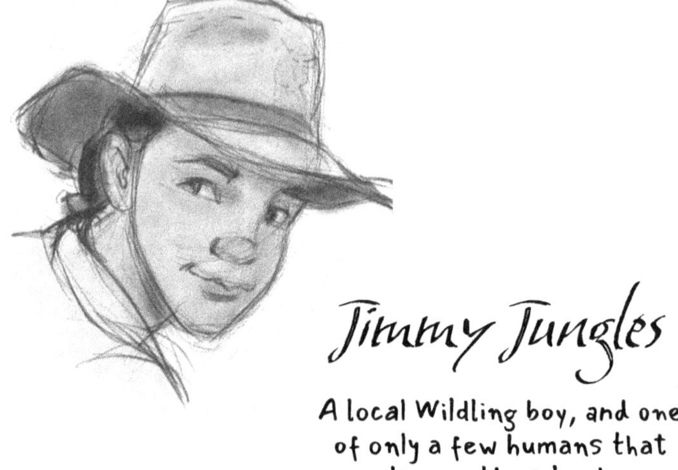

Jimmy Jungles

A local Wildling boy, and one
of only a few humans that
live on the island.

The Wazoo is all I've ever known and I
have had plenty of fun with my animal
friends all these years. But thirteen has
been different. The old fun things I used
to do don't feel the same anymore.

Lately, I've only been wanting to try new
things in an attempt to understand this
odd society of ours. So, I've decided to
write this journal in hopes of describing
my new friends and adventures.

And who knows, maybe I'll even find out
what it is I really want along the way.

Contents

Discover the Wazoo

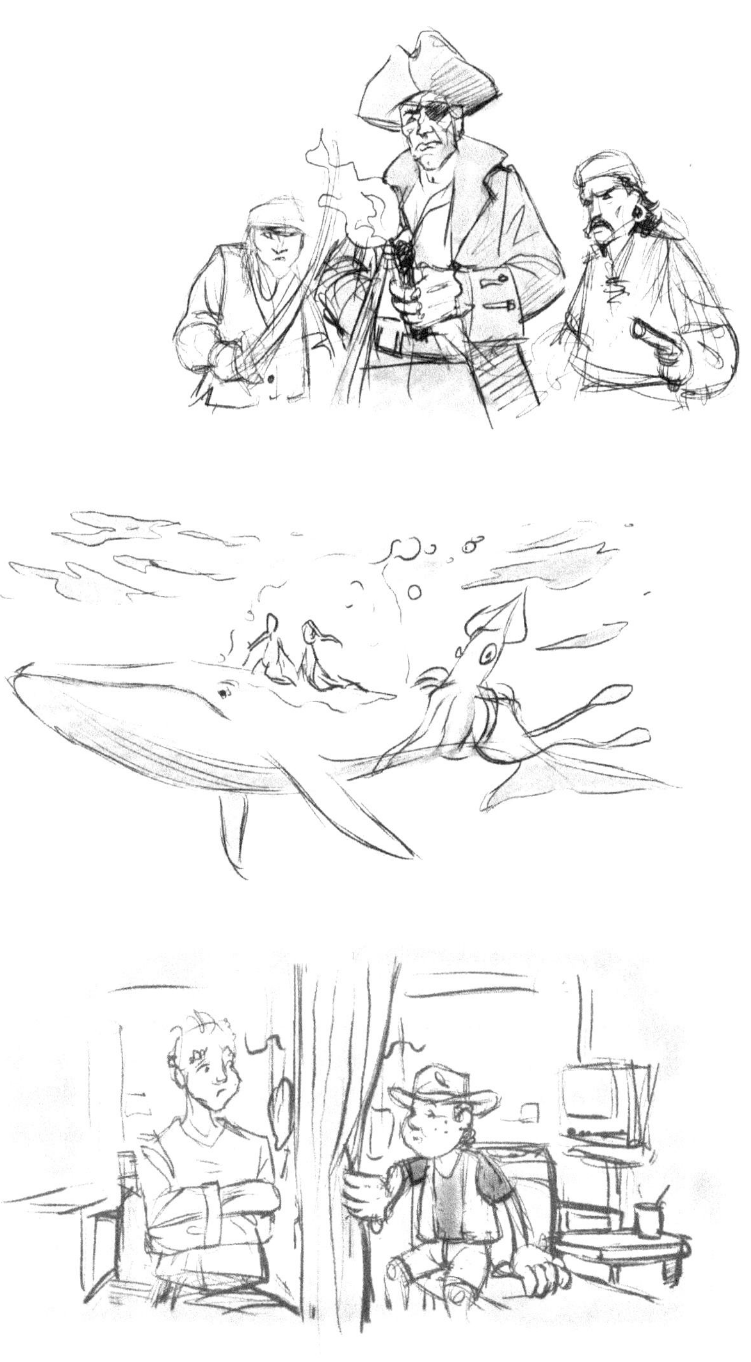

Captain Bacawly

and the
Breakaway Bandits

by

Jimmy Jungles

The Lost Island of the Wazoo

IT ALL STARTED WITH A DREAM. One that took me away from my treehouse home where I would invite all my exotic animal friends, away from a beautiful island where flowers of every color grew through crystal clear ponds, around large ancient boulders, and up thousand-foot-tall trees.

As you can guess, the Wazoo is no ordinary place, and I am one of the few lucky enough to call it home. I could go rhino racing down the mountain sides, play bumper boats in the swirling swamps, slide through mud pits all weekend long, and jump along the bouncy lily pads off Bayuga Bay. This was the only life

I knew, and for better or worse, it was all about to change.

But it all started with a dream. I woke up alone on a rotting wooden floor. Wet dirt pressed against my face while I rubbed my eyes to look around the small, dark room. There was a dry taste of salt in the air, and all I could hear were large waves crashing against the walls, rocking me back and forth. A coldness held me tight as I tried to figure out where I was.

Cwhhhhhh! Cawwcahhhhh!

A loud call came from outside. I slowly pushed open the creaking door and walked down the hallway, taking a bright lantern hanging against the wall with me. Rain slipped through the ceiling above and thunder banged across the sky. As I reached a large room, I raised the light to see a bunch of dirty smelling men with ragged old clothing snoring away, some with glass bottles, others with a long metal stick beside them.

Cawwcahhhhh! Cawwcahhhhh!

The same call got louder from above. I walked past these long black tubes with large metal balls beside them and gently walked up the stairwell. I had never seen anything like this before at the Wazoo, and I was beginning to wonder just how far from home I was right now.

I lightly pushed on the hatch before strong gusts of wind ripped it wide open. Rain poured down harder and felt like little needles as a strong breeze knocked me back. I lifted the lantern, trying to see what was in the darkness around me. Something was moving just up ahead. I could see it staring at me with its large eyes, waiting for me to come closer. I crept up slowly, not sure what was about to appear.

From the shadows emerged a large bird, staring at me with the same awe I saw in it. It must have been over twenty feet high and had dark brown feathers with a bold yellow beak.

Was this giant beast calling in the middle of the night? What did it want? Why was it here? Why was I here? None of this made sense. Maybe it wasn't even real. *A dream!* I thought to myself, just then and there, *this was all just a dream,* I said to myself over and over again. It had to be. And soon, I would be waking up back in my treehouse surrounded by all my Wildling friends and family back in the Wild. As for now, all I could do was to stay calm and wait, hoping this would all be over soon.

Cwhh, Cwhh!

The bird called lightly as it walked closer and leaned down to see me. I could feel my whole body shaking while the large bird tilted its head and stared. After a few seconds, it moved its beak to the side of its wing, shuffling through the feathers as if it were searching for something. It turned its head back around and leaned back towards me, clenching a small, shiny stone, almost too bright to look at. I put my hand out as it gently dropped it. *Was this why the bird was calling me the whole time? How did it even know I was here? What was this stone?*

"Wh-what is this? What do I do with this?" I asked, wondering if it could even understand me, but the bird continued to stare.

Cwwhhhh! Cawwwwcahhhhh!

It called to me eagerly, moving its head towards the sea. But I had no idea what to do.

"What? What is this? Where am I? What am I doing here?" I asked harshly, but the bird moved back, staying silent as it fluttered its heavy wings and flew up into the air. "Wait, where are you going? Come back! Come back!" I said, trying to chase it.

I looked back at the stone. Maybe it was a clue. Maybe if I raised it in the air, the bird would come back. I waved it high, but nothing happened, so I looked into it, trying to keep my eyes open and see past the illuminating light. I was confused. Lost. Not sure what to do, or still even close to knowing where I was. So, I looked around. I had never seen a boat quite this large, nor one with a wheel right at the center of it all. *Maybe I could steer this whole thing with it! Maybe I was supposed to follow the bird or at least go back home.*

Right when I was about to walk over, a pair of doors slammed open, and two men walked outside towards me, one holding a large, scrolled piece of paper open, looking at it carefully while the other one shouted at him. I quickly hid behind a couple of barrels before they could see me in plain sight.

"Are you sure this is it? We *cannot* screw this up, the captain will be furious!"

"I assure you, we are headed in the right direction. I have never seen anything like this before. The boy's map is certainly the one the legends have spoken of," he said as he held up the glowing paper.

"So that's it then? Within days, we shall arrive at the rumored island? Where they say dreams can never die?"

"Yes," the man said calmly, scrolling up the long piece of paper and putting it back into his coat pocket. "The Lost Island of the Wazoo, the wonder of the world, the isle of paradise, hidden from us no longer. And soon, we shall be the first men in history to ever find it."

A tall man wearing a long, black coat walked slowly as he approached the men standing off to the side, his metal boot thumping against the creaking floors. I couldn't see his face but I noticed his tight metal fist and patch on his eye. A large black, red-eyed crocodile with chains shackled around its neck walked next to him and slowly looked around. For a second, I thought it was looking at me, and I quickly turned away from it.

"Who left this yer lantern on me deck?" he asked angrily in a weird accent.

"Oh, I'm sorry, Captain, I will get that immediately! It must have been one of the crew, I'll mak-"

"Are we almost there? Three months I've been at this now, scramblin' the seas, goin' nowhere, all cuz of you!"

"We will be there soon, my Captain. The boy's map has been correct so far," the navigator said, keeping his head down. The scar-faced man turned and quickly lifted him up by the neck.

"For yer sake, I do hope so! Me crocs have been gettin' hungry, *restless* these past few days. Might hav' to give 'em somethin' to eat, a *new* meal ta' taste," he said before throwing him and then quickly walking away.

The two men followed behind their captain, and

all I could think about was what they were saying. *The Lost Island of the Wazoo? My home? Why did these strange men want to come to my home?*

But while I was lost in my thoughts, trying to figure out what they were saying, the lantern hit the ground and shattered. I looked around to see if anyone was around, but no one was in sight. I started to breathe heavily as metal chains clanked across the floor. Suddenly, the black crocodile lunged at me with its long mouth wide open. I threw myself back, trying to kick it away, but it crept faster towards me.

I was standing on the ledge of the giant ship as it tore through the wooden railings with its teeth. I tried to jump away and towards its back, but I was quickly lashed by its long scaly tail and fell into the cold deep sea. I couldn't even open my eyes or move as the cold chill wrapped itself around me again, the ice water brushing through my veins and freezing my body. *This must be a dream. This all had to be a dream!*

Cwwhhhh! Cawwwcahhhhh!

That was the last thing I remembered...

Chapter 2

The Vacuum Incident

I WOKE UP ACHING IN PAIN on my bedroom floor. The dream must have shaken me from my study desk. I don't know how long I was down here, but apart from the pain, my mind kept racing. What was that? Why was I on a large boat talking to a bird with some ragged men looking at a map? What did any of it mean? This was the strangest dream I've ever had. Never in my life did I have one quite like that. Is this what happens when you turn thirteen? You start to get terrifying nightmares every time you close your eyes?

I did my best not to think about it. I brushed off the dust on my khaki vest and wrinkled green shirt before putting my silver tree necklace back underneath it. I hopped back on my feet and sat down at my study table, hoping I had gotten further on my essay than before. Nope. Not a single word added since I had plopped myself into this seat a few hours ago. I was supposed to finish a seven-page paper and I had barely come up with two paragraphs. I couldn't even tell you what I was writing about. These were just words on a page as far as I knew. And the best part about it was that it was all due tomorrow.

"Jimmy, can you come out here please!" Damien, my small gray furred pet dog with large circular glasses asked from outside my door. "Sal, ugh, he's just making a mess! And he invited the Dardo brothers too! It's chaos, absolute chaos!"

"Yeah... I'll be there in a second," I said, rubbing my eyes and yawning as I opened the door.

"They're running around, knocking things over and just throwing food everywhere! It's terrible. I tried to make them stop but they just won't listen!"

"It's fine Damien. I'll tell them to clean it up," I said while putting my notebook and book back into my satchel.

"By the way, did you finish your essay yet?"

Yeah I-uh am alm—"

KLPSHHHH

I jumped as I heard a plate shatter from the kitchen. "Ugh. Sal, SAL! Stop throwing things!" Damien yelled as he ran back across the rope bridge and to the main hut of my family's treehouse. We had a nice home, similar to many of the other Wildlings who lived in the jungle, and I always felt blessed to have such great neighbors in our small town of Laetta.

"Morning, Mrs. Pacaya!" I said to a red, long winged Lagia bird who was flying by. She was one of the sweetest neighbors I had.

"Oh, hello, sweetheart! Beautiful day, isn't it?"

"Hey, Mr. Hobbs!" I said as I waved to my mole neighbor, but I don't think he heard me. He was in his head while dragging a suitcase along, probably frustrated about one of his trial cases as usual.

"Make sure your mom knows this wasn't me! I tried to stop them, Jimmy. I tried my best!" Damien said anxiously, but I was actually surprised, thinking it was going to be much, much worse than it was.

I wasn't completely surprised by what I saw. You see this wasn't the first time Sal got into a food fight with a couple of friends from school. In fact, I was practically used to it by now, I'd even been in a few myself.

"Damien, relax," I said coolly as I pulled my green pet snake out from under a box of Cornley's Power Pops cereal, He squirmed around spilling the small sugary pieces. I couldn't tell if he was actually stuck or just trying to eat. "Sal, what are you doing?" I said as I lifted him up.

"Oh, Jimmy! Hey! Uh-well the Dardos came over, and well, you know how rowdy they are! They started throwing chips at me, so you know I had to—"

"Can so-somebody please help get me out of this bagel!" a small green bird groaned while rolling around on my dining room table. "It's too heavy," he said, trying to nudge it off him. And there were bagels all over the room, on the floor, hanging off the coat rack, heck I even saw one stuck in the tape player for all the movies we'd get. Sal must have literally been whipping them around.

"You are so mean, Sal!" said his yellow bird brother.

"Hey! You threw a box of cereal over my head!" said Sal as he slithered over to confront the two birds.

"Guys! Stop fighting, alright? Just clean it up. I don't need my parents on me again," I said just as I walked into a puddle of milk. I pulled off my soaked socks and left them on the floor as I walked over to the couch to see two other neighborhood friends of mine, Goran, a prickly little porcupine, and Forsef, a light-furred ferret, sitting on my couch completely covered in mud.

"Wh-did you guys just go mud sliding?" I asked before crashing next to them on the couch. I saw their dirty prints everywhere, from the TV, couch, table, remote, even on a can of Cracker O's and on the bag of Salty Split's chips.

"Well, you were too busy looking around for all those fruits and berries with your friends. I told ya, Jimmy, there ain't too many!" Goran said before he shoved more chips into his mouth.

Normally, I would be upset with all the messes I had seen, but I wasn't sure if it was because of my dream or all the angst of trying to start the essay I had due tomorrow. For some reason, I just didn't care about anything today and I couldn't tell you why.

While we were flipping through the channels, a small red bird lifted note cards with its long orange feet, reading them.

"Dury, what are you studying for?"

"What do you mean? We have that language arts test on all the short stories of Haynabok Hurs tomorrow! Don't tell me you forgot!" I threw my head back, knowing this was going to be another week of awful grades. I wasn't even sure if I was passing at this point, but it was close. I don't know what happened. I used to be so good at school, mostly As with usually a B or two. But the classes got harder. More effort was required, and for some reason, I just couldn't find that in me. Somehow, I had gotten by copying a friend's homework, hiding my test grades, but report cards were coming out in a few weeks and I really needed to get my act together.

"WAIT-WHAT TEST?" Sal said as he threw off the bag of chips from his head and slithered over to us.

"What do you mean, what test? We were literally studying for it yesterday!" Damien said.

"Oh, but that was when we were out looking for fruits—which by the way, Jimmy, we still are going to try again today, right? I can't believe we found nothing yesterday!" Sal was talking about the blooming season, where Wazoo fruits would ripen and Wildlings everywhere would go picking for them together. Usually, it was a very fun tradition, but lately, for some reason this time around, the island had hardly anything growing and we were already in the second month of spring.

"I-I really don't care. You guys can go with Amelia if you want."

"Wh-why not Jimmy? You're that behind on your studying and homework. Did you even finish that essay yet?" Damien turned around and asked me again. I

sighed as I rolled my eyes. I hated it when he acted like my third parent.

"Damien, I'm nearly done. But I don't know what's the big deal, always trying to go fruit picking. It's always the same stupid thing we end up doing, okay? And language arts is the easiest class to study for. The essay, yeah I'm almost done, just a little more to go, but I definitely don't want to go picking again," I said, sitting back on the couch and grabbing some chips.

"Well, I dunno if there's even any left. They're all so rare these days," Forsef said as he flipped through the news channels, but suddenly I saw something that for a second looked familiar to me.

"Wait, go back! What's that reporter on the beach saying?" I asked. He slowly went back but I grabbed the remote from him and flipped faster.

"And these strange footsteps found on the beach resemble nothing ever seen before on the Wazoo. Detectives still are not sure if this had anything to do with the disappearance of Hilligan Higbee, a large Oeipek pig, who owns a few shops around the Wazoo, was last seen just as he was closing down his bodega last night before being reported missing by his wife. Investigators have been unable to find the owner since last night and have gone back to his shop to notice a severe break-in did in fact take place. Most notably, a strange, long metal object shown here. It appears to be some sort of blade used for cutting, but authorities are still wondering why such a long one of this magnitude would exist. Hopefully, in the coming hours, we will have more to report on. Back to you, Byaro.”

"Can we watch something else please? This is giving me the creeps!" Forsef said, covering his eyes. But I didn't listen to him or whatever anyone else thought. That metal blade, why had it looked so familiar? Where had I seen it before? Then it hit me, my dream! The men were carrying something almost exactly like that. But still, I couldn't even figure out why or even remember who they were. I just had this dream, yet my memory was sparse. I was just trying to piece it all together.

"AHA! You haven't finished your essay! You haven't even started it at all!" Sal said as he threw my book and spiral onto the ground. "CAUGHT YOU RED HANDED, JIMMY!"

"What? You haven't even started? Jimmy, this is due tomorrow! When do you plan on starting?" Damien said, freaking out as he looked at my paper.

"Uh-I don't know. I was going to figure out my topic later," I said as Damien walked back and forth.

"WHAT! You haven't even picked a topic?" Sal said.

"Jimmy, we had a month to work on it! Why did you lie and tell me you were almost finished?"

"Ugh, Damien just stop. I'll get it done tonight or I'll ask Mr. Dorlin for an extension," I said. Sal and Goran looked at each other before rolling over and laughing.

"What? I'll say I got sick or something this weekend.

"Jimmy, Dorlin is the grumpiest Wildling teacher the Wazoo has ever seen. He loses his patience when his chalk breaks! Do you really think he's just going to magically be nice and give you more time to start on an essay he assigned a month ago?" Sal asked.

"Yeah Jimmy, you really screwed yourself here," Goran said sitting upright.

"Oh, shut up, Goran! And pull your thorns out of my couch!" I said angrily. But deep down, I knew they were right. I just didn't want to think about it or even acknowledge it.

There was a sudden knock on the door, and I immediately jumped up. Was Mom home already? The place was still a mess, and I was <u>not</u> in the mood for another lecture. I walked over to open the door but was relieved to find out that it was only Amelia. She had dark braided hair, clear skin and even a few pretty freckles. She wore khakis just like mine, except they were always long and buttoned up, even on the hot days. She was my closest friend. She wasn't nearly as smart as Damien, but always outworked everyone to get the straight As she earned. Sometimes I felt like she was just trying to compete with everybody, whether they knew it or not.

Amelia came with her two pets, a small, shy Jybooan monkey named Barry, and a rude, impatient, sassy, tiny, purple robin named Riley.

"What in the Heloks happened here?" Riley blurted out as she immediately flew right in. Amelia's jaw dropped as she looked around the house. To be honest with you, I really hadn't noticed how much of a disaster the whole place really was until I saw her face. Spilled food all over the floor, mud all over the living room, and some kind of jam somehow on the ceiling.

"Wh-Jimmy, this place is a dump! We have to hurry and clean this up!" she said.

"Yeah, well, I was working on my essay so I—"

"It's not his fault, he's got the messiest friends in the whole Wazoo! And I don't even know who any of you are!" Riley yelled at everyone.

"Uh, well, I'm Forsef," he said sticking his body out from a bag of chips.

"Don't you remember me, Riley? I'm Goran, we're in the same—"

"Yeah, yeah I know. Mudpit Guy, what about you birdies?"

"We're the Dardo brothers!" They all said at once.

"I'm Derwin," said the one with green feathers, still stuck in a bagel.

"And I'm Dyron," the yellow one said. Barry smiled, walked up, trying to get the courage to say hello.

"Dilrin here!" said the purple one as he popped out of the couch.

"Douooresh!" the blue bird said as he swirled around, putting down the bagel he was eating.

"Dawan, nice to meet ya!" said the orange brother.

"My name is Bar—" Amelia's pet monkey finally got the courage to say.

"And I'm Dury, the only one here apparently who feels any need to study for our test in Ms. Keaton's class," the red-feathered brother interrupted. He was the only one Riley even bothered to look at.

"Ok, so let's get going? I don't want to let everyone pick all the babaloos from us, it's already getting pretty late!" Sal said, looking at the clock.

"No. Why do you guys always want to go fruit picking every year? It's boring. Let's just do something else, something fun," I said.

"Something else? Where is this coming from? And no, we need to clean this up. Your mom is literally walking home right now. She'll be here soon!" Amelia said urgently. I shook my head as I looked around. Luckily, I had the perfect solution.

"Wh-Jimmy where are you going?" Amelia asked as I went into the back closet and got the steel blue vacuum my mom had told me to never use. It was called the Clean Sweeper 9000, the state-of-the-art cleaning device in the whole Wazoo as my dad had put it. It had buttons labeled for everything you could even think of doing: washing, drying, sweeping, wiping, vacuuming, organizing, even arranging! My dad had said he and a few other engineers were able to work on the design. He wanted to try it out for himself before he sold it for entire neighborhoods and communities to share. Indeed, it did not disappoint.

"Woah!" Douooresh said.

"What is this?" Amelia asked as she walked over to it slowly, completely fascinated.

"This is what's going to clean the mess, and in only a few minutes too, and then we can go straight to berry picking," I said as I took the black cord and put it into the outlet. All my friends gathered around, amazed to see something like this in front of them.

There were several levels from *Passive Tidy Up* on the first knob to *Massive Mess* on the tenth knob. I set the dial to the fifth level, *Quick Chores*. The Clean Sweeper named the function in its robotic voice before quickly jumping up and going straight to the sink. Four flexible metal rods stretched out, each with the paws of a different Wildling. Two began washing and scrubbing away while the third wiped the table clean, and the fourth arm cleaned off splattered Jello, jam or whatever the heck it was off the ceiling.

"See, everything will be okay!" I said as I jumped back onto the couch and grabbed a few chips.

"Wow! This thing is incredible!" Forsef said.

"Wish I had one, our hut would be so much cleaner," Goran said.

"Jimmy, your mom is going to be home in a few minutes! There's no way this will all get cleaned in time!" Amelia said, crossing her arms.

"Uh, fine, Sal can you set the dial to ten, please?" I asked. Looking back, this was the moment I most regret. Unlike everyone else, I tended not to doubt Sal because he never really learned to read, or think things through, not to mention his concerningly low attention span. Never did I really care about any of that until today. But boy did I really regret it.

But to Sal's own defense, he really did have the worst vision of all of us and was probably concerningly dyslexic. I mean, I hadn't seen him read a book since the second grade, and we would often have to hear him complain about how difficult it was to read Damien's test answers during exams. But

nonetheless, he persisted and look at him now—a proud seventh grader at Cross Rivers Middle School. I could only wonder what incredible feats were in store for him.

Instead of setting the dial to ten, he must have spun it all the way to twenty, an extreme I did not know existed up until this point. Almost instantly, six more metal arms shot out of the machine as the Clean Sweeper scanned the room and accelerated to each of the messes. "EMERGENCY CLEAN, EMERGENCY CLEAN," it kept saying. At first, I wasn't alarmed as I saw it zip across the room. But it would do contradictory things, like pick up a pile of plates but then put them on a sofa chair and then it would lift up a kitchen chair, only to have another hand knock it back down again. Then it would go back and lift the single sofa and let all the plates fall down! I mean at one point, it was spraying water all over the living room floor, putting snacks in the fridge while spilling more milk than Sal even did all over the place. It even grabbed soapy water and a sponge to wipe the walls clean. I mean, for every mess it cleaned, somehow it made two!

"Jimmy! Something's wrong, it's too overwhelmed by the messes!" Damien said as he dodged one of the long metal arms thrown over him. Soon enough, the arms chased us ripping the pillow cushions, tossing plates everywhere, throwing a chair to the other side of the room, and even flipping over our dining room table. "WORK OVERLOAD, WORK OVERLOAD!" it said in a now louder monotone voice.

"EVERYONE GET DOWN!" I yelled as we all hid behind the couches as the machine spiraled out of control, throwing pots, pans, spoons, food containers, and even the tablemats all over the place before it started to come after us. It grabbed Damien and waggled him in the air. All the Dardos flew out the shattered window while Goran and Forsef ran out screaming, taking my chips with them too.

"You have to turn this off!" Amelia yelled.

"How? It'll yank us if we try to change the dial now!" I yelled back from behind the living room table.

"Th-the plug! Y-you have to p-pullll th-the plug-gg," Damien said while dangling around. If any of us even tried to go for the cord, we'd be dangling right next to him in seconds, so I came up with the next best thing.

"Throw stuff at it!" I yelled, thinking that if we could distract the machine, I could have enough time to crawl past it and pull the cord. Everyone started throwing back all the kitchenware. Now was the perfect chance.

Had this plan actually worked out, I would have considered it to be one of my few brilliant ideas. As I began to slowly pass by all my furniture and scoot through the dirty floor, I could see the black cord just up ahead. All I needed to do was get past the counter.

"ACCELERATED MESS, ACCELERATED MESS!" It alerted and began zipping all around the room. I opened a cabinet door to try and get something to throw at it so the Clean Sweeper would stay away from me.

"Sal? What are you doing here? You're supposed to be helping us turn this thing off!"

"No way, Jimmy, that thing will either run right over or crush me!" Sal said before slamming the door shut.

"Sal, open this and give me something at least!" I said, knocking on the cabinet door to which he opened it slightly.

"No!" he said before slamming it shut again.

Just as I was approaching the machine, ready to pull the plug and end this, the worst, WORST possible thing happened.

"Jimmy? Jimmy, what's going on?" I heard my seven-year-old brother say with his soft voice. He was always kind and sweet, only wanting to read whatever book he could get his hands on if Damien wasn't already going through it himself. "Wh- what is that?" he said as he came downstairs in his pajamas as he rubbed his eyes.

"JACKSON NO! GO BACK UPSTAIRS!" I yelled, but it was already too late. The Clean Sweeper had come over and grabbed my little brother, dangling him by his shirt.

"Help! Help me, Jimmy!" he cried. I completely abandoned my plan and hopped onto the counter to grab him. Instead of pulling him down, though, I was being twirled in the air.

"Jimmy!" Amelia yelled, trying to help get me down before she was grabbed by the foot and raised up.

It all seemed hopeless, and I wasn't sure what the Clean Sweeper was going to do with us to be honest with you. That was until the front door opened and my mom walked in after her long shift at the hospital.

"JIMMY JEFFERSON JUNGLES, WHAT IS

GOING ON HERE?" My mom yelled as she stared right at me.

"MOM, STAND BACK! IT'S GOING TO GRAB YOU," I yelled as the machine moved towards her.

"Cleaning complete!" she said firmly. Instantly, Amelia, Jackson, Damien, and I were all thrown to the ground as the long arms swiveled back into the machine. The light that was shining red turned white.

"*Cleaning operations complete,*" the machine said calmly before shutting down completely, all of its arms quickly going back into it. When I looked around the room, the whole place was a mess. Chairs everywhere, dishes broken, food all over the floor, and little tub containers anywhere but the kitchen. It was an awful mess, and it was all my fault.

My mom had crossed both her arms as she shook her head. She still had her white coat from working overtime at the hospital the night before, all because of the sudden rise in patient sicknesses for some reason. Her eyes were bagged, her dark hair was messy from running around all night, and I'm sure she barely had the patience at this point to deal with a son like me. But I honestly didn't know if she was about to yell at the top of her lungs or tear up and cry about how miserable I made her life sometimes.

"Mom, I-I'll clean it up. Don't worry. You just go to bed."

"You-you think at this point I can really believe that, Jimmy? Hm? Do you really think I can trust you to do anything? Did you even finish your homework? *Don't* you lie to me, Jimmy. Gosh, how do I already know the answer, Jimmy?" she said, putting her hand up before I could even reply. I looked at her and nodded my head silently as my mom did her best to hold back the tears in her eyes.

Chapter 3

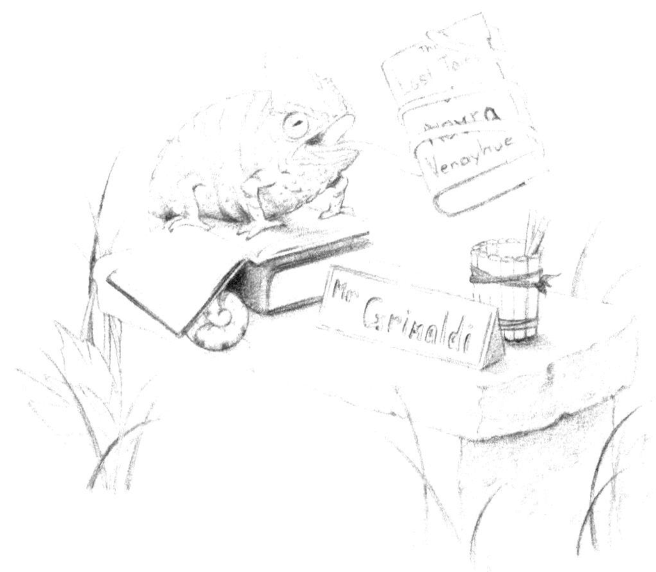

The Old Geezer's Bargain

"FOR THE TENTH TIME, I don't want to talk about it!" I said as I was taking my bike out of the garage. Amelia, Riley, Barry, Sal, and Damien, who had all been kicked out so my mom could *talk to me*, were now all standing, waiting to hear just what she said. My mother knew all too well they'd try to take up some of the blame when it was all my fault any of this started in the first place. But worst of all, I hated how upset I had made her. It made me so mad just to see her sad. *How are you going to get into a good high school if you don't get good grades, Jimmy? You have to try your best, and I know you're hardly even trying anymore. You were so good last year, straight As! What happened? What changed, Jimmy? I don't understand!* Honestly, I wish I knew too.

"His mom is mad because he hasn't finished his essay! That's right, Jimmy, I saw your blank pages!" Riley said.

"WHAT! Jimmy, we had a month, what were you doing all this time?" Amelia asked angrily.

"Ugh, will you just shut up! None of this would have happened if Sal didn't mess up the dial!" I said as I hopped onto my bike and Sal shrank down.

My friends had left me alone so I could sort through all the anger and guilt I felt. My mom was right. I needed to start taking school more seriously and I definitely didn't want to disappoint her with my grades. After all, it never did feel good to constantly be procrastinating all of my school work and studying.

We rode through the trails to the Monek Library, which was nice and almost cave-like in appearance. It was the closest library to my school, Cross Rivers Middle School, so naturally I always had a friend around whenever I stopped by. We parked our bikes and walked past the statue of a long-eared mouse with absurdly large glasses, Monek Mygikski. He apparently would always study here in his young days and eventually went on to become the Pleaser of the Wazoo, the leader of our island.

"How long are we going to be at the library? I wanted to pick fruits today!" Barry complained. Nearly everyone was excited about finding owjees, durangoes, cwiwicks, but most especially the sweetest fruit across the island, babaloos.

"In a while, Jimmy still needs to work on his essay. Besides, we can study for Ms. Keaton's test tomorrow. Then we can go picking."

"No! By then, it will all be gone!" the little monkey replied as he began to flop his body down, throwing a tantrum of sorts. Truth be told, I wasn't really excited about going out and picking fruits anyway. It was the same old tradition I'd been doing all my life. I guess it was just one of the many activities across the island I just didn't find exciting anymore. If only I knew why.

After a while, it got very quiet around me as everyone was locked into their own studying. Damien was already forty pages into a book he had just picked up while Amelia was using her neatly written note cards to study for Ms. Keaton's exam tomorrow with Riley and Barry. Who knows where Sal went off to, but honestly, I was glad he was gone. He was always my biggest distraction.

I sifted through Damien's notes, and my own book, trying desperately to pick one topic. The monkey protests, the boulder wars, the hippopotamus blockade, even bug rights would've been great to write about. Yet, the more I tried to lock down and focus, the more I could only think about the strange men I had seen in my dream. *The Lost Island of the Wazoo. Soon we shall be the first men to find it.* All I could wonder about was why I saw any of it, and if it was as real as it felt. Who knows, though? Maybe this was just another bizarre one that I'd end up forgetting about in a couple of days.

Just as I was getting dialed in, deciding to scrap whatever it was I was writing about and to get into bug rights, someone had been calling for me. "Psst, Jimmy," I heard a whisper from somewhere. I looked up, but quickly went back to focusing on my work. Then a paper ball hit me right on the head. I looked up sternly as Sal waved at me from a few tables away. He wanted me to come over to all the other friends around him, but I shook my head, trying to focus on my schoolwork. I thought they'd all understand, but instead, another paper ball was thrown at me. I didn't react. So, another one was thrown. And another. And another, until I actually lost my mind and shot up from my seat to march over.

"WHAT?" I asked loudly to all of them.

"Jimmy, tell them about the vacuum. They don't believe what we saw!" Sal said eagerly as he laughed. At the end of the day, everything was a joke to him. And he was the only Wildling on the whole island who could actually get away with it.

"Did a bunch of arms really come out from it?" a small blue Ossalow bear exclaimed as he jumped up and down.

"Could it really do all your chores? Really?" said Oki Occugpy, a delinquent platypus classmate.

"Say, Jimmy, you don't mind if I came over to borrow it, right?" Steab Staubaloue, a giant-nosed wombat asked.

Normally, I wouldn't mind talking to all these classmates of mine. In fact, I wouldn't mind wasting hours on end laughing away and having a great time. But I was in a time crunch. This time tomorrow, I had to have an essay finished and be ready for a test, two things I hadn't even started preparing for yet, and it was irritating me to my bones.

"Sal, I have to finish my work, leave me alone! All of you!" I said before marching back to my table. Amelia and Riley had been watching me the whole time. I already knew they just thought I was off wasting more time again.

"Did you finish your essay already?" Amelia asked, but I only shook my head. I didn't want any of them to know that I had hardly started. I continued writing a few sentences before Sal tried calling me over. "Pssst, Jimmy," he said before throwing another paper ball at me.

I lost it, quickly packing my things into my satchel and walking away from everyone.

"Where are you going?" Damien asked.

"I'm going to find a book to help me do some research."

I made my way down to the other side of the library, known as the stacks, where there were aisles of academic books and a few desks here and there. Generally, not many Wildlings made their way to these parts because there was almost no one else around, exactly what I needed.

I sat down, trying to put thought into my words. Actually trying to write, not scribble away. But I found myself scratching most of it after finishing a paragraph. Not to mention I had no idea where it was really going, or why Damien's notes kept mentioning this Ythoa Yyaannsyy Wildling.

I was searching on an old wooden computer in the

basement for a book that mentioned this when a Wildling named Jary Jenfields walked by, surrounded by a bunch of students as he gossiped away.

"...and Mr. Oens lost everything too, but that didn't make the news. I heard Paleggo's house was also broken into, and they stole bunches of food! Oh, Jimmy! How's it going?" the annoying little squirrel said as he ran up to me and stood right on top of the keyboard. "Is it true? Did a vacuum really destroy your house? I heard it was chasing all of you down too!"

"Jary, not now, I need to finish my essay."

"If you need, you could always stay over at my place, though I don't know which tree you'll be able to sleep on..."

"Jary! I'm fine, please can you go?"

"No way you'll be able to stay over, nobody trusts humans, especially since you all have been going around breaking into homes!" Biggsby Baunops, Jary's long eared brown furred rabbit friend said from behind.

"What did you say, Biggsby?"

"That's right, I said it! You no good humans have been going around and stealing from the rest of the Wildlings, that's why my daddy says you should all be thrown off the island!"

"Wh-humans haven't been breaking in anywhere! Why would you say that?" I asked, but Biggsby didn't reply, only looked over at Jary.

"No, no, don't say that! The Jungles family would never do those things! It was, well, the pirates who did it."

"The who? Jary, what are you talking about? What are pirates?"

"Oh, Jimmy, haven't you heard the news of strange footsteps on the shores and all the missing Wildlings? There have been a lot of break-ins, too. And well, some are saying it's these pirates who've come from far away on these large boats called ships."

"What? How come no one's seen them then?"

"No idea, Jimmy, but this isn't the first time. My friend Gibsig says his dad has a friend who has another friend, and his neighbor told him these dirty old men, the pirates, were here thirty years ago. He said they set a bunch of fires, but the Pleaser and media kept it all a secret so none of the Wildlings would panic."

"What? You're telling me outsiders have found the Wazoo? And that this isn't even the first time?" I asked, trying to think to myself. Trying to make it all make sense until suddenly, it hit me. *My dream! Was that what I was seeing? Were those the same men he was talking about? The pirates?*

"But how? No one has ever found the Wazoo! Are you sure this is real?" a long-nosed pink mouse wearing a blue bowtie asked.

"No idea, Cnuk."

"A large ship? You think it just slipped past the coast guards and that none of the police noticed a bunch of strange men running through the woods? And not a single Wildling said a thing? Do you really believe all that, Jary?" asked the white furred lemur as he went on munching a packet of chewy gooey walnuts.

"It's true Swafoo! You have to —"

"Oh, Jary, don't believe everything you hear!" Cnuk interrupted.

"You see, this is why no one ever believes you, because you always say the wildest things!" Swafoo said, shaking his head.

"GOOD MORNING, YOUNGLINGS," said Ms. Napala, our grouchy ostrich librarian, as she marched in while still holding a few books she was in the middle of shelving. Jary was getting ready to explain himself before quickly shriveling back in silence. "This is the quiet section, as you all well know! Be quiet, or I will call security, do you all understand?" she said sternly. We all nodded our heads. "And no eating here either!" she said as she ripped the large bag of nuts and waited for us to separate. But I wasn't finished with the conversation. Not just yet.

I quickly waited for Ms. Napala to walk off before running after Jary.

"Jary, wait up!"

"What is it, Jimmy? I don't want to get kicked out of here. Not again!" he said as he jumped onto several books on the shelf to talk to me.

"Those pirates you were talking about on the large ship. Did they carry large blades, almost like knives?" I asked. Jary thought to himself for a few seconds.

"Oh, you mean swords? Yes they carry those, that's what they use to attack with! Scary things I hear."

"And what do they want with the island? Why did they even come here in the first place? Why did they set those fires?"

"Well, between you and me, Jimmy, I heard they came here to find something, and when they couldn't get it, they started setting large fires to get what they wanted."

"What did they want from the Wazoo?

"Who knows Jimmy. But many died from the fires and the news didn't say it was the pirates, just that it was some sort of accident. And same with the Consulars and the Pleaser, they all kept quiet about it."

"What ended up happening to the pirates that came before?"

"I dunno Jimmy. One minute they were here and the next they were completely gone. I don't think anyone who knew about it even saw them leave. I don't know what happened. All I can tell you is now they're back," Jary said.

"Shhhh!" a small brown skunk gestured before slipping back into the shelf and reading.

While I was off trying to find a book I could use for my paper, Sal was sitting around telling everyone about this morning's vacuum incident as Amelia and Riley were all finished studying, slowly getting more and more impatient as they wondered where I wandered off to. All of them were ready to go fruit picking, but that was the last thing on my mind.

Barry, who was usually the shy one of the group, always tried his best to talk to a popular group of Wildlings from school, mainly Krayter Kaarmadi, a chimp who usually wore a backwards red cap hat and leather jacket. He was perhaps the most shallow and selfish student at Cross Rivers, always spreading rumors, making fun of everyone, and getting himself into detention for who knows what. It wasn't a surprise though, since his father was apparently some rich, bigshot lawyer for many important Wildlings all across the Wazoo.

He was a spoiled brat among many other things, and I did my best to avoid him.

"HEY! YOU CAN'T BE HERE!" said an orange-furred monkey as he pushed Barry away with his tail. He turned back around, looking like he was walking away, but waited before he turned around, crouching away from anyone else who might see him. He was a shy monkey, but don't think for a second that he wasn't sneaky or even a little selfish.

Many of my classmates and upper-class students, monkeys, rhinos, birds, a frog, a deer, and a kangaroo all walked towards the large back area of the library, known as the safari room, and sat around as Krayter jumped onto a stone table and yelled to get everyone's attention.

"Alright everyone, listen up because I'll only say it once!" Krayter said as everyone turned towards him. "First, we're going to go to Uwamwa Forest to hear Peister debate some candidates for his election campaign."

Everyone around groaned at the mention of it, probably because no one wanted to listen to some dumb political speech by a bunch of oldlings, and I couldn't blame them either.

"WHY?"

"WHAT! NO WAY!"

"THAT'S SO BORING KRAYTER! NO, WE'RE-"

"Alright, alright, that's enough!" Krayter interrupted. "Look, I don't really care about this either, but my dad said there are *plenty* of babaloos growing right around there and that we can go picking after it's all done. All he asked is that we cheer on everything the vulture says, and boo at everyone else after they've finished speaking. That's all we have to do, alright? Can everyone do that for an hour?"

"Can I bring my friends?" a long-limbed monkey asked.

"NO! We can't let too many Wildings know, otherwise there won't be enough for us."

"But how many babaloos will there be?"

"Bunches on bunches."

Barry was hiding behind a desk, barely peeking his eyes over a table. After overhearing the whole conversation, Amelia's little monkey pet quickly ran off, happy that he had finally found a way to impress Krayter.

While all of Krayter's friends walked out together like some kind of glorious pack, I walked up nervously to Ms. Napala, the ostrich librarian, who I couldn't tell if she hated just me or every youngling all the same. Though I had seen her smile once, I don't think she had to do it either.

But it couldn't have mattered to me now. I wanted to know everything there was to know about these pirates. I had never heard anything like them ever before, and now it was the only thing on my mind. I mean one crazy dream was nothing, but seeing the same metal blade on TV and hearing a few friends of yours talking about rumors of things you'd already seen, that would drive you a little crazy too, wouldn't it?

"Hi, Ms. Napala," I said gently, hoping she wasn't still upset.

"Oh, good morning, Mr. Jungles. I see you're actually trying to get some work done now." (You see what I mean.)

"Uh, yes. I was hoping you could help me find a book about a topic I want to write about for school."

"Yes of course, we are one of the biggest libraries in these parts of the Wazoo and have many selections! What exactly did you want to look for?"

"Uh, yes, do you have any books on pirates?"

"Pirates? Well, I haven't heard of that before," she said as she typed and searched on the computer. "Hmm, I'm not getting anything here. Tell me, what are these pirates?"

"Uh, they're these dirty humans that live on ships and have these weapons called swords they use to attack others with and uh, well, they go around finding lands to invade and I think they've come to the Wazoo before and well, now again too," I muttered nervously, watching her face as her expression went from shock to confusion and eventually pure anger.

"I don't know what kind of fairy tales you kids have been making up these days, but don't tell me this kind of nonsense Jimmy Jungles! I suggest you go back to your books and choose a serious topic!" she yelled as I nodded my head and walked off.

I quickly sat down and began writing again. I was still nowhere near being done, and mentally, I had completely checked out from writing an essay on bug rights. It was important, but my heart wasn't in it.

But right as I was about to give up, Mr. Grimaldi, the old geezer chameleon who looked like he was at least three hundred years old and was usually always shouting, approached me.

"You! Come with me. Now, youngling!" he said in

his low, raspy voice as I jumped up from my seat and followed him.

"Uh, am I in trouble?" I asked.

"You were the one asking about the pirates, weren't you?"

"Uh, yes, I was," I said, still confused about where he was taking me as we walked down the staircase and into an old, dark room. He flipped the light switch on with his long tongue and I looked around to see stacks of books piled up on each other with cobwebs and dust all around them. There were large swivel plants curled up all over the stony room.

"What is this place?"

"This is my office boy," he said as he jumped on a table that had a plaque etched with his name on it. He extended his tongue again, this time to the tiled ceiling searching for something.

He pulled out a book and put it in my hands. I brushed the dust off of it and saw that it said *The Lost Tales of Nevra Venayhue*, on the front cover.

"What is this?"

"What do you mean, 'What is it?' It's a book about pirates! Do you want it or not?" he asked.

"Uh,yes, but, Ms. Napala said there were no books on pirates. How do you have this?" I asked.

Mr. Grimaldi laughed to himself. "She's too sweet to know anything about them, but I don't blame her. You see, this book has been banned all across the island, every copy burned, well, almost every copy, I should say."

"Really? Can I have this one?"

"Well, I'll tell you what, since you are so young and can still move around, I'll give you this book, but you've got to go and pick me some of these sweet blue babaloos growing around. Haven't got my tongue wrapped around a single one this year," he said, but I didn't listen, too busy sifting through the old dusty pages with fading black ink. The convincing evidence I saw was the old images of the same dirty, rugged humans I had seen in my dream. I was completely mesmerized, asking myself how I had never even seen them in the first place. But I still didn't know if I could believe it all. The men I had seen in my dream, the rumors of pirates that Jary was telling me about. It sounded too crazy without any proof. Maybe this book would explain it all.

"HELLO!" he said as he slapped me across the face with his tongue. "Did you hear me? Do we have a deal or what, boy?"

"Uh, yes, yes, I'll pick you some babaloos!"

"Oh, not just some," he said with a smirk. "I want a dozen bunches for that book!"

"A dozen bunches! How am I supposed to get—"

"So, we don't have a deal then?" Grimaldi said as he began to pull the book away, but I quickly clenched onto it.

"NO! Okay fine, a dozen bunches today," I conceded, having absolutely no idea where I would even get them. "Uh, but sir, can I ask you a question? Who was this Nevra Venayhue person?"

It was quiet for a moment as the chameleon lowered his head and took a few steps away from me. "He was the leader of the pirates way back then, and the first person to ever find the Wazoo," Mr. Grimaldi said seriously as he looked away.

"So you think the pirates are real, too. But why was it all kept a secret? And how did he even find us?"

Mr. Grimaldi quickly turned his head and looked into my eyes. "Don't ask me to do your homework for you, Mr. Jungles!" he yelled angrily as he ripped the book out of my hands with his long tongue and pointed me out the door.

Wazoo Parts and Projects

FOR THE FIRST TIME IN MY LIFE, I was thrilled to do my homework. And to top it all off, I had found a book I actually wanted to read! Every word, sentence, and paragraph.

Yet, as excited as I was, there was still one major problem: where in the Heloks would I be able to get twelve bunches of babaloos? Hardly any had grown this year, and those who did manage to find some were punching and kicking just to keep them. Turns out, however, I was much luckier than I thought.

I rushed to all my friends who, at this point, were wondering where I had wandered off to.

"Alright, let's find some babaloos! Ready guys?" I asked.

"Are we ready? More like are *you*?" Riley uttered right up in my face.

"You want to go picking now? I thought you didn't want to. Did you even finish your essay? *And* there's a test tomorrow," Amelia said.

"What, no! We'll miss out on the babaloos then! C'mon, let's just go for a bit!"

"I heard there's a lot at the Uwamwa Forest, let's go there!" Barry suggested.

"Uwamwa? No way, that's too far north! We'll never make it in time. No, lets just look around here," Riley replied.

"Babaloos? You want to pick babaloos? Those are the hardest ones to pick!" Damien said. "The Tayngo trees are the hardest to climb, especially with all the sludgy goo they have. Let's just go somewhere local and pick a different fruit."

"NO!" Barry and I both yelled at the exact same time. "We have to get some babaloos, they're the sweetest!" I replied.

"Oh, if we go to Uwamwa, Krayter and his friends can help us! Monkeys are really good with trees," Barry said naively.

"Yeah, Krayter, *help us,* I'd love to see that!" Riley scoffed.

"Well then, I don't know what we're going to do! Uwamwa is way too far, and I don't know anywhere else that has those fruits. It'll take us hours," Amelia said, crossing her arms.

We stood in silence and thought as my friends went back and forth for a little while before an idea finally hit me.

"No, it won't! I've got a way we can get to Uwamwa really quickly actually! C'mon!" I said as I ran out of the library and got onto my bike.

"Where are we going, Jimmy?" Amelia asked.

"Just follow me!" I said before ripping down the trail.

My friends, bless them, had absolutely no idea just where I was taking them, and how we were going to get any babaloos, but believe me when I say this was the perfect plan. And it was all going to start with a place I had known my whole life.

"Wazoo Parts and Projects?" Riley blurted out, confused like the rest of my friends.

"Jimmy, why are we at your dad's shop?" Sal asked as we got off my bike and pulled it up against the wall.

My dad had a small shop where he made and perfected all kinds of metal, stone, and wooden parts for machines, vehicles, buildings, you name it. It was the little place that always kept him busy. And he was absolutely obsessed with it too, making sure to work any chance he could, even if that meant perfecting the measurements of a sketch right before bed. I had no doubt he had earned the whole island's respect. And there wasn't a Wildling who didn't know I was his son.

"So what're we doing here? I still don't get it!" Sal asked.

"Well, my dad showed me this one part a while ago called the rotoblade. It was to help make a few small vehicles fly all around the island. It can attach to pretty

much anything *and* we can manually control it too. It's actually very simple. We can put it on the bike, then fly to Uwamwa and pick babaloos without even getting a piece of goo on us!"

"Wow, that does sound perfect!" Sal said enthusiastically.

"So let me get this straight, you want to pick fruits and berries by just stealing a few parts from your dad's shop? Is that it, Jimmy?" Riley said bitterly.

"Well, obviously I'm going to return them! We just need the rotoblades for a few hours. Look, do you all want any babaloos or not? Because I don't mind going by myself if I have to," I said firmly. Almost all of them agreed, well, except for Amelia, who looked confused by all of this.

"I just don't get it, Jimmy, why do you want to go picking all of a sudden? You thought it was boring just this morning," she said. But I didn't want to answer her. I couldn't afford to look any more irresponsible than I already was.

"I don't know, things change, I guess," I said in a low, unsure tone as I walked towards the rusted back door of my dad's shop. The paint was peeling off and there was no doorknob, just an empty hole. It was one of the many menial tasks my dad hadn't bothered to think about. His business was successful, but the place looked like an absolute dump.

When we walked inside, the whole room was hot and stuffy. The floors, which were originally clear concrete, had become covered in dark plaque, dirt, and dust with deep cavities in them. Wires were hanging from the tall ceilings and pipes were running all along the sides of the walls. There really wasn't any other place I'd ever seen like this.

Every machine was covered with rust, mold, and some kind of dark gunk to top it all off. The room we walked into was rattling loudly with a loud cutting sound heard all through the area, while the employees operating these machines wore ragged clothes, worn-down boots, and ear covers so they wouldn't go deaf. Some carved wooden pieces, or operated a metal stamping machine, while the other half of the shop assembled pieces together to make a part before sending them off to be organized into the storage bins a few floors up. But before I could even think about getting on the elevator, I needed to find an old friend.

Ollie Olren was your typical incompetent employee. Constantly forgetting tasks, falling behind on work, and always sneaking off to catch a quick nap. My dad would always complain about employees like Ollie, but I don't think he ever realized he had a real knack for always hiring them.

"Hey Ollie!" I called over to the tall, waddling white rabbit who wore an orange vest with a large, hard helmet over his slicked-back ears. He was carrying a few long wooden pipes on his shoulder before dropping everything to hop over to me.

"Jimmy! What's up? It's been too long!"

"I know, and thanks for helping me build that ramp at Mudpit Falls!"

"Ah, don't mention it, that was fun for the both of us! Anyways, you need something, bud?"

"Actually, I do. It's a new part Dad was showing me, and I can't have him find out. It's called the rotoblade."

"The rotoblade? What are you all going to do with that?"

"Just want to try 'em out and pick some fruits. But don't worry, I'll give it right back!" I said.

"Oh wow, sounds fun. Try to get some for me too if ya can! Just make sure no one sees you sneaking off with 'em. Your dad will kill me if he finds out. The rotoblades will be up on the sixth floor."

"Okay, thanks Ollie!" I said as I took the key tag from him and walked to the elevators.

"No problem, oh, and don't forget to leave the keys when you're done!" he said before skipping off. We walked past a few of the working machines down the hallway and reached wooden doors behind a cubical stack of metal beams going up. I scanned the keycard quickly and eagerly tapped my foot, hoping no one would catch us. I could see Amelia and Barry shaking as we all looked around anxiously, completely paranoid that someone would see us, well, except for Sal, who was practically dancing with excitement.

"We're going to fly into the air!" he said to Damien, who was getting lightheaded at just the thought of being amongst the birds.

There was a small dink noise as the elevator doors opened to a thin wooden plank walkway, barely as wide as me. We took our first steps and the whole structure shook. Clearly, only one Wildling was *supposed* to be walking on it at a time, but that didn't stop us.

We walked slowly, looking at the baskets of parts

on each side, all with their full name and serial number underneath.

"Sal, slow down!" Riley said as he was bouncing on the wooden planks reading off each of the baskets. Eventually, we reached a box which listed:

SERIAL NUMBER P423872
ROTOBLADE
NAVIGATIONAL ATTACHMENT COMPONENT

There were a few dozen of them, each a small, black box with a removable dark gray triangle component sitting on top. It was right there in our sight. I was one step closer to picking the babaloos and getting the pirate book I needed.

There was a metal grabber hanging between the wooden beam we were standing on and the large bin of rotoblades we needed, but we didn't have the usual remote control to activate it. We all looked at Riley, hoping maybe she could get the parts, but she could barely grip them with her legs. "I can try leaping over and getting it!" Sal said ambitiously as everyone shook their heads.

"No, you won't make it," I said.

"Yes, thank you Ji—" Riley said as I jumped up and caught onto the hanging wire, putting my feet onto the back of the large metal grips. "JIMMY! Get back here! You're going to fall!" Amelia yelled. But I ignored her, and swung back and forth, getting closer to the bin before throwing myself into it. The whole scaffold shook aggressively as I held on. For a second, I thought it was all going to collapse right there. But it all became steady, though I began to breathe deeper as my whole body jittered.

My friends held their breath until everything was still and the creaking noise stopped. I grabbed two black rotoblade boxes with a strange triangle attached on top. But this was the scary part. I'd either be able to jump back to the other side and everything would be okay, or I'd fall to my death.

"Come on, Jimmy, you can do this!" Sal cheered.

"Guys, you need to go back to the first floor. I don't want any of you falling off when I jump back on that walkway. It's way more unstable than this side."

"Jimmy, you can grab onto the hanging hook and swing back," Damien suggested.

"Look, I don't have time to argue. Just go down, I'll meet you there in a minute, okay? And take these with you!" I said as I gently threw both rotoblade boxes at Amelia. My friends went down the walkway. When the elevator doors closed, the whole scaffold was squeaking, and that sent chills down my back. But what else could I do? Calling for help would just be a one-way ticket to my dad's office. I had no other choice, a kind of situation I would always find myself in.

I took a deep breath before leaping and grabbing onto the hanging grabber. I almost thought I was going to be okay, that is, until I looked up and immediately noticed the rope slowly ripping off from the ceiling. In a few seconds, I'd be tumbling to the ground. This couldn't have been going any worse, or so I thought.

I only had a few seconds more so I tried to swing one last time and launch myself to the wooden walkway. I was able to land, but even my successes aren't all triumphs. In fact, I'd say a fair amount of them were destined for disaster. Before I knew it, the entire scaffold structure fell back and crashed against the other wall of parts. Oh how much worse it got from there...

Parts were pouring out from both sides as I landed onto a conveyor belt not too far below. Metal and wooden parts were raining down from either side and piling up all around me. I tried to get up but beams from the scaffold and parts continued to come crashing down on both sides. I could see employees holding onto their hard hats and backing away as the mess accumulated. A few even got buried themselves.

I put my satchel over my head to protect it and looked down the sides to see a huge drop coming. I panicked, running back to the other side and immediately began to climb over the large mound of parts still falling and forming onto the large conveyor belt.

But I was too slow, and began screaming as I fell off the edge, flying through the air until I landed onto a larger pile of metal and wood parts that bent my bones and put cuts on my skin. I pushed my arms out and tried to brush off all the heavy parts from the rest of my body. After nearly a minute, I was able to get up with many scrapes and aches all over.

"SHUT OFF THE BELT!" yelled a gopher as a large seal flopped past the dropping parts before pushing back a long control stick. There was a loud beep before the belt finally stopped.

There were employees standing around me shaking their heads and cursing up the Wazoo as they looked around the place. Piles of parts everywhere, sections of the whole company mixed with each other, and scaffolds all broken and scattered. I had managed to create another mess today, one far bigger and wider than any I had ever made before. All I could hope was that my dad and mom did not talk until I picked the babaloos, until I got the book from Mr. Grimaldi. Because I knew more than anyone else that they were going to ground me horribly.

"It's gonna take days to clean this up! Raygu, what happened? Why is this whole place a mess? Who is responsible?" I heard someone shout, but before I could even see who, I dove quickly back into the pile.

My dad was a tall, light-skinned man who usually always wore the same button-down shirt and dress pants. He had clean-combed blonde hair and a scruffy beard to complement his almost always grumpy attitude. If you saw us both together, you'd never even guess we were related. He walked around, looking at the scattered parts all around while shaking his head. I hid underneath, honestly thinking I was going to be able to get away, but one little clue gave it all away.

My dad bent down and picked up a tan hat he recognized all too often. "Raygu," my dad said to a hopper. "Tell everyone to shut down production, we need to all clean this up right now!"

"Yes, sir," the short foxlike creature said before leaping high and off. Everyone ran off, getting to work while my dad stayed perfectly still.

"Jimmy, I know you're there. Come out," he grumbled in pure disappointment. All I wanted to do was run out the back door and avoid talking to him. I didn't like it when he yelled, but I couldn't blame him either. In times like this, I deserved it.

I got up nervously, not sure what to say to stop my dad from blowing up. "Hey, dad," was the only thing I could even think of to not agitate him anymore than he already was. I just wanted to keep him calm, but his eyes were dark and caved. His face was unusually tight, as if he hadn't slept in a week.

"In my office, Jimmy. Now," he said sternly before storming off to talk to his workers. I walked over as he hid his anger. Or at least, delayed it.

When I walked to the front, everyone in the office was in panic. "Do you have paperwork for the Luycnic parts?" asked Yoosa, my dad's kangaroo secretary. She had on a large blue dress covered with white flowers.

"Yes, yes, what about the Wablu order? That's due today!" replied Jynaly, a large hippopotamus who was the other secretary.

"Well, I'm trying to print it, but I don't know why it's not!" said Yoosa as she banged onto the side of the printer and continued to click the start button with no luck at all. "Oh, don't tell me its—aha! I knew it,"she said as she ripped open the bottom of the printer cartridge and pulled out a small gecko sleeping there in its brown trousers.

"Gyoggi, quit sleeping in the printer, your drool is clogging it up again! Get back to work, it's a mess out there!" she said as she tossed him onto the desk.

"Oh no!" he said before scurrying off.

"Oh, Jimmy, now's not a good time to talk! Someone messed up really badly and now there's a huge mess out back! He's got everyone scrambling!" Yoosa said as she had papers all over her desk with purchase orders for all sorts of different parts needed by businesses across the Wazoo. But I couldn't look her in the face and tell her what I'd done. She was just too sweet, and worst of all, she thought too highly of me. One of the few that did.

"Okay, I'll just wait inside," I said as I opened the door to Dad's large office. He had piles of blueprints scattered all across his desk. There were tables and shelves with dozens of parts sitting around that he helped make or worked on. But around the walls and on his desks were nearly a dozen pictures of our family.

I sat down in the chair across from his large wooden desk, looking closer at some of the designs and notes he had written on them. I couldn't understand what the parts were for or what the scribbled little notes even said. But this had been what my dad had spent a lifetime working on.

My dad stormed into the office and sat down. He took a deep breath as he covered his face with his hands. "Close the door," he said calmly. That was the moment I began getting nervous again. "Your mother called me after your little disaster this morning at the house. She said you went to the library to work on your essay because you still haven't finished your homework, and now I find out, in the middle of my day while I am in a meeting, there's been a huge mess on the factory floor made by my very own son."

"Dad, I'm sorry. I didn't know what happened. I was just trying to—" I said before I was interrupted.

"What am I supposed to do now, Jimmy? My whole day of production will have to be stopped just to clean up *your* mess! Do you see what you've done? Your little fun play time is costing me big! Do you have any idea how far behind we're going to be now?"

"I'm sorry. I didn't know this would happen, Dad. But I'll help fix it all. I promise it won't happen again," I said apologetically as my dad sat back in his chair and looked off to the side for a second. He took a deep breath before speaking again.

"You see. This is exactly what I am saying, James. You have responsibilities and you completely avoid them. You want to run around and have fun not even wondering what the consequences for anything you do are," he said angrily.

"Dad, I was, I'm just going to—"

"No, Jimmy. You aren't listening. You never listen to me. Your grades are atrocious. You create a mess at every turn. You can't keep doing this. You're thirteen years old now."

"Dad, I know bu—"

"NO, YOU DON'T KNOW, JIMMY," he yelled before pausing again. "I don't want to hear that you know. You're better than this. But you have poor habits and make poor decisions. You just can't keep living like this, James. You need to change. You need to start taking your life more seriously. Like your mother does. Like I do. Soon, you'll be applying to high schools and colleges, and one day, you'll need to get a job just like the rest of us."

"Okay, I'll try harder at school. My grades will be better."

"James. It's not just about that. You need to stop acting like a child. Do you want to end up as a leaf cleaner or some rock picker? Hm? You want to be doing that kind of work for the rest of your life?" he said as I looked at him quietly and simply nodded. "You need to start thinking about your goals. What you want to do with your life. What you are going to do for society. Someday, you are going to have to amount to something, and I hope you realize that sooner rather than later."

The room was quiet for a while. My dad looked at me as I could only look at myself and take in what he had said. There was no question my parents wanted me to grow up. I just wish I knew how.

"If you don't do well on your essay and test, Jimmy, I'm going to have to ground you, and there won't be any friends or hanging out. It'll be just school and home. That's all until you start taking your life more seriously," he said sternly as he stared into my eyes.

"Okay, Dad, I'll get it done. I promise," I said faintly, looking down in shame.

"Good, now please, just go. I have a lot of work to do."

I walked back outside and saw my friends in the distance, but kept my head down, too ashamed to even look at them.

"How'd it go, Jimmy? What did your dad say?" Sal asked. I walked past him and towards the bikes, knowing full well my face had said it all.

"Jimmy, are you okay? What did he say?" Amelia asked.

"Nothing, let's just hurry up and get to the forest," I said, trying to make sure I had enough time to get the babaloos I needed.

"Jimmy, why do you want to suddenly pick berries? You hardly tried picking any with us yesterday, and now all of a sudden you want to get them, I still don't get it! You should go back and finish your schoolwork. I know you ha—" Amelia asked before I cut her off.

"I tore up my essay, alright? It sucks. I hate it. Okay? But I found a book for a topic I really want to write about. But it's a very rare one, and Grimaldi said he would give it to me if I gave him a bunch of babaloos. Okay? Get it now?" I said angrily.

"That's why you're so motivated, Jimmy? That's why you made a mess in there and got your dad yelling?" Riley said. I didn't respond but instead looked at the two rotoblades Amelia set by our bikes.

I knew what my parents and even most of my friends thought of me. Deep down, I wanted to prove them all wrong. And now I finally had my chance. I was going to pick babaloos and write about something I actually cared about. A topic that would shock everyone. I was going to get an A on this essay. I could feel it. Tomorrow, I would be turning in the best essay Mr. Dorlin ever read, and then everyone would see for themselves that when I really worked hard at something, it was some of the best work anyone had seen. I expected every Wildling at school to talk about it, maybe a few adults would find out about it too. It might even make the front page of the *Riverside Relay*, our school newspaper. And then they would all say, "*Wow that Jimmy Jungles can really write! He really is very talented.*" Principal Fangoria might even ask me to write for our weekly paper, not that I ever would.

Chapter 5

Picking and Dropping Babaloos

IF YOU THOUGHT A DISASTROUS DAY like today couldn't get any worse, boy are you in store for one heck of a surprise. All I was trying to do was pick a few babaloos, yet it seems like that's the last thing that ended up happening.

I walked outside after getting lectured for the second time today. Don't think I never listened. I do, and believe me when I say this, no words hit me harder than my parents'.

I pulled the small gray triangle component from the black box and instantly it spread out to a wider panel. My dad called it the control center which would start the whole flying apparatus. I locked it in right between my handlebars. I was about to get it started, but needed to do one last thing.

"So, what do we have to do, Jimmy?" Amelia asked, completely puzzled by the whole thing.

"Attach the black box behind our seats, and Damien, work on her panel to set up everything," I said as I attached the flying component on the backend of my bike. We were all good to go.

I hopped onto my bike and clicked 'Flight Module'. Suddenly, a wooden rod extended out from the box and three wooden blades popped out and started to spin rapidly.

"Jump on, let's give this a try!" I said to Damien and Sal as they got behind me.

I held on tightly to the handle bars as I began to pedal. I was riding slowly on the ground, but before long, I could feel us being carried into the air.

"Jimmy! JIMMY! Y-you're flying!" Amelia said from a few feet below, barely able to hear anything else she had to say as the wooden blades fluttered loudly behind us.

"Hurry up!" I said, waiting for Amelia to ride up. She was much calmer than I imagined, being nearly twenty feet from the ground. It was Damien and Barry who couldn't stop clutching onto us, closing their eyes, shaking the whole ride over. But never once did Amelia or I even worry about falling and plummeting to our own deaths. We were just amazed by the view.

From up above, I saw the Wazoo like never before. We passed by the Trigian Forest, which I had spent countless days playing with friends in, to see it now as nothing more than a bundle of branches and leaves. We zipped right past it all. This was my home. All I had ever known. But from up here, amongst the birds, it all looked the same, as if there was nothing really special about it to begin with. The only thing I wondered was what was past this island and its surrounding seas, what lay beyond the seemingly endless ocean, and across the bright blue sky. I could only wonder.

I touched the panel to raise our elevation a couple dozen feet because the last thing I wanted in the papers was Wildlings saying they saw two humans flying through the air. Not to mention *three* lectures in one single day would probably be just enough of a reason to kick me out of the house.

I had gotten so comfortable riding the flying bike at this point that I began to tilt us while pedaling as fast as we could go. Damien urged me to stop, but Sal and I were having more fun than when we went leaf sliding at Bungaluggya.

I knew we had arrived at Uwamwa when I saw the tall blue leaf trees start to appear. We slowly lowered ourselves a few hundred feet and squeezed through the branches. We were lucky the area we landed was largely empty, but there was loud cheering and talking going on not too far away, like a big event or something was going on. I didn't make much of it at the time, though I *definitely* should have.

"Not too bad for our first time, huh?" I said, smiling as I looked at Amelia, who was still shaking as she got back up onto her feet. "Don't worry, we'll get used to it."

"Ugh, Jimmy, we almost crashed into those trees!" she yelled.

"That's okay, we didn't!" I said.

"Wow, that was incredible! We were doing what Riley gets to do all the time!" Sal said, jumping to the ground. We turned around to see Damien passed out on the floor. Sal slithered over to check up on him. "It's okay, he's still breathing!"

We strolled our bikes as we walked, looking for babaloos until our curiosity to what big event was going on overwhelmed us enough to finally go check it out. There were crowds of Wildlings cheering and booing as a few stood on stage, speaking behind separate podiums.

"What is going on here?" I asked.

"And to you, Consular Abbondale, how can you simply sit back there and be content with the progress of our lackluster police? The island is under tremendous duress these past few days and I think it is absolutely asinine that we do nothing while we see this horrid rise in crime rates before our very eyes! We should call upon the Venali Guard to further investigate these matters aggressively!" said the tall yellow furred monkey with a red bowtie as he pointed at the turtle standing behind his podium.

The crowd began to boo furiously again, but I could hardly tell what was going on. At the time, I don't even think I had ever even seen the Venali Guard before, but I had heard stories of the vicious group of tigers that lived off the island.

"No, Consular Yackley," the turtle replied condescendingly as he turned and responded to the monkey.

"We must trust local officers to investigate these crimes! We cannot rely on the powers of the Pleaser to override the capabilities of police and the Baroner's control over their local territories." The Wild cheered loudly in response.

"I am asking the audience to not express their emotions at this time so we may preserve the time and hear each candidate speak, please. Consular Precarious, how do you respond to this matter?" asked the tall, well-dressed otter to the red-headed vulture with oddly shaped wings.

"I know that no Wildling has ever lived through such a series of unexplained crimes. And regardless of what you believe we should do, there is no doubt the island is taking a voracious toll on these rampant criminals. Already, we are seeing fewer flowers blooming, fewer fruit blossoming, and bugs of all kinds starving. The island is not well and the police are not acting urgently enough to find and confront the matter. Thus, I believe we should take drastic actions and allow the Venali to hunt down these criminals across the Wazoo to fin-"

"NO! We will not allow the Venali to walk into our society so freely. It has been well documented that these great hunters of the Wild are not only vicious but reckless, and I have no doubt they will cause more damage and destruction than any sort of good," said the tall blue bird in a purple coat.

The Wildlings on stage continued to argue and speak over each other while the otter moderator did his best to create some peace. The crowd, too, continued to shout and protest, though I was still not sure why.

"Come on, let's go find some babaloos!" Barry said as he dragged me by the hand to come back to the rest of my friends. They hadn't walked as closely to the crowd as I did, but I don't blame them. This was all unhinged anger slowly descending into chaos. *Could it be the pirates? Was that what they were arguing about? How to handle them? But how did these crimes make the island not well?* The more I thought of what was being said, the more confused I was.

"What was all that about?" Sal asked as we walked back and began looking around the forest.

"Those are all candidates running for the Pleasership, the highest office of-"

"Obviously, we know the Pleaser is the leader of the island! We're not all as stupid as Sal is!" Riley interrupted as she sassed back at Damien.

"Hey! I know, I was - uh, just confused about what was going on!"

"Well anyway, it's a debate for the election coming up. One of them will have to go up against the current Pleaser, who is..." Damien quizzed Sal.

"Uh-oh, oh! Torry Thortbock!" Sal said. Everyone immediately bursted into laughter, and well I was just glad I kept quiet. I had no idea either.

"Sal, that was in a movie! It's Greygor Guildenhall, the *scary lion* you keep seeing on TV? Come on, you should know that by now!" Amelia said, smiling.

"Yeah, but they were all mad about something, and I don't think it had anything to do with the Pleaser," I finally came into the conversation, saying. "There are a lot of crimes going on, even Jary was talking about it to me."

"Yeah, I heard that too. I don—"

"Look, I found one! I found a Tayngo tree!" Barry said as he ran back to us jumping before grabbing Amelia by her arm and dragging her. We didn't have to walk too far from the event going on to find a tree filled with babaloos.

"What the Heloks is this?" Riley asked as she flew close to the orange goop all around the tree bark.

"That's goo, don't get too close or you'll get stuck!" Damien warned.

"Oh, I can do it! I climb trees all the time!" Sal said eagerly as he hopped onto the tree and got caught just a few seconds after.

"Ugh, Sal, you're still too small!" I sighed as I pulled him off and wiped my hand on the ground to get off all the goo. "Let's fly the bikes up, then someone else takes over while I jump onto a branch."

"I'll come with you, Jimmy. You can hop on the tree and I'll wait for you to get back on the bike," Amelia said. "Oh, and use this for the bunches you pick off!" She said as she took out a bag from her backpack. She really was good at thinking things through.

The babaloos were long curved fruits with a blue peel and orange polka dots, but underneath its skin was the sweetest pink delicacy the Wazoo had ever known. It was no surprise they were so rare, eaten almost as quickly as they were found.

We flew up on my bike, and I stepped onto the branch slowly. I wasn't worried about falling near-ly as much as I was getting stuck if I slipped and fell onto a huge clump of goo lying around. Mr. Grimaldi requested a dozen, which I thought almost impossible until I actually began to look around and move carefully through the tree. Believe it or not, there were babaloos in almost every direction I looked and only took a few tugs to pull a bundle right off.

It didn't take me long to get to a dozen bunches, just a few more for the rest of us, and then I was as good as out of here. Everything seemed to be going well as I filled up the bag Amelia had given me, but as I strayed further out into the branches of the tree, I began to hear the same debate going on. The Consulars were continuing to argue but about something different this time. Still though, I found myself intrigued by it all, which was odd because normally I had not cared too much for what politicians were saying around the Wazoo.

"Yes, we need to consider creating more hospitals above all else. It should be our number one concern!"

"Oh, preposterous! There's no disease! We need to focus on our economy. Expanding Wazoo business across the seas will transcend the island's capabilities and help us all live better lives, you must see this!"

"And risk getting hunted? Let the Wazoo be found? Lose our rarities to the rest of the world? Oh, you are so reckless, Peister Precarious! We should be counting down our days if you ever take the high post!"

"Patience, please! I am asking the Wild to restrain from any outbursts!"

"Look, Jimmy, I got some!" Sal said as I quickly turned to see him carrying a bunch of babaloos by his mouth.

"Sal! What are you doing here? Go back now, we

can-" I whispered angrily, trying not to have anyone beneath us know we were here. But before I could even finish, a large eagle wearing a blue police uniform flew in.

"HEY! YOU KIDS CAN'T BE UP HERE! GET DOWN NOW! CAN'T YOU SEE THERE'S A DEBATE GOING ON?" yelled the angry officer. I was so frightened, I began to shake as I fell back.

"Oh, Jimmy, grab my tail," Sal said. I knew he meant well, but honestly, did he really think that was going to help? I can't complain because I actually did it, and he started to scream before he jumped up, and we both fell off the tree.

It must have been a twenty-foot drop. I mean, we weren't that high up in the tree. Still, we came screaming down, disrupting the whole professional and very sophisticated debate with our childish demeanor. You'd think the police would have some mercy on two younglings nearly falling to their death. Turns out, they don't, especially when you find a way to land on a few 'important' politicians...

The good news was I got all the babaloos I wanted and many extra on top of that. The bad news, however, was that I somehow made it look like I was attempting to kill a politician. It certainly didn't help that the whole audience was screaming. I mean, I was just a little thirteen-year-old! And the police, boy, were they awful, rushing over and quickly throwing Sal and me on our backs before cuffing us up, like we were savages or something!

"Oh, sir, I'm so sorry! I didn't mean to fall on you!" I apologized desperately to a very hurt vulture, who was moaning in pain as I had somehow managed to make his wings look even more deranged than before.

"Mr. Precarious, are you alright, sir?"

"DOES IT LOOK LIKE I'M ALRIGHT?" he yelled, raising his very bent wings up in the air. "Somebody, fix it now, I can't walk around looking like this!" he said to a few medics before screaming at the top of his lungs as they tried to realign them.

"MOVE, EVERYONE, OUT OF THE WAY! I WANT TO SPEAK TO THEM," said a very large, bright brown rooster with a blue uniform and shining badge. "WHO PUT YOU UP TO THIS! WHY DID YOU TRY TO AS-SASSINATE A CANDIDATE SEEKING THE PLEAS-ERSHIP? HUH? WHAT IS YOUR AGENDA?" he yelled as he stood over me, immediately trying to interrogate my intentions.

Sal and I looked at each other blankly before shaking our heads and speaking over each other. "NO-no! We-we were just picking babaloos, see look!" I said, pointing with my chin over at the spilled sack of baba-loos just a few feet away. "I didn't know we'd fall and crush him! It-it was his fault!"

"My fault? How did you lose balance all of a sud-den?" Sal quickly denied.

"Because you freaked out when I tried to grab your tail! You pushed me back!"

"Oh well, you know you're not supposed to squeeze hard!" he argued back, but at this point, it was useless.

"Uh-huh, sounds like a bunch of excuses to me!" said a long-legged gerbil also in uniform. "Bucknic, take these CRIMINALS away and lock them up at

Konokalok Jail. Attempting to murder a political candidate, huh? That's thirty years easily!" he said, huffing to himself. A long, skinny monkey officer walked over and carried us around his waist.

"No, please don't take me to jail! I still have to finish my homework!" I bawled out loudly.

Chapter 6

The Pleaser of Dreams

AT THIRTEEN YEARS OLD, I had begun doing many different things to try and have new experiences, but going to jail was not one I *ever* expected to have. Worse yet, this would be a tough one to explain to my parents, especially after being a disaster child all day today.

We had been thrown into the back of a police van made mostly out of dark wood. It had long grass growing all around it, green and orange lights shining up from the top, and *Garagwa Police* written on the side.

"Are we really going to prison? I don't want to go, please!" Sal cried out loud as he was being carried, unable to move with the tight cuffs banded around him.

"SHUT IT! You stupid kids shouldn't have been trespassing in the first place! Much less crashing onto the stage!" the tall monkey said as it opened the doors to the police van.

"WAIT! Hold it right there!" someone came yelling in. The vulture, whom I had just landed on and whose wings I'm sure I broke, was walking with the tall rooster in a police outfit next to him.

"No Officer Mooney, we will not start arresting younglings at the Wazoo. I assure you of that."

"But sir, they made an attempt on your li-"

"Well then, do a better job securing the area! Now release these children immediately or your captain will have to deal with my lawyers!"

The officer stayed quiet but brushed its long brown feathers forward as the monkey kept the door open and waited for us to get back out before taking off the cuffs.

"Yeah, don't mess with us! He's going to get his lawyer. In fact, we're going to get all the lawyers! Then you'll see!" Sal said, I guess trying to mock them? The vulture, whose name I had not even known then, walked us back.

"So sorry about that, younglings! Security is severe for these sorts of things. Please be a little more conscious where you go next time."

"Oh, no, sir, thank you for letting us out! And I'm sorry for falling on you, and breaking your wings."

"Oh, these things? They've been broken my whole life. You know, I've never actually flown. But anyways, what's your name, boy?"

"Uh, Jimmy, sir. Jimmy Jungles."

"Ah, very nice to meet you. I am Peister Precarious," he said. "Anyways, it was nice meeting you. Both of you do yourselves a favor and not drift too far off anywhere, alright?" The Consular said right as he was about to walk away. But I couldn't let him go without asking him a question that had been burning inside my head.

"Mr. Precarious, sir, can I, uh, ask you a question?"

"Oh, sure, Jimmy, ask me anything."

"Uh, those crimes going on around the Wazoo, all the break-ins you were talking about on stage, do they have anything to do with pirates?"

Peister fell silent for a moment as he stared back at me. I could tell he was completely baffled.

"Uh, well, you are certainly asking me an interesting question. There was, a long time ago, a rumor that spoke of people who called themselves pirates. But I have not seen any significant evidence or indication from intelligence."

"There is! That blade found on the beach is called a sword, something they use to attack each other. There's a whole book about them I've found. I'm actually using it to write an essay. But I think they're here, and they're going around stealing from Wildlings."

"A book, you say? Well I-I don't know what to say, Jimmy. I've never seen a pirate. As for the break-ins, we do need to solve this. I have never seen such recklessness by anyone."

"Okay, fine, but one last question. Have you ever heard the name Nevra Venayhue before?" I asked Peister, who looked back at me as he looked down and thought to himself. I could tell he was shocked.

You certainly know quite a bit, but I'll tell you this if you can keep it a secret between us," he said as I nodded. "I do remember a man named Nevra Venayhue. He was believed to be a man who came here many years ago. Some even say, he was the first, and as far as I know, the only man to ever find the Wazoo."

"And what happened to him?"

"I don't know. This was in an intelligence memo given to us many years ago from sources I couldn't say. From what they told us, though, he was no longer an issue. I assumed he died."

"Oh, okay, well, uh, thank you, sir."

"Yes, well, remember to keep this a secret, please! And stay out of trouble, too!" he said as I walked back. I didn't get all the answers I wanted, but he had given me enough confirmation that I needed to know that the Wazoo really had been found, most likely by pirates. Why it wasn't all over on the news or something everyone knew about was beyond me. But it was true, and I think it was time we all knew the truth.

I walked back to the crowd area. Most of the Wildlings were gone, but I was still looking for my friends. I had no idea where Sal went off to, but eventually I did find them all together. Amelia was dragging our bikes with her as they looked around for me. I dropped a few bags of babaloos down to them as I went picking. Now I needed to get them over to Mr. Grimaldi and finally get this essay finished.

"Oh, there you are, Jimmy! Boy, you were really talking to that old bird for a while! That's the one he crushed!" Sal said to everyone.

"You guys didn't really get arrested, did you Jimmy?"

"Uh, no, he's just making that up, it was just a misunderstanding. Anyway, where are the babaloos I gave you Amelia? I need to give them to Grimaldi before the library closes today!"

"Well, I had them, but *no one* wanted to help me move the bikes," Amelia said, staring at Damien.

"What, I can't! It's too heavy for me! I can't even keep it on my paws."

"Guys, where are the babaloos?" I asked again firmly.

"I don't know, Barry was carrying them. Where is he?" Amelia wondered.

I looked down in the forest and was completely shocked. Barry was standing with Krayter and all his phony friends, smiling away as they were all eating the babaloos I had picked.

"WHAT IS WRONG WITH YOU, BARRY? I NEEDED THOSE! AND I PICKED THOSE BABALOOS FOR US! AND NOW YOU'RE JUST GIVING THEM ALL AWAY!" I yelled, unable to contain my anger.

"Oh, hey, Jungles, great fruits you got here," he said laughing with everyone else. I quickly ripped the bag from his hands, but there were only three bunches at this point.

"DON'T EVER TALK TO US AGAIN!" I said, yelling at Barry before stomping off.

Barry went and walked away with Krayter and his friends, going who knows where. I didn't even care. Betraying me for a low life Wildling like Krayter. Believe me when I say there was no greater insult than that.

"Jimmy! JIMMY! Don't just yell at him!" Amelia

yelled, as I took my bike from her, and threw the mostly empty bag behind my shoulders. I had no time to listen. It was Sunday, and the library would be closing soon. I didn't even think about how Damien and Sal were getting home, and Amelia definitely gave me an earful about that.

I rode as quickly as I could until I was out of sight before turning the flying apparatus on. When I arrived, the front door was locked, and there was a closed sign right up front, so I banged as loudly as I could until I was able to annoy someone to come over.

"MR. JUNGLES, THE LIBRARY IS CLOSED!"

"No, I just have to talk to Mr. Grimaldi really quickly to-"

"You should have finished your schoolwork earlier! Goodbye!" Ms. Napala said as she tried to close the door, but my foot was jammed in already. I screamed in pain.

"Please, Ms. Napala! I can't fail the seventh grade! Please!" I said, begging before she finally called Mr. Grimaldi.

I waited a few minutes walking around outside before the old chameleon came out from the side door with the book.

"Alright, hurry up. Ms. Napala knows this is on the banned list," he said, running to me faster than I ever thought possible for someone his age. I quickly turned around, hoping he wouldn't notice.

"HEY! WE AGREED TO TWELVE! THIS IS ONLY THREE!"

"I know, but please, I'll pick them later! I-I just

really need this book for my essay due tomorrow! No way I can get an extension on the assignment, Mr. Dorlin hates me already!"

"Well, I can see why!" he said.

"Please, sir, I-I'll get you more. I'll pick you *thirty* bunches more and give them to you! I promise, otherwise you can stop me from ever checking out a book again. Just please, I really need that book today Mr. Grimaldi!"

"Thirty?" he asked.

"Thirty," I said, knowing full well in the back of my mind I wouldn't keep that promise.

"If I don't get them this week, I'll get you and all your friends banned from the library, do you understand?" I quickly nodded my head and put the book in my satchel. I never did fulfill that promise, and Damien was *very* upset with me when he found out why his library card had suddenly been suspended indefinitely.

"Come on, get him out, Upta!" Krayter yelled at his blue monkey friend. "Pull harder! Lohabbii, help them out!" he said, pointing from a few feet away. You see, after eating all of my babaloos, Krayter and his friends only wanted more and thought if little Barry Barnell could reach them, why couldn't they?

Eventually, after a collective effort, they were able to pull out Gharoosh, though there was still some orange goo pressed against his body.

"You said it was easy picking those babaloos! Why were you so afraid to go up and pick some more?"

"Well, I, uh—"

"NO, tell me right now how did you get those baba-loos with Jimmy Jungles? He can't even climb trees! How'd he get a whole sack of them?"

"We-uh we used his uh-bike that—"

"A bike? You're telling me a bike helped Jimmy Jungles get all those babaloos? Does that make any sense to you? Oh, you are just the stupidest little monkey in the whole Wazoo! C'mon guys, let's just get out of here," Krayter said as he walked away furiously.

Barry was now alone, and very sad after having disappointed all his friends today. He was dragging his hands low against the forest grass as he sulked all by himself. But little did I know Barry Barnell was about to have the dumbest bit of luck I think I'd ever heard of.

While wandering through the woods on his way back home, Barry managed to take an unfamiliar path. I don't know if it was because he was lost in his thoughts or pacing around from his anxiety, but he hopped through trees until he stumbled onto an old, disgruntled Jacuta tree, shuddering with irritation as Barry continued to weep and wail. These are nasty things, usually found in the Heloks, that swat at anyone nearby. Somehow, this was way down south, closer to where I lived. I have a theory that Jacutas get up and walk around at night, though I've never been able to prove it.

Just when Barry got close, this tree grabbed him with its leaves, twisted its whole trunk, and launched him, who knows, maybe a hundred feet? A thousand if a Wildling could survive it.

He was thrown into a tall, brittle Dhalfi tree, whose

branches were known to collapse as soon as they came in contact with any sort of pressure. Barry quickly fell down and landed onto a metal cart sitting on two thick pieces of twine. He got up, peeking around trying to figure out where he was and what in the Heloks he was sitting in. Just as he tried to get out, the cart sped rapidly along the twine trail and dove through a pile of leaves on the ground.

He did not enter a hole but a very deep tunnel leading into an underground cave, one of hundreds the Wazoo had all around. The cart sped rapidly down, Barry could barely even hold on and struggled to control his anxiety.

BANG!

The cart smashed against the back wall of a cave and made a resounding echo. Barry was shaking as he looked around. He was in a large room brightened by torches standing against the wall. At first he was terrified, but soon enough, Barry felt nothing but absolute joy. At the very bottom of this cave were piles upon piles of babaloos, a real dream come true. He almost couldn't believe it, I surely couldn't when he told me. But it was true. The sanctuary did exist, and it was nothing short of a wonder.

Of course, the little monkey's first thought was to scoop as many as he could into a bag lying around and throw it onto a cart, not because he wanted it for himself. No, no, no. It was for everyone *else* at Cross Rivers who would all now want to talk to him. It was the dream of every elementary student to be so popular, one he was now lucky enough to live.

While Barry was overwhelmed with joy, I was already back home and fifty pages through *The Lost Tales of Nevra Venayhue*, written by a little lizard known as Agwes Augwarn. Captain Venayhue arrived on the island over thirty years ago with a group of men all savages alike, hunting Wildlings to eat on the island, and hiding in the interconnected underground caves of the Wazoo. Several eyewitness reports stated that ruthless humans attacked them. Others noticed their houses being broken into for resources. Regardless, however, more stories were kept suppressed from the Wild to prevent widespread hysteria. News was withheld from Pleaser Worwick Whaktabi himself as the intelligence agencies continued to investigate the matter.

A man by the name of Chatlan Mandabel was able to be reprimanded one night after setting a trap near the town of Bayaanga. He was interrogated for hours, and authorities were able to learn many details that he identified himself as a pirate lord on the high seas for many years before being ousted in wars against the Ankler Family, a notorious group of ruthless pirates who ruled many lands and many seas. He joined Captain Venayhue who was forming a coalition against the Ankler's control, but after numerous wars were lost, he sought refuge for his remaining family and friends. At least sixty men traveled with Captain Venayhue on his large boat, which, in their culture, is referred to as a ship, which these humans called the Red Roaring. However, it fell under attack and sank, thus the surviving crew came to the Wazoo on small boats.

As much as I loved the book, it made me angry when here and there, there were pages purposely ripped out which detailed the whole story. Instead, right as I was about to figure out just how these pirates found the Wazoo, it was missing at least twelve pages. It made me absolutely furious, but nevertheless, I kept writing. One way or another, I was going to find a way to complete this essay.

The man was detained as they sought to gain further information and negotiate with the invading group. At some point, however, the discussions turned into ultimatums (which the dictionary said was a fancy word for demands), and that fires were set out as the Venali Tigers began to hunt and capture humans they found lurking about at night. In total, eight men were captured, though six of them died from the attack and fires, while the remaining two were unable to provide sufficient information.

The Wild was a frenzy, and many thousands injured, if not killed, as fires were continuously being set until one fateful day when Pleaser Whaktabi called upon the seven Keepers to raise the Royal Army. They had pinpointed just where the pirates had stayed and planned a secret point of attack. Supreme Commander Greygor Guildenhall led the army, but he was surprised to discover that not only were the pirates ready, but they had set up an entire fire trap in the caves and surrounding areas.

Many pirates and even more Wildlings from the army had died in the rampant fires, which were eventually calmed by emergency fire crews all coordinating together. Still though, many of the pirates were able to take their boats and escape the Wazoo. What was even more shocking was that the prisoners were no longer found in their cells. Many believe there were Wildlings on the island conspiring with these outsider raiders. But to this day sufficient answers have not been collected, and the pirates have never been seen again.

It was nearly two o'clock in the morning when I finished reading, and writing for nearly ten hours straight. My eyes were burning, but I wanted to reread my essay to make sure there were no grammar errors in my sixteen-page paper. Yet as much as I tried, I couldn't, and I fell asleep almost instantly, unknowingly about to have another memorable dream.

Before I had dreamt I was on a large ship at night, looking at the biggest bird I'd ever seen, and overhearing a few men talking about coming to my home in search of something. That was all before a crocodile charged after me, and I fell into the sea. When I opened my eyes, I could see I was lying on some strange beach shore, the cold salty water brushing against my soaked body. This island was a lot smaller than the Wazoo and there wasn't a single Wildling in the luscious green forest as I walked around.

CAAAAACWAAA CAAACWAAAAA

The same large eagle I had seen before was now standing on a rock, looking down at me as I got up from the sandy shore of some strange island.

"What am I doing here? Where am I?" I said as the bird landed and stared at me. It then spread its large wings before flying off. But I didn't want it to go. I was still angry. And confused. So, I ran after it, wanting answers, wanting to know why I was here.

The bird came to a halt right in front of a cave and looked over at it before staring at me. "What do you want from me? What is that?" I said to it, but it only continued to call and look from the cave back to me. But I only stood still and looked at it. "What's in there? I'm not going!" I said, but the bird continued to stare at me blankly before waving its wings and flying through the large crevice. Again, I followed it, wondering where it was guiding me to. I still had no idea what this bird wanted from me.

CWAAAA, CAAACWAAAAAA, CWAAAAAA

I continued to follow the bird as its calls were now turning into echoes, but it was completely out of sight, and I could feel the sweat sliding down the side of my face. The air was thick and smoky, while the cave walls burned my palms, but I continued to walk, wondering why we were here.

There was a large center dome with hot lava flowing between the small flat stones off to the side. *Was this a volcano? Why was the bird bringing me in here?*

I walked carefully around it, still looking for the eagle, but began to hear voices echoing from the end of the cave as there was a bright light flashing from far down.

I paced forward slowly to hear the voices grow louder. A conversation was going on, and someone was angry.

There was a large flame in the shape of a lion speaking to a goat with twisted horns and a long beard all in the form of water. I had never seen anything like it in my life. I hid behind a rock and peeked my head out to see what was going on.

"The Wildlings will know, and if they find out, the entire Wazoo will go into a panic! Not to mention, this could greatly affect my election! The Watchers are already gaining more traction because of the increase in crime," said the lion, embers from its body falling to the ground.

"We are nowhere near that yet, Greygor. Do not fret. You must continue your talks with the pirates to ensure their peaceful departure," said the goat as it slowly approached the lion.

"HOW? THE PIRATES ARE GETTING MORE RECKLESS BY THE DAY! THEY CANNOT BE CONTROLLED. THE CAPTAIN SAYS IF HE CANNOT FIND WHAT HE IS LOOKING FOR, HE WILL UNLEASH HIS RAGE ON THE ENTIRE ISLAND. IS THAT SOMETHING YOU'RE WILLING TO RISK GIYATAR? THE LIVELIHOOD OF THE WILD?" yelled the lion, flames blazing from its mane and back.

"Pleaser Guildenhall," the goat replied calmly. "The Wildings still do not know. But I assure you, we cannot give them what they seek. The power would be too great in their hands. We can give them all the other rarities this island has to offer, but not *that*. You must be willing to go to war with them once more and forcefully extract them all."

"No, these pirates, they do not care for anything or anyone, but themselves! I am supposed to be who the Wild relies on! I am the Pleaser of the Wild, the Pleaser of Dreams! The one to ensure that dreams can *never* die! If the Wildlings were to discover my association with them, it would shatter their hope. It could even flop the election! Think about what that could mean for the future of the Wazoo! You must reconsider."

"I cannot do that!" said the goat.

"OH GIYATAR, YOU HAVE BECOME SO NAIVE! THE MEDIA ALONE WILL CRUSH MY CHANCES, AND THE WILD WILL LOSE TRUST IN THEIR PLEASER!" the lion yelled. "MUST I REMIND YOU ABOUT THE HUMANS AND THEIR WAR CULTURE, THAT THEY WILL BURN THIS ISLAND TO THE GROUND LIKE BEFORE! ARE YOU WILLING TO TAKE RESPONSIBILITY FOR THAT?"

"Well, then you should *NOT* have let them free last time! You were the one who trusted those pirates for whatever negotiation you set up. Letting them escape, allowing the whole island to be set ablaze. That was your fault, and because of it, now they have returned! You must find and arrest them again!"

"You are not listening. *These* pirates are different from the ones before! They are more advanced, subtle, yet also more ruthless and demanding. But more than that, I believe a Wildling is working with them, helping them hide themselves amongst us. Though I have hardly any idea who would do such a thing."

"Unless you can find who is helping them, there is nothing else we can do, Greygor. In the meantime, you must find a way to work out a deal. At least keep them under control and summon the army to find where they hide! It is our only way," said the goat as it sat down

before slowly fading away while the lion remained, roaring furiously as it paced back and forth.

Did the eagle want me to see this meeting? To hear that our own Pleaser was working with the pirates? I crouched up and began backing away, wanting to leave without being noticed. I was walking to the dome when I accidentally kicked a rock against the wall and it echoed. I shot up and looked back at the giant lion now staring, before it began to chase after me.

"WHO ARE YOU BOY? WHAT ARE YOU DOING HERE?" he yelled. I ran as quickly as I could, retracing my steps as I tried to remember how to get back outside as the lion was gaining up on me, its hot flame body heating my entire body as it got closer and closer.

CAAAAAA CAWCAAAAA

The bird called as it flew down from the dome and grabbed me by its legs. It flew us out but the lion only charged faster with its gust of fire nearing.

RRRRAAAAWWWWWWWWRR

The lion yelled loudly as we reached the outside. It leapt in its last attempt to stop us. I could feel the flames pressing against my skin, and screamed from the burns. I knew this was all a dream, yet the pain had felt just as real.

Chapter 7

The Lost Tales of Nevra Venayhue

EVERY WILDLING BELIEVED THE WAZOO could never be found, that we were away from the rest of the world, if there even was anything else out there. Some believed this small island was all there was. But the rest of us had always known there were other lands and civilizations living their own lives, though we could never really prove it. I mean, our ancestors had to get here from some place, right?

Regardless, the story I had spent all night writing up would change the way every Wildling saw the Wazoo. That our little island was a lot closer to other lands than we realized, and that maybe we were just a small

part of a vast and endless world. One far different than our own way of life.

As much as I had read and wondered about the pirates, there was still much I couldn't tell you. *Why did they sail across large seas on ships and attack one another? Why were they always stealing? Why did they never want anything close to a stable life like we had at the Wazoo? But most importantly, why was Greygor Guildenhall, Pleaser of the Wazoo, working with them?* None of it made sense. I know it was only a dream and that I couldn't prove anything. But still, I heard and read too much for all of it not to have at least a little bit of truth.

I was eating my nutmeg bar and staring off into the distance, completely ignoring the conversation my friends were having while we were sitting in the basement classroom near Coyyky Hall. It was our usual hangout spot before classes began, and I was trying to catch up as much as I could on months of lessons from the books we read for class: The Expeditions of Ferales and Hobbts, Carwigwa Running Shantoe with Haynabok Hurs, and Buggington Farm Riots.

"Okay, let me quiz you. First question, who is Oopa Ohoon?" Sal asked.

"Uhhhh," I muttered, sifting through Damien's cleanly written notes.

"He was a grizzlebeetle who first assembled meetings to discuss efficient farming labor techniques to increase food production," Damien said.

"Oh, is this the Cikabaad Convention?" Amelia said as she sat down with Riley.

"Okay, okay, give me another question," I said as I continued reading the notes.

"What did Gespego Guarls ask Keeper Umaagar Uuoilyesh in the Inquiry Trials?" Damien asked, and again I went blank, trying to remember when we were even taught that.

"Uh-who? Can you repeat the question?"

"Wow, Jimmy, when you don't care, you *really* don't care," Sal laughed.

"Oh, shut up, Sal, I knew you were as clueless as me before you studied all day with him yesterday!"

"Well, maybe if you weren't always behind on another homework, you'd be able to study with us for a change!" Riley sassed back.

"Hey, at least he finished his essay for class today, right, Jimmy?" Amelia said, trying to boost my mood through the hopelessness of ever doing well on Ms. Keaton's exam.

"Yeah, I worked on it for ten straight hours last night. It's sixteen pages," I said.

"SIXTEEN? What did you even write about?" Riley asked as she swirled up in the air.

"Woah, what's your topic? It must be something really interesting!" Amelia said. I was really debating on whether I would tell them or just wait until we had to read it in class, but I just couldn't contain myself. So, I began to tell them about pirates, led by a man named Nevra Venayhue, who found the Wazoo over thirty years ago and how they were now back, though I didn't have all the evidence to prove it was exactly them.

"Found the Wazoo? I'm pretty sure that's impossible Jimmy. After all, the Asiyokulinnya trees have kept us hidden for millions of years, it's hard for me to—" Damien said, probably ready to go on for an hour.

"Look, I can't tell you everything. I don't know how they know, but they've been able to come here before, and now they're back. That long metal blade we saw on one of the shores on TV, it's called a sword. And they travel around on large boats, called ships. I bet you they're hidden somewhere around the island too," I said, deciding not to go any further and tell them about the dreams I had.

"A large boat just hidden away? Jimmy, that's impossible, the coast guards would have said something about it by now!"

"Well, I'm telling you, there are pirates here. Everything that's going on now, the break-ins, the missing Wildlings, all the damages in the Wild, it all happened thirty years ago. And I'll tell you something else, I think Greygor Guildenhall has something to do with it."

"Greygor Guildenhall? The Pleaser of the Wazoo? You think he knows all about this?"

"Yes, I was able to get a whole book on it, too! Look." I told them as I pulled out *The Lost Tales of Nevra Venayhue* from my satchel.

"And it says the Pleaser was involved? I don't believe that," Damien said, flipping through its pages. "Jimmy this book, it's missing half its pages!" he said, completely heartbroken. I didn't want to tell them about the dreams I had about the pirates, mostly because I'd sound crazy, but also because, well, I didn't even know if I could believe them myself.

"Is this why you were rushing to the library with those babaloos Jimmy? To get this book?" Amelia asked nervously.

"Sounds like a bunch of crazy talk Jimmy. Let's just hope Dorlin buys it," Riley said right before the class bell rang and we all got up, walking to first period. I put the book back into my satchel, not knowing that it would be the last time I'd ever see it.

A few periods had passed and I had studied as much as I could from Damien's notes for Ms. Keaton's tests, which were always much easier than Damien had made them seem (thank Gideon for multiple choice). I walked into Mr. Dorlin's class early and sat down, reading through my essay as he rampantly punched away at his keyboard from over his small water bowl. He was a normal brown perch fish with obnoxiously large glasses over his face and a stern attitude that would surely make you wonder why he was that way.

"Kaaswol, that's four tardies for you! One more time and I'll be giving you a detention slip!" he said as the little panda who's giggling quickly turned to nodding with a frown. "Okay, class, we will be reading the essays due today. If you have not written the seven-page minimum, you will be deducted five points. If your sources are incorrectly cited, you will be deducted five points. If your handwriting is sloppy, you will be deducted five points and be expected to provide all necessary translations," he said, throwing his fin up into the air. He began calling students one by one randomly throughout the room. Everyone sank into their seats, nervous and hoping they wouldn't get called on.

We all sat quietly, most of us listening, as Mr. Dorlin scribbled away with his notes, angrily huffing and fussing under his breath as the students read on.

"S-sin-sink h-holes are a v-ver-very comm-common issue in the jungle which is why hogs try to live in gr- grasslands an-and the-the iss-issues of la-land dispute ar-are com-common."

"Alright, time is up. Thank you Hardeeth. Jimmy Jungles, you are next!" he called, just minutes before class was set to end.

"You got this Jimmy!" Sal whispered as I stood up and began shaking, feeling my own heart beat as I tried to stay calm. *You'll do great. There's nothing to worry about.* I said to myself.

"We, the Wildlings, have enjoyed many privileges while living on this island. Plenty of food, nature that supports us, an economy that tends to all of our needs, and laws that always seek to protect us against any danger that may come our way. Well, I should say most dangers. We all have heard the many tales of our island, that it is the wonder of the world, a land where dreams can never die, but most importantly, an island that can never be found. Well, I am here today to present to you that not only are we not alone in this world but that the Wazoo has been found multiple times over the years by a group of mysterious men never mentioned in the papers, nor reported by the police. This group of outsiders is known far and wide as the pirates and have dwelt upon our lands thirty years ago and are here again now.

"All of us have seen the reports on the news. Strange footsteps on the shores, a mysterious long blade, and more crimes than ever before. A lizard by the name of Agwes Augwarn was able to talk to several intelligence agents about a man named Nevra Venayhue, who brought them all here long ago. They ransacked Wildlings, murdering many, and created careless fires all across our land."

As I was going on and on with reading my paper, I looked up to notice many classmates were shaking, if not covering their faces, or ducking their heads. They were all scared, so much so even Dorlin had heard enough.

"Mr. Jungles, just what are you talking about? None of this *ever* happened!"

"It's because it wasn't reported on Mr. Dorlin! But I do have a source," I said prepared as I walked back to my satchel and scrambled through it for my book.

"Well? Where is your source?" he asked.

"Wh-I just had it. Maybe I put it in my locker. I can go bu—"

"Well, I have never heard of such things, but any expert can assure you the Wazoo can never be found!"

"Well, there were large fires that took place thirty years ago when Greygor Guildenhall raised the army and it-"

"What? There was no army! And the fires happened because of the energy factory incident; gemstones accidentally conducted enough electricity to set on uncontrollable fires! There are pictures and evidence of this everywhere!" Mr. Dorlin yelled, but the rest of the class was happy, almost relieved, to think none of this was true. That I was just going on an imaginary, conspiratorial rant. Eventually, they began to laugh. They all thought I was a joke. I sensed it all across the room as the sweat started to drip down my back. The class bell suddenly rang and many of my classmates jumped up, ready to head straight to lunch. "Class dismissed, please leave your essays on my desk and do your homework for this week's lesson due Monday. I hope many of you now see the importance of doing it ahead of time," he said, looking at me sternly as they giggled to themselves.

I was angry. I wanted to pick that small fish up from his bowl and yell at him myself. Whatever. Couldn't expect much better from him anyways. Mr. Dorlin always had it out for me. He and Principal Fangoria. Can't say I was even surprised. I threw the essay onto the desk and stormed out, but as I walked down the hall, I could see many students already looking and laughing at the sight of me. The whole school was going to start talking about it, and I'd be a laughingstock to everybody by the end of the day.

I scrambled through my locker, throwing everything out as I searched. *I just had the book, where was it? How could I have lost it already?*

I slammed my locker shut, not even wanting to go to lunch. All my friends would think I'm crazy, or worse, start feeling bad for me. I headed to the cafeteria when good ole' Jary Jenfields came by.

"Hey, Jimmy, *hehe* I hear you're a conspiracy theo-rist now, *hehehehe!*" the small squirrel said as he rolled over and laughed annoyingly.

"Ugh, go away, Jary!"

"What did your parents say? Are they still mad at you for ruining the company? And the house? Oh, did they find out you also crashed on to that debate stage and almost went to jail yesterday? Wow, Jimmy, you really do mess up a lot of things," he said. To be hon-est with you, I don't think he was trying to make fun of me, but that's not how I took it then. Immediately, I chased after him, trying to put my hands around his furry little tail.

"Ooh, Jimmy, stop! Why are you so mad? Don't be mad at me, I was just kidding around!" he scurried down the hall to the corner stairwell right before I was able to put my foot *gently* on his tail and grab him.

"I-I'm sorry, pl-please don't hu-hurt me, Jimmy!" he said, gasping for air and wiggling his tiny feet under my palm. I loosened my grip, but not by that much. "I had just heard, well, from everyone really, and was just letting you know what they were all uh, saying! I was-I was uh, *helping* you really, don't you see?" He was lying through his teeth. Everyone always has something to say until you confront them, I've learned.

"I don't care, don't say anything about me ever again. Keep your nose out of my business! Do you un-derstand?" I yelled as he quickly nodded his head. "This was all your idea, too! You told me about the pirates, now you're making fun of me? You knew it was some crazy lie this whole time?"

"Wh-no I didn't lie to you! It's a rumor I've heard from a lot of Wildlings! I've heard it many times, but I didn't tell you to write a whole essay on it! Okay, don't blame that on me! Now can you please let me go?" he said desperately.

"Then why'd you keep saying all those things out loud? How did you even know I fell onto a stage?"

"Oh well, Krayter wouldn't stop telling his friends, and Barry Barnell got a bunch of babaloos that he brought for everyone. Did you know he's really good at getting them? Do you know how he does it? I never expected a little monkey li—"

"Oh, Jary no. SHUT UP!" I said, losing my patience and yelling. "I don't want to hear any more rumors! Now do you know where my book is? Who took it? I need my source or Dorlin is going to fail me!" I said finally letting him go.

"Sorry, Jimmy, no idea."

"Alright then, can you at least tell me where I can find Peister Precarious? I really need to talk to him!"

"Peister Pre — is that one of the Wildlings running for Pleaser of the Wazoo? The one who's bones you crushed?"

"*Yes*, yes, it is, Jary," I shook my head. He really did, somehow, know every little thing about everybody.

"I think he's at the Arcadium today. There's some big discussion going on or something. But what is it? What do you have to tell him?"

"Thanks, Jary," I said before quickly turning around, not wanting to tell him any more of my business that he didn't need to know. I knew exactly what I needed to do next. I was going to tell Peister everything. About how I kept having dreams of pirates talking of coming to our island, about all the evidence I found of a man named Nevra Venyahue finding our island and living here, and, more importantly, that Greygor Guildenhall, our very own Pleaser of the Wazoo, had been working with the pirates this whole time.

Chapter 8

Arguments at the Arcadium

"JIMMY, WHERE ARE YOU GOING?" Amelia asked, following me as I was about to head out the doors.

"I-I have to go," I said simply, not wanting to explain myself, unsure if she or any of my other friends would even understand what I was thinking.

"Oh, come on, Jimmy, it wasn't that bad. Everyone will forget about it, alright? Let's just get lu—"

"No, you guys won't get it. I need to leave. I need to talk to Peister again. It's important," I said as I walked out the front doors.

"Peister? The vulture Peister? Why do you want to talk to that old bird?" Riley asked, completely confused.

"Look there's not a lot of time, but I need to go to the Arcadium right now. If you want to know why, come now, otherwise I'll tell you later," I said, but almost surprisingly, my friends immediately followed, well except for one.

"You want to ditch school? Again? Why Jimmy? You know I hate asking everyone for help to catch up!" Damien said as he hopped up on my bike.

"Oh, you do better than them on the test anyway, why does it even matter if you miss a few classes," Sal sassed back.

Now, in case I haven't gotten to explain it before, the Arcadium was the name of the chamber where all the chosen Consulars of every territory would get together as one body, known as the Assentory, to make laws and decisions for the whole island. I had been there a few times on my weekends to see the very beautiful gardens, great sculptures, and the most incredible arches overhanging it all. But I had never been there when actual work was being conducted, nor were we probably allowed. At the very least, this would all be interesting. I just hoped I wouldn't end up in handcuffs again.

We landed at Arcadia on the upper east side of the island. There were many tall white statues of birds, similar to the one that had been in my dream, standing upright all throughout the forest. We hid behind trees from the main marble floors and past the purple Kulinyan bears who guarded the area to hide in the tall bushes overlooking the large open pit were the Consulars would sit.

"Oh, we should not be here! We should not be here!" Damien said, shaking at the sight of the viscous bears walking around.

"Jimmy, are you going to tell us why we're here now? It looks like something is about to go on! Why do you have to talk to Peister right now?" Amelia asked urgently. I'm sure if she was just as nervous as Damien, and as confused as Riley. Sal, on the other hand, was completely amused, calling out all the funny clothes the Consulars wore.

"I will Amelia, just wait," I said as a penguin with yellow slicked back hair on its head waddled down the steps to a stone stage at the bottom of the chamber and gently hit the gavel against the podium.

"The Assentory is now in session! We have been called upon to the Arcadium by the Elders of the Primary Council to resolve the recent increase in crime and rising infection rates across our islands. We will have open discourse before we reach a final vote on the Pleaser's order for a complete lockdown of our society. Consular Yackley, the time is yours," said the penguin.

The tall, thin monkey stood up to applause as he took off his top hat. He had wide sideburns and a long blackcoat. I remembered seeing him before on the debate stage and how much the audience was cheering him on then too. He was very well-liked and apparently leading every poll in the Watcher Pack at the time.

"Thank you, Vizer Iwick, and I must commend the Elders for calling upon this session. The Pleaser, and his Waker constituents, are all heavily out of line for suggesting the entire island be locked down. Rather, we should allow the Venali tigers to roam freely upon our land and hunt down these thieves!" Yarbis said before sitting back down. The Vizer then called upon Lopolla Lyren, and the shiny, pink-shelled turtle sat up to speak.

"Must we all be reminded of their prior history that made them become banished from freely roaming the mainland in the first place? What my colleague *and candidate* fails to recognize is that we, the Wildlings, are facing an incremental crisis that is not being discussed. Hospitalization has gone up nearly twenty-five percent among the Wild in the past few days alone. Furthermore, reports are now coming in that show not only has this year's blossoming of the many fruits on our island been delayed and lacking, but they carry an extreme infection experts are calling the Balooza," she said as the entire audience gasped and muttered. "Our island has seen many diseases in its history, but due to the recent behavior of nature, it is abundantly obvious our island is not well, and we may be facing problems more significant than when Synacara spread over fifteen avons ago. Thus, I recommend to this council that we comply completely with the Pleaser's orders and pass this resolution," Lyren said before sitting down. The Assentory broke out in complete argument as many stood up and shouted.

"Oh, this is preposterous. What about the younglings who go to schools? What about the millions who need to work? Because of an increase in crime, must all the wild suffer? This is utter bombastic nonsense!" said a brown-furred gorilla in a suit with a fat tie as he threw down his briefcase on his desk.

"That is enough out of you, Mungis!" said the Vizer as he banged the gavel several times.

"As my colleague has just informed this council, there is an imminent breakout coming for us all. Clearly, the island has not been well. There is no use denying it, Consular!" said a red, sharp-shelled pangolin.

"Consular Showven! What we are talking about is the sheltering of all our citizens for normal and everyday life! The Wildlings will lose their patience, and I assure the Pleaser, he will feel the wrath of the Wild should this notion pass!" said a large purple lobster.

"I would just like to state that the recent increases in robberies and missing Wildlings are higher than they have ever been before. To an extent, I do agree with the urgency of the Pleaser, and that we do need to entertain a potential, widespread shutdown for the mere safety of the Wild!" Peister said standing up. Immediately, many members began to laugh out loud, while others remained quiet to listen.

"What? Why are you agreeing with the Pleaser?" Peister's own colleagues blurted out.

"Not enough votes from yesterday's debate? *Oh, I forgot, you got crushed!*" said a large white pelican, falling backwards and laughing as others burst out too.

BANG BANG BANG

"There will be no insults spewed in the chamber! Need I remind you all we are in session! We are in *formal* session!" The Vizer said as he continued to hit the gavel until everyone was silent. "Please continue with your synopsis, Mr. Precarious."

"These are no ordinary times. Should a full and complete lockdown take place, there would be no opportunity to establish our widely sought trade routes, a plan that would boost our own economy and the livelihood of every Wildling! Furthermore, there has been much evidence and personal accounts that these criminals are human invaders. I remind my colleagues of memo CD6370 released and revoked thirty years ago. I understand many, myself included, were not a part of this body. Regardless, however, I am willing to cite this as circumstantial evidence as a *possibility* to help explain underlying circumstances. We must act seriously before more tra—" the vulture said before being interrupted by many outbursts from all around.

"The trade route? Now is the time you see fit to discuss the trade route?"

"Humans stealing from us? Why there are hardly any on the island itself!"

"What, do you suggest we deport all humans from our island? Is that what you recommend? Not a single police report has even indicated them, and you stand here in the historic chamber saying such hateful, speciest remarks? Have we resorted to conspiracies already?"

"Are you suggesting we just raid every human household for full proof? Disregard their Wild rights guaranteed under our Grand Charter? I tell you what, you are going far above and beyond the Pleaser's notion and I would be damned if we come down to it!"

"A desperate attempt at votes. A desperate attempt Peister, that's all this is!"

BANG BANG BANG

"ORDER! THERE WILL BE ORDER!" Vizer Iwick demanded as he smashed the gavel.

"Might I have the chance to clarify! I must!" Peister asked the floor, and the penguin nodded. "I am not recommending any radical treatment for humans on this island. The court system of assumed innocence for every Wildling is the law of the land, the will of the Wild! Nor do I concur with the absurd claims that there is any rampant disease spreading throughout our island. But the Wild should beware, there is a special group of sophisticated perpetrators among us. Perhaps invaders from another land who may have found the Wazoo somehow. I would be willing to allow the Venali tigers to search the premises or at least consider a temporary or limited lockdown in certain regions of the island!"

"We must not entertain the conspiracies of Mr. Precarious nor Ms. Lyren!" said Yarbis Yackley. "They are simply conjuring a mere fantasy and poisoning the peace of the Wildlings' mind, and I will NOT have it. I say before this council today with full confidence that there is no impending disease nor any foreign invaders!" he said as many of the Consulars stood and cheered. "Furthermore, let me emphasize with the highest certainty that it is *impossible* to find the Wazoo. IMPOSSIBLE! It has never nor will ever be done!" More applause broke out, with many Wildlings beginning to stand. "Rather than entertain the ideas of these ridiculous Consulars, we must take our time seriously and focus on the pressing issues of crime. To let all the Wild know, no matter what is at stake, this is a land of dreams, a land where dreams can *never* die! And most promptly, we must let the Pleaser know we do not believe in his fear-mongering ways, that we will *NOT* give in!" he said, raising his arm out to the cheering.

"Wow they really all hate Peister!" Sal said as the chamber broke into aggressive arguments again. Vizer Iwick continued to smash his gavel as he tried to stop all the across the aisle yelling going on.

Suddenly, a few white tigers walked forward above the entire chamber, behind where the Vizer had stood. The Venali surrounded the entire Arcadium, a few jumping on top of the tall stone arches and looking down at all the terrified Consulars beneath them. A lion slowly approached and sat on top of the small hill over-looking the entire chamber.

"Is that who I—" Amelia asked before I cut her off.

"That's Greygor Guildenhall," I said in awe. The lion looked just as I had seen in my dream, his tall bulky fig-ure with a long brown mane that ran near to the back of his legs.

The Pleaser sat silently as all members of the As-sentory looked up at him. They were all in shock, even Vizer Iwick did not know what to do. "Oh, Pleaser Guil-denhall, what an honor it is to be in your presence," he said as he and everyone else bowed, well all except for one standing member, Yarbis Yackley.

"I would like to add that the Pleaser is not a mem-ber of this council nor has he been summoned by the Elders to be here! I request he not interfere with our discussion and permit us to continue evaluating his notion," Consular Yackley said firmly. Greygor took a brown paper from his palm and handed it to one of his Venali guards, who took it with his mouth and slid down into the side of arcs before hopping down the floor. Everyone in the chamber was terrified as the Vizer received the note and read it out loud himself.

"The Pleaser has overseen this meeting today and believes this serious council gathering has turned into a charade for campaign slogans and theatrical performances. Therefore, he will ask the courts for approval for a full lockdown of the island. Any resolution from this chamber has been formally dismissed," Iwick said as Greygor got back up and walked away, the Venali tigers following him.

"Outrageous, this goes against the wishes of the Elders to examine the best courses of action! The Pleaser has breached his power! We will sustain until the Assentory has agre—"

BANG BANG BANG

The aisles began to fill as Consulars protested as they left the Arcadium, a few still shouting and arguing. I kept my eyes searching, looking for Peister, while also trying to avoid being seen by any of the bear guards around.

"What's going on? Why did the Pleaser stop this meeting? What is he trying to do?" Sal asked as we walked slowly through the bushes near the exit.

"I-I don't know, he really wants this lockdown for some reason," I said, already having my suspicions that it was to help the pirates.

"Jimmy, where are you going? Come back!" Amelia asked. But I didn't listen. I needed to find Peister, figure out what just happened, and tell him what I knew. I just hope none of the nicely dressed Consulars would notice a thirteen-year-old kid trespassing.

I was lucky they were all too furious at each other to even bother seeing me. But I walked past all their noisy commotion and saw Peister walking into the forest. I ran after him, just hoping none of the Kulinyan bears would jump up and attack me. I called out to him, and he quickly turned around in complete shock, immediately ending a conversation with a constituent.

"Wh- Jimmy? What are you doing here, boy?" he asked as he put one of his broken wings around me and walked further away from the rest of the Consulars. I wasn't sure if he didn't want to get humiliated again with the jokes, or if he was just embarrassed to be talking to a youngling in public. "You have no business being in a place like this. I suggest you turn around immediately before security sees you."

"I can't, I have to tell you something," I said right before I went on explaining everything I knew about the pirates, how I had dreams about them, how I did research about them in a book, and even that I heard Greygor talking to a goat known as the Watchwaker, whatever that was.

"*The Watchwaker*? You mean to say Greygor Guildenhall was talking to Watchwaker Ghanji about pirates in your dream? Is that really what you are saying?"

"Yes! He knows all about them. He may have even helped them get here, somehow. But we have to do something, we have to let everyone know. I know it was ju—"

"Just a dream? Are you kidding me Jimmy? Dreams are the most powerful phenomenon known to the Wild, how did you even manage to slip into Greygor's?" he asked curiously, but I had no reply. I didn't even know why, much less how. All I could think of was the tall bird that guided me. "We must act Jimmy. Because, to be honest with you, my colleagues and I are wondering why he seeks to lock down our island and release his personal guards. Something very dangerous is going on. But we need proof first."

"We have to go to the papers; I can tell them about my research and everything I've found."

"That still won't be enough. We have to do something else, something drastic," he said, looking away from me. I stood confused, and not at all ready for what he was about to say next. "I will need your help if we are to do this Jimmy."

"To do what?" I asked.

"I'll need you to break into the Pleaser's Palace. Find evidence of any sort, whether it be a recording between Greygor and someone else, or some sort of letter he wrote. Regardless, I will need proof the pirates are here and that he knows."

"WHAT! You wa- how? How can we even do that?"

"I have an idea how I can get you in, Jimmy. Just give me a few days to sort through things, then I can write to you when I am ready. But you will be safe, I assure you that. No one will even know you were there."

"Wh-Peister, I don't know. Can't you get someone else? Another Wildling?"

"Not someone I can trust, Jimmy! Not someone that will keep this a secret. Besides, you seem to have a knack for sneaking into places you do not belong, don't you?" he said, staring. "Still, though, I understand if you wanted something in return for doing a task as dangerous as this. Tell me, is there anything you want? I am a Consular after all. My influence is quite extensive, to say the least."

I stood, thinking to myself for a moment. There weren't many opportunities anyone would get asked this.

"Well, I wrote an essay about pirates for my history class and my teacher is probably going to fail me, can you convince him to give me an A?" I asked naively. Peister thought for a moment before turning back to me with a large smile.

"An essay about pirates? Similar to what we talked about earlier? Hmmm. How about I take it up a notch," he said, but I was confused with absolutely no idea what he meant. "I'll put your essay on the front page of *The Wilder.*"

I nearly fainted from shock alone. *The Wilder? Would I, at thirteen years old, really have an article in the biggest newspaper all across the Wazoo?* It seemed too good to be true. And indeed, it really was. I agreed without even hesitating.

The Pleaser's Palace

MS. KEATON WAS NOT TOO THRILLED when she heard why my friends and I had to miss her exam, but we all decided to make up the excuse we were too sick with the Balooza that was going around (though none of us had hardly any idea what that was just yet). Luckily, she let us make it up after school.

But that was all a few days ago and now it's the least of my worries. Today I was going to break into the Pleaser's Palace, a castle located on one of many little islands known as the Ivory Islets just off the coast of the Wazoo. My plan was to leave right before Dorlin's class and sneak back after recess, but that's only if everything went well. Peister's letter made it seem like he knew exactly what I needed for this, and that everything would be fine. Still though, I couldn't help but shake at just the notion of trespassing by the most vicious beasts the Wazoo had ever known. I mean, they had been banned from coming onto the mainland for millions of years, and with good reason, I assume! How exactly was I going to do this?

"What's wrong, Jimmy? You seem really nervous about something? I've never seen you jitter this much," Amelia said as I sat shaking my pencil during study hall. "I'm sure you did fine on the test," she said, but that hadn't even crossed my mind.

I took a deep breath before sitting back up and looking around. I didn't want anyone to overhear me or see Amelia freak out. I had told her what Peister wanted me to do, what I was going to leave to do in just a few minutes. She was speechless and thought, rightfully so, that I was on a mission to kill myself.

"Jimmy! You know how illegal all this is? You can't do this, there's no way you'll be able to sneak past Venali! They'll kill you right when they lay their eyes on you."

"I know Amelia, but I already agreed! And besides, if I don't, the pirates will just roam around without anyone ever finding out! You know what those men are capable of? Every Wildling is in danger if I don't do this."

"But pirates, Jimmy? You really think they're here at the Wazoo? I mean, from your essay alone, they don't sound too smart. I'm sure they'll get caught soon. It's not worth risking though. Please, don't do this."

"I have to," I said right before getting up and going

up to our sloth monitor. "Mr. Ekels, can I get a pass to go to the library please?"

"Mr. Ekels, can I get one too please?" Amelia said, walking up right behind me. I raised my eyebrows and shook my head, but she did not back down. "I'm not going to let you do this! Not alone at least," she said as we walked out of the front doors. I wasn't really worried until she barged into this. Somehow, I could live with myself getting hurt, but the chance at losing Amelia, my best friend since I was a kid? Now I was really beginning to panic.

We flew over to Horresaak Bay on the northeastern side of the island but found no one there to take us to the palace. We had been sitting on a giant rock for a few minutes. Peister's letter said we had to wait for someone named Terren to come meet us on shore, but I was beginning to have my doubts.

"Should we turn around?" she said after fifteen minutes of silence. We had been panicking this whole time, but now we were wondering if Peister had lied to me just to get back at me for falling on him.

It wasn't until I began throwing shiny little blue rocks into the shallow end that I heard a loud splash and a giant reddish-pink squid suddenly emerge from the water with its many long tentacles stretched out. The Wildling had large yellow eyes and peered back and forth at Amelia and me as we walked up.

"Jimmy Jungles, is that you down there? Oh, and a friend I see! No worries, I can squeeze you both in with me," he said in a high, cheery tone.

"Are you Terren?" I asked.

"Why, yes, yes, I am! Come now, we have to hurry! We have much, much to do!"

"Wait, I just wanted to ask before we go, how are we goi—" Amelia began to ask before we were grabbed with his long tentacles and held us in the air.

"Alright kids, we're about to make a deep dive. How long can you both hold your breath for?" Terren said.

"Uh, maybe a minute, I think," I said.

"Oh, okay, I'll try to swim quickly then! Now take a deep breath both of you."

"WAIT WHAT'S HAPPENING!" Amelia yelled as he straightened his body before diving into the sea. We passed by many Widaroh fish, which had long yellow strings coming out from their wing side and Batmets, which changed their shiny complex scales from bright pink to dark green and a pretty orangish-blue. But we hardly had the time to admire any of this beauty, nearly gasping for air at this point.

We must have sunk thirty or forty feet deep when I saw a large dark blue whale waiting. We landed immediately on top of it, but what was most surprising of all was that there was no water around us anymore. Amelia and I coughed as we were catching our breath from this unexpected bubble of fresh air underneath the sea. Amelia and I looked at each other, completely confused. "H-how are we breathing right now?" I asked, looking at Terren.

"Ougou whales have an ability to create an atmosphere above them for their air, to breathe but also use as a weapon if predators attack. "Go ahead, see for yourself. Stick your hand out, younglings," Terren said as I put my hand out towards the sea. None of the water leaked inside, and I was able to pull it in and out with almost no trouble at all, like we were in a barrier or something. In all my time at the Wazoo, I had never known a Wildling that could do something like this.

"But sir, you still haven't told us the plan! We don't even think we'll be safe. There will be tigers everywhere. Maybe we should turn around," Amelia said.

"No, you kids will be safe. Trust me, they won't even see you coming," he said as we traveled deeper into the sea. "Ugaash, take us to Lakora's cavern," he said as the whale let out a high-pitched moan.

Ugaash moved swiftly through the water, passing by large prickly purple gharofish, little orange yiglots, arrowhead seahorses, and wide humfish creating air bubbles as they swam as a large pod together through spiral jellyfish with all around types of tall and long wrinkle coral nearly as long as one of Terren's tentacles. We passed by all this until we came upon jagged rocks that had a wide canvas opening.

We were rising back up through the narrowing cavern when I saw small yellow lights moving above us. Terren grabbed us both and shot straight up towards the flickering lights. They were little starflies circling around the air, lighting the dark cave around us.

"Okay, come here younglings. This is how you will get past everyone," he said, pulling out a long green weed tarp. "This is Caecuweed. It will hide you from any of the Venali tigers lingering around," Terren said as he handed it to us.

I picked it up and held it over my body, to which

Amelia quickly became shocked. "Jimmy! Half your body is gone!" she said in disbelief. I was shocked. I threw the whole thing over myself and began to run around, Amelia's head scrambling as she tried to look for me. "Wh-where'd you go Jimmy? I can't see you anymore," she said stunned.

"This thing is incredible!" I said as I reappeared behind her and she jumped back a little. "I've never heard of anything like this before on the Wazoo!"

"Ah yes, not too many have. The sea has many kept secrets, you see. And not too many know of this, but please do be careful children, if not the Venali may still notice. They are renowned in all the Wild as the best hunters. Please be careful."

"Okay, and what do we do? What do we have to find?" Amelia asked nervously.

"As Peister asked, we need anything that may prove there are pirates. Documents or even a conversation. OH! Which reminds me, take this," Terren said, handing us a small shell attached to a wooden block with a long coil of thin plant stem coiled inside. "This is a recorder. Push in the little swirl here to start it and push it on the other end when you want to stop. The Pleaser should be in the Crown room at the very top. Just get to the second floor and go all the way down the hall until you see the large stairwell."

Amelia nodded her head as Terren placed the recorder onto her hand. I took her by my side with the tarp. "We can do this, it's not the first place we've ever snuck into. We just have to move slow," I said, reassuring the both of us.

"The exit is just through the grass patch at the end of the cave. Make sure you lock it before you come back here, okay? Do be careful, younglings! I will be waiting for you right here," Terren said as we walked through the cave path, lit by the starflies still buzzing around. We looked at the walls and saw large drawings of lions with smoke coming out of their noses and mouths as they attacked other Wildlings, until the very end when a large turtle with spikes on its head came crashing over them with a wave. I had no idea what any of it meant, but it was fascinating. Cave art wasn't something I had seen a lot of, nor did I expect to see any of it here, but it didn't matter. We had to keep going.

There was a stone lock right at the end of the tunnel. When I unlatched and pushed against it, sunlight immediately ripped through and blurred my vision.

I hadn't known very much about the Ivory Islets. Only that it was named after the many large elephants that roamed its ground. But when I looked around, there was a large, beautiful, luscious, garden with long, curved hedges, tall, bright yellow trees with aisles of indigo roses, blue ivies, and red tulips just to name a few.

As we came out from under the hill opening, we walked through the garden, passing long-headed woodpeckers flying around as warblers chirped loudly. We walked closer to the palace and past a large white marble fountain that had a giant turtle with the same crown thorns on its head as the one on the cave walls. There was a description written right in front that I pulled Amelia to go over and read:

In memory of Taatuwah Tyromar, Watchwaker of the Wazoo, the pioneer of peace, crusher of cruelty, Dreamsire to all who suffer. For the everlastment of dreams, the end of untold fantasies, know thyself and the truth of all truths, all is given, now and forevermore.

Amelia and I had the Caecuweed blanket over us as we stood and looked at this majestic statue. This Watchwaker statue was of the same turtle I had seen on the walls in the cave just below. This was now the second time I was hearing about a Watchwaker, after hearing Greygor talk to one, yet I still had no idea why they were so important.

"Do you know what a Watchwaker is?" I asked.

"Yeah, they're the spiritual leaders of the island, sworn to protect dreams. It's a tradition that's been going on since the very founding of the island," Amelia said.

Just ahead were a few gray, large-headed elephants roaming around the garden, each with extraordinarily bright, colorful patterns: spirals, shapes, flowers, even drawings of different animals, as if it was all telling a different story. Behind them was a tall, tan stone palace with green vines growing all around the sides and hanging from the main entrance. The Pleaser's Palace had many trees growing from it and large archway openings on the ground and upper floors. It had an elegance unlike anything I had ever seen before.

At this point, we had yet to see even a single Venali

tiger. You'd think, coming to the Ivory Islets, that they would be everywhere, keeping an eye out for any threat. But it wasn't until we walked slowly through the vines over the large archway that one popped out of nowhere and walked past us to the outside. I pressed Amelia back as we both leaned against a wall. Venali tigers were known to be aggressive, and were one of the few species I had ever heard of that could turn invisible on command.

My heart was racing, my body was shaking, and I tried to breathe as quietly as I could while we walked past half a dozen white tigers on the first floor of the palace. Though we were hidden by the Caecuweed, their eyes were piercing at me as if they sensed something. If they didn't see us, then they could probably smell us. I kept us on the move as they slowly approached.

We walked up along the spiral staircase as quietly as we could and saw nearly two or three dozen Venali standing their post or roaming the halls. Amelia's eyes jumped up, and I took in a deep breath. We had to get to the Crown room, and we saw staircases just down the hall.

Between the archway windows were paintings of many Pleasers of the past, so beautiful that we couldn't ignore staring at them for just a few seconds while slowly creeping along the hall.

A few tigers we passed sniffed the ground and walls aggressively as their furs stuck up. They looked around confused, not sure what was triggering their senses. If we had any time, it wouldn't last for long.

We walked up against another set of spiral staircases

that led to a single door. Beside us was a tall portrait of a tall white ram with horns that curled and pierced forward as it stood high on the mountainside looking up at the sky. I knew instantly it was Gaelor Gideon, the first Pleaser of the Wazoo. Almost everyone on the island knew who he was and how he fought for freedom and peace on the island many millions of years ago.

Two Venali tigers came walking down the hall of the Crown Room. Amelia and I stood still against the wall, holding our breath as we waited for them to walk downstairs.

We were about to enter the top when another Venali walked out in front. "What is your business here?" it asked firmly, looking right at us. I looked behind and quickly put my hand over Amelia's mouth as I pushed us back against the wall. Another white tiger came from behind and passed us by.

"I wanted to report that the first vanguard has been sent out, but crime has steadily increased in Delaor and Swyvyk. The criminals may be localized around there, but we are still tracking their route as we speak," said the tiger right in front of us.

"Very well, I will alert the Pleaser as soon as he is finished," said a tiger as he turned and began walking back to the room.

When we reached the top, we entered a large round room with tinted blue windows. Greygor Guildenhall, the large blonde furred lion with a long brown mane, had been sitting behind his stone desk. He had piles of papers all over it and a small hamster with a pink sweater and large glasses writing furiously as the lion spoke to a fat pig wearing a blue suit and pants with a monocle over his eye.

" ... not sure if more security will even help! These filthy pirates just run around and ransack whatever it is they can get their hands on. I have yet to catch even one of them as we speak!"

"Amelia, get the tape out, we have to record this," I whispered as we walked closer to the ongoing conversation.

"My liege, I would do anything and everything possible to help the Wildlings of the Wazoo. Might I suggest a plan to help with appeasement of our situation?" said the fat pig.

"Oh, what deal are you trying to strike up now, Hortley?"

"Well, Mr. Pleaser, I believe what we truly need is to establish an agreement that benefits both pirates and Wildlings alike. A deal that could fill both our pockets would surely urge them to temper their behavior."

"And just what are you thinking exactly?"

"How open are you to the establishment of a trade route to the outside world? Where our very precious plants, fruits, and gems could be exchanged for valuable resources and an expanded economy in return?"

"Oh, another suggestion for the trade route, how wonderful! You're beginning to sound like that crazy parrot Peister Precarious! Let me be perfectly clear when I say the Wazoo has *never* interacted with the known world. We are to remain hidden and avoid all direct contact. That has been the will of the Wild since our inception and I will NOT be the first Pleaser to break such tradition!"

"Well sir, you must understand these are untraditional times. And I assure you, the Wazoo has been found for the very first time, I presume, in our history. This gracious lockdown you are vying for could work to our advantage. It would be fortunate if we sought an agreement and created a symbiotic relationship with our aggressors. What better proposition than a business that-"

"THERE WILL BE NO SUCH THING, HORTLEY!" Greygor yelled angrily. Hortley quickly froze up before nodding his head.

"I understand, my liege. I hope in due time you will reconsider," Hortley said as he grabbed his cane and got up, slowly walking out of the office. But Greygor was still agitated even after the fat pig left. There was a tall, light blue bird with a wide yellow beak and skinny legs, quietly listening in the back.

"Sir, I must say the negotiations with the pirates are not getting better anytime soon. We must seek some way of satisfying them. They are growing impatient and becoming more reckless by the day. It will not be long before Wildlings discover they are indeed on the island. Perhaps what Hortley is suggesting would be beneficial to -."

"I AM PLEASER OF THE WAZOO AECHUS, DO YOU UNDERSTAND? I HAVE CONTROL OVER EVERY PEBBLE ON THIS ISLAND AND COMMAND THE ENTIRE ROYAL ARMY. I COULD CRUSH THEM AT WILL LIKE I HAVE ALREADY DONE BEFORE!

AND YOU ARE MY PATRON, THE LAST ONE TO EVER QUESTION MY JUDGMENT!" he said getting up and shouting down the blue bird.

"My Pleaser, my Pleaser, I must apologize for any offense," Aechus said as he bowed. Meanwhile, the brown hamster had jumped off the table to search the ground for Greygor's glasses that had fallen off. "Of course, I believe you have complete control over the situation. I would never question *your* judgment. You are doing everything possible, but there is a rising sickness among us. All can tell the Wazoo is not well, that something is a little off sir. Many have already sought critical care as numbers rise daily. We must be ahead of this and sign an order today for a complete lockdown."

"The Consulars have already rejected this notion when I disclosed this to them a few days ago. It seems many are more interested in setting their campaign against me rather than actually carrying out the will of the Wild. But no matter, our best chance is to go to the courts directly, or warn the Wildlings of this disease without mentioning the pirates at all. But I do not intend on cooperating with Mr. Hasselback's effort in the backend to set up any sort of business practice with those savages. That greedy pig will surely be the end of us, should he profit from it," Greygor said as his temper now calmed down.

"Sir, it is Elder Uraganu, he was wondering if you still wanted to meet to discuss plans to prevent another attack. Should we move this or ma—?" said a small guinea pig after picking up the phone.

"No! Tell him I'll be right there!"

"Okay, it's in the West Branch at the Sangrin Room with many Consulars as well."

"Please come be my scribe during this, Chachina. Have your staff work on finishing the court documents later," he said as his small secretary jumped off the desk with her notepad. "Aechus, you must come too, but remember, no mention of the pirates to any of the Elders," he said as the bird nodded before dreadfully coming along.

As Greygor and Aechus walked down the office entryway, Amelia and I waited a few seconds before taking off the Caecuweed.

I quickly ran behind Greygor's desk as Amelia stood still, in shock from hearing everything we had just heard. "Amelia, stop the recorder!" I said as I quickly skimmed and scrambled through all the piles of papers on the Pleaser's desk. "What are you doing? Don't just sit around there, we have to move quickly!" I said trying to yell but also whisper at the same time.

"I-I just can't believe any of this. I mean that whole conversation was- was unbelievable Jimmy! You were right! There really are pirates at the Wazoo- we've been found!" she said. I thought I'd feel better that she said that, but the more I looked at her, I could see how broken she was.

"It's okay Amelia, everything will be okay. Alright?" I said, hugging her as she began to tear up. "But we really need to get this done, not for us, but for all the Wildlings who need to know, okay? Do you trust me? Ca-can we do this?" She nodded and we both rummaged through Greygor's desk again. We already had the recording, but I knew deep down we would need physical proof. Proof Wildlings could see for themselves.

We shuffled through many papers as fast as we could until we finally came across a wrinkled old paper, water-stained and with almost illegible handwriting. "I think I found it," I said to Amelia as she looked over. I read it outloud.

WE HAVE BEEN AT THE WAZOO FOR NEARLY 10 DAYS NOW. WE HAVE NO REASON TO BE STUCK ON THIS DUMP ISLAND AND WILL LEAVE AS SOON AS WE FIND WHAT WE NEED. BUT YE HAVE BEEN NO GOOD TO US N' MY CREW IS GROWN IMPATIENT.
I SEE YOU STUPID ANIMALS LOOKIN' FER US. STAND DOWN OR WE WILL STAR' KILLIN' AND LEAVIN' BODIES 'ROUND. MY MEN ARE NOT AFRAID. DO NOT TEST US.
HELP US FIND THE DREAM, OR FEEL THE WRATH OF ME CROCS, AN' THE WHOLE ISLAND BURNED TO THE GROUND.

-IRONBOOT

Ironboot? Was this what they called Nevra Venay-hue? But as I began to get lost in my thoughts wondering, I turned to see Amelia shaking anxiously.

"They're going to kill Wildlings? Burn the island?

Oh Jimmy, they really are savages!"

Honestly, I felt exactly the same as she did, but I didn't want her to get any more worried than she already was.

"I don't know, but we have to get this to—" I was saying before we heard commotion coming from the staircases to the Crown Room. Amelia quickly ran over to me and threw the seaweed tarp over us. We backed against the wall as the tigers came into the room.

"I'm telling you Hargaan, I-I can smell it," said one of the Venali tigers to a large gray tiger with thick black stripes and a scar over his face.

"Well, where is it T'kaajy? You kee—" he said angrily before staring right at the desk we had just defiled. They quickly walked past us and began to sniff the entire desk. "D-do you think what I am thinking?" asked the dark, scar-faced tiger.

"I think someone just raided this office. The Pleaser never keeps it this messy, and it- it smells like humans too!"

"But how? Humans could not have gotten past us! We have guards all around the Palace! Someone would have mentioned it."

"I don't know, but I am telling you, I smell it here, I smell humans here along with a strange seaweed," said the white tiger as he smelled around the room. "The stench is strong. I-I think they are still here *IN THIS ROOM!*" he said as he sniffed and jumped against the wall not too far away from us. I slowly stepped closer to my right, hoping to make a quick and quiet exit from the room. But they walked closer. We covered our mouths, waiting.

"Nothing! You smell nothing T'kaajy, you spend too much time in the hot springs and eating eluhawheat! Let's go back down to our patrol," said the tiger, still following behind his friend.

"Perhaps you are right, Hargaan," he said slowly as he turned back and walked slowly. Amelia and I held our breath until suddenly the tiger's eyes shot wide open and jumped right on top of us. We fell back as the tiger clawed and bit the tarp off of us. We tried to regain our footing as I tugged the Caecuweed out from under the tiger's jaws, knowing full well that if we didn't have this, there was no way we'd be able to make it out of the palace grounds.

"HUMANS!" the gray tiger yelled before it roared ferociously.

We headed for the stairs and ran down as I threw the Caecuweed back over us, but we were making so much noise it was almost pointless to even be wearing it. We reached the second floor, gasping for air as the tiger roared again, but we didn't even waste a second looking back.

We came to a stop suddenly when we saw the floor packed with tigers all roaming and arguing with each other. Somehow they already knew. Quickly I turned and guided us carefully into a room, peaking in to see it was empty before I slowly closed the door.

"WHAT INVADERS? HOW?", "WHAT DO YOU MEAN THE PLEASER'S OFFICE HAS BEEN RAIDED?" "HOW COULD THEY HAVE ESCAPED?" "HOW DID WE NOT SEE THEM BEFORE?" I overheard them all arguing, but I knew we didn't have much time. We

needed to find a way out of here.

"What is going on here? What is the meaning of all this ruckus? I am in the middle of a very important meeting!" someone said in a deep voice. I slowly creaked open the door and looked down the far hallway. Greygor Guildenhall was surrounded by Venali tigers, all bowing down before him.

"My lord, I am so sorry to bother you. But it appears someone has broken into the Palace and stolen from your crown. We are looking everywhere, but we cannot find the humans who did this."

"WHAT! HOW DID THEY GET PASSED HARGAAN?" he said before slashing his claws across the tiger's face. "SEARCH EVERY FOOT OF THE IVORY! I WANT THEM BROUGHT TO ME AT ONCE!" Greygor said again and they all rattled off, sniffing and searching aggressively while many others ran downstairs.

"Looks like it's cleared up, this might be our best chance!" Right as we were about to open the door wider and slip out, a tiger pushed it back and barged into the room. Amelia and I walked back slowly against the back window. "Sakuut, come here, something happened here, I feel it!" he said, sniffing. Another tiger walked in and didn't say a word, but instead sniffed around the walls.

"This is the same scent I picked up from the office, Camugar. They were here, they definitely were," he said, sniffing the other side. The tiger's face was right in front of our bellies as it sniffed the floor. I tried to scoot us closer towards the door, but suddenly the tiger turned and jumped on us.

"What is it?" asked Sakuut.

"THE PERPETRATORS!" he yelled while clawing the seaweed off of us, shaking as the tiger was now on top, staring at me with its wide black pupils. The tiger had gripped my leg and started to pull me back with its sharp white teeth, digging into my bone. Amelia got up and leaned against the wall before kicking it right in the face! The tiger was stunned. I took the Caecuweed, but the other tiger jumped over trying to grab me. Amelia pulled my arm but we fell through the arc window right into the bushes several feet below.

The tigers roared from the room we were just in as they peered out the window and looked directly at us. I could hear the other tigers running out as they rushed towards us from around the castle. We threw the Caecuweed over us and ran.

I thought we had a good gain on them, but one white tiger out of all the rest was quickly outrunning them, and worst of all, it was able to see our tracks even as we walked past all the sand and back into the garden.

We tore through the hedges and flowers, the hill with the secret passage within our sights, but the tiger was only a few leaps away from us, its long yellow fangs practically hanging over our backside.

"Keep running straight to the passage, I'll meet you there," I said to Amelia as I let go of the Caecuweed and began running away in my own direction. The tiger quickly turned and followed me, ignoring Amelia as she called my name. "Go Amelia! Go!" I yelled as I ran through a few hedges onto a grassy field. I was running away for a while but hadn't seen the tiger that was chasing us. For a moment, I thought it went after Amelia. Suddenly, out of nowhere, the tiger reappeared from behind and jumped on my back.

It turned me around and roared in my face, staring at me with its wide eyes."THIEF! WHAT HAVE YOU STOLEN FROM THE PLEASER?"

"I-I didn't st-"

"LIAR!" it yelled as it clenched its jaws onto my arm and dug in with its teeth. I screamed as I bled. I tried punching its face, but the tiger didn't budge. *This was it. This is when I would die*, I thought at first. But out of nowhere, an elephant charged and threw the tiger off me with its large tusks.

Run, youngling, more are coming! The voice was somehow loud yet also coming from my own head. But I didn't have time to even think. I quickly got up and ran back. I saw many tigers running past me and towards the field as I climbed back into the passageway underneath the hill and shut the latch. I was panting heavily, lying against the rocky walls as I tried to catch my breath.

"Jimmy, are you alright?" Amelia asked as she looked and saw my torn clothes and open bruises. "Oh no, you're bleeding!" But I didn't respond, still trying to catch my breath and get the image of the tiger's eyes out of my head. It was quiet for a few seconds before I could think about what needed to be done next.

"Amelia, give me the Caecuweed. I'm going to hide it in my satchel," I said right before we walked up to Terren to tell him we lost it.

Chapter 10

The Breakaway Bandits

WE WERE LUCKY TERREN BELIEVED we lost the Caecuweed sheet he had given us, even though Amelia was still confused why I lied to him. I figured after a terrifying bout like that, we may need this again at some point. And who knows, it may be handy to disappear at a moment's notice.

A few days had passed since we gave the recordings and letter to the giant squid, who said he now had to give these to a few pesky little monkeys who wouldn't stop poking him in the eye. I hoped Peister was going to hold his end of the bargain though, I still hadn't received my graded essay back from Mr. Dorlin, and I wasn't necessarily in a rush to get that back.

News broke early Monday morning on every single paper I could think of, each with its own twist: *The Wazoo Has Been Found, Unfriendly Next Door Neighbors, Greygor Guildenhall's Biggest Scandal, Incoming War.* Over the next couple days there was a panic, even the newscasters had no idea what to make of it. Zheyban Zwitszer, a fast speaking, black feathered Bnuken bird was somehow even more incomprehensible than usual as he flipped out during *The Early Bird Show.*

"Breakingnewsohdowehavesomebreakingnews! Itsappearswehavebeeninfiltrated,INFILTRATED,b-yagroupofraidersknownasthePIRATES!Whatanunbe-lievablestorycomingforwardrightnow.Butdon'tfreak-out,pleasewedon'twantanyonefreakingout,even thoughI'mfreakingout,youdon'tfreakout,okay?Okay!" the black bird spattered out in a few seconds before taking out a brown bag and huffing in and out of it. They cut to break almost immediately.

Others went right into the details of the letter, con-fused by its very essence, Jasalee Japayla tried desper-ately to figure.

"Okay, please tell us more about these human in-vaders, are they so uncivilized they must go along with obscure names like this, an 'iron boot'?"

"Yes, if I might clarify, it might be a nickname for the purposes of intimidation."

"So they just go around and intimidate everyone with their name, but it has to have some meaning, doesn't it? I mean, honestly, how can any Wildling or human in this matter travel so many megafeet of ocean, swimming or sailing, with an iron boot? It just seems so absurd for anyone to believe this.”

“Yes well, we do not know the nature of these iron boot people, and the letter alone is not enough to affirm their existence, but if the leaked tapes are as valid as we believe they are, then not only is the Pleaser aware of their presence, but is actively hiding them from the rest of the Wild.

“Yes, it does seem the Pleaser did acknowledge them, and indeed seems very worried. But it is of utmost importance that the Assentory bring forth the whistleblower of this entire situation. Do we have the slightest clue as to who that might be just yet?”

“Well, we are not entirely sure, but we estimate that it may be someone in Greygor’s administration. However, there have been speculative stories of a potential break-in as well.”

“A break-in? Do you mean at the Pleaser’s Palace? Oh that is simply impossible!”

“These are only rumors, maybe even murmurs. But we are still investigating the matter.”

“That is still astounding to say that anyone could get past the Venali - well I can’t imagine it at all! But yes, it could have been someone on the inside that the Pleaser himself trusted, still though it is very difficult to imagine. But while we wait for answers to these investigations, the Wild is still awaiting for an official statement by Pleaser Guildenhall himself on his potential corruption or at least negligence to the Wildlings.”

“Turns out Jimmy really called it!” Sal burst out loud when we arrived at our usual corner before the first bell rang. "And you all thought he was crazy, isn't that right, Riley? And Amelia, Damien! But I believed you Jimmy! Those pirates, they're here! And now even the news won't shut up about it!"

"Well, I'll be the first to say, looks like your kookie essay had something to it after all!" Riley said in the only way she knew how to apologize. Amelia, however, hardly looked at me. Everyone else thought she just wasn't interested in all the talk or maybe upset at what she heard, but I knew why she chose to stay quiet. I knew exactly what she was thinking. I felt it myself.

Class resumed that day as usual, and I was still anxiously waiting to get all of my grades back in. My dad had told me to do better, but only now did it finally hit me.

D+
Complete lack of effort.
Conspiracy work with no sources.
<u>Pointless</u> and <u>Uncoordinated</u>!

I shook my head walking out. Even with the news, Mr. Dorlin didn't seem to flinch a bit at how much he hated me. Worst yet, there were red scratch marks, scribbles, large rudely worded comments all over it. I mean, the whole thing looked like it was bleeding! I'd have to rewrite the whole thing before I sent it out to Peister. I just hope he kept his promise of publishing it in the paper.

Ms. Keaton's class hadn't gone any better, and I crammed my C test into my backpack as we were packing up for the day.

"He's corrupt! Greygor Guildenhall is corrupt! We need Yarbis Yackley to kick him out this election," Eiidwic, a small red Sykaa deer said as it walked around with a bunch of posters on its side with a few bright green frogs on its back, shooting confetti as they went down the hall. Krayter, however, started ripping them all down and putting Peister posters up and chased after the deer once he saw him. I couldn't blame either of them, and couldn't hope more that Greygor Guildenhall would lose. I mean honestly, how do I almost go to jail for falling off a tree, but the Pleaser invites pirates to our island and nothing happens to him! It all sounded backwards to me.

Amelia had done a pretty good job hiding the fact that we broke into the palace and were the whistleblowers, though I wasn't sure how much longer she could hold out. Everyone had their breaking point. We were only Wildlings afterall.

"Amelia? Did you do badly on the test? Why have you been so quiet?" Riley asked her as she landed onto her shoulder.

"No, I just - uh didn't get a lot of sleep," she said lightly, but the truth was she had been stressed the whole weekend. We helped reveal the truth, but now it was a matter of who we could trust to actually get them off the island.

"Well, I got a B on my test! We have to celebrate that!" Sal said as we neared back to my house. Suddenly, we came and saw a chair laying right on the lawn of my house.

"What the-?" I said looking up and seeing the front window broken again. "Did someone turn the cleansweeper on again?" We ran up the stairs to my front door, which had a big dent in the center as if it had been kicked open.

I had never seen my house quite like this before. Kitchen drawers pulled out and stacked onto each other with silverware, plates, and even my food. Not to mention the fridge was left open, food thrown all over the kitchen. I knew exactly what mom would think if she saw all of this. I'd be grounded for a year at the least. Might even have to start sleeping in the garage.

"WHAT IN THE HELOKS HAPPENED HERE?" Riley said, freaking out. Just then, I heard something rumbling from upstairs and a tall, fat man came down to my kitchen with torn pants, a ripped shirt that barely fit over his enormous belly, and probably more hair on the sides of his face than on his head. He came down carrying a few drawers and was startled as he saw us.

"Who you be? This my loot!" he said, holding the drawers he was carrying to the side. A few plates and cups fell off and shattered on the floor.

"Calic, I told you we need to be careful," said a shorter, skinner man carrying piles of clothes from my parent's room.

"HEY PUT THOSE BACK!" I yelled as the man dropped everything and ran behind the counter. He was shaking erratically and silent as he took deep breaths.

"O-Oh, I'm so sorry. Wh-wh-who are y-you?" he said, barely able to hold his dull knife straight.

"Me? I'm the person that lives here! What are you doing in my house?" I said as the big oaf moved up a bit closer and was starting to get angry.

"This my loot! Get yer own!" the fat man with several missing teeth said again.

"What's all this ruckus about?" a dirty blonde boy a little older than me said as he walked over from my room. He wore a long ragged brown coat completely unbuttoned to show his torn blue shirt. He was carrying a few of my mom's gems and necklaces.

"Hey put that stuff down! Stop stealing my stuff!"

"'Fraid I can't do that, captain's orders."

"Captain?" I asked before suddenly realizing. *These were the pirates, and they were breaking into my house as we spoke.* "You- you're all pirates! You're with Nevra Venayhue and have a large ship called the Red Roaring a-an-and you're going to set the whole island on fire!" I said, walking towards them all and pointing as I made my accusations.

"Wh-hold up, hold up. Nevroy who? What you talkin' 'bout boy?" he laughed while making a wide smirk as he looked at his two friends completely confused.

"You're a pirate! You're not from the Wazoo!" I continued to accuse, but the boy did not flinch and instead reached in his pocket to take a bite out of a purple ecotta.

"Firs' of all, I ain' no pirate. Get that in ye damn head, boy. I'm Head Rebel of the Breakaway Bandits, understan'?"

"Ok, but you're with Nevra Venayhue, or Ironboot as the letter said. He brought you here, but why?" I yelled, but the pirate trio laughed again.

"Boy, jus' where you gettin' yer facts from? Ole' Ironboot is who we call Captain Bacawly, an' he ordered us to get him some supplies an' riches, but to be honest with ya, I ain' seen many places as nice as this 'round these parts. Captain will be most pleased, no doubt."

"No, you're not taking anything, that's all my stuff! My parents' stuff! Put it back and leave now!" I said.

"Jimmy, we should call the police," Damien said as he shook.

"WHAT IN THE HELL! Is that a talkin' doggie?" the trenchcoat boy yelled in amazement as he came down trying to pet Damien.

"Yes, I can speak perfectly fine," he replied while backing away.

"Calic, this lil' animal right here can speak better than you ever could!" the pirate boy said, chuckling.

"He's not an animal, he's a Wildling. We all are," Amelia said as she crossed her arms while shaking. We were all a little frightened as he slowly approached us.

"Oh, well I'm *so* sorry miss, I would jus' hate to offend ya," he said sarcastically as he raised his hands before taking another bite of the ecotta. "Was yall's names anyway?" he said turning around and looking right at me.

"Uh, Jimmy. I'm Jimmy Jungles. And who are you?" I said backing up as he turned around to walk back to the piles of drawers in the kitchen. I looked down and saw a long metal blade hanging off to his side. He was no ordinary bandit like he claimed, he was a lying pirate.

"Jimmy Jungles, huh? Why that's quite some name. They call me Wyatt Picker, an' the big oaf over here is Calic the Knobhead," he said pointing to him while he chewed down on some bread from the fridge. "An' this skinny pea we call Winsley Shivers," Wyatt said as the frail pirate waved lightly. Somehow, he was more uncomfortable with the confrontation than any of us.

I didn't know what to say, but I knew these three, along with the rest of his group, were behind all the attacks and robberies taking place. "And where are your pirate friends hiding? Hm, robbing the whole island? Tell me where Captain Bacawly is hiding!" I demanded.

"First of all, I tol' ya I ain' no damn pirate, okay? We might be rude, dirty scum, but we ain' nothin' like Ole' Ironboot's heartless crew! We the Breakaway Bandits, an' don't make me tell you again!" he said angrily while pulling out his large sword and pointing it at me. "An' second mos', I ain' gon' tell you junglefolk a thing 'bout where we hidin'. I can tell y'all gon screw up this whole plan already! An' believe me when I tell ya, you don' wan' messin' wit' ole' Ironboot. He's got crocs, an' they ain' the talkin kind a animals if ye get ma' drift. So you'd be best be stayin' 'way," he said seriously as he walked up and stared me dead in the eyes. I nodded.

"Alright well, you can't take my stuff! Put it all back. My parents, th-they're going to kill me if they see the house like this with everything gone!"

"Yer parents? Whatchu mean ya got them parents?" he asked as he walked back and took another bite from the ecotta.

"You know like a mom and a-a dad that like, well you know, look after you while you grow up? This whole place is their house, and well I live with them," I explained slowly, shocked that I even had to.

Wyatt was silent as he continued to chew while looking around. "Hm, that be soundin' like some work!

Anyway Jimmy, we best be on our way. Come on now boys, round up," he said as they all picked up the stacked drawers laying around in my kitchen.

"Wait! STOP! You can't take this stuff I nee-"

"Can't, captain's orders. I ain' told ya, but me 'n him got a deal goin'. I lend him my map an' after this whole bout all over an' he come gettin' what he's lookin' for, I get the Renegade all to meself," Wyatt said as he walked out the door, not even bothering to help his friends carry anything.

"Wh-what map? Wait, STOP! Can you at least tell me if he's found the Dream?" I asked quickly, wanting to know so many things.

"The what? Boy, this ain' no time for sleepin', we got begettin' back to the ship!"

"Wh- so you-, nevermind, but can you just please not take all our stuff, we really need all that you know!" I begged, but he immediately shook his head.

"'fraid not Jimmy, captain's orders!" he said as he marched out my front door. I should have run after him, but at that moment I could only think about how messy my whole house was and who my parents would blame.

Chapter 11

The Early Report Card

A FEW DAYS HAD PASSED since my house had been broken into. Wyatt and his other lowlife pirate friends seemed slightly less terrifying than the media and I had imagined them to be. But still, they were probably walking around continuing to rob, somehow going unnoticed by most Wildlings and police. That was another thing I wished I had asked.

I was lucky I had my friends to back me up about the pirates really breaking in, otherwise I don't think my parents would have ever believed me. Still though, Riley never left a detail unnoticed, and immediately started to barrage me with questions about what I meant when I asked them about the Dream, a little detail the media tried to not even mention. I just lied and said Peister told me about it, though I'm not even sure if he really had a clue what it was. I sure as heck didn't. But I knew I couldn't tell *any* of my friends that Amelia and I had broken into the Pleaser's Palace and leaked it all to the press. Don't get me wrong, I wanted to, but I just wasn't sure if they could handle it. I barely could.

I had been walking to school when reporters flooded around me, many of them holding microphones and talking in front of a camera while others were just flashing away with pictures. I had never been bombarded by the press before and had absolutely no idea what to say to them when they threw their questions at me.

"Jimmy! How did such a youngling like you write this bombshell article about the pirates? Have you had any special encounters?"

"Wh- no I just did a research project from what I saw on the news," I said, doing my best to lie. The last thing I needed was more questions from these reporters, but they relented on despite my trying to brush them all off.

"Do you or your family have any familiarity or connection with these human pirates upon our land?"

"What? No, of course not! Not all humans are pirates!"

"There are many speculating as to who the whistleblower could be? Is that you or one of the pirates you might know Jimmy?"

"Wh- whistleblower? No! And I'm not a pirate either," I said as I walked past all the reporters and finally made my way into school.

"JIMMY JIMMY! LOOK!" Jary said as he ran up with several other of his squirrel friends. He was holding today's edition of *The Wilder*. "You made the front page! I quickly took the paper and scanned it with my eyes.

A young Wildling boy by the name of Jimmy Jungles wrote a bombshell report for his classroom last week that detailed pirates were in fact dwelling on our land nearly thirty years ago! Similar patterns of crime and sickness spread during this period but the Pleaser and intelligence agencies were adamant about hiding this information- the truth! The paper continued to go on, mentioning parts of my article that I had read out loud in class. The teacher, Mr. Dorlin, was surely shocked by the article, but stated he was not surprised by such a reveal. "One can never know what to truly expect from Mr. Jungles, but surely it was one of the most profound, forthcoming articles I have ever read from a middle school student, I can assure you that!" All these nice words for the paper, yet I doubt he'd even consider changing my grade. As news from the still unknown whistleblower comes to light, and the Wild is learning the truth of the state of affairs on the island, that the Wazoo has actually been found, information from the young Jimmy Jungles gives us an important perspective into the nature of these pirates, and may bring us one step closer to finding them! Quite an important piece of journalism from our local middle school student!

"Wow Jimmy, the front page! That's amazing!" Sal jumped up emphatically.

"Gotta say...not too shabby! Looks like your essay wasn't so crazy after all!" Riley cheered.

"Unbelievable Jimmy! You know how many reporters fight for that spot? I can't believe you just mailed this in a few days ago and the papers took it right to the front page!" Damien said in disbelief. I just hope he didn't ask too many questions about it later, or else I'd have to tell all of my friends exactly what Peister and I had agreed to.

"Yeah well, I guess everyone is only talking about pirates nowadays. I just wish Dorlin would change my grade. Fat chance that happens though."

"By the way, did you ever find out where you kept that book?" Damien asked.

"No idea, still can't find it! Someone must have picked it off. I bet I was sitting in class or got bumped in the hallway when those Kuibida mice came and ran off with it. Little rascals are always stealing," I said, shaking my head.

But as exciting as it all was, Amelia stayed quiet, knowing full well what I had to do to get in the papers.

But that's not what bothered her. It was something else, something even my friends couldn't wrap their minds around. And I couldn't blame them either. Every headline of every newscast or paper only read along the lines that the Wazoo has been found, strange humans from abroad, or what could possibly exist beyond the island. But despite the fact the reporters and news outlets had talked about the pirates all day and night, they still wouldn't get into the full extent of just how cruel and gruesome they really were. And my fear was that we all might find out.

As the day went on, I only received more and more praise from students, who came up to talk to me in the halls, or ask me questions while in the middle of class. It's funny how quickly things can change. Most of them were laughing at me or thought I was crazy just a week ago, and now, they were all in awe of me. The Wild was truly an unpredictable place.

But for each Wildling who came up wanting to talk to me, I could only think, in the back of my mind, if they only knew the truth, if they all were saying the same thing, even if it was a rumor. *Did they think I was the one who broke into the Pleaser's Palace? That I spied, recorded, and gave away confidential information to the press?* I couldn't help myself from shaking as I thought that with one quick blink, a group of Venali tigers could appear out of nowhere and drag me away if they read the papers.

I finally got a chance to talk to Amelia when Mr. Ekels gave us study hall passes to the library after *everyone* would not stop staring and whispering as they watched me literally just do my homework. We were working at the back table, and Amelia, somehow, had kept her cool though she definitely wasn't. I thought I'd try to avoid the topic, but I couldn't resist. I had to know if she was feeling okay.

"So," I asked gently as she continued to keep her head down and write on. "How've you been?" I said as she continued to write silently before slowly looking back up at me.

"Uh- fine." she replied awkwardly before continuing her work.

"Amelia, come on. Just say what's bothering you! You've barely even talked since we broke into the Palace and even less when those stupid pirates came to my house. You haven't even congratulated me for making the paper!"

"Jimmy, I've just been busy, a lot is on my mind, that's all,okay?" she said as she went on to lifelessly do her homework, but I wasn't having it.

"Just- just say you're scared! Seriously, say something! Anything! Tell me how terrified you are about the pirates being here! Tell me you're worried, that you're panicking every night! Please, something! Anything!"

"WHAT JIMMY? What do you want me to say? You want me to congratulate you for all of your crimes? Stealing from your dad, stealing from the Pleaser? And lying to everyone along the way as *you* dragged me into this so *you* wouldn't get hurt? All so you could get *your* name in the papers!"

"Wh- is that why you think I did all of this?"

"It's not just that Jimmy! It's the fact that you're

willing to risk your own life, and refuse to listen to a thing I've said. And you know what, it's a good thing I did come because if I didn't Jimmy, and the tigers caught you or pinned you down an-and, I'm not sure we'd even be talking right now!"

"Well, I didn't force you to come! And what did you expect me to do? I told you what was going on before anyone else did, didn't I? I knew there were pirates at the Wazoo, and I was right, wasn't I? Now we all know, it's all over the news. But that's the problem, we only know they're here, not how or why, or what they even want!"

"So? You're just going to keep on doing all these crazy schemes to make things happen? Lie, steal, break who knows what laws, risk your own life all so the police and patrol do their jobs and catch the pirates?"

"This isn't fun for me, Amelia, believe me. I have suffered plenty because of it. But someone needs to do something!"

"Ok, and we have police, patrols, even the Royal Guard looking into this, why can't you just back off Jimmy? Step away. We're only school kids you know. Our only job is to do well in school, yet that only ever seems to be the last thing on your mind."

"Well, if you don't want to come along and help, or at least hear anything, then don't talk to me!" I said before I took all my things and marched up. I *thought* she was worried about everything going on, not that she was secretly mad at me this whole time. I mean, I was doing what was best for everyone, wasn't I? I couldn't understand how she could've been angry at me at the time, but I would have to think about all that another time. These were turbulent times at the Wazoo. Small things were suddenly changing, and all of it was just beginning to add up.

Not too long after I walked away from Amelia and into a private study room, which I was only able to have to myself for about three minutes before a goofball bird Douooresh Dardo, an always snacking ferret Forsef Farcuswa, and an orange, spiky furred duck Boignagan Basstler, all barged to talk about the trending news.

"You were on the news Jimmy! Like on the TV! And everyone outside is asking about you. They can't wait to see you again!" Boignagan cheered.

"Yeah! And why didn't you tell us you were friends with that famous Consular fella - uh lets see what was his name again? Pacooter? Pradanda? Hm," Douooresh said, thinking out loud.

"Oh, there he is, coming in!" Forsef said as he waved at someone. At first, I didn't mind until, well, I actually turned around and saw who it was.

"Oh Jimmy, there you are! I've been looking all over for you!" a small little squirrel said as he barged in. Jary Jenfields somehow always managed to find me when I least wanted to talk to him. "I've been getting plenty of interviews, and I told them all about your Consular friend, you know Peister Precarious, and how he's been helping you figure out how to solve your dilemmas, like when you got arrested, almost, and how you're working with him a lot and how you come to me for some help too, you know when you need to know what's up."

"You what? NO, I'm not friends with Peister, stop saying all of that!" I replied anxiously. Though Peister had helped me, I couldn't risk Wildlings knowing more than they needed to, otherwise it might not take long for rumors to start forming, and somehow a few of them might figure out the truth, even if it was just a lucky guess. Still though, I could get caught for what I did, and getting thrown in jail was the last thing I needed right now.

"BIG NEWS! BIG BIG NEWS!" said Gunter Gobiyan as he came waddling in as he carried a large square TV. The television obsessed koala never let it leave his side and somehow convinced every teacher at Cross Rivers it kept him focused throughout the day, but in reality it really just kept him from falling asleep.

"And with the final tallies coming the towns of Apaloosha, Ogwamani, Yitswa, Tegusigalpa, Bahvanna, and Hegladarra, WCBN can now confirm Peister Precarious is the winner of the Watcher Pack, securing the nomination after the last few shards were casted earlier this morning from a runoff that went on since last night. Yarbis Yackley, who led this campaign the last three months and was presumed to be the nominee, has fallen significantly after just a week of the news about Pleaser Guildenhall's pirate scandal. Wildlings seemed to find validity after the vulture warned the Wild that lingering invaders inhabiting the island, hidden by our very own Pleaser, now seem to be proven true. As a result, Consular Precarious was able to earn the trust of many Wildlings and transcended the polls rather quickly, but what do you have to say Qwioc?" Dygaan Dryeke, a thin yellow bat with purple glasses asked.

"Yes, it does appear Peister will now be the Majoriat of the Watcher Pack and will become Aspirer, challenging the Obliged, Greygor Guildenhall, Pleaser of the Wazoo for over thirty years now. Criticisms from hiding the pirates and his strict lockdown for Balooza prevention, set to expand very soon, show him already trailing the new candidate. But we shall see, the first of three debates is set to take place next week with Peister set to name Yarbis as his Patron. Both of them, no doubt, will challenge the decisions of this administration. And, surely, the Pleaser will have much to answer for," Qwioc Quigmiaac, the tall, dark night raccoon said.

"Well that's some big buggin' news for ya, ain't it Jimmy?" Jary said. "Your politician friend could really win it all!"

"Wh- I told you he's not my friend!"

"Oh, is he still mad you fell on him?"

"NO! And enough with all the rumors, Jary!" I said, finally losing my patience with him.

"Well either way, it looks like all that whistleblower news breaking out really helped him up! I wonder who it was? Do you have any idea, Jimmy?" Jary asked, though I felt he was somehow suspecting me.

"Uh- no, I have no clue," I said, feeling myself shake, anxious at the thought of everyone finding out.

"Well, whoever did really helped Peister, that's for sure!"

"I bet it was one of the Venali. I heard they're the meanest Wildling in all the Wazoo!" said Douooresh.

"You think a Venali guard did this? No way, it had to be someone from the Watchers, you know the Watcher and Waker Packs are always spying on each other don't you?" said Boignagan. *"What if it was Peister who did it? What if he was the one who broke into the Palace?"* the orange duck said, covering his beak in shock. Jary nearly fainted just at the thought this hot gossip might be true. He was just about ready to tell half the school at that moment. You could see it on his face.

"What! That broken bird can't even fly, and you think *he* snuck past all the Venali tigers? Give me a break!" Forsef said.

Gunter hushed us all several times, worse than the librarians do I might add, as he continued to flip through the channels while the rest of us continued talking about the pirates, that is until the intercom went off.

"ATTENTION, ALL CROSS RIVER STUDENTS PLEASE MEET IN THE AUDITORIUM AT ONCE. WE HAVE A SPECIAL ANNOUNCEMENT," Principal Fangoria said in monotone.

Students lined up in the stone bleachers outside, all curious as to what could possibly be important enough to interrupt a school day, though most of us hadn't minded it a single bit. There were reporters and cameras standing around waiting as our stern, tie-wearing goose principal, Ferrallis Fangoria, spoke into a microphone.

"Thank you everyone for being here. We have a special announcement to make today and that is one of our very own students, Mr. Jimmy Jungles, has won an Outstanding Wildling of the Week Award by *The Wilder* for his bold efforts to closely examine our society and best serve the Wild. Please youngling, if you could come down here to accept this award."

Almost immediately, the whole school cheered, as many stood up and applauded. I felt the flashes on me as many cameras honed in as I walked toward my principal who did his best to hide his grim face. A tall long necked lizard stood beside us, and handed me an oval shaped crystal with my own name printed on the bottom. I couldn't help but smile as we all posed for pictures. Apparently I was the youngest to ever win the award. I almost couldn't believe every Wildling was proudly cheering me on. Well, almost everyone.

"In my office after this, Mr. Jungles!" Principal Fangoria whispered in my ear. I knew this was all too good to be true.

I hadn't quite gotten into this before, but Mr. Fangoria had a, well, let's say a brief history with me. He could never prove that I was behind many of the incidents that took place at school, but had always suspected I was behind them one way or another. This would be, in my guess, probably the fiftieth or sixtieth time I'd been called into his office for a 'talk' that always felt like a police interrogation. I only wondered what he could have possibly found wrong after I *literally* just won a public service award.

I gently pushed open the wooden door, and sat down on the stone chair. He was typing away angrily on his computer before turning to me, putting his wings out and together as he looked at me.

"Oh you really have done it to me this time, Mr. Jungles! Do you know that?"

"Oh wh-"

"Shut up!" he said as he banged on his keyboard. "I have had it up to here with you! You and all your shenanigans! Food fights, paint splatter on the school walls, skipping classes, jamming the xerox machine, Vuyupa flowers under teachers desks so they'd fall asleep in class. All of it I can't prove, but I know it was you! But this, THIS!"

"Uh well, what's wr-" I tried asking again.

"You know how many parents I have calling me concerned about their youngling's well-being? That a student could possibly be associated with pirates? Not to mention the whole Wazoo thinks we let any student come up with whatever crazy conspiracy they want! Oh you have really done it this time," he said, going off on his rant. But honestly, I was confused.

"Sir I didn't do those things and what's wrong with being in the newspa-"

"Oh, you naive little boy! Don't you know, the media will print and say anything that sells! Anything that turns eyes for a little bit of money! And your baseless article which your own history teacher has said is a hoax is REALLY making headway this time."

"But I won an award, isn't that goo-"

"Not if we're getting all this bad attention! You think anyone wants to send their student to a school that prepares their student to make CRAZY public remarks? NO! But no matter, I have found the perfect solution to put you in your place- an *early report card!*"

"What! You can't do that!"

"Oh yes I can, and will, along with a very rotten

letter to your parents about your classroom behavior. You will learn your lesson Jimmy Jungles. One way or another, you *will* learn!" he said before dismissing me back to class. But honestly, I hadn't even the slightest intention of sticking around. Not when my livelihood was at stake. Gideon knows what my dad would do if he saw my report card.

When I rode up to my house, I could see good ole' Rutgis Rhaines swiftly swing along the trees as he delivered the mail from his bag. I ran up the stairs as he was filling up our mailbox with envelopes.

"Rutgis! I'm so glad you're here!" I said to the large dark gorilla as he was sifting his mailbag.

"Heya Jimmy boy! How've ya been? Stayin' out of trouble, I hope," he said ironically.

"Oh, you have no idea. Got any mail for us? I can take it!"

"Hey wait a second Jimmy, I saw you on the news! You reported about those pirates! Good job son!" he said as I smiled. It felt even nicer when someone other than my friends and classmates complimented me. I took all the mail we had and ran inside. I hoped I remembered to thank him, but I quickly sifted through the pile until I finally saw an envelope from Cross Rivers Middle School with 'High Priority' written on it. I was quickly relieved, that is until I ripped it open.

> Dear <u>Jimmy</u> Jungles,
> You silly boy.... Did you really believe I would be foolish enough to send the letter to YOUR house? Of course not! Not a single Wildling has

ever schemed this school as much as you have. I have called and mailed your home many, many times. And yet somehow, every detention slip and letter comes back signed with <u>NO</u> changed behavior. Even the phone calls I have with your mom and dad seem too suspicious... And even though I cannot prove it, I know <u>YOU</u> are behind it all! Which is <u>EXACTLY</u> why I have sent a letter and report card <u>DIRECTLY</u> to your father's workplace, Wazoo Parts and Projects! I may not have the evidence I need to expel you just yet Jimmy Jungles, but mark my words, that day is coming!!! Oh, and by the way, I told him I would be sending you home early today, so he should be there any minute now...

Ferrallis Fangoria
Principal of Cross Rivers Middle School

I had to have the worst school principal in the history of the Wazoo. Who writes to their students like this? Does this crazy goose just hate all children? I didn't know what to do at that moment. I was only twenty minutes away from my dad's work, plenty of time to go there, snatch the mail, and get back to school. But right as I was about to leave, I opened the door and saw my dad standing right in front of me...

"Oh, hey Dad, you're home early," I said nervously, trying to control how much I was shaking.

"What is this Jimmy, what is this letter?" he said in a low stern voice as he barged into the living room. "I don't even know where to begin with you," he said as he stared at me sternly. "Look at these grades! You told me you were going to get better!"

"Oh, you know how Fangoria is! He exaggerates everything and he doesn't even have any proof that I d -"

"JAMES JEFFERSON JUNGLES, I DON'T WANT TO HEAR IT, NOT AFTER I SEE THIS KIND OF A GARBAGE REPORT CARD! YOU SPEND ALL YOUR TIME RUNNING AROUND *WITH FRIENDS*, ACTING LIKE SOME, SOME KIND OF *HOOLIGAN*! WHERE ARE YOU GOING TO GET IN LIFE IF YOU DON'T WORK HARD JIMMY? YOU COME IN AND MESS UP MY FACTORY, NOW I HEAR ABOUT YOUR BE-HAVIOR AND GRADES? UNBELIEVABLE. I RAISED YOU BETTER THAN THIS JAMES. YOU ARE MUCH, MUCH BETTER THAN THIS," my dad shouted as he paced back and forth, trying to control himself.

"Dad, Fangoria makes up everything! Look see, I won an award. I'm in a few newspapers, and even got mentioned in the news! I think I can really help m-"

"I DON'T WANT TO HEAR ANY MORE OF YOUR PROMISES JIMMY. YOU'RE GROUNDED. NO FRIENDS, NO TV, NO RUNNING AROUND PLAY-ING. JUST HOME AND SCHOOL, THAT'S IT! NOW GO TO YOUR ROOM," he said as he pointed me out of the kitchen.

"But Da-"

"GO TO YOUR ROOM NOW!"

I walked out and slammed the door. There was so much on my mind at that moment. So much I wanted to explain, but didn't get the chance to. I guess it didn't matter. Nothing was more important than school apparently, and any huge public acknowledgement was *nothing* compared to the glory of grades.

I hit my bed a couple times and screamed into my pillow. I just didn't want to be here. I wished I lived with some other family, someplace far away from my parents. We were not alike, not alike at all and clearly valued very different things. I don't even understand how I was born to them, maybe it was a mistake somehow. I hoped there was. Because to me, I saw a lot of things were more important in life than grades, there had to be. But apparently, I was the only one.

Chapter 12

The Great Debates

LATER THAT DAY, as I went to the kitchen to grab a quick snack, I caught a glimpse of a press conference my parents were watching. After all the talk today of the whistleblower, Greygor was *finally* going to make a statement about it all.

"As you all have heard, we have been found by a group of outside invaders, known formally as the pirates, responsible for the increase in robberies, vandalism, kidnapping, and the spread of a gruesome disease. The WIA notified me of their presence nearly a month ago and I have made it my top priority to find and neutralize this threat. While I did not choose to come forward immediately with this information to prevent hysteria, I have and always will uphold the Wild's best interest. The reports that I have somehow colluded or have any grounds of cooperation with these fiends is simply absurd, used by my opponents to undermine my authority and resolution to the matter. I hope every Wildling remains safe during this period and will surely do all I can to protect everyone, thank you," the Pleaser said in an official statement.

"Well Irepa, that was Pleaser Guildenhall finally coming forward and responding to leaks from his own cabinet regarding the pirates and allegations that he is working with them."

"Yes Ascah, it does look like the Pleaser was finally willing to admit knowing about them for a while, but who can really know just how involved he or the intelligence agencies were with them and what it will take to hunt them down. Regardless however, the Pleaser's poll numbers have dropped quite significantly, and he stands six points behind the newly chosen Aspirer of the Wild, Peister Precarious."

"That is certainly concerning for the Waker Pack with the election only a few weeks out. He will have to find a way to turn things around rather quickly. Perhaps the Great Debates coming up can help clarify just how involved he was and what he intends to do to protect all of us in these wild, wild times."

"Wow, sounds like he's going to lose," Sal blurted out. Quickly, both my parents turned their heads and stared before turning off the television.

"NO TV Jimmy, you're grounded!" Dad said as he

looked out at me. Somehow, someway, I was going to make it to those debates to talk to Peister about making another plan. There was still a large pirate ship hiding somewhere on our island and not a single Wildling could find it.

A few days had passed since my dad had lectured me about my awful report card. I thought getting grounded from going anywhere was bad, that is until the newspapers about Greygor's new 'solution' to the pirate and disease became official.

"A lockdown? What's that even mean? Why is everyone so angry about it?" Riley said as we all sat around the cafeteria chatting.

"It means there are only a few spots we're allowed to go! And that police and local patrol will make sure we don't stray too far from the trails," Damien explained.

"WHAT! We can't even go to Mudpit Falls then?" Sal yelled as he threw his tail down in frustration.

"Nope, we'll get strikes taped onto us. Three and we can't leave our house. Five and we go straight to jail."

"That has to be illegal! Isn't it illegal? Sal asked.

"That's ridiculous, why can't he just find the pirates! I mean, how hard is it to find a large ship in the middle of the jungle? I asked.

"It says here the Pleaser is taking this precaution to keep us safe from the Balooza that has been going around. Hospitals apparently have been getting more and more packed since the pirates came here."

"The what? Balooza? It's just a little sickness, why is everyone freaking out? It's not that big of a deal," I said.

"Oh, it's a big deal alright!" said Jary, jumping out

from underneath the table. I instantly shook my head and yelled at him for eavesdropping on us, but he went on as if nothing happened. "Have you heard about what happened to Kattap-"

"JARY! Go away!" I yelled right as he ran off. I guess he remembered what happened last time he made me mad.

"Yeah, apparently being around the wrong tree or even eating the wrong fruit will give you a sickness like none other. Maybe it's for the best we-" Amelia was saying.

"But this isn't about anyone getting sick Amelia! Greygor's helping the pirates try and find the Dream, so he's keeping everyone he can away!"

"What even is that? The Dream?" Sal asked.

"I don't know, but I-I have to talk to Peister again. He's the only one we can trust right now," I said confidently at the time.

"But Jimmy, aren't you grounded?" Amelia asked as I sat back and rolled my eyes. As if that was going to stop me.

The Great Debates were to be held at Ereffree's Glaze, better known as the Pleaser's Memoriam. Damien had mentioned to us that Eghes Ereffree had made large white marble pillars raised with carvings of the faces of our leaders of the past, who we often refer to as the Ancients. I don't know how many Wildlings could tell you their names or even what they had done, but over the many millions of years the Wazoo has existed, this was the hall of the most remembered, the ones who stood the test of time to help shape the island we have today. And I didn't think there was anything more respectable than that.

We flew over right after school ended. I thought that was early enough, but we barely managed to squeeze a spot up front. Many from all parts of the Wild had come to watch. There was much at stake for everyone. I was just waiting for my opportunity to talk to Peister, but I guess we would have to wait.

Krayter was there with many of his other friends, but that's not what upset me at all. Somehow, Barry still had babaloos he was sharing with everyone else. Despite the fact that the whole island was locked down, the little monkey had somehow managed to pick fresh fruits without even a trace of the Balooza! (Deep down, that was what *really* made me believe this whole lockdown was just a nonsense lie.) All of them were snobbishly eating fruits, talking louder than any other group around them. Maybe I'd be lucky enough to see them all get the Balooza, I heard a few Wildlings started bloating up and flying away with the wind. That is what the news said would happen, after all. I didn't know how true that really was, but boy do I wish I got to see that. And in a way, I got exactly what I had hoped for.

There was a giant white stone stage surrounded by large pillars. Two wooden stands were placed on either side and a small desk was placed onto the grass. A small toad with large glasses and tall straight legs was wearing a checkered vest as he stood up to face the audience. Nednis Nelly was always known for his honest, objective reporting, though he spoke in a low monotone voice that could make any Wildlings fall asleep.

"Thank you all for being here tonight! This will be the first of three Great Debates the Wazoo will host to help Wildlings everywhere decide who will reign as Pleaser. Each candidate will be given three minutes to respond to my questions. Please be silent so we can get through as many topics as possible. But first, let us all give a warm welcome to the current Pleaser of the Wazoo, Greygor Guildenhall, and the Aspirer of the Wild, Peister Precarious!"

The audience stood up and cheered as both the lion and vulture emerged slowly from the forest area behind the monument. Peister waved ambitiously, even with his broken wings, and looked enthusiastic while Greygor barely made a face, simply nodding before walking up the stage.

"Thank you both for being here. My first question goes to you, Mr. Precarious. As we all know, these are pressing times for the island. How would you protect the Wildlings from the ongoing pirate crimes and what would your plan be to eradicate them from the Wazoo?"

"Thank you, Ned. Well, it certainly does appear that the Wazoo has indeed been found. And though we know very little of these pirates, I take this threat very seriously and am content to see Barons of every territory assemble patrol forces. But we must remember who is to blame. The leaks from the few brave individuals in the Guildenhall administration understand his lack of action and ineptitude on the matter. These leaks revealed his prolonged cooperation for intentions we still do not know. Furthermore, his newly named solution on the matter, this lockdown, has made life on the island more hectic and unbearable. All for what? What is the Pleaser's intention? I ask you all to wonder. To prevent us from living the free life because of pirates we can not find? To stop us from eating the freshly grown fruits gifted to us by the Ancients? We are NOT caged animals! The Pleaser has completely overstepped his authority on the matter to lockdown the island without the approval of the Assentory. Surely the courts will overturn this egregious enactment in no time."

"And to you, Mr. Pleaser?"

"Well, this is all just absolutely ridiculous. The fact of the matter is I had nothing to do with the pirates finding the Wazoo. But I know one thing, that not only are they a threat, but so is the disease they bring with them. You yourself alerted the Assentory just a few weeks ago that the Wazoo was not well, that the island's nature is indeed feeling off and that we might all suffer the consequences. Why abandon such beliefs just to oppose me? Why resort to these foolish games? I try to protect the wellbeing of every Wildling from lingering threats, and you dare say we are caged animals? It is absurd how irresponsible your words have been in times of crisis. The threat from Balooza should be taken very seriously. This unnatural disease is significant as infection rates have shot through the roof! For our own safety, no Wildling can be allowed to dwell off into the forest, surrounded by contaminated trees, fruits and even fellow Wildlings.

"This right here is the lie from my opponent. Mr. Pleaser, I have worked with several Barons of the island to launch a special investigation into the matter, lest we were able to stumble upon your true intention for this lockdown. Mr. Dumsdree, please step forward with your findings," Peister said as he looked off to the side of the forest. Several large bears came forward, rolling large wooden barrels with the description 'Wazoo Trading Company' stamped on top of them. The bear opened the tops and dumped fresh fruits all over the ground. "It appears that while you have been working so hard *protecting* us from the Balooza, you are packing our fruits away, and sir, might I ask you who was doing the packing?"

"Uh well, they were tall humans with strange clothes, nasty attitudes. We scared them off pretty quick though."

"The pirates! That is who was packing these fruits, that is who these fruits are going to, and only now have all Wildlings finally learned the truth of your true intention with this lockdown, and I will *NOT* have it! Mr. Dumsdree, please have your team distribute the fruits to our fellow Wildlings!" Peister said as several bears came towards us rolling the barrel. Fruits were being passed around, even thrown in the air as we all ate in delight.

"NO! DO NOT EAT THE FRUITS! THE BALOOZA IS A REAL THREAT! THIS IS VERY IRRESPONSIBLE OF YOU PEISTER!" yelled Greygor as Wildlings booed back and continued to eat. I personally grabbed small, round green ganaches that were thrown into the air and began to eat them.

LIAR! LIAR! GREYGOR IS A LIAR!
While half the audience yelled, the other half, including myself, went ahead eating as we all chanted against the corrupt Pleaser. "Jimmy, put that down!" Amelia yelled as she eventually grabbed them out of my hand and threw them.

"What, why'd you do that!" I yelled angrily.

"Yeah, I wanted some!" Sal complained.

"Mr. Precarious, this is NOT a trial! You cannot accuse and bring forth unevaluated evidence to a debate stage," Nednis Nelly warned.

"I had to expose the truth! But ask the Pleaser why he would conceal this at all? I'm sure we would all love to know."

"Pleaser Guildenhall, your response?" the frog asked.

"This is outrageous! I have fought long and hard for the sanctity of this island and am not willing to give it up for the sake of profits! Obviously, this is the doing of none other than Hortley Hasselback, with whom I have no association. Only a scoundrel like him would do such a thing!"

Hortley? Hortley Hasselback? Where had I heard that name before? It took me a minute before it all came back to me when I was at the Pleaser's Palace. Greygor had just been meeting with that fat pig wanting to arrange some deal. *Why would he lie about being involved when they had just met a few weeks ago? Were they both involved in this business deal?* I thought to myself as questions continued to race into my mind.

"Mr. Precarious, please there is no evid-"

"No, Ned. Fresh fruit was being hidden away from

the Wild for the sake of profit! This is nothing short of scandal that the Pleaser has allowed pirates onto our island for his business intentions. It must be said and known by all how corr-"

"Oh, but is it really *me* who is working with pirates? Are you really saying that you have had no association with them? It is you, afterall, pushing this trade route idea in the Assentory, one that would surely spell disaster for our island."

"My interwater trade routes plan has NOTHING to do with *YOUR* profits, nor any association with pirates!"

"Interesting. Hocbuk, please set up the video footage recovered from *our* investigations committee."

"What video? You cannot just launch an investigation without the approval of the Assentory or local Barons, this is more abuse of power by the Pleaser."

"EXCUSE ME! Must I reemphasize, this is NO TRIAL! SECURITY DO NOT LET THEM ENTER!" the small Nednis Nelly said to no avail. At first, the police refused to let long limbed, red Mokunk monkeys walk any further to the debate stage, that is until the Venali tigers began to slowly approach.

They set up a large white tarp between two stands and placed the projector a few feet away. The video was blurry, struggling to gain focus and still shaking as a tall man in a black coat slowly walked into a dark room, dragging some kind of metal across the floor before sitting at a desk. He then placed his metal fist onto the table, before looking directly at Peister, who had been shaking in the video the entire time. *Where had I seen this man before?* I thought to myself until I remembered the dream I had on the ship a few weeks ago. It was the man who wrote Greygor the letter, the one Wyatt called Captain Bacawly.

"H-h-how c-can I h-help you, s-s-sir?" he said anxiously.

"Shut up ye stupid parrot! I am gettin' sick of all ye animals. An' I don't want to hear any more about this profit trade garbage ye keep tellin' me 'bout!" he said, pounding his metal fist against the table.

"Ok, well whatever it is y-you want, I'm sure we can do our be-" Peister said, shaking as he looked down underneath the table. But the crocodiles the captain brought with him were looming underneath the desk, closing in and clenching their jagged teeth towards Peister.

"You see, me croc knows I don' like you. But he knows ye too good for us, an' he knows what I do to folks that anger me. I'm tir'd wastin' me time! An' me croc here is waitin' for me approval.

"But the money we cou-"

"I DON'T CARE! It all means nothin'. I wan' real power! More than what any money can ever buy. An' the lion has been useless to me, but that fat pig. He tells me you'd know where I could get what I wan'. Well? d' ye?"

"I-I think so."

"Good, so yer goin' to help me then? Do we have an accord?"

"Y-y-yes I-I will lo-look for whatever it is you want," Peister said, continuing to shake.

"Good, 'cause they tell me you're ma' best chance. Don' let me down now, otherwise I'll be comin' back to make a nice roast outta ya. Understan'?" Bacawly said staring before he and his crocs began to walk out, but not before one of them widened its red eyes and whipped its tail at a small bunny butler. The video went black but we all heard its long teeth crack the small bones.

The whole audience was shaking after watching the video. *How could Greygor show us a video like that?* A few Wildlings screamed, others cried and barfed as they heard the crunching noise.

"I think we can all see just how associated Mr. Precarious is with them, but what I wonder about is just how long this bargain was going on for? This trade route idea he has carried for so long in the Assentory, was it not just confessed that the pirates were involved? I mean, just how many lives lost do we have to blame for your cowardice?" Greygor said, looking right at Peister.

"Well now just hold on a minute there, Pleaser Guildenhall, as I've said before, this is no trial. But I am sure we are all curious to know, just what is your current association with these pirates, Mr. Precarious? Are you still performing favors for them? How long ago was this meeting?"

"Wh- l-lies! These are all lies! I-I was uh-threatened! T-thwarted by these fiends! They broke into my home and threatened to kill me! Lies Greygor! Say no more, I have been unlucky enough to go through the same trials and tribulations as many of the Wildlings today. And all because of you!"

"Well, it appears, Mr. Precarious, you have agreed to help the pirates with the consequence being your very own life. But please tell us, if you may, what exactly is it that they want? What would you be able to give them that no other Wildling could? It appears Hortley Hasselback, the wealthiest Wildling on the island, has even endorsed you for some reason."

"I-I do not know what it is these fiends want. Look Ned, I was attacked, alright? I would have agreed to anything to stay alive, but what we need to focus on is protecting the Wild!"

"Then why not report this matter to the police? Why not cooperate with the intelligence agencies? It's because Mr. Precarious is HIDING something from us all, and we cannot elect someone who chooses to engage in secrets," Greygor said, brilliantly flipping the narrative everyone accused him of just a week ago.

"No Mr. Pleaser, that is absolutely a lie! How dare you question my loyalties to the island. I-I have worked long and hard over the years to ensure-"

"*BOOOO!*"

"*LIAR!*"

"Then why are you so associated with the pirates? You have met with him. In fact, he was looking for you! Do not deny the video!"

"*THEY'RE BOTH CORRUPT!*"

"If I might ask the audience to - to please quiet down so we can get through all the questions! As for you Wildren, please, civilize yourselves! As I have said before, this is a formal debate, not a trial! The Wild deserves better from both of you and not these unproven accusa-" Ned said, trying to keep everyone calm, but both Greygor and Peister continued arguing over each other as the audience continued to angrily chant. *LIARS! LIARS!*

And just when I thought there was no way any of this could get any worse, a few Wildlings who had eaten the fruits suddenly began to hiccup or sneeze out purple bubbles. Many in the crowd began to groan in pain as they laid on the floor.

"Jimmy? Jimmy are you alright?" Amelia asked me. At first I didn't know what she meant, I was still focused on the debate afterall, but suddenly, I felt the need to itch all over my body as large boils quickly grew. That's when I first noticed.

"J-Jimmy- you're orange!" Sal shrieked as he slid away from me. I thought that was the worst part, that is until my shoes began to tear open as both my hands and feet nearly tripled in size.

"Whabs gobin' on? I thon'th feeth gooth," I said as the whole area started to spin uncontrollably as I coughed up bubbles.

"EVERYBODY, STAND BACK NOW!" said a police officer as many came running to the audience. After a while, I heard ambulance sirens coming from far away while I lay flat on the ground, breathing heavily while looking up at the sky.

Chapter 13

Wauttapuck General Hospital

"ARE WE ALMOST THERE? THE PATIENT IS EXPE-RIENCING BLOATING SYMPTOMS!" yelled a tall yel-low gorilla as it evaluated me in the ambulance. I don't remember getting in, but I could hear the sirens buzz-ing through the woods. I felt so dizzy from seeing every-thing spinning around me that I only just noticed the small air sockets forming underneath my now bright orange skin.

"Administer Cerpac immediately Hedabaz!" the sheep nurse said as she was busy attending to a crying long-nosed Narqoota who threw its long claws around as large red thorns poked out of its unusual blue polka dot fur. There was no common look for the Balooza I guess, but you knew almost at once if you had it.

Nurse Hedabaz grabbed my leg and pulled me down as I began gently floating upwards. He buckled me to the gurney, but still I could feel myself jiggling as my body continued to expand. The medicine injected into me caused the bloating to go down, but I was still a long way from getting better.

"Hurry up, Westafor, before the patient starts bloating again!" the gorilla nurse yelled at the small weasel. The driver instantly hit the speed pedal and we all fell forward as the vehicle shot faster down the road.

The ambulance eventually came to a sudden stop, and I was immediately pushed out into a noisy hospital floor. Hundreds of nurses were running around attending their many sick patients, and purple bubbles were floating all around the air. Don't even get me started on the nasty odor spreading around. I'm sure many Wildlings hadn't showered in a week, and I'm not just talking about the patients, either.

The yellow gorilla walked up quickly to the nurse at the front desk, a deer named Nurse Ita, who had looked tense as she aggressively typed away on a keyboard and had large stacks of patient charts right next to her while yelling away into the phone. "Hello! Where are you Nebbayu? Patients in 2142, 608, and 1437 are all free to discharge! Quickly please, I'll need to fix eighteen more urgent care patients right away!" she said intensely.

"Uh, ex-excuse me, this patient needs to be medicated quickly before his symptoms exacerbate again! Can you find us a room?" he asked.

"A room? You think we can find anyone a room at this time?"

"Well, he needs to be treated immediately, or his bloating will return, and we might have to go to surgery! Please, there has to be something!"

"What, he has the Balooza and is bloating too? Oh for Gideon's sake, you should have told me that first!" she said in shock as she looked quickly through the database. How lucky was I to not only have the Balooza, but probably have the worst kind of it all. "Okay, let me find where I can squeeze you in. Did you finish charting?" she asked but the gorilla was taken aback because he had apparently completely forgotten to do that. "Wh- you haven't even started this!"

"He was bloating really bad and started to float, I had to get that under control, and we had a couple others in the amb-"

"Ugh, if you don't want to do your job, then I don't want to hear it! What's your name, youngling?"

"Ub, by nabe is Thibby Thungleths," I said, startling myself as I listened to what I had just said.

"Okay, Thibby, I'll put you on the schedule now, Dr. Plesco will meet with you shortly in room 2934."

"Wait, 2934? Up in the psych ward? Isn't that the room with the – *the crazy patient?*" he whispered.

"Well, he's been stable lately, and honestly, that's the best we can do for now. Hurry along, nurse Hinz!" Nurse Ita said angrily as she picked the next patient chart from her huge stack and continued to type away.

Both doctors and nurses ran erratically across the halls, jumping on beds and sometimes even patients in order to get to their next one. But just as I was reflecting on how badly the lives of Wildlings had been, I saw my mom in the distance, taking scrupulous notes at a cow who was blue with now orange spots. I turned around and threw the blanket over my head, just hoping she wouldn't see me, not like this.

I nearly nodded off asleep as we were waiting and going up in an old rumbling elevator. When we finally arrived at the twenty-ninth floor, I immediately noticed the dimmed lights and dirty gray walls. I was pushed along the bumpy, cracked floors which sank as we rolled over them. We passed a ragged counter where nurses were catching up on paperwork and opened a rotting wooden door to lead us into a cramped smelly room with a long white divider covering the other side.

"Oh, a new friend? Hi new friend! What's your name?" said the mysterious Wildling on the other side of the curtain. Nurse Hinz walked over and immediately shushed him.

"There's an important case going on, the doctors need to focus to get him to feel well!" the gorilla said to the patient behind the curtain as he tried to catch a peek.

"Oh no, what happened? Let me help!" the patient said, trying to get up from the bed.

"Mr. Sutterman, do not -uh! Extra care, may I please have extra care for patient two in 2934?" the gorilla called over the intercom before two other nurses barged in to control the Wildling patient. But I was in too much pain to even pay attention to what was happening on the other side of the room. My arms and legs started to get more air sockets forming as the very itchy feelings started to come back again.

"It hurth! It hurth all over, how muth longer unthil the thoctor comths?" I asked with my tongue still swollen and in aching pain around my hands and feet. I didn't even want to know what I looked like. I just wanted all of this to go away. I even started to kick the end of the hospital bed as I felt my mind getting too overwhelmed.

As I sat there waiting, the whole room now spinning as I continued to cough out large purple bubbles, my body and face both began inflating again. Suddenly, the front door slammed wide open, and a tall, wide owl wearing a white coat walked in.

"Alright, who's next? And where are my charts, nurse?" he asked, scribbling something quickly on a piece of paper. As the doctor looked down at me, I instantly noticed the heavy caves around his bloodshot eyes. It looked as if the Wildling hadn't slept in weeks, yet he was as upbeat as ever while evaluating my body. "Okay, so tell me, Mr. Telywinkle, how long have you had swivel feet and lizard tongue for?" he asked before looking up. "Oh my, you've turned into a carrot, too I see," he said, squinting as he closely observed me.

"Wait, what?" Nurse Biala said as she hopped on to my bed and then onto the doctor's shoulder to look over my chart. "No, this is the patient from 2193; we're in 2934!"

"Oh-OH! Yes, of course. I just wanted to - er go over that with you," he said while shuffling through his clipboard. "Alright let's see what this says. Hmm... nope can't read that. Okay, yes somewhere here, just give me a second, one second, please. OH, who put that there?" he said, startled as he knocked over a tray of food and an IV to the floor while shuffling through his charts. I really don't think he even knew just how tired and out of it he actually was.

"Ith hurbs, ith hurbs ebywbear anth I canth thalk goob eiber," I cried, unable to stand the pain any longer.

"I see, I see. A swollen tongue, orange skin, and boils. Yes you definitely have the Balooza. Let's just see what we can do before it gets any worse. Let's definitely get ten pecks of Lagoon Iberexyn. Anything else I should be aware of?

"Yes, he was also bouncing around all bloated in the ambul-"

"WHAT! HE HAD THE FLOATING BLOATING HOPS? OH, I HAVEN'T GOT TIME FOR THIS! Just prep him for surgery and I'll take care of him while I do the six other Wildlings I have scheduled for uh- OH GOODNESS ONE HOUR AGO! Why haven't you told me I was late to the surgery, nurse?" he yelled as he nervously looked at his watch.

"No, no, no! No floating and no hops yet, only bloating! I administered Cerpac on the way over."

"Oh, thank Gideon, okay, that would've been a real overboard morning, even for me."

"Uh, it's almost 6 pm," said the gorilla nurse beside him.

"Yes, yes, that's what I said. Anyway, nurse Biala, please administer Iberexyn and leave the patient here overnight! Now I must-OH," he said, crashing into the wall while walking out. "Ah! Surgeries. I must go do my surgeries. Please fill out the rest of the chart, thank you!" he said, throwing over the clipboard before dashing off.

"Wait, you need these charts! Do you even know what procedure you are doing? Dr. Plesco? DR. PLESCO!" the skunk said as she chased after the very lost doctor.

"Oh yes. Great idea!" he said emphatically yelling from down the hall.

As we waited for my medicine to arrive, nurse Switters and nurse Lysen had their paws full, still struggling even more with the mysterious patient behind the curtain.

"Mr. Sutterman, you need to eat your queatmeal! That's why you're so upset," said the dog.

"NO SCUP! THIRTEEN YEARS IN HERE, AND ALL YOU'VE EVER GIVEN ME IS QUEATMEAL! I WANT REAL FOOD FOR ONCE! Berries, honey, jelly, juice, sweets, anything else but that moldy dirt!" Mr. Sutterman said, banging onto the table.

"What's going on?" asked a tall, upright bunny nurse who walked in and crossed his arms as he saw just what was going on in here. "Mr. Sutterman, by my own records, you haven't eaten anything in three days. We're not allowed to give you any fruit because of the Balooza spreading around, so you just have to eat your quea-"

"NO!" the old man said stubbornly again.

"Alright, that's it. Hold him down, I'll feed him," the bunny said as he came closer. There was a brief silence as they forced the spoon closer to his mouth and force fed him. From the small outside window, a thin, long green plant stem suddenly began to crawl into the room and threw the two nurses holding him down against the wall before grabbing the bunny off his feet and holding him upside down in the air.

"YOU EAT THE QUEATMEAL!" Mr. Sutterman laughed as the green plant then took a spoon full off the floor and shoved it in the bunny nurse's mouth. I couldn't see with my own eyes, but I could tell that it tasted gross as the bunny nurse groaned before quickly spitting it out and pressing a red button against the wall.

"Oh, I warned you, Mr. Sutterman!" the bunny yelled before grabbing the radio out of his pocket and speaking into it. "Patient is out of control and dangerous to the staff! I'll need a straitjacket for room 2934 immediately!"

The patient continued to laugh until a large panda marched in holding a large white straitjacket.

"N-no, no. NO! I don't want that, I don't want that!" he screamed as he tried to kick the panda. I could only hear all the bumping around as nurses fell into supply drawers trying to hold him down.

I guess I was too ill to even remember all of the details; the whole room was still stretched out and spinning while it continued to change colors. Things got quiet quickly, and almost immediately, the large panda came over and picked up the largest syringe. Boy, did I hope my eyes were just messing with me, but something felt like they weren't. The nurses quickly turned me around, and before I knew it, I was getting injected in my lower, 'lower' back. It stung worse than a Juowhavian bee sting and flushed my mind with only bad thoughts: pirates in my dreams, screaming parents, getting lectured by a principal who clearly hated me. All of it hit me at once like a nightmare in daylight and made me want to never return to the hospital ever again. But eventually, I passed out to a blissful sleep.

I must have been out for at least five or six hours by now, but when I woke up, I looked at my arms, and even touched my face, and felt nothing wrong. My skin was not as thick as leather, no boils, not even one itching sensation. I grabbed the mirror on my bedside just to be sure, and I saw that I was truly back to my normal self.

My toes were peeking out of the large holes in my shoes as the soles had almost completely been ripped off at this point. I grabbed my hat from the table next to where I lay as I got up, ready to head out the door.

"H-help! Help me p-please," sobbed the patient behind the curtain. I turned back right as my hand touched the knob. I had almost forgotten there was a Wildling in the room with me, and how much trouble he had caused. I walked over and pulled the curtain back to see a frail old man with a long white cloak wearing a tightly secured straitjacket. All of his exuberant, vibrant energy from a few hours ago had somehow ceased. Now, all he could do was look down and shake erratically with a tight, almost lifeless face. He was in pain, barely able to even whisper.

"Uh- are you okay sir?"

"I-I ca-can't feel. Th-the voices wo-won't stop," the old man said sobbing. *"I just want it to stop. MAKE IT*

STOP!" he cried, throwing his head around as he cried uncontrollably. *"Take this off, please! It hurts. Take this off and get me out of here, I don't want to be here! Get me out! Please get me out!"* he continued to wail, but I had no idea what to do. This was the same man who somehow got a plant to come in and attack the nurses, unless it was just the Balooza making me hallucinate. *Why was this old man even kept in the hospital to begin with?* I thought long and hard as he trembled in pain.

There was not a single zipper on the straitjacket, and I couldn't find a single way to take it off. *How did they even get it on? How was it making him hallucinate with so much pain?* I searched quickly through the medical drawers and pulled out some oddly shaped scissors and cut through the abnormally rigid material, somehow thicker than cloth, but tough like some thorny Mekaaly plants up in the Heloks. It was uncomfortably tight, and all I could do was wonder how. It took a while, but finally I was able to get it off before gently putting him on a wheelchair I swiped from the hallway.

I strolled us out of the room, hiding behind a wall to make sure no one saw us. From what I heard when I first got to the hospital, every nurse and doctor probably knew who this Mr. Sutterman was, well everyone except for me, that is.

"The butterfly, follow the butterfly," he muttered, slowly gaining back his consciousness and strength. I had no idea what he was talking about until I actually looked around and saw a small orange butterfly that was swiftly flying through a somewhat busy hallway.

Someone was sure to catch us. I tried to tell him it was going to be a bad idea. *"Follow the butterfly, it will guide us out,"* he said before passing out again.

It only took us a few minutes to get caught, and that's when Mr. Sutterman really began to surprise me. "Hey, you there! Where do you think you're going with that patient? Come back here now!" said Nurse Dummens, the giant panda who injected me earlier.

I thought this was it for us, that we'd surely get locked back in our room, but suddenly the hallway began to lightly rumble as a cracking noise came from the walls. Almost instantly, water came pouring out, spilling with a force strong enough to knock over a hundred-ton panda and push it down the hallway. But I didn't have time to watch, the butterfly was fluttering around the back stairwell door, waiting for me, I guess.

"Eighty-eight, eighty- nine, nin-," the yellow gorilla said to himself as he hit a string ball against a paddle.

"HEDABAZ! QUIT SCREWING AROUND! Did you move the patients? The door was left wide open! Where are they?" Nurse Biala asked as she came up behind him.

"W-what? I don't know, I didn't even move them," he said as he quickly dropped the paddle and straightened up.

"Then where are they?" the skunk asked.

"THEY ESCAPED! THE PATIENTS HAVE ES-CAPED!" Nurse Dummens said as he was still being brushed down the hallway in a stream of wet paperwork, medical supplies, and medications, a few other screaming nurses along with him.

We came out just a few floors from where we started. I had no idea how this butterfly knew where it was going, nor why Mr. Sutterman had trusted it so much (how did he even know it was here?).

"WHERE IS SUTTERMAN? WE CANNOT LET HIM ESCAPE THE HOSPITAL. DO YOU UNDERSTAND ME? FIND HIM IMMEDIATELY AND BRING HIM BACK HERE!" a wolf security officer yelled into a radio. "HAVE THE POLICE SURROUND THE AREA!" We were hidden in a hallway with patients all around. I quickly took a bedsheet off one of the beds and threw it over Mr. Sutterman. That should buy us some time to get us further along, or so I thought.

I pushed us as fast as I could down the hallway, the butterfly leading us to the elevator.

"Excuse me, no sheets over the patient's head, what are you-agh!" a bird nurse said as her eyes popped open. "What is Mr. Sutterman doing down here? SECURITY! THIS BOY IS TAKING THE MISSING PATIENT!" she yelled over at the large gray wolf, who instantly jumped onto the desk and hunched down its head to stare right at me. I gulped before quickly pushing the wheelchair as fast as I could, the security officer growling as he chased after me. The elevator doors opened, and we quickly slid in. I pressed the twelfth-floor button, the lowest floor it could go to, at least twenty times until the doors finally closed. I could hear the wolf pounding against the door.

I was panting as I looked back at the elevator numbers. We snuck out from the twenty-ninth floor and got chased all the way down to the twenty-sixth floor. Gideon knows what we'd see when we got out.

"CODE RED, PATIENT ESCAPE! CODE RED, PA-TIENT ESCAPE!" I heard over the intercom as lights flashed in the hallways. Somehow, no one in the elevators noticed us in the back corner. There was, afterall, a sick elk with its legs all tied up together as it continued to jerk, that is, until a foot slipped out and kicked all the nurses around. There was also a large kangaroo who had large blue bumps around its body and a five-foot tongue wrapped around its body (oddly enough, he turned out to be a classmate of mine.)

I ran us out onto the fourteenth floor, not giving a care to the world where that butterfly wanted us to go next. If the whole hospital was hearing about us right now, I'd be willing to bet they were waiting for us to reach the lowest floor the elevator could go. We needed some place to hide out and wait until all the police and security had given up looking for us.

There were a few officers scrambling around the floor, but I managed to find an empty room in this packed, Balooza-infested hospital. I quickly placed him onto a bed as he was still shaking and moving his eye-brows. *Should I just leave him here?* I thought anxiously. The whole hospital was looking for us, and would definitely lock me up if I got caught. I didn't know what to do, but a gut feeling told me I should wait for Mr. Sutterman to wake up. And boy was I glad I listened.

A nurse came in a while after. I tried to keep my cool, knowing full well we were not registered to be in this room.

"Oh, I'm so sorry for keeping you waiting. We've just been so busy that I'm only getting to my rounds now," said a sweet pink koala as she grabbed a bag and put a tube into Mr. Sutterman.

"Yeah, that's ok, I figured," I said smiling, hoping deep down she wouldn't recognize Mr. Sutterman.

"Is this your grandpa? How long has he been sick for?"

"Uh, yeah, for a while now. I've hardly seen him," I said nervously, trying to keep my cool and hope she wouldn't ask any more questions.

"Aw, that's sweet of you to bring him to the hospital. Not many kids do that nowadays. We'll do our best. I'll try to have a doctor come check up on him soon. Has the chart been filled out already?"

'Uh, yeah, we're just waiting. But no need to rush, he's been like this before. This is actually the best he's been in a while."

"Aw, ok honey, I'll let them know," she said before slipping back out.

Nearly an hour went by before his eyes slowly opened and he turned to me. "W-where are we? Did-did we escape?" Mr. Sutterman said softly.

"No, we're still in Wauttapuck General, but on the fourteenth floor," I said as an awkward silence followed. I had tried so much to help this man, but I hardly even knew what to say to him. "Uh- Mr. Sutterman - sir, what's going on? Why do they all want you back in that room?" I asked, though I had easily another hundred questions, first of which was *what in the Heloks did you do to those nurses?*

"Well, thank you, youngling. Say, what was your name again?"

"Oh, I'm Jimmy. Jimmy Jungles, Mr. Sutterman."

"Well, nice to meet you, Jimmy, and please, call me Seuss," he said, peeking out the window on the door. "Looks clear around here, not a lot of nurses or security. Now's our chance to go."

"Uh, Mr. Sutt- or uh, Seuss, did you have the Balooza or -uh any other problems? Why did they tie you up an-"

"Oh, Jimmy, I'm not sick, is that what they told you?" he said, coming over and putting his hands gently on my shoulder. " There's nothing wrong with me, but they needed some excuse to lock me up! I've been stuck here for thirteen years! And I've had enough. All day, they put that stupid jacket on me, fed me the same garbage food, and left me all alone to my own thoughts. I've had nothing for far too long, and have gone through more suffering than any Wildling ever has! So please Jimmy, don't feel guilty. Don't believe all their lies! Never did I imagine such a sweet place like the Wazoo be run by fiends!" he said, shaking anxiously as he talked. "Will you help me Jimmy? I'll give you anything in return, I promise."

At first, I didn't know what to say. I had so many questions. *Why was he in the psych ward to begin with? Why did they lock him in that vestm and why was he acting so strangely with it on? How did he even move that plant to attack the nurses? How did he know the butterfly was here? And the water pipe burst that happened on the twenty-ninth floor, was that him?* It all made no sense to me, and I wasn't sure if I should even be talking to him, he was still a stranger after all.

But I heard the cry in his voice and saw the desperation in his eyes. I knew then, I had no other choice. "Ok, Seuss, I'll help you, but you still have a lot to explain to me after this is all done, alright?" I said.

"Thank you, Jimmy, you don't know how much that means to me. Now come on, let's get out of here," Seuss said. We carefully slipped into the hallway while keeping our heads low as we passed by many busy Wildlings rushing to see their patients. So far, we were in the clear.

The Code Red alert had gone away, and not a single officer was in sight except when we reached near the end. There was a large seal sitting in front of the elevator, peering around and speaking into his wooden radio anytime a Wildling needed to use the elevator. On the other end, the staircases were blocked off by a spiky pink-headed Lecotto bird. "They're blocking all of the doors. What are we going to do?" I asked, but Seuss did not seem concerned at all. Seuss closed his eyes as we stood just down the hall. Suddenly, I heard a large burst from a room, a door was broken down as nearly a dozen purple octopuses came walking out, splattering goo all over the floors as they squirmed through the floors, walls, and even the ceiling and nearly ran over the bird guarding the stairs. "Officer Picoli HELP, THEY'RE TAKING ME AWAY!" the security guard said as the small green, long rat nurse followed after.

"GET BACK HERE ALL OF YOU!" said the seal as he charged over at them. "Alert, alert! Octopuses are escaping. I repeat, Octopuses are escaping!"

"Now's our chance, Jimmy," Seuss said as we ran to

the elevator doors and pressed the first floor. We were almost there.

We arrived at ground level to see dozens of officers all around the area. I pressed us back against the wall as we went down the other side of the hall to a far more crowded hallway with irritated patients and stressed nurses. I saw a cart of dirty sheets and blankets when the brilliant idea hit me. "Seuss, get in this, quick!" I said before throwing a blue button-down shirt around me as he jumped in and hid. "Where do we go now? There are too many halls, and the police are everywhere!"

"We'll just follow Jayayla!"

"Jayayla?" I said, completely confused until I looked up and saw the same orange butterfly from earlier. I quickly pushed towards the fluttering critter and followed along until we came up to a place that looked familiar.

AMBULANCE EMERGENCY DISPATCH

Was that what we were going to do? I just hoped Seuss knew how to drive. I thought we were in the clear until we came upon two familiar faces, one deadly wolf who almost caught us on the twenty-sixth floor, and a tall rooster who had nearly arrested me when I fell on top of Peister almost a month ago. I kept my head down as I walked towards them and had to shush Seuss a few too many times, who was cheering far too soon.

"They couldn't have escaped! We have the whole place on lockdown!" Officer Mooney said.

"Yeah well, I'm sure with a Watchwaker anything could happen. Did you hear he flooded the entire 29th floor and let out fourteen Octopi? Who knows where he could be by now!" replied the wolf as he gently began to sniff around.

"Well I heard the old geezer escaped with a Balooza patient, a young Wildling boy named Thibby Thungles," the rooster said as they passed us. I took a deep breath. Maybe they wouldn't notice us. "Something off Darnell?" Officer Mooney asked.

"That smell, I-I recogn-wait a minute! YOU THERE! STOP RIGHT NOW," the wolf yelled, I guess, somehow remembering my scent from over an hour ago.

I pushed the cart through the open lobby as fast as I could, but the cart was just too heavy with Seuss in it. *Should I abandon him here? Take off and escape for myself?* After all, they only wanted Seuss.

The wolf was at my back, ready to leap on top of me and hurl me to the ground. I was five seconds from surely getting tackled by Officer Darnell until Seuss stood on the cart and pulled me in, letting the cart just roll down on its own.

"IT'S HIM! IT'S THE WATCHWAKER! GET HIM!" Officer Mooney yelled. The wolf clenched onto the side of our cart, trying to slow us down by pressing its feet to the ground. I looked into its deep blue eyes as it stuck its teeth out, growling at us. That's when Seuss really showed me a real glimpse of his powers. When I began to see him as something more than just an old man locked up in a hospital. When I finally began to understand what a Watchwaker really was.

Seuss stood up and put both his hands along the side of the cart as he closed his eyes. Without me even knowing, the whole floor turned to ice. Wildlings everywhere fell to their faces. Others spun in circles. Officer Mooney slipped right off running after us and over into a counter, his feet and feathers hanging off the desk.

Seuss then reached his hand over and touched the wolf on his snout as he leaned onto our cart. Within a second, ice grew from around its face all the way to its legs. The wolf was completely frozen and stuck in the middle of a hospital lobby as went on strolling through. I looked back, my jaw dropped completely as I rubbed my eyes to stare. I could not believe what I had just witnessed.

"IS HE FROZEN? HOW DID YOU DO THAT?"

"No time to worry about that, Jimmy," he said softly as he whipped his right arm in the air and steered us down a short flight of stairs and crashed us through one of the hospital entrances. Wildlings, patients and medical staff alike, were all staring as we launched right past them to the outside, back to the Wazoo.

Seuss threw his arms open again as he looked right at a parked ambulance. Its back doors opened suddenly and we slid perfectly right inside while ducking our heads. I was panting, just trying to calm down from all the mayhem I had just witnessed.

"Do you know how to drive one of these, Jimmy?" he asked as he looked back to see if anyone was coming. Of all the crazy things he *could* do, this was apparently something that stumped him.

I hopped up front and turned the keys hanging in the ignition before I bolted us through the parking lot.

The cart started to scoot around behind me, and Seuss nearly flew out as I made a sharp turn onto the main trail. It was a really good thing I had told him to close the back doors.

Chapter 14

Advice from a Watchwaker

IT WAS THE MIDDLE OF THE NIGHT, and I was still a long way from ever getting home. After driving out of a hospital with a patient, whom I helped escape from the psych ward, and also happened to have some strange magical powers, you'd have to see for yourself to truly believe. And to think, all of this happened just because I got a 'little' sick for a few hours.

"Let's go to Palipilo Forest!" Seuss said, pointing me to go off the main trail. Eh, whatever. It wasn't too far from my house, and at this point, I was just happy to be out of the hospital without my parents ever knowing what all I've been up to.

It was quiet for a while, Seuss looking out the window and laughing, glad to finally be back outside after thirteen long years. But in the meantime, I was thinking which of my hundred questions to ask this bizarre man. I mean, I had heard *of* a Watchwaker, but never in my wildest dreams did I ever imagine any Wildling could do what I had just seen at the hospital: moving plants, breaking glass to let the octopuses roam freely, freezing the floors, and I'm pretty sure make a gust of wind to push our cart out of the hospital. I just had to know how he had made it all happen.

"Do you have powers, Seuss? Like magical powers?" I asked, but Seuss looked ahead with a blank expression on his face. I don't think he wanted to answer, or even knew how to explain himself. But I had to know, so I persisted. "Why won't you tell me? I helped you escape Seuss. I feel like I should know if that was a mistake. If you're dangerous..." I said as I stopped the ambulance.

He looked down and scratched his head before taking a deep breath. "I'm just a dreamer Jimmy. I can have dreams that let me engage with the Wild like few others ever could. And a few know this about me, and have locked me up because of it, but please, let's not dwell too much on it," he said as he opened the car door and stretched his hands wide. I came out and walked around as he gazed at the night sky and the forest around us. He was happy just to be free again, to be out in the open.

"Who locked you up, Seuss? Was it Greygor Guildenhall?" I asked, wondering if he knew who that even was and what he thought about him.

"Oh, you'd be surprised, Jimmy. Many Wildlings don't like me. The politicians of the island, the secret agencies we have roaming all around, and many other rich Wildlings as well. They all have never liked me since the island came to find me. They always feared I was a threat to them, especially when I became Watchwaker. That's why I've been heavily medicated and restrained in that psych ward. For thirteen years, I've been their prisoner. Until you came, Jimmy. You came and gave me my life back, and I'll never forget it."

Everyone? Why? We have had other Watchwakers? Heck, we even had one right now! What was so different about Seuss? I thought to myself, trying to make it all make sense. But just as I turned back around to ask him something else, Seuss ran off suddenly, deeper into the forest. "I don't underst- Seuss? Where are you going? Come back!" I said chasing after him.

It was the middle of the night, pitch black and quiet except for the crickets chirpinf and wylese gently chiming. I continued walking through the dark forest, the moon and stars glowing far above as I passed through a few shrubs. "Seuss? SEUSS? Are you there?"

"Up here Jimmy! Hurry, before they leave!" I heard him say from on top of a hill. I walked up slowly with a few more butterflies passing me by. When I reached the top, I saw a swarm of butterflies all flying together like a flock as they swirled around.

He stood on top of a large rock and stretched his arms wide as he smiled. The butterflies flew around him, almost as if they knew him. "Oh, I missed you all so much!" he said, smiling.

"Wh-what are all these butterflies doing here? I've never seen so many at once, and why are there these sparkles floating around us?" I asked. For as long as I'd lived at the Wazoo, there was still so much I did not know about it.

"These are one of my favorite creatures, Jimmy, sweet little Avirraris," he said as one flew into his palm. It had a glowing, bluish-purple pattern on it and released delicate sparkles from its wings. I had never seen such a beautiful butterfly in my life, and here I was surrounded by a tornado of them fluttering around the night sky. "These wondrous beauties carry with them so many dreams, and bless us all as they fly by."

"They carry dreams? How can they do that?"

"Oh, Jimmy, dreams are everywhere. They are the reason we wake up and do what we do. What we live for. What we need. And the best part of it all is that they are always given to us," Seuss said, standing back up. The butterflies flew quickly around where we were standing, as if they were in awe of us. I was anxious, not sure what was about to happen, but Seuss was not at all afraid. He held his arms out and laughed as he looked up, butterflies flying through us as more sparkles fell to light the night, like little floating stars. "This is a world of dreams Jimmy," Seuss said softly.

To be quite honest with you, I was completely confused. *A world of dreams? What does that even mean?* More importantly, though, I wanted to ask him about my own dreams, how everything I'd seen had come true one way or another.

"Are all dreams normal, Seuss? Have you ever had strange ones before? Ones that you didn't even know why you had them?"

"Sure, all the time. And I love them. They always make me think, or at the very least add to my perspective. But why do you ask, Jimmy? Has something been bothering you?"

"Well, I've been having strange dreams lately. They take me away from the Wazoo and everyone I know. And I've seen strange things. I knew about the pirates before they came to the Wazoo, and even the corrupt Pleaser talked about working with them. It-it just makes me so, so afraid! And worried! I just want all these bad dreams to go away! Do you think these butterflies could help me sleep?" I said, but I could tell he was confused. He had no idea what I was talking about, and I don't blame him. He had been locked away for thirteen years, and probably had no idea what I meant by the pirates.

"Our dreams, Jimmy, are much deeper than we think, and oftentimes, we can learn from them. I could help you with that, if you want," Suess replied. I only nodded, not sure exactly what he was planning.

He stretched his hand, letting one of the butterflies fly gently onto his palm. Sparkles from its wings fell into his palm, and he moved it towards my face. "The best way to get over our fears, Jimmy," Seuss said, pausing as he waited for the butterfly to fly away, a small pile of sparkles sitting on his palm, "is to confront them," he said before blowing the silver dust into my face. I turned my eyes and face away, but as I looked back, the whole world around me was suddenly changing.

Everything, the night forest, the butterflies, even Seuss, had all disappeared and I was standing on a small island underneath a bright purple sky.

But this was no normal island, nothing like the Wazoo from the looks of things. There were many dark purple clouds floating through an aura of bright lights glowing in the sky. I could not see the moon, but instead only the many dozens of shining stars above. "Hello? Seuss?" I called out to hear only my own echoes. I was lost again and began to walk around.

There were many tall stone statues like those at the Wazoo, but these were not of any Wildlings I had ever known. They were all humans, holding some kind of long stick and all wearing strange robes or metal sheets over them as they stood straight. To be honest with you, these were odd statues and I had no idea what I was looking at. *Was this all that Seuss had wanted me to see? What did this have to do with what we talked about?*

As I wandered throughout the forest, I began to see small, brown furred monkeys walking around. They were shorter than Barry and certainly couldn't speak. Instead, they looked at me with their big eyes and shrieked. I couldn't tell if they were afraid, angry, or maybe even excited that I was there, but they threw their arms in the air as they jumped around. Soon enough, they were walking up and climbing onto me. *Why couldn't these Wildlings speak? Where was I?*

As I was moving them off of me, one of the small monkeys pulled the circular crystal out of my pocket and raised it up. It was still as clear as when the bird had given it to me in my previous dreams. But to be honest with you, I had completely forgotten that ever happened, that I even had it on me.

A monkey raised it up high, and the rest gazed at it as if it was showing them something. They all watched silently until another monkey jumped and grabbed it for himself. They all chased after it, continuing to steal and fight each other until one of them finally ran off with it, the others screeching loudly as they followed. I tried to keep up.

Eventually I found myself in a glade with a circular stone table at the center with large and small sparkling gems embedded into it with long lines connecting them all. Around it were more large human statues, each of them holding the same long rods in their hands, some wearing necklaces made of rocks.

But as much as I wanted to figure what all of this was, I could only concentrate on all the monkeys surrounding me, standing on every statue, hopping across branches and climbing every rock, all of them shrieking and jumping loudly as the monkey who had my stone was now on the highest branch of all the trees. It started to yell before looking up at the sky and spreading its arms wide. Suddenly, it began to rain and all the monkeys around jumped and danced. They were celebrating.

While the water drenched us all, I could see an orange-furred monkey, heavily bruised and scratched, jump quickly onto the branch and snatch the stone from the brown monkey's hands before knocking him off onto the ground. Instead of raising it to the sky, the monkey stared into it and began pointing to random monkeys in the crowd. The rain quickly stopped and fires suddenly grew. Many screeched as they themselves were set on fire. The orange-furred monkey watched in delight, and not too long after, the whole grove was blazing.

Many of the monkeys ran as fast as they could, but I had my eyes set on the monkey who had my stone. I chased after it, running past flames and waiting for it to come down from the collapsing trees.

Eventually, it jumped down almost in front of me. I stepped on its tail and wrestled with the monkey, trying to rip the stone from its palm as it continued to punch and kick at me repeatedly. We rolled closer to the fire, but even when I had my hands around the stone, I kicked the orange furred monkey off of me as it tried to fight back. Soon though, the monkey was caught by flames, screeching as it spread on its body until it fell down and lay lifeless. I turned around and ran to shore alone, somehow unscathed by any of the fire.

The stone was now in the palm of my hand as I escaped. Not a single monkey was around me. As I came closer to the water, though, I began to hear voices from far away. "HELP! PLEASE, SOMEBODY HELP!" When I looked, I saw someone tied in a small boat with a few other animals. I came up closer and then realized it was my friends trapped on this island with me somehow. *Was this really them? Why were they here with me?* I thought to myself before quickly running over to them as fast as I could.

"Wh-what are you guys doing here?" I said as I

began to untie the rope around Amelia's arms.

"Help Jimmy! Help!" Damien begged from a cage.

"Behind you, Jimmy!" Sal said. I turned around and quickly ducked as a pirate slashed his sword at me. The rotten tooth pirate charged at me again. I looked back to see more pirates coming from the distance on the other side of the shore. *Where did they all come from? What did they want with us?*

I was completely defenseless. All I had was the rock in my hand. It would have to be good enough. *Maybe I could use it like the monkeys had somehow?* I really didn't know, but pointed it right at them just like they did, hoping it would keep the pirates away. But there was no fire that formed, nothing that stopped these angry pirates from charging towards me and my friends.

Instead, the water rose quickly up to my ankles. Pretty soon, I could no longer see the ground. Even the pirates were confused, standing still as they were now floating in the water.

"Get in, Jimmy!" Amelia said as I quickly hopped into the small boat. I took the oar and started to paddle away as fast I could. Soon enough, there wasn't a pirate anywhere in sight. I thought I could take it easy, panting as I stopped rowing in the middle of the now large sea.

Clouds quickly started to come and thunder roared across the dark gray sky above us. I looked back to see pirates in their large ship heading towards us. *What! How? Why?* I thought to myself as I quickly started paddling again. *This was all just a dream. This all had to be a dream. But why Seuss? Why all this?*

There was something black underneath the surface

of the water, coming closer, and pulling the oar that I was using to sail us away. Amelia grabbed me before I could be tugged away by the oar into the water. Two black crocodiles suddenly appeared on either side of us, ripping apart the wooden oar into small wooden pieces as they stared at us with their large, menacing red eyes.

I quickly took the stone back out of my pockets, hoping it would do something to keep us safe. Anything really. But nothing happened, so I began to pant heavily as I hit the crocodiles with my last remaining oar before steering us away.

A strong force started to pull us forward, faster away from the crocodiles. I had no idea how or why until I stood up and saw a whirlpool right up front. I tried to move us away but could not. Eventually, the oar was thrown out from my hands and we spiraled deeper and deeper into the layers of the sea. Thunder continued to bang across the sky. Soon the water was over us all.

I opened my eyes, panting as the sweat ran down my back. It was still dark outside, and without a single crocodile or purple cloud in sight. I got back up on my feet and started to walk back home. Seuss approached me almost immediately. "Oh, Jimmy, good, you're awake! How was your dream?" he asked. I didn't know how or what to say. He said all my bad dreams would go away, and here I was having another nightmare, probably worse than any I had before. So I told him about it and we talked while heading to my house.

"It was a stone, you say? One with powers? Well, that's not just any stone, Jimmy, it sounds like *Nguvuyaabi*," he replied.

"Well, whatever it was, it didn't help me at all! I'm not sure what the point of that dream was, Seuss. What did I confront? I didn't get anything out of it!" I said angrily.

"Ah, Jimmy, the dreamstone is an ancient tool, used to express what lay in our deepest imaginations. To show not only what we are capable of, but what surrounds our dreams as well."

"But what does that even mean? I'm just always afraid? Why shouldn't I be? I was being chased! My friends were in danger and everything was turning into a disaster!"

"Jimmy, sometimes our dreams are not just about what we see. Or what happens to us. They are bastions of our own consciousness that give us an opportunity to reflect. To rethink our lives by revealing to us how we feel and perceive. In a way Jimmy, we *are* the dreams we have. That whole experience, everything that happened *was* you!"

"You mean that I was the pirates? And those crocodiles? The fighting monkeys? That's all supposed to be me?" I asked, completely confused.

"Yes! I noticed that too. All the fighting. All that anger and unsteadiness throughout your dream. You've built up quite a bit of it. It tells me a lot about what's been going on within you. But I don't blame you either. Life can make us feel many ways, Jimmy. But we have to remember, this is a world of dreams and our only responsibility is to make sure it stays that way for everyone. No anger or sadness should ever get in the way of what we must do."

I was speechless. *We are the dreams? A world of dreams? Really, he said it again? What was he even trying to tell me? I knew I was angry and worried, but shouldn't I be?* This was all too much. I was just too tired to think about it anymore. Not to mention I had school tomorrow and still needed to find where the pirates were. I stayed quiet as we walked, pretending I was thinking. But when we finally got to my house, I knew I couldn't just say goodbye. Seuss was not only a friend I had made, but a Watchwaker also, one of the most powerful Wildlings that might have been on the island. And, most importantly, he might be our only hope against any pirate attack.

"Seuss, I need your help. We all do. There are these pirates from far away who have come onto our island. No one knows where they're hiding, and they keep hurting and stealing from us. It just doesn't make any sense how they're able to keep doing this without getting caught. Do you think you can help get rid of them, please?"

Seuss looked away, thinking to himself for a moment. "They *found* the Wazoo? How is that even possible?"

"I have no idea. All I know is they're looking for something called the Dream."

He raised his eyebrows as he stared back at me. "The Dream? They know about the Dream?" he asked, but I could only shrug. I wasn't sure if it was the dreamstone he mentioned or something else. Seuss thought a little more to himself before turning back around to look at me. "Hm, we definitely can figure something out. Do you think you can meet me at Yakbuka tomorrow afternoon? I'll be in the twisted Swylobi trees with some old friends, not too far away from the large pile of boulders," he said. I quickly nodded my head, barely able to keep my eyes open any longer.

Chapter 15

Odey's Honeybar

THE NEXT DAY, Sal and Damien were both very relieved to see I was not all fat and orange anymore. I was completely cured and looked like I hadn't even been to the hospital. But the best part about it all was that my parents hadn't known a thing. Sal, or Damien, but most likely Sal had convinced them I was staying late with Amelia to work on some project and that I'd be sleeping over at her house. Let's just say the morning started with my parents knocking on my door and me jumping out from my back balcony. Luckily, it still ended with a few pieces of toast and bacon being thrown out from the kitchen window.

When I arrived at school, Amelia nearly dropped all her books as her mouth fell wide open. I guess having my hair turn green, burping bubbles, and having literally both my hands and feet stretched out left quite the impression on her. A few hours passed with my friends constantly asking me questions every chance they got. I kept it casual for as long as I could. But they knew there wasn't any way a person as sick as I was with the Balooza would be released already. And they hadn't even known I was nearly as bloated as a balloon at one point. It wasn't until we were sitting on the tower on the playground that I figured I might as well tell them how. I almost immediately regretted it, though.

"YOU BROKE OUT OF THE HOSPITAL WITH AN OLD MAN? THAT'S AWESOME, JIMMY!" Sal blurted out.

"Sal! Don't encourage him. Why would you do that, Jimmy? He might have needed attentive care! He could die if he's out of the hospital for too long!"

"No, he was suffering in there! If anything, they were making him die! And besides, Seuss can help us get rid of the pirates, I know he can. He has these strange powers and he might be able to help us find them!"

"Jimmy, you can't! We have to turn him in to the police, put him back in the hospital!"

"WHAT! Did you not hear what I just said? He could help the whole Wazoo! And besides, it was probably Greygor who locked him up in the first place! We can't do that. He might be our only chance at stopping them."

"Look Jimmy, I know you just want to save the Wild, but there might be something wrong with this man, and I'm not sure we should trust him right away. He might not be as safe as you think he is."

"He's a Watchwaker, Amelia!"

"So, you're just going to work with someone from the psych ward Jimmy? You're not even a little worried?"

"Amelia, it's not that simple. I saw things, things you wouldn't believe. He's not lying to me, and trust me, he's not dangerous!" I said, walking away. It was useless. Getting them to believe anything. It was just like the pirates all over again. They didn't believe me then, and they certainly weren't going to believe me now.

"Jimmy, come back, we just want to tal-"

"No, just leave me alone!" I said, angrily marching off and leaving school. I didn't want to talk to any of them, but maybe this was what Seuss was saying. The whole point of my dreams. All the anger and worry I had. Maybe I was carrying too much of that with me while also throwing it at everyone else. But what else could I do? Ignore everything? Go around playing as if nothing was going on? And to be honest with you, in these past few months, it seemed like I was knowing myself less and less. As if I were becoming someone else and I didn't even know it.

I rode my bike to Yakbuka forest, famous for the yellow longtail Bembea monkeys that wouldn't hold back on throwing a coconut at anyone who overstayed their welcome. I walked towards the twisted Swylobi trees Seuss had mentioned to meet at. There were dozens of purple Rukakan monkeys, 'flingtails' as we called them, twirling around the air shouting to the mountains as I passed them by. Seuss was right, there were large stacked boulders, but he was nowhere in sight.

"Seuss? Seuss, are you here?" I called towards the trees as I walked around, only getting stared back at as a few coconuts were thrown my way.

"HEY KID! I'M NAPPING!" I heard someone say as I walked along until eventually a Bembea rolled upside down in front of me. "Can I help you?" he said with his eyebrows hanging low and a coconut in his hand.

"Uh, yes, is Seuss Sutterman here?"

"Oh, Seuss, who, uh I may or may not know, l-let me check. But just so I understand, who are you?"

"I'm Jimmy, his friend."

"Ok, I'm Yoki. Just give me a second Jimmy," he said before quickly twirling his tail back up the tree and yelling at someone. *"He's alone. Yes, that's what I'm saying, he already knows him! No, he's just a boy. Well, of course, they all lie, but not one this young. Okay, well I trust him!"* I heard being muttered to some other monkey friends I presumed. "Hello, yes, please come with me!" the monkey said as he came back down, quickly grabbed me, then coiled his tail to shoot us up.

I was being swatted by leaves and branches as we swished up, passing many little blue squirrels, whistle-birds and hopping kangetts (smaller kangaroos). After a few hundred feet, Yoki placed me onto a branch, sitting right across from Seuss, who was enjoying a nice byungyubaat, a very chewy red jelly desert from a local bakery.

"Jimmy, there you are! You're just a little early, I'm almost finished making my gift for you!" he said with jelly dripping down the side of his mouth as he jumped back up.

"A gift? Why?"

"For helping me out! I've been catching up with all my friends. Turns out, you can miss quite a bit in thirteen years, heck, I can't even recognize half my friends!" he laughed as he carelessly walked across a branch. "Come with me!"

"Uh, Seuss, where have you been staying? Do you have a home?" I asked.

"Oh Jimmy, the whole Wazoo's my home! I'll sleep in any bushell or branch I set my eyes on."

"But aren't you worried about the police?"

"Eh- they barely managed to catch me the last time. That too, I was betrayed. But I doubt it'll happen again," he said, ripping a berry off the tree and eating it. Just seeing that after having the Balooza made me cringe.

I walked over the thin, shaky branches slowly, looking down and trying to make sure I watched each step while Seuss was whistling and waving to the many monkey friends who swung by. "Hey! How are you? Oh, by the way, have you seen Sabayabayu?" he asked, but they quickly shook their heads. He continued walking and calling, "SABAYA! WHERE ARE YOU? Hm, where is he? He said he would be here by now!" Seuss wondered.

"SEUSS! I'm over he-" a gray, hunchbacked monkey with a strange umbrella hat said waving over before suddenly tripping over and falling, barely grabbing onto a branch. "Ohf! Almost lost my glasses there!" he said with a congested, squeaky voice.

"Oh goodness, Sabaya! Are you okay?"

"Yes, yes I am, though I am feeling a bit dizzy, but no matter!" he said, raising a finger and pointing up in the air. "For I have gotten exactly what you have asked for. Come closer, please, I will show you," he said as he took out his pocket and showed us a few weird twines I had never seen before.

"Oh, Sabaya, you found them! Tringets and Turdimot! This is exactly what I needed. I hope they weren't too hard to find."

"Oh no, it wasn't so bad once I passed the rutweb and kicked off the thorny whip plants and rolled out of the spiky rukghoo beds, though I may still have those warbiny bumps from when they stung me," he said, scratching his head. "But yes! Absolutely not a problem at all, but I don't think I'll be going back to the Heloks anytime soon," Sabaya said.

"Well thank you very much. And sorry for all the trouble! Here, I want you to take- now I know I put it here somewhere," he said, shuffling through his pockets "Ah yes, here please take this!" Seuss said, taking out a shiny red ruby. I was in shock, gems were very rarely seen on their own in the Wazoo, yet he already had one just a day after escaping the hospital.

"Wh- this is a pure Reinhart ruby! Oh my, this is a magnificent marvel of metamorphic science, a natural heirloom of the Wild! Thank you, thank you so much Seuss! You-you have astounded me," Sabaya said to him as he was chewing on another piece of jelly from his pocket.

"Oh! Well, no worries! I appreciate it!" he said before waving goodbye to the monkey, who was staring at the stone as he walked straight into the main bark of the tree.

But before I could even turn back, Seuss was already squatting down, sticking his tongue out of the side of his mouth as he stretched and coiled a few of the plant twines around a very large vine he had. He then pulled it all apart after assembling it. "Perfect! Jimmy, take a look at this," he said with a big smile, but still, I had no idea what he had done. "Here, climb onto my back, I want to show you how it works!" I did what he asked, and to my complete surprise, he jumped off the tree.

"NO, SEUSS WH-" I tried yelling before we fell nearly a hundred feet. Almost instantly though, he raised his arm towards the sky, and the vine stretched and coiled around a branch long enough for us to swing back up. As we bounced through the air, many Wild-lings awed or laughed as we passed by.

I still had no idea where Seuss was planning on taking us, but I can tell you that when we did finally stop on a tree, my whole body was shaking from the excitement of swinging through more jungle than your average chimp could even imagine. "Th-that was amaz-ing Seuss! I've never done anything like that in my life! What is that thing?"

"Ah, just a little something I made. I call it the vine-whip, but I want you to have it in case you ever need to get anywhere in a hurry. And don't even worry about falling, it's made to grab onto your own arm. Just loos-en your grip as soon as you swing up, so it knows to let go of the branch, then just throw it forward again," Seuss said as we walked across a few branches until we

reached the largest beehive I had ever seen with dozens of bees buzzing as they zipped past us. When we got closer, I read the wooden sign.

ODEY'S HONEYBAR

To be honest with you, on any other day, I would be more than happy to come to a place like this. But I just couldn't stop thinking about the pirates. They were still here wreaking havoc, and that was the only thing on my mind. "Seuss, we need to ta-"

"Check this out, Jimmy! It's one of my favorite restaurants. Come on, you'll love it!" he said as he ran ahead. When we walked in, there were tables filled with Wildlings all throughout the large dome, eating away at stacks of honey-laced food. A few of them were so large, that I had wondered just how exactly they managed to get up a few hundred feet on this tree. But I guess at the Wazoo, you really shouldn't be surprised by anything you see.

"Please come with me!" said the small Wyibyn bear wearing a fancy blue vest and tie. "Here are your menus. A waiter will be with you shortly."

"Uh, excuse me, excuse me!" Seuss said right before the small bear was able to walk off. "If Odey is around, could you tell him Seuss is here?" he asked before scanning the menu.

I won't lie to you, being out with Seuss made me very nervous. He did, after all, have a natural way of standing out in public to say the least. "Seuss, we need to talk about the pir-"

"There he is!" someone in a low voice said behind me.

"OOODDEEEYYY!" Suess said emphatically as he got up.

"It's been too long, old friend!" said an enormous bee with jelly marks over its face and large gut. I rolled my eyes and shook my head, wondering when we were ever going to talk about the pirates.

"Yes it has, I can't believe you actually opened your own place!"

"I know, isn't it great? You see? I told you I would one day have the most delicious food the Wazoo has ever seen! Come sit, order anything you want, it's on the house! You, waiter, come here," Odey said as he flew over to the table and looked at the menu. "I want you to get Seuss and his friend here, one of everything, understand? One of everything!"

"Oye, ok sir!" the small twiddlebird said before zooming off to the kitchen, barely skirting waiters carrying trays full of plates.

"Wowee! Thanks ,ole' pal! How's business going?"

"Not bad, been a little bumpy now and then, especially with all this pirate and Balooza news going around. But we're managing. But outside of that, my jams an' jellies an' honeymelts have been selling off really well by the jar. That Hortley fella, as big an' stinky as he is, knows how to run a business, I tell ya! Given me plenty a good advice too," he said in his low jolly voice.

Seuss froze for a second, shaking and taking deep breaths as Odey went on and on about his business partner.

"Is that our food?" I said, trying to deviate his attention and steer the conversation someplace else.

"Yes, yes! Have at it!" Odey said as many birds and koalas helped to carry several filled trays of food. Seuss immediately turned and jumped in his seat when he saw it all, before quickly grabbing the wafer dripping with honeygoo right away. "Don't forget to try the hard chocolate cracks, bansambun bread, Goinitzka jam, Gungubamunga, and everything else! Seuss, you call me after you're finished and we'll catch up buddy!" he said before buzzing off.

After a while of stuffing our faces with all the honey and jam we could possibly squeeze into our bellies, we sat back and laughed talking about how we barely made it out of the hospital. But I couldn't resist. I had to say what was on my mind. "Seuss, can we talk now? Do you know who Hortley is? Hortley Hasselback?" I asked, but he immediately turned his head away. I could tell Seuss knew him by the way he reacted to Odey talking about him, but how?

"Oh, Jimmy, don't remind me of such things," he said, dismissing my question as he got up. I followed him as we walked outside. Seuss casually gave another gem, this time a blue sapphire to the bear host, who nearly fell off his seat at the sight of it.

"I know, Seuss, but please can you tell me? There are pirates searching all across the island and I still have no idea why. Please, can you just tell me," I begged. He paused for a few seconds, thinking to himself, before answering.

"Jimmy, he- he was the one who betrayed me. Got me locked up in the hospital because I wouldn't help him make some money or whatever it was he was planning." I remember the large pig asking Greygor to work with the pirates on the trade route. I think Captain Bacawly was talking about him in the video, as if they had known each other somehow. *Did Hortley do it? Did he bring the pirates to the Wazoo or at least know about them coming? Was this all his doing?*

"I don't understand, Seuss, what does this have to do with them wanting the Dream?"

"Jimmy, that is one of the biggest secrets of the Wazoo. Not many Wildlings have even heard of *Sepannagharum* before."

"What is it, like a weapon?"

"It could be, Jimmy. To the untrained eye, it is just a fruit, but to those who eat it and know its full potential, they have the ability to control many minds and find worlds that should never be known! In the wrong hands, I cannot imagine what would be done."

"Do you think Hortley is behind this bringing the pirates? I know he is working on some big trade scheme. But do you think he would really help the pirates?"

"Listen to me, Jimmy! The pirates cannot get their hands on this fruit. I don't even know how these outsiders found the Wazoo. Greater forces are at play here. If what you've told me is true, it must be Hortley, but still, I do not know how."

"Well, is there any way you can find them, Seuss?"

"I'm afraid not, Jimmy. I've tried asking the butterflies, but they claimed they haven't seen anyone out of the ordinary. This is all not making any sense to me. We must find Hortley quickly. Is there anyone you think you can ask about his whereabouts?"

"Peister! He might have some idea where to find the pig and possibly the pirates too. They did just break into his house after all... He might be able to help us."

"Perfect Jimmy, speak with him. In the meantime, I will do my best to come up with a plan to get rid of them," he said urgently.

"Trying to leave without me, eh Seuss?" said the large bee as we walked to the edge of the branch.

"Ha, you wish!" Seuss said, smiling as if our conversation never even happened. "By the way, that was a great feast you served us!"

"Ahh, least I could do! Now come on, I want to take you to Gobika, see the farm where I make most of my jams!"

"Ooo, yes, please! But one second Odey. Here, Jimmy, take this," he said, handing me a small white flute. "In case you ever need to talk to me, call a butterfly with it and they'll tell me exactly where to find you!" he said before being grabbed by the enormous bee and buzzing off, laughing loudly off in the distance.

Chapter 16

A Patron's Parting

A WEEK HAD GONE BY and I still had to make it up to my friends after bursting out at them for thinking Seuss was dangerous. I really do my best to avoid formal apologies and instead go for the casual 'lets do something fun approach.' I know it's not exactly right, yet somehow, I managed to get away with it.

Mudpit Falls was technically closed, but enough Wildlings snuck in over time for even the police to forget all about it. It was there that I first showed them the vinewhip Seuss had made. They were amused, seeing me ski through the mud as fast as I did. But it wasn't until they saw me practically flying through the air that they finally started to come around on the crazy old man I was now friends with, though Amelia still had her suspicions.

As we were cleaning the mud off ourselves, I told them about the whole, well, partial plan I had made with Seuss, that I would find a way to talk with Peister and see if he knew anything about where the pirates could be, or at the very least where Hortley was.

"Peister? Didn't you try to do that last time? Let me think, how did that go? Oh yeah, you ended up IN THE HOSPITAL!" Riley said, mocking me.

"She's right, Jimmy, I heard he really bolstered up his security after Bacawly broke into his home and intimidated him. Don't expect your luck to be so easy this time."

"Well, that's different, Riley! I caught the Balooza! Besides I still have the Caecuweed, and now the vinewhip, so it'll be easier. Even if his security team sees me, I'll be able to get away in time."

"No, Jimmy, you take too many risks, you're always going to do something dumb! This is a horrible idea! Why do you even need to talk to him? He doesn't know anything about the pirates!"

"No, but he knows Hortley I bet."

"Wh-Hortley? What are you talking about, Jimmy?" Riley asked.

"Yes. Hortley Hasselback. That's who we're looking for. Do you guys know him? I heard he's the richest Wildling around and probably owns Wazoo Trading Company, that's why he was mentioned in the video leaked during the debates," I said also not wanting to mention that Amelia and I saw him at the Pleaser's Palace.

"I-I think so, but what does he have to do with any of this?" she said carefully, trying not to give too much away.

"I think he's the one who brought the pirates here. Not Greygor, not Peister, or anyone else. I think he brought them here for his own wealth."

"What? No, Greygor brought them here! You said you saw him in your dream trying to do something with pirates and the media keeps talking about all the proof they got from the whistleblower!" Riley said, as I glared at Amelia for a second.

"Well, I was wrong. I think Hortley is behind this all. He's pushing that trade route more than anyone else, and Seuss said it was he who betrayed and threw him into the hospital. That's when I got the idea, or at least, started putting it all together. I mean, it all makes sense, doesn't it? Seeing that he has the most to gain out of all of this."

"Oh, again with that old man, seriously? Are you just going to believe everything he tells you?" Riley sassed.

"No, I think Jimmy's onto something. Hortley brought them here to get all this going. I mean look at those barrels. All the gathered fruit was packaged and stamped. Someone has to be organizing all of this. The Wazoo Trading Company, I don't know where it is exactly, but I bet wherever the main site is, that's where the pirates are hiding!" Damien said excitedly.

"Exactly!" I responded, happy that at least one of them was now understanding my plan.

"So, why does the news keep implying it's Greygor who's behind th-" Sal asked.

"Oh, don't listen to the news, they don't know just as much as anyone else would. They never have the answer to anything anyway. But Peister will know. I'm sure after getting broken into and especially after having every Wildling see or hear about the video of him with the pirates, I'm sure he'll want to do something big to clear his name."

"We all started to walk out of the hot geyser room, where Wildlings could clean themselves up afterwards. Amelia had stayed quiet for a while now, and I wasn't sure if it was because she disagreed with my plan or she was just focused on getting the last bits of dirt out of her long hair.

"Well?" I asked.

"Well, what?" she replied.

"C'mon, you know what I'm going to ask. Do you think my plan is any good? I mean we were there at the palace. We saw Hortley pushing the trade route idea to Greygor. And my plan makes sense, doesn't it?" I asked genuinely, hoping not to get into another argument with her. I really did hate it when we fought.

"It's not your plan Jimmy, I'm just worried. Anything can happen these next few weeks. All I can think about is that letter and the video. That the pirates want to burn down the whole island, and I-I just don't know how much time we really have," she said, sobbing a little as she crossed her arms.

I went over and gave her a big hug. "We'll do our best to find them, okay? We will stop them."

I thought the next few days would be calm and easy, or at least I really hoped so. After everything I had been through, from almost getting arrested, breaking into the Pleaser's Palace, to getting the Balooza, and escaping from the hospital with a wanted fugitive, all I wanted was a peaceful time to at least try and get my grades up. I was on my parents' last nerve to say the least. But peace was the last thing any of us got.

"Big news, big, BIG news!" Gunter, my koala friend, said as he marched into the library with his TV while we were all sitting around working on our book report for *Spudfly and Yupee* for Ms. Keaton's class. He put the TV down in front of all of us.

"...thank you for being with us today Skhoka, now if you don't mind telling us where you are exactly and what is going on over there?"

"Absolutely Hnan, there were reports over the past couple of weeks that fights between Pleaser Guildenhall and Patron Aechus Albrite have reportedly escalated over negotiations with the pirates, the increase in crime, and the spread of the Balooza. Then it was quiet until today, where the Patron turned in his resignation and is now expected to give a very important announcement any min- oh here he is," the reporter said before the camera panned over to the stone podium where the tall light blue shell beak stork stood.

"Thank you for being here today my fellow Wildlings. I have formally given my resignation from this administration. I have simply seen too much and cannot afford to be a part of passive actions when millions are suffering and stressed from the chaos these pirates have brought to our island. But, I am also troubled at the few good leaders this island does have. Peister Precarious is certainly no solution, and neither is Greygor Guildenhall for our beloved Wild. We should all be seeking the guidance from someone who will not play into these petty games, and who is willing to do whatever it takes to capture the pirates. As someone who knows the innards of our very struggles for nearly twelve years, I believe I can bring these solutions. Therefore today, I am declaring my candidacy for Pleaser of the Wazoo to ensure the promise that all the dreams of this remarkable homesake never die. Thank you all so very much," he said walking off and ignoring the flashing cameras and perpetuating questions coming at him.

We were all shocked as we watched what had just taken place. The entire study area now filled with Wildlings gasping and gossiping, all wondering what this meant. *Why did they break apart? Are the pirates going to attack soon? Is the Pleaser or Peister going to lose?*

EXCUSE ME! WHOSE TV IS THIS?" Ms. Napala yelled as she walked in. Every student backed away while Gunter stood still and clueless.

"Uh, i-it's mine, but it's imp-"

"NO TVs allowed in the library! I will be taking this to my office!" she said as she grabbed it and walked away.

"No, No! Ms. Napala, I'm sorry, I'm sorry. It was big news. I won't do it again, I promise!" my koala friend said crying as he chased her down.

"Three Wildlings in the election now? Like two wasn't enough of a headache!" Sal said, absolutely confused at what he had just watched. But no one said it all better than Riley.

"What is even going on? Are there rules anymore? I mean things are just getting wilder and wilder by the day!" And indeed they would be.

A week later all of my friends and I left right after school to head straight to Calajaa Forest. Even getting there an hour early seemed too late as the area was already crowded with Wildlings all along the Ino River, a long and thin river that ran through the whole Wazoo from the south of Badaan all the way north to Curtaka. I quickly waved goodbye to my friends as I took out the vinewhip and swung into the air. I headed to the back area of the forest where the candidates would prepare. There was a rock with Peister's name inscribed on a little wooden hut. I sat in the tree branch, hiding behind the leaves, waiting until the vulture arrived in a chariot led by dark black panthers, each with piercing yellow eyes.

Peister walked into the hut and quickly shut the door while at least a dozen panthers surrounded the area. It was now or never. I quickly put the Caecuweed and carefully slipped in.

He was walking back and forth, flipping through flashcards with talking points he wanted to hit for tonight's debate. "Peister," I said as I unveiled the seaweed sheet around me. He quickly jumped up and the note cards fell all around him. "We need to talk!"

"Jimmy!" he said as he rushed over to me. "What are you doing here?" he whispered as he opened the door to make sure his guards were not alerted. "And why, for Gideon's sake, do you still have this blanket? You were supposed to give it back!"

"Wh- Peister, that doesn't matter! We need to talk about the pirates!"

"Don't you talk like that to me, boy! Now go away, I'm preparing for the debate!" he said arrogantly.

"Ok, I'll leave, but please tell me what you know about Hortley! I think he may be working with the pirates, though I can't prove it."

"What! No, who told you that? Is that what the news is saying? Wh-ah-no, you know what, I cannot talk right now! I need to be ready for the questions, we'll have to figure out another time!"

"But Peist-"

"OUT! Or I will call security!" he said, standing next to the string bell at the top of his hut.

I don't blame Peister for being too upset, mostly because he was right. Marshull Manics was hosting the debates, and if it was going to be anything like his regular show, I knew these candidates would be in for a far worse time than even the Heloks could do to them.

You see, Marshull Manics was perhaps the most notorious 'news anchor' all across the Wazoo. This suited-up moose was known for creating the tensest environments for his guests, throwing personal attacks, accusations, and untrue narratives at them just to get them all riled up for views. He was often dubbed the most entertaining and sensational TV show at night, but I just wasn't sure how great he was for everyone's head. I had a bad feeling he was going to stir the pot the wrong way. And unfortunately, I tended to have a good hunch about things.

"THANK YOU ALL VERY MUCH FOR BEING HERE! I AM YOUR HOST MARSHULL MANICS, MODERATING TONIGHT'S DEBATE WITH NOT TWO, BUT THREE CANDIDATES," the moose announced passionately. He graciously welcomed each of them, but something tells me that sweet tone was going to die quickly.

"Pleaser Guildenhall, there have been many pressing disasters under your own leadership. Your own Watcher Pack is collapsing as your once greatest advocate is now on the stage against you. Not to mention the steep increase in crime rates, and the plummeting health of all Wildlings due to the Balooza. My first question to you, Mr. Pleaser, is how do you even have the audacity to walk onto this stage right now? How can you even live with yourself?" Manics asked. I instantly rolled my eyes as members in the audience started to chant in anger, causing the provocative moderator to hush the crowd silent.

"Th- this is absurd! I have run the Wazoo perfectly for the last thirty years and now you-"

"Mr. Pleaser, just answer the question. How long have you and Patron Albrite been colluding with the pirates? And did Mr. Precarious play a role in all of this?"

"Wh- Manics, I have never worked with the pirates!" Peister blurted out.

"Oh, is that why they came to your house? All of this is recorded on video. I think we all deserve to know, Consular, what the nature of your relationship was with them and how you upset them?"

"Oh, you cannot be ser- THEY BROKE INTO MY

HOME MANICS!" he replied, throwing his broken wings into the air.

"Okay, fine, don't answer. Pleaser Guildenhall, explain to us all why you fired the Patron and in which scenario did he mess up?" he asked. Greygor was completely flustered, not sure where to even begin his answer, but Patron Albrite stood up firmly.

"How could you say that Manics? You and all your foolish exaggerations! Just because I left the Palace and run my own campaign, you believe I was fired? This is all utterly ridiculous! I have served this island and the Pleaser faithfully, but the tragedy of these pirates finding our island is my only focus!" Aechus Albrite said, angrier than I had ever seen him before.

"And sir, does it bother you that you are undermining the ENTIRE Waker Pack? Now giving more leverage to Consular Precarious. Who knows, if anything you two may be working together to take down the Pleaser!"

"CHEATER!" They all kept chanting while others booed. Aechus became agitated, and waited for the crowd to quiet down before answering.

"Absolutely not! I think there would be nothing more despicable than if Peister Precarious were to become Pleaser of the Wazoo! His trade route proposal, his desire to establish an industrial relationship with the outside world, incremented workforce, and Gideon knows what else would turn the Wazoo into nothing more than a circus show!"

"Oh, you cannot be serious!" Peister shot back. "The Wazoo is *the* wonder of the world, with more rarities and safety of our dreams than any part of this world has ever known! But we have an opportunity to create a better lifestyle for all of us! Are you so against that? Perhaps it does make sense, seeing how you do not seem to mind turning your back on your own pack." This is what Manics did. Create so much tension that the candidates would stop arguing with him and would argue with each other.

"Alright, you can avoid my question for now. Mr. Pleaser, are you in any way associated with this trade route, or at all believing in this far-fetched theory?" Manics asked.

"No, I am not involved nor do I believe it would be good for the sake of the Wild t-"

"And look at this, you are LYING as well Mr. Pleaser. It was recorded nearly two months ago that you had a meeting with Hortley Hasselback regarding the trade route. Why are you so willing to hide your support for the matter?"

"Wh-no, I had met with him to dissuade the greedy pig from pushing forward his trade-"

"*BOOO!*" The crowd started saying to all the candidates as they screamed in anger. Just as they finally arrived at the topic I had wanted to know most about, Hortley's involvement in all of this, the arguing among them went on as they desperately tried defending themselves and attacking each other. I didn't see the point in all this useless fussing. It was only making the crowd angrier, and the Wild less trusting of any of them. The fighting had gone on, though I doubt a single Wildling was getting much out of it at this point.

After this disastrous debate finally ended, I quickly swung back onto the tree to look for Peister. Strangely enough though, he walked right past his hut and off deeper into the forest. *Did he forget we were supposed to be meeting? Why did he not enter his chariot? Where was he going?* I was confused.

"Peister? Where are you going?" I called him from behind.

"Wh- Jimmy, how do you keep finding me? Go away!"

"Wh-no! We need to tal-"

"Not now, Jimmy. Please, just turn back now!" he was hoppling off even faster. But I wouldn't give up that easy.

"Peister, PEISTER!" I said following him, looking around to make sure no panthers were peeking from around the corner. I had the vinewhip in hand, ready to slash and escape at a moment's notice.

Suddenly, a long, wooden, caterpillar-like car rolled in front and stopped us right in our tracks. "What is this?" I said as it circled around us. Peister gulped as a black panther jumped down from a tree and said nothing, only staring their bright yellow eyes right at us.

"The boss would like to meet with you," the panther said as the door opened. Peister walked in nervously. I was looking up at the trees, squeezing the vinewhip in my hand and just about to escape. "You too, boy," he said in a low voice. *The boss?* I didn't want to risk it, but more importantly, I wanted to know just what in the Heloks was going on right now.

I sat down next to Peister on a cushioned leather couch and looked across to see a fat pig wearing a blue suit. He was flipping through pages of notes while eating a large white cake.

"Ah, welcome, welcome! It is nice to see you again, Peister," the fat pig said with a greedy smile. "And same to you, young man. Jimmy Jungles, wasn't it?"

"Hortley? Why are we here?" I said, thinking to myself, just trying to put it all together, until it finally hit me. "So, this whole time you've been working with Hortley? And when I broke into the Palace and found evidence against Greygor, that was just so you could win, wasn't it? You've just been lying to me - to everyone- this whole time, haven't you? All for what? Money? Power? Is that it?" I yelled as I looked at him, but Peister looked down and away, refusing to acknowledge anything I had just said.

"Very intuitive boy, I like that. But please, don't blame him, he was just doing what he was told," Hortley said, taking a handkerchief and wiping his face. "Don't you see, Jimmy, it's not for me, this is the will of the Wild! Believe me when I say, youngling, we really have not amounted to much as a society. Many would see us as nothing more than mere animals living together without the slightest ambition. But we can be *more*. I assure you, we can be much, much more! Soon, we will be able to exchange everything from our rare gems to unique plants, and even all the elegant fruits this island has to offer. We will create the *most* powerful economy any land has ever seen, putting us at the center of the entire world! And with only a few sacrifices to make."

"Give away our fruits? How? That's all infested by the Balooza, you ca-" I began to say until it finally hit

me. What Hortley had really been doing. "*YOU!* You caused the Balooza to spread. It wasn't from those pirates! You did it!"

"Very intuitive boy. *Very intuitive*," Hortley said, impressed with me, but I wasn't having it.

"So, that's why you're trying to have Peister win this election? And tear down Greygor in the process? To get richer than you already are! Is that what this is all about?"

"Let me ask you, boy. Do you think Greygor is capable of change, hm? To do what it takes to create a greater society? Many do not see it that way. And many others have helped me in my pursuit to create this trade route. Peister, you, even Greygor's closest advocate, have all come around to see my vision in some way."

"WHAT! *You* made Aechus betray Greygor too? How? How can you just control everything and everyone like that? And Peister, he's your little puppet, isn't he?"

"Don't be so terrified, Jimmy. These are new times. The pirates are only a momentary distraction. A means to an end," Hortley replied with a sneer laugh.

"A means to an end? They're stealing from the Wild, hurting Wildlings everywhere! And it's all YOUR FAULT!"

"Well, I cannot disagree with that. My hold on them is lessening by the day. They seek things other than our initial agreement. It seems the promise of riches were not enough. But no matter, I hear you have a new friend, Jimmy. Someone who could aid our cause. Is this true?"

"Y-You mean Seuss? How do-"

"Oh, never mind how I know, boy. I am sure, by now, you know of his extraordinary abilities. Powers the Wild has never known with greater capability than even Giyatar Ghanji himself. The Watchwaker could be very helpful to us in stopping this tragedy and controlling the pirates. You must know that."

"Seuss is not going to help you! Not after you locked him up! I'd never tell you where he is! You don't care about anyone and I'm going to make sure the press and everyone in the Wazoo knows it!" I yelled. Hortley was getting disgruntled again as he sat back, making a smug face.

"THAT'S ENOUGH OUT OF YOU, BOY! You really don't understand business, politics, or just how anything in this world really works! Perhaps it was a mistake stealing that book and making you depend on Peister. You are just as useless and pathetic as all the rest of them! Move out of the way, Peister, so my guards can take this boy straight to Kyrokky. Maybe there he will learn some sense. Cyter, take him away!" the fat pig said to the panther as it slowly walked towards me.

I jumped towards the door and opened it. "Where do you think you're going?" Another panther standing on the roof of the car said before grabbing me and lifting me to the top. A few more of them climbed from inside the limousine to the top.

"Boss said we have to take him to Kyrokky," one of them said, looking down at me as he licked his lips, "but I guess he wouldn't find out if we just ate him instead."

I reached into my bag and took out the vinewhip, trying to let it wrap around my hand and swing away. "Just what do you think you're doing?" a panther said, walking over me with its long fangs hanging out.

Suddenly, Venali tigers jumped out from a tree above and landed onto the moving vehicle. The panthers quickly turned around and hissed at them before they attacked each other, biting into each other's skin and tossing each other around. I raised my hand, ready to get pulled into the air by the vinewhip, but almost immediately, I was knocked off by a panther diving at me. My head slammed into the ground before I could fly off the moving vehicle. It all went black as all the roaring eventually faded away.

The Twisted Caverns

I WOKE UP WITH A HEADACHE and a slight swelling on the side of my head. As my vision started to come back to me, I looked around to see I was no longer laying outside in the Calajaan Forest, but in a room, laying on a bed. At first I thought it was my room until I noticed the stone floors and walls. I lifted the ice pack off of my head and got back onto my feet. I had no idea where I was but it all looked familiar.

"Ah, good! You're awake!" said a long-legged Eekit bird wearing a nurse's outfit.

"Uh, ma'am, what hospital is this?"

"Oh, this isn't the hospital youngling, this is the

Pleaser's Palace!" she said. I ignored everything else she was telling me as I saw orange eyes staring at me from the slightly opened door behind her. This was the last place I should be. If Hortley wanted to throw me at Kyrokky, I can't even imagine why the Venali tigers wanted to bring me here. After all, I had stolen from them and made them all look stupid. I began breathing heavily, worrying that even my nurse would be scared of a white tiger from barging in.

"You boy, come with me!"

"No, absolutely not! He's still not well. He is supp-"

"The Pleaser demanded his presence once he awakes! Now get up, boy, and come with me.

"Harix, you are out of li-"

"UP NOW!" the tiger yelled as I quickly shot up. I was looking for my things, but they were nowhere to be found.

Many of the Venali guards unveiled their invisibility and stood still, watching me with anger as I walked down the hallway. I was the one who had made them all look bad, and caused all this trouble for the Pleaser in the news. I was shaking and tryinh to keep my eyes down as I passed them all by.

We walked up the spiral stairs and entered the Crown Room. Greygor Guilenhall was staring off into the window by his desk as fire from the chimney crumbled the wood. It was nearly as warm as the volcano I walked through in my dream when I first saw him.

"My lord, I bring before you the thief," Harix said, bowing. "How shall we avenge you?"

"Thank you, Harix, you may leave now," the Pleaser said calmly, as the tiger growled on its way out.

It was quiet as I stood alone with the lion, waiting to hear what our very own leader of the island might say after I stole from his office. He was the Pleaser after all. He could do anything he wanted to me, and no one would have to know a thing about it. I was scrambling to come up with a defense, going to blame Peister and Hortley for lying to me and giving me everything I needed to steal from him in the first place.

"How are you feeling, Jimmy?" he asked softly, still not looking at me.

"Uh, bet-better, sir."

"Good. I hear you were with some awful Wildlings before the Venali came and rescued you. I hope you realize how lucky you are. We arrived just in time," he said, turning around and walking towards me.

"T-that was you who sent them? Why?"

"It was important that we kept an eye out for you, having a relationship that close to Peister is dangerous. He is willing to work with anyone who helps his cause. And some Wildlings will do anything for power, Jimmy, as I am sure you know by now."

"Are you talking about Hortley, sir? I know he brought the pirates here, and now he can hardly control them. All for his trade route idea. For his own wealth."

"His influence is deep. No matter which side we are on, everyone always finds themselves having to work with him. Look at my own pack, half of them are already on his side, throwing away the values I thought they stood for."

"What are you going to do sir? The pirate attacks are getting worse by the day. It's only a matter of time before they burn down the island."

"I am very aware of the destruction they could do to our island. They are putting the Wazoo in a corner, spreading fear, and forcing me to make compromises. All for the sake of peace," Greygor said, looking at the ground.

"You're talking about the Dream, aren't you?"

"How do you know about that?" The Pleaser was surprised as he turned to look at me.

"I-I talked to Seuss Sutterman about it. He said it could be used as a weapon," I replied, not wanting him to say that I read it off a letter on his desk.

"Like I said, Jimmy, I do not like the negotiations I am having to think about. But it may be our only choice to get the pirates off the island permanently, and ensure they never return."

"But how? I still don't understand how they found the Wazoo in the first place."

"They have a map, Jimmy. A very special map I nearly destroyed decades ago. Never did I imagine it would come back to haunt me."

"A map, sir?"

"Yes. But none like I have ever seen before. It shines and changes what it shows. They have found the Wazoo through wicked means. And I have no doubt it has the origins of sorcery."

"How did they get it?"

"I have no idea. But I told the Captain I must have the map if he wishes to possess what he desires.

Still, though, I will need help to get it when I go to the Ohwahgon tomorrow. Can you meet me at Lake Astoria in the Induwaaz forest by dusk, Jimmy? From there we will make our way."

"The Ohwahgon? What's that?"

"Yes, Jimmy, the Watchwaker's temple. I will arrange for a meeting with Giyatar Ghanji and in that time, you will search for the sacred fruit."

I immediately felt my heart jump. *Me? Of all the Wildlings we have on this island, why does it always have to be me?* With all due respect, sir, why me? Why not the Venali? They're the best hunters, I-"

"No! One little thing that irks them and they'll start to attack everything. And I cannot afford the rest of the island hearing about this. Not now. I need someone who can help keep this quiet. You can use the Caecuweed to hide yourself," he said, looking down at his office to where the blanket and vinewhip were laying. "I'm sure you've been able to sneak around plenty of places with it before," Greygor said, looking down at me.

"Okay, but sir, I've been through the Induwaaz plenty of times, and I don't ever remember seeing a temple there."

"Well, Jimmy, that's because it's not always there," he said as a large white tiger, bigger than most of the others, walked into the room. "Caadjy, I want a boat arranged for this boy to be taken to the mainland. Be sure NONE of the guards approach him in any way. He is very important to me. Do you understand?"

"Yes, my lord," the tiger said, bowing. I followed it as the giant beast guided me out of the palace and to the dock before another large tiger chased after us. The guard stood tall in front of me.

"The Pleaser has commanded this boy to be taken back to the mainland. Return back to your post, now Hargaan!"

"This boy keeps sneaking into this sacred isle! And all the guards blamed me for letting him pass the grounds! I have been stripped of ALL my accolades!" yelled the large gray tiger with strange black streaks as many Venali quickly ran up and slashed their claws at him before tackling him down.

"Do not worry about him, just get on the boat," said the large white tiger as the gray one was being dragged away. I stepped onto the small pontoon and looked around, not sure who was going to take me back to the mainland.

"Jaqwee!"

"Yes!" said a fish as it popped its head from under the water while chewing on a long plant.

"Escort this boy back to Wazuba Bay and keep this off the record!"

"Yes, Caadjy!" said the shiny blue fish as it saluted the tiger with its long fin. I could tell now, this was a fly fish, but even then, it couldn't be strong enough to push a pontoon. It wasn't until he swam around while blowing the small coral whistle that I saw the hundreds of fly fish around me.

"READY YOURSELVES! HOLD ON TIGHT, BOY!" he said as I squeezed the railing. Before I even knew it, I was zipping across the water, the Pleaser's Palace quickly fading into the distance. I was whipped and zipped all across the water as we nearly dodged every obstacle lying in the water. When we reached the shore, I only remember everything spinning, and that I could barely stand straight when my feet touched the dry sand.

The next day, all I could do was act calm in front of my friends, that Peister and I had only gone away to make a plan to save the Wildlings...Don't get me wrong, I didn't like keeping secrets from them, but sometimes it's important to do things just for the sake of your own sanity. That was a lesson I've learned all too often.

I really wasn't worried until Amelia suddenly appeared at my locker right as we all were heading for lunch. But as it turns out, she had other thoughts on her mind.

"Hey Jimmy," Amelia said as I closed my locker. I wanted to talk to you."

"About?"

"Uh, Barry, actually. His friends have been mean to him lately, and well, he has been crying to me this whole week about it. He told me and everyone else he's sorry."

"So?" I said angrily.

"*So*? Jimmy, he wants to hang out with us again! But he knows you're still mad, which is *why* he's been avoiding us."

"Well, he shouldn't have given away all my babaloos! You know I still owe Mr. Grimaldi a bunch of them. And besides, those were for us!"

"Oh, Jimmy, can you just get over it! This is such a

small thing, and you know he's been trying to be Kray-ter's friend forever. Yesterday, he told me they wouldn't even let him come with them because he didn't have any more babaloos, *okay*? Clearly, they're just using him."

"Well, I could have told him that from the beginning! But he wanted to forget us and act like we're nothing to him. Fine. But that's his fault, and I don't think we have to feel bad at all."

"Uh, you know you just have such a rotten attitude about everything you don't like! If someone questions you, or does something you don't like, you just throw fireworks into the air and march off. But if that's how you want to handle it, fine! I'm just going to say, Jimmy, it's important to forgive someone. Because they would do the same for you," she said before walking off. That was the difference between me and her. Even when Amelia was angry, she was still able to make a good point.

After lunch, I went to Ms. Keaton's class, still dwelling on where I had to be tonight. I didn't like being alone with my thoughts for too long. It keeps you away from everything else going on. Being stuck in your head, letting your mind drift to wherever, it all just takes you away from the heart.

"Alright, class! Please break up into groups with a few partners around you to work with! I want the full worksheet based on what you read and what we talked about done by the time class ends," she said after about twenty minutes of teaching. I was with Calquwa, a twist horn deer, and Yurton, a yellow tree frog, while Sal and Damien were working with Amelia off up front while Riley and Amelia's human friend Vyla, who was perhaps one of the sweetest and quietest Wildlings there was, were working with Thunker, a light brown marmot (ground squirrel) who always wore a bright tie to school.

I was lucky to have great partners who not only did the reading, but fully understood it, too. I was able to sit back, agree a little here, disagree a little there, and know that I was going to get a hundred percent on this and thank goodness for it.

While everyone was trying to talk and come up with answers, I couldn't help but notice Barry working with Krayter and his other friend, Dezgon, a giant Gillan monster lizard.

"You seriously don't know any of this Barry?" Krayter griped. "First you stop giving us fruits, now you don't even do the reading for us. Just get away from us, you're so useless," he said while turning his chair away. "Hey Huedo, over here!" Krayter called over to a large headed orange bird who quickly turned and flew over.

Barry tried to wipe the tears out of his eyes before running out of the classroom quickly. I looked back at my friends, who were too focused on the assignment to even notice.

"Hey guys, I have to go get something from my locker real quick!" I said to my partners.

"No problem, Jimmy!" Yurton said. I quickly grabbed my satchel and walked out of the classroom fast enough for Ms. Keaton not to even notice.

I called Barry's name as I looked down the hallway, but he was completely out of sight. It wasn't until

I opened the door to the flight of stairs that went up, that I saw him sitting there, sobbing while sitting on a step. He looked over and almost immediately got up, shaking as he looked at me. "Oh, no, Barry, I'm not mad!" I said, trying to get him to calm down. "Why are you crying?"

"Because I-I spent all this time trying to make Krayter my friend, giving him all the fruits I could get, but now I can't so he doesn't want anything to do with me. And I can't even go back to you guys because you're all mad at me. No one wants to be my friend!" he said before curling up and crying again.

"No, I'm not mad at you! I was just upset, that's all."

"You're not?"

"No! It was uh, well, I'm sorry, Barry. I don't know what got into me. I should have just told you sooner."

"No, I'm the one who should be sorry. I got these fruits and berries and only thought of impressing Krayter. But I ignored all my real friends. I'm sorry, Jimmy," he said. We ended up sitting around there for about ten or fifteen minutes, laughing about how Krayter was always mad at his 'friends'. Then I asked him how he hadn't gotten the Balooza from all the fruits he had gotten. It was then that it all began to make sense. "Oh, no Jimmy, I don't get them from the jungle! I found this cave where they're all usually picked and placed in for some reason. But not anymore, they blocked the hole with this wooden plank and I haven't been able to move it."

"The hole?"

"Yeah, that's where all the babaloos are kept. They

store them down there. Then these tall scary-looking humans come and take them in barrels and roll them out."

"Wait, what? You mean the pirates?"

"Well, I don't rea-" Barry was saying, scratching his head. " I only saw them once there, but ever since then I couldn't even go back."

"Barry, you have to show me. We need to go there now!" I said standing up, realizing that this might be where Hortley had been running his whole operation from, where the pirates might be hiding!

"But we still have schoo-"

"It doesn't matter, c'mon let's go!" I said as I pulled his arm and walked out of school, not even letting my other friends know where we were going.

The Makaykhe Forest was only a few miles from school. It had been a while since I had dwelled in this part of the Wazoo, and it was most known for its pillow trees that had soft thick leaves that many Wildlings would use to sleep with. A few trees carried these unusual leaves together while others had bent branches or trunks just trying to support them. Needless to say, it was a struggle moving through this area, pushing against all the heavy bundles until we finally arrived at the spot Barry had been coming to all this time.

"You see, I can't move it," he said, pushing away the large leaves that were covering the flat wooden board. I got on the other side and helped Barry lift it off.

"Wow, that looks deep. Do you just jump in?" I asked.

"Oh no, Jimmy, there's a, well, let me see where it is!" Barry said, climbing a tree and jumping across the branches. Out of nowhere, a silver cart came sliding down, traveling across a tan squigglywood lianas track that I hadn't even noticed until now.

"This is what I've been using to get down and up from the cave!" Barry said, jumping out. I could tell this was all Hortley's doing. They'd take the fruits and throw them in and let this go all the way down to a cave spot to be packed.

I jumped in as Barry pushed the large lever forward. We moved forward slowly, holding onto the edge tightly before we took a huge plummet that made me shake erratically.

The cart shot down nearly fifty feet as we were spiraling down against the tracks in a dark cave, keeping our head low to avoid hitting the tall stalactites hanging over us. The wheels pressed against the lianas as the noise of the rolling cart echoed. I just hoped no one heard us as we came down.

As we got lower, I saw a few torches lit and hanging against the sides of the wall. We were getting close, and I could see barrels and piles of fruits all bundled at the bottom.

The cart then came down before pounding against a rock and throwing us out right into a pile of fruit. I had never seen so many fruits all together in my life, and of such different colors and varieties as well. Bright blue bocas, yellow iweets, pink galoongges, purple oiykets, and most notably, the long, curved polka dotted babaloos.

"Why are you mad, Jimmy? We can take whatever you want!" Barry asked as I walked around and shook my head.

"I-I'm just-" I said, struggling to put into words exactly what I was feeling. "Disgusted. This should be out in the Wild for everyone, not all hoarded up in a cave."

Barry had begun scooping a bunch of the fruits into a sack while I opened the barrels labeled 'WAZOO TRADING COMPANY.' This was exactly the evidence Peister brought to prove an underground business was operating, though Hortley must have given it to him to use *against* Greygor, accusing him of selling out the Wazoo. It was a clever plan by Peister and Hortley, especially considering the media had been crushing Greygor at the time.

We had about four sacks filled up and tossed them into the cart when we suddenly heard voices from down the cave. I quickly dove us into a pile of fruits and shushed Barry.

"I'm getting sick of this damn island! Keep gettin' bites 'n scratches just from the plants," a tall man said.

"Oh, shut yer mouth. You actin' like you been hurt. Poor ole' Cyrik got 'tacked by a rhino, an' can't walk no more!"

"Well I can't stan' an' this Yuriy. You'd think there'd be gold with all the praise, but not a lick of it's here! Wonder of the world my stinky rump it is! Only thang we gots is some useless fruit an' some diseases that make no sense. You hear about Griswalt?"

"No, what happen to 'em?"

"You ain't heard? He turnt green!"

"WHAT! Griswalt's green? When this happen?"

"Just the other day! Poor fella got his tongue all

stretched now an' he been hoppin 'round like a frog! Captain said to jus' keep him in a locked room for now."

"The hell happened?"

"Don't know, guess he musta tried one them Wazoo berries. That's why Captain said don't be eatin' nothin' less we killed it!"

"I agree. Anyways, what you drag me out here for?"

"Thought I heard a noise like someone was back here, but looks like this cart just came down an' smashed against the stone. Look at this mess 'round here."

"Jus' tell one a them tiny boys to clean it all up," said one of the pirates as they were now walking back down the cave.

"Come on, Barry, let's follow them," I whispered. Barry raised his eyebrows and shook his head, but that didn't stop me from dragging him along as we lay low and followed behind them. I had to know where they were going.

"-an' I don' know why Captain put that kid in charge of e'erything. Just makin' a mess is what it is."

"Oh, that yappy one? I hate him. 'Pparently, the kids got a map to whole Wazoo. Heard cap'n was gon' give up the Renegade if he take us to the Wazoo an' get what he wants."

"WHAT! Ain't no way Ironboot givin' up his ship. He'd much rather rip off his own leg than do that!" one of them said as they reached the end of the tunnel and walked outside. Barry and I hid behind a rock as we looked around to see, sitting right there in the middle of the Wazoo, a large, brown ship held up by wooden stumps and a long, thick lianas vine that ran from under the ship to down the hill. There were a few dozen pirates, all sitting or laying around, minding their own business. I was shocked. Not a single Wildling could find them, and here they were as plain as day.

I really didn't understand how they were able to hide from the local police, island patrol, or even the Venali until I looked at the trees around the hideout. Hanging on every tree branch was a seaweed blanket that looked like curtains. *Caecuweed!* The same plant Hortley had probably given to the giant squid who brought us to the Pleaser's Palace. In a sick way, it really was all connected. It was all making sense to me now. Hortley had truly been playing with me this whole time, using me like a puppet and I didn't even know it.

I tried to keep calm, not get into my head too much. After all, there were pirates right up ahead who would gladly cut us with their swords if they got even the slightest glance at us. We hid behind a bush as I tried to think about what to do, wishing I brought the Caecuweed for moments like this. But I guess that's what I get for trying to play hero too quickly.

"Let's go back, Jimmy, before they see us!" Barry said as he tried to pull me.

"No! I need the map, it's right up there!" I said as I ran along the edge of the side and towards the ship. There was a long net hanging on the side and I climbed up as Barry followed. I could feel my whole body shaking. We reached the top and hid in the corner, looking back to see if anyone had noticed us, but we were in the clear so far as the other pirates continued drinking, showering, talking around a fire, or rolling barrels into the bottom storage of the ship.

There was a wheel at the top of the staircase of the ship and right underneath were two large doors that went into a room, just as it all was in my first dream of the pirates. This was where I saw Bacawly come from. It must be where the map was. I just hoped he wasn't there now.

I slowly creaked the door open and peeked around to see it was empty. I quickly slipped us inside and shut the door behind me, searching the messy room. There were skulls and bones all over the floor along with chains hanging from the ceiling. I rummaged through the desk drawers until I saw a blue, thick cloth-like material and pulled it out. Without even opening it up, I could tell it was special, bright sparkles floating around from it. I unrolled it to see a map of the entire Wazoo, with dashed lines and markings of areas all around our island, places I had not even heard of before. It didn't just show the island, it showed the whole journey to get here as well. It was almost unbelievable to see. Never had I held something as magical as this before.

"Do you have what you want Jimmy? Can we go now?"

"Yes, yes, let's go!" I said as we quickly turned to the door and opened it. Right in front of us, however, was a tall, gangly pirate with a black beard.

"Stealin' from the captain now, are we?" he smiled as he showed his rotting green teeth. But before I could even answer, he swung a club right onto my head and knocked me out cold.

"Jimmy? Jimmy, can you hear me?" Barry said,

shaking me. I rubbed my eyes as I tried to look around, but everything was still a blur. It took me a while to see that we were locked in an old rusty black cage. "Are you okay?"

"Yeah, I'm fine. Where are we?" I asked as I got up.

"We're still on the ship! Oh, after that nasty pirate man hit you, he dragged us down here and threw us into this cage. He said they were going to feed us to crocodiles, Jimmy! How are we going to get out of here?" Barry shrieked as he clanged against the metal cage door.

It didn't take me long to realize they had taken the map back from me. I began to pace around, trying to think of what we could do or say to stay alive. After a few minutes, I heard the latch slam open and footsteps coming towards us.

"Well, well, well, if it ain't my good ole frien' Jimmy Jungles," said a rugged blonde boy with his mischievous little smirk, and the same worn-out trench coat as he walked towards our cell.

Chapter 18

The Forest Fire

"QUITE A PREDICAMENT you found yourself in, huh Jimmy?" Wyatt said sarcastically, leaning against the cage. He was clearly enjoying every minute of this. "Ya shoulda known better, ya' can't be stealin' from folks!" he said laughing, mocking me from when I caught him breaking into my house.

"Wyatt, enough! You need to get me out of here!"

"I don't know Jimmy, you been 'cused a spyin' an' stealin' from the Captain. Many of us woulda called that *mutiny*."

"Wyatt, give me that map back! The entire Wazoo Army will storm here if you don't let me out, so could you ju-"

"*Army?* Last I checked, you was locked right up on in here."

I heard more footsteps as another person came walking down. This time it was a small boy, no older than Jackson, wearing a large black hat with a feather on its side.

"Ey Wyatt, quit screwin' around! Captain wants to have a talk with the prisoner now!" said the boy.

"Shut up Kenny! What you think I was down here fer?"

"Don't I know that already! You gon' do everything ole' Ironboot wants, cus' you thinkin' he'll jus' hand you his ship when this all said an' done. When you gon' learn, Wyatt? He jus' 'notha no good pirate, which is why we gotta plan-" Kenny said, pointing as Wyatt unlocked us from the cage and pushed us in front.

"Oh, Kenny, I don't wanna hear nuttin' about your sne-" Wyatt said, cutting him off.

"A sneak attack!" the young boy in the black coat interrupted as Wyatt rolled his eyes.

"You wanna get crushed by Bacawly's iron boot and fed to his crocs, go right ahead Kenny. I won' stop ya, but you be careful which a them fools you tellin', cus' some of 'em ain't tryna get killed like you, an' I won't defend none of y'all mutineers neitha'," Wyatt said as we walked out to the top of the ship. I looked down to see all the pirates looking back and staring. A few were banging on pots and pans with a stick while others howled with their shirts off as we walked towards them.

"*You done did it now, boy!*"

"*Where the crocs? I wanna see 'em eat 'em up!*"

Barry clenched onto me as I stood waiting by a small fire.

"Glad ye be joinin' us, spy!" a man with a deep voice said behind me. I turned around and stared. It was the same man I had seen from my dream, with scars all across his face, a large metal fist on his left arm, and an old, metal boot on his right foot. Around him were two crocodiles, with the same piercing red eyes, looking right at me.

"I'm not sp-"

"SHUT YER TRAP BOY, ELSE I'LL FEED YA TO MY CROCS RIGH' NOW!" Bacawly yelled as he lifted me up in the air. "I KNOW EXACTLY WHAT THIS IS, THE LION SENT YOU! OR THAT FAT PIG! ALL BUN-CHA LIARS!" he said as he threw me down.

"No, sir, we didn-"

"WELL, I'LL TEACH 'EM ANIMALS! CALIC, GET THE CATAPULT!" he said to the large oaf that had broken into my house with Wyatt. He pushed in a large wooden spoon and then put a large bundle of hay right in its hold. One of the pirates then lit a torch and threw it in, causing a large fire to be ablaze. "YOU TELL THE LION I WANT THE DREAM BY TONIGHT, ELSE IT'LL BE WAR AND I'LL BURN THIS WHOLE ISLAND TO THE GROUND, GOT THAT?"

"O-okay yes, I will get it for you," I said, nodding my head. "Just please don-" I was saying before he took his long sword out and cut the rope, sending the fire over the skies and into the Wazoo.

"NOW GET! YOU TOO, WYATT, MAKE SURE THIS ALL GETS DONE OR THE DEALS OFF!" he said as Wyatt threw his hands into the air in frustration.

I quickly ran, Wyatt following me after a few seconds, as I chased towards the direction of the fire, passing the hanging Caecuweed curtains, and went deeper into the forest.

"Slow down, Jimmy! Do ya even know where we goin'?" he said, but I didn't respond. I only focused on where the black smoke was coming from. It was only when I arrived that I saw trees and plants all on fire, as they fell and crashed into the wave of flames now surrounding us.

A black bear roared as it ran with its children barely able to keep up. High-hoppers (small red kangaroos) jumped over us and onto the trees. The entire jungle seemed to have a rush of Wildlings coming this way, screaming as the flames grew higher and stronger around us. "THIS WAY! COME ON JIMMY, MOVE!" Wyatt screamed as he pulled me away, dodging Barry and me from a collapsing tree. But we were trapped, completely surrounded as there were fires in every direction.

"Grab my tail!" an Egassauan longtail monkey said from above. We were quickly pulled up as the fire had completely spread throughout the ground. A team of chipmunks and ferrets was running around in their orange outfits as they sprayed water out of the long hoses they held.

Blue elephants with painted signs on their bodies slowly approached, somehow levitating large bubbles of water before whipping them against the flames.

"What in the hell am I looking at?" Wyatt asked as we swung further and further away by longtails.

"Those are Wambagyues," I said, but I had only heard stories of them. This was the first time I ever actually saw what they were capable of doing.

The fire was still spreading, but the longtails had found an area where they had died out, though the entire wildlife had been burned down, leaving nothing but black ash behind.

The school! The fires are headed that way! I thought about how much danger my friends and classmates were in. I quickly got back to the ground and began running off.

"What? We can't go back that way, Jimmy, that's where the fires are!" Wyatt said, but I didn't care, I went anyway, and Barry followed. "GET BACK HERE JIMMY, WE GOT A JOB TO DO!" Wyatt shouted as I ran off.

I pulled out the long white flute Seuss had given me and blew into it. Surprisingly enough, it didn't take long for a butterfly to come fluttering around us in the burning woods. "I need Seuss! Tell him to meet me at Cross Rivers Middle School!" I said as the little green critter flew away almost as quickly as it had come. I continued on, running right past firefighters and pelicans cooling off the fires while ignoring their calls for me to turn around. All I could think about was Amelia, Jackson, Sal, Damien, Riley, and all my other friends in danger. I'd jump into the school if I had to.

When I finally reached the school, Wildlings were all gathered outside. The fires had died down, but all of Cross Rivers was now black and falling apart. Many students were crying or screaming, while others lay on the ground with burn marks as nurses attended to them. There were at least a dozen ambulances surrounding the school as the medical staff were constantly running back and forth. Sirens were sounding off. Wildlings were weeping out loud. All of it was overwhelming to see. My own classmates were hurt, and my own school burned down. I had never seen a more horrific sight.

"AMELIA! JACKSON!" I called around looking for them in the crowd. "SAL! DAMIEN! RILEY!"

"Over there, Jimmy," Barry pointed towards the hill. I quickly ran up.

"Jimmy! Oh, you're okay. I was so worried about you," Amelia said as she came and gave me a hug.

"Jimmy! There was a huge fire! We all had to run out of the school, and then the elephants came and put it out!" Jackson said, as he was covered almost completely with black ash. I greeted all my other friends, who were luckily all safe and sound.

"How did it start? I've never seen a fire that large before!" Sal asked.

"I-I don't know, let's just get out of here," I lied, not wanting them to freak out any more than they already had been. I just wanted us all to be at home and safe.

We were all walking back home through the Nooyenan Forest, the long route home. Aevory's Thicket was completely closed off, most of it burned down and evacuated already. It was usually a beautiful sight on the way to school, I would hate to see what it all became.

"Jimmy? Jimmy, are you there?" I heard someone call from afar. I quickly stopped and looked around. I was worried. *Had Wyatt found me? Was he going to tell my friends the entire plan?*

"Who's there?" Amelia asked me. I shrugged as we all looked around and heard a loud thumping noise growing louder.

"Stop Boart, BOART! STOP!" screamed Seuss Sutterman as he rode a large bull and crashed into a large tree right in front of us. Seuss was a bit wobbly, but somehow okay. The tree, on the other hand, was permanently damaged. "Boart, I said slow down a few acres ago! Why didn't you listen?"

"BOART WAS SLOW! WHY YOU MEAN TO BOART?" the large black bull yelled as stomped on the ground, the rings around his ears and nose all shaking.

"I'm fine, just relax," Seuss said as he put a yellow gem into Boart's bell collar. "Thank you for the ride Boart!"

"BOART, THANK YOU!" the bull replied before stomping off again.

"Jimmy, I got your call! We need to talk!" Seuss said.

"Okay, le-" I said, wanting to talk to him alone. But my friends had never seen him before and stared as he came closer.

"Hi there, younglings!" Seuss said, walking past me and greeting everyone with a large smile. "I'm Seuss Sutterman, Jimmy's friend," he said with a smile, but all of them were creeped out, well, except for Jackson, who was completely fascinated.

"But you're old," my little brother said.

"Old? No, you should have seen the Wildlings I had to hang out with. Now they're old!"

"A-are you the person Jimmy took from the hospital? The one with the powers?" Damien asked.

"Powers? Wow, I wish I had powers. But I know how to do a few cool thi-"

"Are you the one who started this fire? Huh? The one we nearly died in?" Riley said angrily.

"Riley, stop!"

"WHAT? You did say he was crazy, didn't you? He probably accidentally started this whole thing a-"

"RILEY ROBINS, THAT'S ENOUGH!" Amelia yelled.

"Why don't you guys just go home, and I'll catch up, okay? I want to talk to him about the fires. Go get some rest, please. We all need it right now," I said as they all walked away, almost unwillingly. I was glad, though, I didn't want them to know anymore about the plans I had made, or how the pirates had created all of this havoc.

"Seuss, sorry about that. They're all still traumatized by the fires. All of us are. We almost got killed today."

"Yes, I-I tried to stop it when I heard, then I got your message so I rushed over. I'm just glad you're all okay. But I haven't the slightest idea how any of th-"

I told Seuss everything that happened the last couple of days: trying to talk to Peister, Hortley admitting that he brought and is working with the pirates, being saved by the Venali guard, my meeting with Greygor, and all about our plan to go and steal from the Watchwaker in just a few hours. I told him every last detail of it all. Though I had just met him, Seuss was, oddly enough, the only person I felt I could tell anything to. He wouldn't argue, judge, or even disagree like my friends would usually do. On the contrary, he always had a way of bringing a bit of wisdom and laughter to our conversations. It was part of what made his presence so calming.

"This was my fault. This is all my fault! Hundreds, maybe thousands of Wildlings hurt, all because of me. I should have just turned back," I said sobbing as tears ran down my face.

"Jimmy, no. It's not your fault, okay? These pirates, I know how they are. They don't care about anyone. If they don't get what they want, they get angry, and they'll hurt everyone in their path. Don't blame yourself," Seuss said.

"They want the Dreamfruit. Tonight. And if we don't give it to them, they're going to burn down the whole Wazoo. I told Greygor I would help him, but I still don't know what they'll do with it. What should we do, Seuss? I-I have no idea," I asked desperately.

"Ah, that's exactly why I was glad you called Jimmy," Seuss said, reaching into his white clock and pulling out a purple fruit with a light purple aroma and sparkles floating around it.

"I-is this the Dream? The Dreamfruit?"

"No ,Jimmy, it's a fake."

"A *fake*? Where did you get it?"

"I didn't, Jimmy. I made it myself! And this should be believable enough to give to them, and once they finally do realize it's not real, they'll hopefully be far away from the Wazoo by then. Go ahead, take a look for yourself."

I really didn't know what to think, I mean it looked almost exactly how Greygor had described it, though I hadn't seen the real one before. But I just didn't know. "So when are we going to give it to them? I can tell Greygor that we already have it and don't need to steal it anymore!"

"That's another thing I wanted to talk to you about Jimmy. I'll need you to do this," Seuss said, scratching his head.

"But- why Seuss?" I asked.

"Jimmy, I'm the most wanted Wildling in all the Wazoo. I have to watch my tracks. And this exchange that you said is happening tonight, there'll be the Royal Guard, maybe even police too. All of whom know who I am. If they see or catch me again Jimmy, I-please Jimmy. I can't go back. Can you please do this?" Seuss asked, almost lost for words. I held it in my hand for a while, letting its purple aroma pass through my hands before I put it into one of the inside pockets of my vest and said goodbye to Seuss.

When I reached my house, everyone was lying on the couch, silent as they listened to the anchors talking about the fire that broke out and all the forests that were affected. It didn't seem to spread more than ten miles with the school being on the tail end of it. Still, though, too many were injured, and I didn't even want to know if anyone had died. Then, Greygor Guildenhall appeared to give a statement:

"- still gathering evidence for the fires that have broken out today, but I want to emphasize the importance of community help and collaboration. We are only as strong as we are dutiful to each other. To know that no

Wildling, no matter how different in species or belief, can ever be our enemy, is our most sacred calling. We will do our best to determine who is responsible for this fire and ensure something like this will never happen again. May the Ancients look upon us all. Long live the Wild, long live the Wazoo, the only land where dreams can never die. Thank you," the Pleaser said before walking off back to the palace, passing on all the questions being thrown at him.

There was an awkward silence as we all sat, letting what Greygor and the rest of the newscasters said sink in. Noone knew what to say, we could barely look at each other.

"I put Jackson to bed. Oh, and your parents called. I let them know we were all okay and back home. I think your mom is on her way, though."

We talked for a while about how terrible this fire was. Deep down everyone knew this was no accident, but an attack by none other than the pirates. But just when I felt I could finally tell them where the pirate hideout was, karma had a way of coming back and haunting me as usual.

A rock suddenly smashed through a window right by the front door. "What the-?" I said getting up and looking out.

"YOU GET OUT HERE, JIMMY JUNGLES! I KNOW YOU'RE UP THERE!" Wyatt yelled from just outside my front yard.

"Wyatt, what is wrong with you! You broke my window!"

"Oh, shut up! We're supposed to be on a mission,

remember? Now come on!"

Right then and there, I had an important decision to make. Give Wyatt the fake dream now and have him go away, or go with him and Greygor tonight to steal the real one from the Watchwaker. To be honest, I couldn't tell you which was the better choice. They both had their risks.

"Not now, we will go later tonight! Just, uh just come inside! And be quiet too!" I said, hoping none of the neighbors noticed a boy dressed in rags with one bad attitude walking around.

"Ok, guys, everything will be okay, just don't freak out," I begged.

"What's going on, Jimmy?" Amelia asked, but before I could even explain anything I had gone through today, Wyatt barged through the door.

"Thought you could lose me, did ya now, Jimmy?"

"You were talking to a PIRATE? What's *he* doing back here, Jimmy?" Riley asked angrily as she flew up to me. I tried to calm them down, but instantly all of my friends started yelling, very upset that the pirates burned down the school and much of the wildlife.

"You g-get out o-or we're going to call the police and tell them pirates are here!" Amelia said, getting up and backing away.

"Oh- what I say 'bout callin' me a pirate, ya crazy talkin' junglefolk!" Wyatt said angrily as he unsheathed his sword and pointed it.

"Everybody, calm down! He didn't cause the fires, alright? In fact, he's trying to stop Bacawly with me! Why don't you guys just uh, sleep at Amelia's tonight, huh? That way, I can take care of a few things with Wyatt, okay? How's that sound? We all deserve a little space to calm down anyways," I said, looking over at Amelia and the rest of my friends as Wyatt put down his sword as my friends nodded before walking out, more quietly than I had ever seen them.

I had no doubt there was bound to be more arguing and pointing the blame at each other. But we didn't have time for any of that. There was a lot to do tonight. And besides, I had other issues to worry about, most of which was that I couldn't risk my parents finding out there would be a bandit staying over tonight.

I kept Wyatt in my room as we waited for night to arrive and brought him a few things from my pantry. "Mocha Crunch, it's like chocolate, and those are Grit crackers." He ate it almost unwillingly, making weird but then delighted faces.

"Hm, not too bad. But you junglefolk really don't have any meat or bread 'round? This a bunch of goofy food right here," he said, walking around, looking through my books and notebooks. "Damn, you been doin' all that readin', huh Jimmy?"

"Yeah, it's for school, it has really been dif-"

"Ah, but they ain't teach you 'bout life do they?" he said, wagging his fingers. "Bout how t' get what ya want. How to fight 'n 'fend fer yerself. Bet you don' even know how to use one a these," Wyatt said, pulling out his sword.

"Is there like a technique to it?"

"Interested, huh Jimmy? Go ahead, give it a try," he said as he handed the sword to me. "Just keep your stance a lil' wide an' control yer swings. There you go," he said as I tried to maintain my balance while also trying not to damage my room or furniture. But I didn't know how he did it, carry one of these around, ready to go life or death with people at any moment. I wondered if he'd ever killed someone with it.

"Jimmy, can I talk to you?" my dad asked as he knocked.

"Quick, hide under my bed!" I said as I gave back the sword and told Wyatt to crawl under my bed, which he eventually gave in to.

"Yeah, Dad? I said as I ran over to my desk.

"How are you, son?" he asked as he barged right in.

"Uh, fine, just you know, doing some homework."

"Good. I-I just wanted to say I'm glad you're safe. Your mother and I were, well, very worried about you," he said as he sat down on my bed and patted me to sit down next to him. "But you have to know there are a lot of crooks around these days, creating all this havoc. Making everyone frustrated. But I wanted to tell you to make sure you understood how important it is to stay safe and away from all of it. And also do not let anything you see or hear distract you from your future, Jimmy. Don't let it make you lose hope or work towards accomplishing something. We have to do what we can to put ourselves ahead. We can't always be worried or angry about things we can't control. We have to focus and do what little good we can. No matter what happens, James, you can't forget who you are and what you have to do for yourself. Do well in school, participate in activities and be a leader; all of it is important. I might not have said this to you before, but I'm very proud you won that award."

"You are?" I said, completely shocked.

"Of course! Youngest to ever win Wildling of the Week, getting on the front page of *The Wilder*, that's all quite an accomplishment, James! I know I was mad when I saw your report card, but I wanted to tell you I think it's good you do stuff like that. Not a lot of kids do. But still, don't get involved in all these protests with angry people. You need to focus on yourself. Empower yourself. You really can do anything you put your mind to on this island, *trust me*, I have lived it. I have seen it all before," my dad said as I nodded my head. "Now have you thought of an answer to my question I asked you before?"

"Uh, what question, Dad?" I asked, not sure what he was talking about.

"In my office, a few months ago, when you made that mess. Remember what I asked? What do you want to be when you grow up? Have you thought about that?"

"Uh, well, maybe I could be a journalist, I was thinking," I said unconfidently, not sure if that was what he had wanted to hear, or even if I would be happy with that. But my dad sat back, and nodded his head as he thought to himself.

"I think that wouldn't be so bad. You'd fit in pretty well. But I think you can be even more than that and, deep down, I think you know you can be bigger than that too," he said, looking right at me. "But we'll see James. Keep working hard and dreaming big. You never know what you can accomplish if you believe in something. And who knows, you might even surprise yourself," my dad said before patting me on the back and walking out. I had never heard him talk to me that way before. I was so surprised that I nearly forgot that we had to get going. Though, it didn't take long for Wyatt to remind me.

"'Ey, jungleboy, you all done now? I'm dying over here!"

"Oh! Sorry, yeah, you can come out," I said. It was getting late now as I looked up at the clock. Already nine o'clock. "Let's get going."

"Who was that? Yer parents?"

"Yeah, my dad, didn't think he'd ever say he's proud of me," I said as I reached to pull the Caecuweed and vinewhip hidden under a loose wooden tile.

"I mean if you really need all that happy talk," Wyatt said as he looked at everything I had in my hands. "Wh-now just what the heck is all this fer?" Wyatt asked, confused as I opened the back door of my room to get to the balcony, the vinewhip already firmly wrapped around my arm and Caecuweed around my shoulders.

"Put your hands around me and hold on tight," I said as we were standing out on the railing of my room. Wyatt went on cursing as we swung from a nearby tree all the way until we landed on the ground.

"Now jus' how long you been doin' that fer Jimmy?" he asked after rolling around in the dirt.

"Come on, I'll tell you on the way," I said as I helped him up.

Chapter 19

Into the Ohwahgon

"A LION? Did you just say we're meetin' a lion?"

"Yes, he's a friend and is going to take us to get the Dreamfruit."

"An' this lion just knows everythang? He's not gon' tear off our faces off er nuttin'?"

"Wha-no! He's the Pleaser of the Wazoo, the leader we chose to keep us all safe."

"Leader of the island? This Wazoo really somethin'," Wyatt said, shaking his head in disbelief. "Bunch a crazy talkin' animals tellin' ya what ta do. I tell you what Jimmy, when this all said and done, I ain' ne'er comin' back here, I swear," he said.

"What's it like where you're from?" I asked. Wyatt was quiet for a second, looking down as he thought while we walked on a steep dirt path. We were getting closer to the lake.

"Dirtier than 'round here. Buncha no good police chasin' down my crew 'n e'ryone else, tryna throw 'em in prison. But we get by. Other than that, I would say it's the same as these parts. Jus' a buncha animals tryna tell everyone else what to do," he said, but I really didn't know what he meant exactly.

We finally arrived at Lake Astoria in the middle of the night. I tried to get Wyatt to tell me more about where he was from or what it was like, or even what these Breakaway Bandits were about, but his lips were as good as sealed.

"Ain't nobody give a damn Jimmy, now c'mon," he said as we looked around, but all we could see were the flashing fireflies flickering their green lights and a few wolpeetas clicking away in the otherwise silent night. There was no one in sight as we stood around waiting, and I was beginning to worry Greygor had changed his plans.

"Aye, where the lion at Jimmy? You said he'd be here!" Wyatt asked impatiently. "We gotta meet Bacawly soon, n' he ain't the waitin' kind." I didn't know how to respond, but as I began to look around, I heard light, gentle footsteps along the grass, but still could see no one. That was when I knew they were angry. But before I could say anything to them, two Venali tigers suddenly appeared and threw Wyatt and I to the ground.

"The Pleaser said you were to come alone! And you bring a pirate with you? Why? To burn this place too? To assassinate the Pleaser? STATE YOUR PURPOSE!" one of them asked persistently as it stood over me, his piercing white eyes staring at me as I felt his heavy breath push against my face.

"Aye, get off me! I ain' no damn pirate! An' I ain't start no damn fires neitha! You can thank jungleboy fer that one!" Wyatt said, trying to kick the white tiger off of him.

"ENOUGH! HYUCC, KAIZAAN, COME BACK HERE," said Greygor as he slowly emerged from the woods, a dozen or so Venali tigers appearing out of nowhere and surrounding us.

"Wh-how'd those other tigers jus-" Wyatt asked, completely stunned at what he was seeing.

"They can turn invisible," I whispered.

"My lord, look! A pirate's weapon," one of the tigers said as he grabbed the end of Wyatt's sheathed sword with his teeth and dropped it on the floor. "These boys are a threat to us sir, here to kill you! We must interrogate them to see if the-" he said before looking to the Pleaser and suddenly bowing.

"ENOUGH! Jimmy, why did you bring this pirate here?" Greygor interrupted angrily as he walked slowly towards me.

"No, sir, it's not what you think, he freed me. He tried to stop Bacawly from starting the fires. Please don't hurt him!"

"SO YOU WERE THERE WHEN IT STARTED!" a tiger said, walking forward.

"TELL US WHAT HAPPENED BEFORE I TEAR YOUR HEAD OFF! WHAT DID YOU DO?" another tiger yelled.

"Well, I uh-" I said, stumbling over my own words. "I-I tried to take the map we talked about, sir. I tried to get the map they used to find the Wazoo, but I got caught. And Bacawly got mad, so he set off a fire and said if we don't get him the Dream by tonight, he'll burn down the rest of the Wazoo. I tried to stop him. He tried to help me, but we- we couldn't. I'm sorry," I said, sobbing.

"SO IT WAS YOU!"

"*A confession!* My lord, permission to escort these criminals to prison immediately for disobeying your commands. They must be tried for the treason they have committed before the Wild!" the tiger said, bowing his head to the Pleaser again.

Greygor let out a loud roar as all the Venali backed away from us. "I SAID ENOUGH! The boys are to come with me and all of you are to return to the Palace at once!"

"But my lord, the will of the Wild does not tolerate this behavior. Their actions are punishable by death! We cannot trust th-"

"*Must I ask again*?" he said in a low, cold tone as he looked around at every member of the Royal Guard, who were all bowing their heads as he spoke.

"No, of course not my sire. We will return to the Palace at once," the tiger said. The Venali all then vanished suddenly as we saw their step marks walk away from us. I just hoped Greygor's word was enough to keep them away.

"Does the Captain still expect to meet at Racuhvwa tonight by the red rocks?" Greygor asked.

"Uh yes sir, cap'n said as long as he gets the Dream tonigh', terms will be met an' we'll be on our way, 'long wit' givin' you the map."

"Very well," he replied as he walked through the dark Induwaaz Forest. I had never been here late at night, nor had I known there were this many Wildlings out, many of whom were hardly ever seen. A purple Yoddalinga monkey swinging across a branch as it called out to the others awake. A little white Shanoa kitten came up to smell our feet but ran as soon as Wyatt threw his arms at it.

Eventually, we reached a tall, dark green vine wall that was nearly ten feet high. Never had I seen or heard anything like this.

"What in the -" Wyatt was saying.

"*Ssshhh!* We have to be careful here and keep your distance from me, too. Don't lose the Caecuweed," the Pleaser whispered. Greygor pressed his paw against the vines, which slowly began to spread out and created an entryway. I quickly threw the Caecuweed over Wyatt as we walked in.

"Once you have the Dream, find a rock and throw it against the wall of the room you see me enter. We'll leave together," Greygor said as we slowly passed by tall swaying grass from a gust of wind that seemed to be roaming around the area. As we walked down the pathway, we saw many large twisted plants that looped in large circles and had large blue and purple petals with small metal chimes dangling from the ends of them making a soft, beautiful melody.

We were only a few feet away from the Pleaser as we now passed many willow trees. We saw, from a distance, a large tree, perhaps a few thousand feet high, with glowing purple leaves around it. *How was this never talked about? Every Wildling on the island should have noticed this, yet Greygor insisted that it wasn't always here! How did that make any sense? Unless, somehow, someway, we were no longer in the Wazoo? But that made even less sense!* No matter how long I lived here, it always seemed like there was something I discovered that made me feel like I never knew the island at all.

Suddenly, large winds brushed down at us as we all crouched, wondering what was above us. We looked up and saw a large white owl with black zig-zag patterns flying over us before landing right in front of Greygor.

"What in the hell is that?" Wyatt asked.

"*Shhhh!*" I said, clutching tight onto the seaweed sheet that kept us out of sight.

"*I am Oorook, Gatekeeper of the Ohwahgon! State your purpose! Tell no lies!*" The large owl spoke loudly without even moving its beak.

"I am Greygor Guildenhall, Pleaser of the Wazoo, here to meet with the Watchwaker on a most urgent matter!"

"*I see,*" the large owl said as it leaned over with its eyes popping wider before stepping back and looking away for a moment. "*The Watchwaker tells me you have shared many dreams with him already, yet you come in person only days before your election? How... unusual.*"

"This matter is most important! A fire was cast among us by a clan of outside invaders earlier today. I require his help immediately!" Greygor said as the owl stayed back tilting its head before closing its eyes and pausing for a second.

"So be it! The Watchwaker will see you now. You may enter this sacred shrine, but do not stray! Do not lurk beyond your stated intentions! Do not overstay your welcome. Do not disturb the peace!" the owl said before it flew back up and away. Greygor slowly walked further to the large black root pathway leading up the tree. Around us were dozens of clear, sparkling butterflies letting out stunning small glitters, almost like the ones Seuss had shown me.

We stayed crouched and invisible while following Greygor up the tree path. The wind continued to blow lightly as I could see small Xicoekhaan foxes with swirling designs on their long blue and purple fur running around as they nibbled on the grass beneath the tree.

As we reached the top, there was a light blue misty aura around as the trees sparkled and the leaves glowed bright purple. It was all amazing, like nothing beautiful I had ever seen before. There was a small room off to the side. Greygor slowly approached it and passed the long sheath of leaves hanging at the entrance. I looked past and saw a gray goat with curled horns and a long beard sitting down. It was Giyatar Ghanji, the Watchwaker I had heard about so many times.

"What a privilege it is to meet with you, Dreamsire. Thank you for your presence, my eminence. What an honor and blessing it is to be here," Greygor said as he bowed.

"Alright, now's our chance!" I whispered to Wyatt as we walked past the Watchwaker's Den and into a large dome with dark blue chimps hanging on branches with their eyes shut. I wasn't sure if they were sleeping or not, but we walked slowly towards a large spiral staircase along the edge of the tree.

Each step was narrow and creaked as the wind pushed us forward. I tried not to look down. We were hundreds of feet high at this point, one false misstep, heck, even a crack, and we'd be tumbling down to our deaths.

"Where we goin' now, Jimmy?" Wyatt asked when we reached the top, where there was nothing but large glowing crystals. They had this odd effect on us, almost like we were being pulled in to look at them. I began to walk closer as I continued staring at all the many personal things it showed to me: my friends smiling as we slid down the mud pits and swung around with the vinewhip, my parents lecturing me, me winning the public service award, even memories of when I was just a child learning to walk, or to my first time on a swing.

"C'mon Jimmy, let's have to keep movin', quit standin' 'round," Wyatt said as he wiped away his tears from whatever the crystals showed him. "Wh-where do we go now? This whole place a maze or somethin'," Wyatt asked. As we tried walking around, peering through many dark tunnelways, a white sparkling butterfly with a shining white aura flew around us. I spoke to it, asking it to show us where the Dreamfruit was kept. Quickly, it began to fly and we followed after it.

Wyatt stared at me, thinking I must have been crazy, but from what Seuss had shown me, butterflies were very sensitive and intelligent creatures, capable of connecting the whole Wazoo.

The butterfly guided us past larger crystals and a few more tunnels until we reached a small twig room hanging off the edge of a branch. The whole room was dark, except for a small purple glowing object hanging near the far wall. I walked quickly towards it but stopped immediately as a few twigs cracked and the entire room started to shake us off our feet. "We have to go slow!" I said to Wyatt, who was swearing as he tried pulling and cutting off a small weed that had wrapped itself around his leg.

The clear butterfly fluttered around before I came up closer to the shining magenta fruit with a dark blue aura coming around it. This was the Dreamfruit, what Seuss had warned me so much about. And now here it was, in the palm of my hand.

"This is it, Wyatt. This is the Dream," I said before I tried pulling it off. Not only was it getting *more* difficult, but I became drowsy just being around this strange sparkling aroma, as if I was about to collapse and fall asleep. I could feel my whole body slowing down. I saw the stars shining, and many strange men looking up, gazing up at the sky while holding their long staffs, large birds flying though the air, and an eye opening as it emitted bright light around all the surrounding darkness. I had no idea what I was seeing, what thoughts and images were entering into my mind at the moment as if I were in a trance.

"Quit yer sleepin' Jimmy!" Wyatt said as he slashed his sword across the stem and pulled the Dream off from the tree.

"Wyatt, what are you doing? You can't just cut at things like that! The tree knows we're here!" I yelled instantly before grabbing the Dreamfruit back from him. Suddenly the whole room began to shake as Wyatt looked around confused.

The white, gentle butterfly that had guided us was now fluttering around erratically before bursting into dust. There was a rumbling getting worse as the whole room tilted sideways before long dark purple legs poked through the twig floors. We looked at each other instantly and knew we had to leave. But before we could, a few spiders punched from the top and dove in to look at us. Wyatt got up on his feet, his sword still in hand, and slashed at the two spiders in front of us as we crept to the side wall to get back to the main branch. We needed to get to sturdy land before the whole room fell down to our deaths. The spiders spat sticky webs at us and stuck us against the wall. I tried not to move too quickly, but Wyatt lunged forward before his foot fell through the floor. "Agh!"

I reached in trying to help him up, but the spiders were nearing, hitting at us with their large legs. I grabbed Wyatt's sword, sitting against the side wal,l and cut one of their legs. The leg bent awkwardly and the spider ached in pain before I went to pull Wyatt back up.

We tried to leave, but the whole room shook as the spider in pain smashed down against the floor. More spiders started to come in, and the room tilted further and further back, the floors too steep for us to even walk on. The whole room started to crack before it completely snapped off, and we were falling through the air.

The room crashed down onto a branch with a lot of black mud all around us. The spiders were stunned, and slow to move. "We have to hurry, they're getting up!" I said as we ran down a large branch, looking for some way to get to the bottom. The blue chimps who were hanging in the branches around us were now staring at us with their bright orange eyes. They had all known we had stolen from them, and they were angry, jumping down and slinging mud at us as they shrieked. We weren't going to make it far at this rate.

"Hold on to me tight," I said to Wyatt as I took the vinewhip out from my pocket. We flew across the branches a few times, all the chimps stopping what they were doing just to stare in awe as we made our way back to the main branch floor and dashed down near the Watchwaker's den. I was supposed to throw a rock against the wall when we were finished. I was supposed to let Greygor know to come with us.

"What're we waiting for?" Wyatt asked.

"Nothing, let's go," I said as we quickly ran down the walkway back to the ground. I could see the vine gate slowly begin to close in. We were running out of time.

"HAVE YOU NO SHAME?" a loud echoing voice said from above. *"YOU HAVE STOLEN FROM THE WATCHWAKER! HALT OR YOU SHALL BE DECIMATED!"* the large owl said as it hovered its long pointy legs right over our backs. But right as we made it to the gate, it grabbed Wyatt and slowly started lifting him away.

"Aye, get off me!" he said as he tried to swipe his sword. "Help Jimmy!" he said. I slung the vinewhip and grabbed onto Wyatt's foot, using all my strength to pull him back down. Wyatt hit the ground but not before getting a chance to swing at the owl's leg. It wailed in pain as we got up to our feet and dived out of the Ohwahgon. The opening shut before we could even look back.

"Well, that was something, wasn't it?" I said after a few seconds of panting, just trying to catch our breath.

"I don't even wanna. You still got the Dream, right?" Wyatt asked as he lay flat on the ground. I pulled the real one out and lifted it so he could see. But now was the tough part. I had to decide which of the Dreamfruits I was actually going to give to Bacawly. And to be honest with you, I hadn't the slightest idea.

It had been pretty quiet on our way over to Racuhvwa. I guess the stress of running through the Ohwahgon was too tiring for Wyatt, or maybe he was just as sick as he could be of the Wazoo, and I couldn't blame him for that.

"Excited to leave? I asked.

"More 'n you know it. Everywhere I turn, there's some animal just waitin' to kill us."

"Good, tell all those pirate friends of yours to never come back either," I said as we both laughed.

"But I tell you this Jimmy, tha's all gon change once ole' Ironboot get his lil' Dreamfruit. All this nonsense will be ova' an' I can have his ship an' runaway wit' the bandits, fin' our own 'ventures. We'll be living the right way. Heck, maybe someday I'll even show you 'round, if yer up fer it." I didn't know what to say, and let it fall silent again as we continued on our way.

We arrived at Clavawaus Grove, not too far out from where the Twisted Caverns were. There wasn't a single person in sight as we waited, and each second that passed, I was only getting more nervous. "Damn pirates are always late. The hell is he doin' anyway?" Wyatt asked impatiently.

I shook my head, not really listening to him, though. We were only a few minutes away from meeting them, and I still hadn't the slightest idea what I was going to give, or if they'd even recognize the fake.

A little while had passed before we heard rummaging coming from the other side and a large bright flame coming towards us. Three pirates emerged, one of them holding a torch, and I shook immediately, still traumatized from all that happened earlier today. A black crocodile held by chains to Bacawly was gently walking closer to us.

"Well, boy, 'ave ye got it?" said the one wearing a bandana. Wyatt looked straight at me as I pulled out the fruit from my pocket and held it up. But just as I was about to give it, Wyatt stood in the way.

"Hol' up. Where's the map I gave ya?" Wyatt asked as Bacawly reached in his pocket and pulled out the sparkling map and handed it to him. I then walked up and gave the Dreamfruit to a tall clean man with a long button down white shirt who studied the sparkles and outside carefully with his monocle.

"Well, Ed? Is this the right one?" Bacawly asked. I was shaking, taking deep, heavy breaths, hoping he wouldn't notice.

"By all measures, and description, I believe this is it, sir. This is *Sepannagharum,* the Dream, my captain," he said as he handed it to him. Bacawly smiled before snatching it and walking away.

"Well, guess this is it then Jungles," he said as he handed me the map. I thought this was the last time we'd ever meet, and just when I was actually starting to like him too.

"Have a safe trip back, Wyatt," I said as he smirked and nodded his head.

I was on my walk back home, thinking about everything that had gone on in just the last few days. From learning about the Dreamfruit, planning to find the pirates, to all the fires spreading, and going to the Ohwahgon, it was all too much, more than what anyone would believe possible from a thirteen-year-old, that's for sure. But just when I was relieved to think it was all over, I heard more rummaging coming from the woods. *Had a Wildling seen everything? Or was it one of the Venali, lying in wait to find me alone and get revenge? The police? The pirates? Seuss?*

My heart was racing until Greygor Guildenhall suddenly showed up and looked at me. We were supposed to make this exchange together, before I decided to leave him.

"Jimmy! Where are you going? We have to trade for the map!"

"Oh, I already did, sir."

"YOU WHAT?" Greygor yelled. "You were supposed to wait for me, remember?"

"I know, but we were being cha-"

"IT DOESN'T MATTER, YOU'VE MESSED UP EV-ERYTHING!"

I was confused, not sure what I did wrong. "Mr. Pleaser! Mr. Pleaser!" said a small, little Aardobac tou-can flying over with a camera hanging over its neck. "Have no worries sir! I got plenty of footage from the exchange, I can edit you in, and we'll be set for the pa-pers!"

"Hmmm, if you say so, Takaaya. Just be sure the anchors air it in the morning," Greygor said, turning away from me, but I began grinding my teeth as I felt all my muscles stiffen.

"So, this was your plan? To look like you fixed ev-erything in order to win your election? Was that what this was all about?" I said angrily. As much as I wanted to believe Greygor was nothing like Peister or Hortley, the truth of the matter was, they all did whatever they could to make sure their image was not only protect-ed, but revered as much as possible while they attacked their opponents. Lying to me and any Wildling they needed to. All for their reputation. All for power.

"Jimmy, this is the nature of our island. What the Ancients have intended for us. These are the games we all must play," Greygor said, turning away. "Now, please, go home and enjoy. Let me do my part for this island. To ensure that the Wildlings and all our dreams are protected," he said, but I didn't bother to reply. I took a deep breath and walked away. I just wanted no more of today. I wanted all the problems we've had the last few months to be over once and for all.

As I lay down in my bed, I could only hope that everything would be better now. That the pirates would be gone by tonight and every Wildling would be cheering tomorrow. I pulled out the real Dreamfruit from my vest pocket and stared at it as it let out the mysterious dark blue aura. This is what so many men had fought so willingly for, what they believed possessed unlimited power. So many wars and deaths all in pursuit of this measly fruit. I rolled over to my side and put it in my nightstand drawer. I would have to find someplace better to hide it in the morning.

Chapter 20

Election Day

NEWS BROKE EARLY THE NEXT DAY that a 'peace treaty' was reached between the Pleaser of the Wazoo and pirates a few hours after the fire broke out. Every television network showed photographs of Greygor Guildenhall standing across Captain Bacawly with his crew and crocodile beside him. How the toucan was able to simply put the Pleaser into an image was just beyond me.

You'd think the Wildlings would have been happy to hear all this. I expected public celebrations, and imagined everyone eating fruits completely worry-free as we celebrated this newfound freedom. After all, we

had been terrified by the pirates for the last two months, you'd think it would be what we least deserved. Oh, how wrong I was.

The Wild was restless. There were constant yelling matches and fights breaking out during what was supposed to be a peaceful protest. At first, I was confused. These were supposed to be good times, happy times, times we craved and wouldn't have traded for anything else in the world. I mean, the pirates were gone! But that was not how the Wild felt. There was tension, anger, and rage at almost every corner of every trail.

"*...a reported thirty Wildlings were injured by several Mindalee giraffes, who went on a rampage and swung violently at Guildenhall supporters in what looks to be advocacy for Peister Precarious. This is only one of several attacks that have taken place over the last few weeks as this election frustration has escalated,*" Kay Kalenae reported.

But it wasn't just the tension itself that was bad, but the news as well! News that I thought was supposed to be calm and informative of everything instead seemed to be changing for the worse as only a few polarizing reporters got all of the attention, most notably Marshull Manics.

"Come tomorrow, *your highness*, your reign shall end! I promise you, no WILDLING will ever support a despicable, *deceitful* creature like you. We all know you worked with the pirates. Everyone does. And not once but *TWICE*, letting large *FIRES SPREAD* while you sit in your big, *fantastic* castle, counting all the RICHES you made DEPRIVING *US* of all of the natural fresh fruits! The Wild is SICK of being POOR, SICK of having NO RESOURCES to live. You have done EV-ERYTHING you COULD to stop Peister from winning, sending YOUR pirate FRIENDS to his house to intimidate him, but he will have *OVERWHELMING* support from the Wild. He will CRUSH you. I have no doubt you will be PROSECUTED, and thrown in JAIL for the rest of your CORRUPT life!" Manics said in his typical screaming-rant orations. It was as if the news was either supposed to give you a headache from all the worry of the world, or make you feel enraged by someone. As good as it all was, we were now just letting it all fall apart right before our own eyes. For a while, I thought this is what we were meant to be, what we really were deep down. Maybe it made sense that we were known as the wonder of the world. That others only saw us as animals.

"GOOD! He deserves to go to jail!" Sal said, jumping up after watching a clip of the rant from *Manic Hour*.

"WHAT! You actually believe all this garbage?" Riley asked.

"You heard the moose, Greygor let the pirates in and caused all these problems! Why couldn't we get any fruit this whole time? And the Balooza, *everybody* knows the pirates brought that while we were being stolen from!"

"Is that a joke, Sal? Do you not remember Jimmy explaining how Hortley admitted to bringing the pirates here to get rich from the trade route plan? That broken bird and fat pig almost got Jimmy killed! Don't tell me you think th-"

"Peister Precarious for Pleaser! That's who I'm casting my shard for today. Don't even bother trying to change my mind!"

"ARE YOU STUPID, SAL? YOU CAN'T BE SERIOUS!" Riley yelled, ready to go off on another one of her infamous rants. But just before a shouting match could break out in my living room, my dad marched downstairs.

"What is going on down here? Who's screaming?" he said angrily, not even finished tying his tie as he looked at the TV screen. "NO! I don't want any of you kids watching or talking about politics. You're too young to be worrying about and listening to all this petty nonsense! It does nothing for you. Focus on school first! Focus on getting somewhere in life!" he said as we all stood still and nodded. I don't think my friends had ever been lectured by my dad until today. "Do you all understand?"

"Yes, Mr. Jungles," all my friends said at once.

Our school was still covered with ash from the roof down as repairs from the fires were still underway. Yet despite all of this, Mr. Fangoria must have thought it was crucial to conduct classes for our own well-being, I guess. It was either that or there just weren't enough kids in his own neighborhood to scream at all day long.

For a few weeks now, all of my classmates gathered around Hunnagan's Hills just west of Cross Rivers, as schooling had technically resumed, though it hardly seemed like it. It was basically one large open study hall, where teachers and their helpers would come around to give us a few lessons and help us with our homework here and there. But to be honest with you, there was far more socializing and laughing going on than anything else, which obviously led to arguing and protests happening in the school, especially on election day.

It was not a bit surprising that when we walked in for lessons that day, Krayter and his delinquent friends had already been there protesting or.... campaigning maybe? I honestly couldn't tell you the difference at this point.

PEISTER FOR PLEASER! PEISTER FOR PLEASER!

And just across from the group of chimps, Whargo Whelkens, a loudmouth mongoose and son of the Consular of the Waker pack, Whavrow Whelkens, were rooting for Greygor Guildenhall. The poor little mammals only wish they had Krayter's megaphone, but that might have actually done it for them in the end.

"KRAYTERIUS KARMAADI, *WHAT* DO YOU THINK *YOU* ARE DOING!" Mr. Fangoria said as he waddled up and swiped the megaphone from his hands. "There will be *NO* campaigning today! Every student twelve and up will be allowed the opportunity to cast but must return to their tables and continue with the lessons of their teacher until it is your time to cast. All Cross Rivers rules still apply. No television, no protesting, no arguing, and most importantly, *NO TALKING!*" Mr. Fangoria said before turning back around to yell at all the other protesters. I knew deep down he was enjoying this, don't try to convince me otherwise. I was just glad he wasn't yelling only at me this time.

"Are you seriously going to cast your shard for Peister, Sal?" Riley asked again. Dad meant well yelling at us to stop fighting, but for some Wildlings like Riley, they just couldn't resist the argument.

"Why shouldn't I?" he asked as Riley rolled her eyes and began arguing with him again. All my other friends got involved, worried about Peister winning today. As for me, I did my best, for once, to ignore everything around me and focus on my schoolwork.

"Jimmy, you can't let him do this! Tell him he's wrong!" Riley said as she flew up to me.

"Honestly, they're both criminals," I said casually, still filling out my worksheet from Mr. Dorlin's class.

"WHAT! ARE YOU SERIOUS JIMMY?" Riley blurted out before being shushed down by everyone. "Out of everything you've seen and done, do you really think they're both the same? Peister almost got you killed!"

Maybe she was right, maybe she wasn't. But I knew that I was perhaps one of the few who actually saw both sides of this game. A game that everyone plays to win, and the Wild had all to lose. Needless to say, I didn't even bother responding to her.

When it was time for our turn to head to the booths, we all got in line, ready to cast our shards. Wildlings sitting at desks handed us the small gray rocks that could fit in the palm of our hands. However, smaller Wildlings like ants or small ida birds would have to carry it and decide together, something Damien told me was a rule passed long ago since smaller Wildling populations were often far larger than everyone else's.

The whole thing was odd, especially since it was my first time ever casting for someone, and as I stood there looking at the bins for Greygor, Aechus, and Peister, I honestly couldn't tell you who I felt was better. Who I felt was any good for the Wild. I was almost forced to make a choice among three Wildlings who bent the law, kept their secrets, told lies, controlled media outlets, and worst of all, worked with the pirates. This was no hero's choice. So, I took a pencil and wrote my name on a sheet of paper before rubberbanding it onto a stone and putting it into a fourth bin. It was the only choice that didn't make me feel guilty. And besides, who had done more for the Wild than me?

I walked back out from the booth, wondering to myself if that was the right choice and, more importantly, if that's what I even wanted to be. Was that the big job my dad was talking about? He had said I needed to think of something bigger than being just a journalist. But Pleaser of Wazoo? Could I really govern over every Wildling? It seemed way above anything I could have imagined for myself. But, in his words, 'you'll never know what you can accomplish if you work hard and dream big. Sometimes you may even surprise yourself.' I kept thinking about that as I walked back to our table.

A little while went by before Gunter came running up carrying the same old TV he dragged with him everywhere. "Look, results are already starting to come in," he said as he looked around before placing the television onto the table.

"Alright, and it has finally arrived, ELECTION DAY!

Thank you everyone for joining us at WBC and participating in this most sacred Wazoo tradition of ours.

"Yes, a few territories have already finished. So far, we have Greygor Guildenhall ahead 113 slates, Peister Precarious 64 slates and Aechus Albrite 7 slates. But there is still much, much more time to go. Back to you, Rian."

"Looks like Greygor is going to win again..." Sal said, sighing.

"Did you really cast your shard for Peister? Please don't say you..."

"No, I decided to go with Aechus! Greygor and Peister are both corrupt!"

"WHAT! Sal, nobody is going to cast him as Pleaser. There's no way he's going to wi-"

"I cast for Aechus, too," Damien said, almost immediately regretting it when Riley turned around.

"YOU TOO! BOTH OF YOU ARE IDIOTS! ABSOLUTE FOOLS WHO ARE GOING TO LET PEISTER WIN," she yelled before flying back to Amelia and Barry. "Who did you cast your shard for? Don't lie to me!" Riley asked as she pecked at Barry's head.

"Ow, ow, stop! I-I chose Greygor!" Barry said as he ran behind Amelia. "I did too! Riley, you need to stop, you're being ridiculous."

I had thought about ignoring Riley while she was in her own mania, but she had been harassing everyone for so long, all day, maybe she deserved a little torture from the truth.

"I wrote in myself," I said proudly. All my friends immediately leaned in, their jaws dropping in complete shock.

"WHAT? CAN YOU EVEN DO THAT? OH, JIMMY, WHY?"

"Listen, I got rid of the pirates, and well, I mean, who else was a better choice than -"

"BUT YOU'RE NOT EVEN TRYING TO BE PLEASER!" Riley yelled. She could talk about it all she wanted to, scream all day, or even gossip about it with Jary Jenfields, I didn't care. I was happy with my choice, and honestly, I thought it was the only right one to make.

No one had paid much attention to Riley's ranting as she flew around intimidating our classmates. Mostly because there were about thirty arguments already breaking out completely on their own. But while we were all glued to the TV, the teachers had all taken note of the ensuing chaos and were trying to control it as much as possible, while they could, though taming the Wild is no easy task. Eventually Principal Fangoria lost it, using Krayter's own megaphone to make an announcement.

"THAT'S ENOUGH! I HAVE HAD ENOUGH! EVERYONE RETURN TO YOUR HOMES. SCHOOL WILL BE CANCELED FOR THE REST OF THE WEEK. YOUR LESSONS AND ASSIGNMENTS WILL BE MAILED! IF INCOMPLETE, YOU WILL RECEIVE FAILURE MARKS!" Principal Fangoria yelled.

I wasn't going to be the first person to complain that school had gotten canceled for the whole week but knowing that we still had to continue with our lessons and homework was going to be a hassle, and Damien knew he had to get ready to work extra, extra overtime. That evening though, we didn't even think about school, or politics, or even what our parents would think.

"Oh, Kanannepaakka! Kanannepaakka!" Damien said, jumping up after he rolled a seven on the twelve-sided dice, pushed up and landed on the spin-wheel area of the board to pick a jungle card that got him three orange gorillas. I can't tell you everything about how this game works, but it was enough to knock off Sal's four purple tail lions and climb Mount Tu' Bubaabowee.

"Oh, I was so close too! How do you always win!" Sal said, throwing his tail over his face.

"Okay kids, time to go to bed!" Mom said as she walked in wearing her new stitched pink pajamas. I looked at the clock and couldn't believe it was nearly nine o'clock already.

"Wait! Can we just see if Greygor won by now? Please, Mrs. Jungles, before we go to bed?" Riley flew up and asked. Mom put her hands to her side and sighed.

"Alright, five minutes, but then I want all of you to go to bed," she said as she went and got the TV remote before handing it to me. Everyone was jumping with jitters as she walked upstairs. I have to admit, though I didn't cast my shard for him, I was still hoping he would win. The Wazoo would be far better off without Hortley running a single thing.

"So Huuwic, where are we with the slate count thus far?"

"Well, Vekow as it stands now with the latest counts coming from the Fahhshii and Taluk territories, we have Greygor Guildenhall still leading 531 slates to 308 slates against Peister, Aechus trailing well behind at 64. While it looks like there is no path forward for the trailing candidates, Elder Ouwaan and the rest of the Primary Council have still *not* begun their expedition to Ipanoppagus for a formal declaration just yet as no candidate is nearing the necessary 783 shards to win, but they have assured news outlets they will make their way there by noon tomorrow to make an announcement for the Pleasership. Back to you, Vekow."

"Alright, well, that certainly does keep us on our feet, but please stay tuned tom-"

"This is so stupid! Why won't they call it for Greygor already? He's up two hundred!" Riley yelled as Amelia immediately hushed her, not wanting my parents to hear any more of the same commotion that upset them this morning. But for once, I actually agreed with Riley. It looked like Peister and Aechus didn't have a chance at all. And I'm sure Hortley knew this too. Still though, why support him if that were truly the case? It all just wasn't making any sense.

We all got to bed and promised for the sake of our sanity, we wouldn't talk about the election for the rest of the night. As we all laid down waiting to fall asleep though, I'm sure that was the only thing on everyone's mind. But we would just have to wait until tomorrow.

I woke up to the cruelty of all my friends hitting me with their pillows as they jumped and rolled all over my bed. "C'mon, Jimmy, we have to get to Ipanoppagus! Before it gets crowded! Stop sleeping!" Amelia said as she continued to shake me. My eyes were barely open as I brushed my teeth, and I hardly had enough time to put my shirt on before Sal just tugged me out of the bathroom. Why was I the only one who was always so groggy in the morning?

Somehow, someway, by the great grace of Gideon, my dad still hadn't noticed the stolen rotoblade parts on my bike. That itself told me I was lucky not to be grounded again. That morning, however, we rode through Aveory's Thicket before flying off to a small town called Ipanouwa, where the Elders would announce the winner and hopefully end all the nonsense protesting and fighting going on. At this point, though, I was sick and tired of saying I was sick and tired of it all.

When we neared, there were already long lines of excited Wildlings and angry protestors waiting to reach the Bowwug Valley. Luckily for us, we were able to skip out on all of that without even the security birds noticing us. Boy do I hope no one ever took these bike parts away from us.

Damien had told us these were considered holy grounds, where the second Watchwaker, Ipa, would often come to share his dreams while standing on a large boulder, speaking to the rest of the Wild. It was crazy to think I lived and walked around the Wazoo that so many Wildlings experienced millions of years ago. It made it all seem more important than any single moment when you really thought about the grandeur of it all.

"Charlene, oh Gideon, Charlene, get back inside, there's a pair of Wildlings with a razor coming to chop

us! Get my stick, I'll attack 'em with it!" said an old shabanzi tree bear sitting on a rocking chair on the front deck of his tree house.

"Ward, oh Ward, you're holding your stick!" said the wife as she ran inside.

We walked slowly to the blue grass valley, pushing our bikes as we saw a mountain top with a large white boulder at the very edge looking over everyone. Just right up ahead of us were Greygor Guildenhall, Aechus Albrite, and Peister Precarious, who was walking around nervously while Hortley Hasselback sat back behind him with a steady ease. Around them were the Venali tigers and Noranu panthers, who had been viciously fighting with each other just a few weeks ago, were now standing around, barely even looking at each other, as if the whole feud had never even happened.

A short gray monkey with a tall moon crescent walking stick and long white beard stood up and raised his hands.

"My fellow Wildlings," said the Elder as he was handed a green leaf with notes. "Your shards have been cast and counted. And now we have the total slates won from each territory of our great island. For Acheus Albrite, the Wildlings have awarded 96 slates to our Patron of the Wazoo! For Peister Precarious, the Wildlings have awarded 601 slates to the great Consular from Hagragada," he said. The crowd began to cheer and jump. "And finally, to the current standing Pleaser of the Wazoo, the Wildlings have awarded 779 slates!" The crowd erupted and jumped up and down in excitement.

GREYGOR! GREYGOR! GREYGOR!

BOOO!

"SILENCE! SILENCE PLEASE!" the Elder yelled as the crowd hushed down. "Now, while results have concluded Greygor Guildenhall the most slates of the island, it is required that the Majoriat of this election acquire a pure majority of 783 slates across all territories of the Wazoo. Therefore, I, Ouwaan Ohwys, Elderen of the Wazoo, and Chieftain of the Primary Council, declare with the powers vested to me by the Watchwaker that the Wazoo has no winner for this election. This is as the Wild wills it to be!"

The entire crowd immediately bursted into an uproar of frustration, booing the Elder and yelling their complaints and chanting for their candidate.

Pleaser Guildenhall was furious, roaring at the Elder from down below as Peister paced anxiously, Hortley throwing his legs down, telling him to calm down.

"STAND DOWN! STAND DOWN! THE WILD WILL CIVILIZE, THE WILD WILL CIVILIZE BEFORE WE PROCEED!" he yelled, stomping his stick against the rock.

"Wait, so nobody won? How can nobody win an election? What's happening?" Riley asked nervously.

"I-I don't know. I've never heard of this," Damien said, scratching his head. I had never seen him so lost before.

To the side along a trail, a large white stone tablet was being carried on long wooden logs by dozens of strong Wildlings. All we could do was look at each other as we tried to figure out what was going to happen. next.

Chapter 21

The Grand Charter

"SILENCE! SILENCE EVERYONE!" Ouwaan yelled, trying to calm the raging crowd. There were a group of long-haired, blue monkeys with strong, orange eyes standing around him. "I have brought before the Wild the Grand Charter and have read the words of the Ancients," he said, putting on his glasses and reading off the notes one of the blue monkeys gave to him:

"The decision of Pleaser shall be granted upon the Wild in the summer of the sixth year from the onset of the previous determined election. It shall be the will of the Wild that a Wildling becomes Pleaser if they win over half the slates entitled across the territories of the

Wazoo. Should no contender win this majority, it will be the responsibility of the Assentory to decide the next Pleaser of the Wazoo by majority. Should this representative council fail to reach a majority or be inconclusive, it shall be the decision of the seven Keepers of the Wazoo to determine the next Pleaser."

Elder Ouwaan rolled up the longleaf and looked back at the crowd, who were still angry at all of this and began to chant again *GRANDSTAND!*

"SILENCE, EVERYONE! I HAVE SPOKEN THE WORDS OF THE ANCIENTS! THIS IS THE WILL OF THE WILD!" Ouwaan said, trying to calm the crowd. But the crowd raged on.

GRANDSTAND! GRANDSTAND! Both sides continued shouting. Never had I seen either side agreeing on anything, except for the disdain they had right now.

"So be it! So be it!" said Raignor Quorok, the tall red emu, who walked in front of the Elder. "Should the Wild be unwilling to accept the Elder's counseling, then I bid the contenders of this race to take the Grandstand!"

The crowd cheered, but a few of us looked at each other, not sure what any of this meant. "What's the Grandstand?" I asked Damien.

"Whenever the vast majority of the Wild disagrees with something an Elder of the Primary Council says, they can call a representative of the Wild, in this case the candidates, to take the Grandstand and to summon the Watchwaker," Damien said.

"But I don't understand, that's what Elder Ouwaan read from the Charter! How can we just ignore it?" Amelia asked. We all looked at Damien, confused as to why or how all of this could be happening right now.

"I-it's just what the Charter says," he replied plainly.

"What? That's crazy!" Amelia said.

"So, they're going to get the Watchwaker involved? Does this mean Peister can win?" Riley asked as she panicked.

"Why would the Ancients allow any of this?" I asked, but even Damien shook his head, completely confused.

"Okay, but what will the Watchwaker do?" Sal asked.

"He can decide anything: how to settle this, who the winner is, heck he can even name himself as Pleaser!" Damien said.

"ATTENTION ALL! I will now call upon each contender in this race to take the Grandstand. If *any* of the three oblige, the Watchwaker will be summoned by the will of the Wild!"

"This was their plan! Hortley, Peister, they're going to take over the whole Wazoo!" Riley said, flying around erratically. *Maybe she was right! If the Watchwaker had known Greygor was behind stealing from the temple, Giyatar Ghanji might just choose Peister out of spite!*

"Aechus Albrite, Peister Precarious, and Greygor Guildenhall, please withstand your council and step forth! Do you concur with the Elder's resolution, or do you wish to take the Grandstand?" the Raignor of Ipanouwa asked.

"Raignor of Ipanouwa, I concur with Elder Ouwaan," Aechus said bowing.

"Very well! What does the Consular of Hagragada

plead?" he said to Peister, who was still talking with Hortley and a few other lawyers at his side, who themselves, it seemed, couldn't agree.

STAND! STAND! STAND! His supporters, along with many other Wildings who had not wanted him to even win, chanted together saying.

"Raignor of Ipanouwa, I concur with the Elder's resolution!" Peister said bowing. The whole arena was shocked, including us. I mean, wasn't this his opportunity to win somehow?

BOOO!

All eyes turned to Greygor Guildenhall, who was still pacing back and forth, thinking about what to do. He was the frontrunner of the whole race, yet he still could not secure a majority of the shards, all because Aechus, his *own* Patron, didn't believe in him. But did he want to risk it all for the Watchwaker, whom he had just stolen from a week ago?

"Pleaser Guildenhall, do you concur with the Elder's resolution, or do you wish to take the Grandstand?"

STAND! STAND! STAND! The crowd chanted to Greygor, who now stood idle and away from his council. He had more slates than anyone else in this process, only four away from winning it all. I'm sure he believed he was the rightful winner of this whole election deep down, as many in the crowd did also. The real question was, would the Watchwaker see it that way too?

"I-I concur," he said after pausing for a while.

BOOO! The crowd erupted. *CORRUPT! THEY'RE ALL CORRUPT!* Wildlings yelled out loud.

"So, it is said!" Elder Ouwaan finally spoke, waiting for the angry chants to die down a little. "The Assentory will be tasked to decide the next Pleaser of the Wazoo. All Consulates are to report immediately to the Arcadium in accordance with the will of the Wild!"

The crowd only responded in an uproar as they began to push and fight each other once again. We tried to make our way out of the mosh pit that was forming, but every Wildling there had only felt the need to argue and fight each other.

"Let's get out of here!" I said as we stood together and tried to squeeze past everyone, Riley flying up to tell us where to go.

When we arrived home, all my friends wanted to do was watch the garbage on TV and take in all the tension and drama they had just witnessed. "Grandstanding an Elder during a political procedure, I have to say I've never heard of such a thing! Please Chek, tell us what is going on? What were the Wildlings thinking?"

"Well, as you know Hijaac, the Wild has always had the right to call upon the Watchwaker when they do not agree with an Elder. That is an ancient right, one preserved throughout our history, but as you said yourself, during an election to seek the Watchwaker? Well, we would have to go quite a few million years back to even hear of such a thing!"

I knew only bad would come of it. And I was right. Wildlings were flustered, arguing with each other constantly, even poor Damien was dragged into it. But as for myself, I wanted no part in any of it. Mostly because I had other thoughts on my mind.

As my friends sat around and argued, all I could wonder was what Hortley was thinking? *How could Peister win if most of the Consulars were part of the Waker Pack, not his Watcher Pack? Was this really their plan all along, to make sure no one won the election?* Something still seemed odd about all of this, but surprisingly, I was not angry, only wondering what, if anything, I could do to stop Hortley from getting the power he so eagerly wanted.

I walked into my room and locked the door before opening the loose plank of wood near my bed. The Dreamfruit was still there, shining with the same glowing aura around it.

"Jimmy? Are you there?" Amelia said, knocking as I walked back to open the door.

"Yeah, where'd you go?" Sal asked as he slipped from underneath. "OH LOOK, A MAP!" he said, ripping it out from the wooden plank I hadn't quite closed all the way.

"Sal put that back!" I said as he quickly and unknowingly slipped it into my satchel. But I was too busy with my own thoughts. I still hadn't told them about having the real Dreamfruit, and after a day like today, I'd hate to panic them even more. I put the purple fruit in my vest pocket before walking out. It was said to be a powerful fruit, capable of entering others' dreams. And what better time to use it than right now when the whole Wazoo was in jeopardy?

"Come on, let's go," I said as I grabbed my satchel.

"Wh- where do you want to go now?" Amelia asked.

"To the Arcadium, we have to stop Peister from winning."

"But Jimmy, Greygor has the majority, he can win it!" Damien said as I got on my bike and turned on the flight module.

"No, Damien, Hortley has a plan, he *always* has a plan! And I just have this bad feeling that something is going to happen. Now, are you guys coming or not?" I asked, ready to take off.

We flew our bikes north to Arcadia, a small town with old stone statues carved hundreds of thousands, even millions of years ago, that were still so well preserved. I saw the tall arches overhanging the Arcadium, with many Consulars already lining up behind the doors, and others gathering in large groups talking. We landed a little further off and hid our bikes.

"What are we doing here Jimmy? We're not supposed to be here. Look at the Venali, and all the police walking around! We have to turn back. We have to turn back right now!" Riley said.

"Jimmy, I-I uh don't want to get in trouble again," Barry said anxiously. He had been quiet pretty much all day, I'm sure not truly even knowing what was at stake.

"We will be fine, alright? Just stay here, I'll be right back," I said, telling them to stay hidden behind the bushes facing the empty Arcadium. I took out my vinewhip and jumped through the high branches in the forest, looking for Greygor. I followed a few of the well-dressed Consulars below me as they all walked in a back area of the forest.

"Pleaser Guildenhall!" said a beautiful rainbow lorikeet.

"Ah yes Tabitha, I've been looking for you. Tell me, do we have the shards to win?"

"Well sir, as it stands, we are at 227 shards guaranteed, Peister is at 219, and Aechus has the rest at 13."

"So, 22 of my associates have vouched for Peister? There is no way we can convince just three to join us? That is all we need."

"I'm afraid they have been persuaded as they see a lucrative opportunity with Peister and Hortley."

"And what of the Aechus supporters, are there any concessions we can make?"

"I can try, but it will be difficult. Not to mention we are running short of time."

"Then we will have to make concessions for things they seek for their own reelection. We are so close, and I do not want this to go to the seven Keepers. Though they are wise, I do not expect them to resist Peister and Hortley's temptations, whatever it is they might be. We must win now!"

"I will do my best, sir," the bird said before flying away.

Greygor was confident, sure he would win. But I had seen how sneaky Hortley was, knowing about Caecuweed, convincing me to break into the Palace for a reward getting published into the paper, hiding the pirates, even spreading the Balooza so the fruits wouldn't get picked. He was very keen at finding his opportunities. I didn't know what exactly he was planning this time, only that Greygor needed a better plan.

A white Venali emerged and bowed before the Pleaser.

"My lord, the Jungles boy has returned. He is hiding in a tree watching us. Do we have your permiss-"

"Wh-get down here, boy! NOW!" Greygor yelled, looking around at the trees. "What are you doing here? This is not the time to be messing around," he said, walking towards me after I swung down.

"I'm sorry sir. I-I just wanted to speak with you. We cannot let Peister win this election. We need to - well stop him! I know Hortley is behind you not winning the election among the Wild, and I know he's planning something here! I just have a feeling."

"Jimmy, I assure you we will win. Neither of us has the numbers, and I still have my advisors talking with a few. Just in the last hour, I was able to convince ten of them to support my cause. More will follow. I promise you. And if not, we will win in the Keeper's Court."

"Yes, but sir, I just wanted to let you know there are other ways you can win," I said, pulling the Dreamfruit out of my pocket and showing it to him. "Seuss Sutterman told me it could be used to enter dreams, an- and influence others. We could use it now, to save the Wazoo, stop the pirates from ever returning, and make sure Hortley never causes any harm ever again!"

"Jimmy, how do you still have this? What did you give to the pirates then?" he said, shaking his head.

"Well, yes, I couldn't give the real Dreamfruit to them, so I gave them a fake Seuss had made. But we could use this now to prevent any more disasters, Greygor. Please, we have to!"

"Jimmy, I know *just* how powerful this fruit is! But I will not use it to win this election. That is *not* the way!"

"B-I just know Hortley is planning something. Plea-"

"I don't want to hear any more of this. Go! And never return. Next time I see you trespassing, I will order my guards to arrest you, do you understand?" I nodded slowly before he walked away. The Venali appeared suddenly and escorted me out of the area before turning invisible once again.

"Well, what did he say? Is he going to stop Peister and Hortley from winning?" my friends asked as I walked to them with my head hanging low.

"We'll just have to see for ourselves," I said anxiously. I could feel my whole body jittering as Consulars began to enter the large dome arena. The Venali tigers climbed the tall white arches as their Pleaser walked down the aisle alongside Peister, Hortley, and Aechus Albrite.

"CONSULARS OF THE ASSENTORY! Gather around, casting for the next Pleaser shall now commence!" said the tall penguin, Izohr Iwick, as he smashed his gavel against the podium several times. "These are, without a doubt, pressing times for our small island, and we must work promptly to ensure procedure is followed by the will of our great ancestors," the Vizer of the chamber said.

Every Consular sat down at their seat desks, with small white monkeys running across the aisles, dropping gray shard stones in front of them.

"What! We cannot begin now! We must hear from each of the candida-"

"That is enough Mungis! You do NOT have the stand!" Vizer Iwick said as he slammed his hammer repeatedly against his podium. Many other Watchers began to stand up, revolting against what they were afraid was a rushed and losing cast for their side.

"This council cannot proceed until we have heard the fin-"

"ORDER! ORDER! Enough of your shenanigans, Mungis! If the Consulars disrupting this session does not cease immediately, they will be escorted out of this Chamber! There will be order!" the Vizer said interrupting as he pounded his hammer once again. "Now, please come forth and drop your shards into one of the three baskets below, the Tempotee monkeys shall tally the count. Only then shall we know what this body has chosen," he said, slamming his gavel.

The two candidates who were not actual members of the Assentory, Pleaser Guildenhall and Patron Albrite, sat at opposite desks on the bottom floor of the entire arena, looking anxiously as Consulars walked down the steep sloped aisles to cast their stones. It was, by all means, a nerve wrecking moment as everyone watched with heavy anticipation. Peister's allies, the Watcher Pack, and a few of the bribed Wakers, had done their best to delay the casting, trying to convince anyone they needed just a few more minutes, but Vizer Iwick was having none of it.

However, while everyone was being given stones and walking in line to cast, I saw one monkey gently put a stone onto Aechus's table, even though he was not a Consular and could not cast. It was much darker shard than the others and emitted a strange green light from it.

"Do you imagine a greater life? One full of promise and fulfillment through your own great prosperity?" I heard suddenly from a dark, strange voice. I turned back confused as to what was going on. What was that voice? Why was it whispering in my own head? *"Do you envision a day where all your dreams come true, whatever they might be? A world run entirely by you, where only good can come? Do you wonder?"*

"Jimmy, what's going on? Are you alright?" Amelia asked as she looked over at me holding my own head in pain.

"I, uh Aechus, look at Aechus! Why does he have a shard? He's not a Consular, he can't cast!" they said looking over as I sunk to the ground, still holding my head. It was then that the flashes started to appear. Aechus stood at the Pleaser's Palace, surrounded by the Venali tigers, as Wildlings all around applauded him, giving speeches, while humiliating Greygor Guildenhall in a debate.

"All will come to praise you! None will stand in your way! All your hopes can become reality and with the deepest reverence amongst all your peers! Believe Aechus! Believe! All your greatest pleasures lie with this important sacrifice. Join Peister. Join him, and only reward can come."

I turned back around, trying to ignore the flashing images of Peister and Hortley talking to Aechus about a deal. *You must do it! We can change the whole Wazoo! See how great you can be!* The voice said. *"Believe*

Aechus! Believe!" I kept hearing. I turned around to see Aechus's eyes turning green as he shivered in his seat, like he was being controlled. I didn't understand how this was happening, and not a single Wildling had even noticed.

"The shards have been counted, and the final tally is in! Please rise!" Vizer Iwick said as Elder Ouwaan slowly approached the floor. "A required 230 shards is necessary to be declared Majoriat and thus the next elected Pleaser of the Wazoo. For Patron Albrite, 14 shards. For Consular Precarious, 216 shards. And finally, for Greygor Guildenhall, 229 shards. Thus, the Assentory has failed to award a majority of its stones, and theref-"

"WAIT! Wait!" Aechus said, standing up. "I wish to make a statement as to my candidacy!"

The whole crowd was silent as everyone leaned in to see Aechus speak on the floor of the Chamber.

"I have talked with Consular Precarious, Aspirer of the Wild, and have decided to pledge my candidacy to serve as his Patron. I submit all my shards to his cause," Aechus said bowing to the Vizer.

The crowd uproared immediately.

"WHAT IS THIS CORRUPTION!"

"YOU CAN'T DO THAT!"

"THIS IS UNHEARD OF!"

"SILENCE! SILENCE EVERYONE!" said the Vizer as he slammed his gavel against the podium. "Patron Albrite, are you saying, right here and now, that you are joining Peister Precarious's ticket for Pleaser of the Wazoo as his Patron and vouching all your shards towards him?"

"Yes, yes, I am," Aechus said as the uproar grew. The penguin Vizer was completely shocked, not sure what was to happen next or if any of this was even allowed. While half the Chamber complained, the others chanted in celebration.

PEISTER! PEISTER! PEISTER!

"And Consular Precarious, do you accept this claim and make Aechus your Patron?" he asked, shaking with anticipation.

"Yes, my Vizer. I accept this proposal with wide wings and an open heart!" Peister proclaimed from the center of the Arcadium.

"Well, it does.... does so appear the Precarious ticket has been able to secure 216 shards from Peister's Pleasership, and 14 from Aechus Albrite as Patron to his ticket. Thus, the final count is 230 - 229. Peister Precarious, you are hereby named Majoriat by this council, and thus it has been determined you will be named the *next* Pleaser of the Wazoo!" Vizer Iwick said, slamming his gavel against the podium.

"WHAT CORRUPT BARGAIN IS THIS?" Greygor shot up and yelled as the rest of the chamber uproared. "THIS CANNOT BE, MY ELDEREN, THIS IS SCANDAL!" the lion went on, looking at the long bearded monkey who was thinking to himself.

"The Vizer has abided by the Chartered laws and-"

"NO! THIS CANNOT BE JUST! I TAKE THE GRANDSTAND! I DEMAND THE WATCHWAKER! I DEMAND THE WATCHWAKER IMMEDIATELY!" Greygor shouted.

"Pleaser Guildenhall, you cannot take the

Grandstand, this is the granted procedural and decision of this chamber. Peister Precarious will become the next Pleaser of the Wazoo. This is the will of the Wild!" the Vizer said as he pounded the gavel.

"THIS IS ILLEGAL!"

CORRUPTION! CORRUPTION! chanted a few of the Consulars as nearly half of them were retaliating against the decision. Greygor marched up from his seat and continued to shout at the Elder, who had simply walked away. The chamber was in utter chaos as a group of Venali tigers now jumped down from the arches down to the floor, roaring and trying to create space between the newly named Pleaser and the raging crowd. The blue monkeys that were hanging over on the arches also dropped down, separating the still angry Pleaser from Elder Ouwaan. The whole arena was in disarray. Sal looked around, confused at what was going on, while Barry put his hands over his ears and closed his eyes, no longer able to take in all the chaos.

"This can't be real! This can't be legal, right, Damien?" Riley said hyperventilating as everyone stared over at him.

"I-I I've never heard of this, I can't tell you!"

"Jimmy? Jimmy, are you okay?" Amelia said, shaking me, the voice coming back in my head again.

"Well done, Aechus! Well done indeed! This is only the beginning! The best has yet to come!" said the dark voice.

Suddenly, a large shadow came over us. At first, I thought it was a cloud, or maybe a large bird until the flaming rock came crashing into the tall overhanging arches and landed on the chamber floors. Many others followed suit as large pieces of white stone came crashing down. The Arcadium was under attack.

"WHAT IN THE HELOKS WAS THAT?" Sal shot up, saying as we all backed away. "What is going on?"

The doors to the Chamber banged open, and tall pirates unraveled the Caecuweed from on top of them and came storming in with dozens of black crocodiles walking down the aisles as the Royal Guard jumped up front.

RRRRRAAAAAWWWWWRRRRRRR

I had no idea what was going on. *Why were they back? Did they know the Dreamfruit was a fake? How?*

"Jimmy, what do we do?" Sal asked.

"You guys head back home. I'll talk to them!" I said before taking out my vinewhip and lashing it against one of the all arch pillars still upright.

Captain Bacawly reached the aisle and grabbed Peister by his neck before raising him up high.

"WHERE IS IT? TELL ME RIGHT NOW!" he said, shaking the vulture before throwing him aside. He then walked towards Hortley, who scooted away as fast as he could before being kicked down.

I tried dodging all the fast-moving crocodiles and tigers who were lashing at each other. But Bacawly was away from all the fighting, now putting both Peister and Hortley in a net before having one of his men drag them out of the Arcadium.

I chased after them, trying to bring them back, ready to whip Bacawly and anyone else who tried to attack me with my vinewhip. I ran up the aisle, tailing the pirates sliding them off, but before I could even reach back to the main trail, someone tripped me at the doors.

"Put these chains on 'fore you even *think* 'bout gettin' up jungleboy," Wyatt said as he foot pressed against my back, pointing his sword right at my neck.

Chapter 22

An Unexpected Departure

"WYATT, WHERE ARE WE GOING?" I asked, not able to see anything with the bag he put over my head with my hands chained together.

"Shut up Jimmy! I don' wanna hear anotha' damn word outta you!" Wyatt said bitterly.

"Where are these stupid pirates taking us? I-is that Jimmy?"

"Wh-Jimmy? Are you okay? Oh you take that bag off him now!"

"Amelia? Sal? Is that you?" I said, not being able to see any of them until after Wyatt ripped the bag off over my head and the sudden light blurred my vision.

"What are you guys doing here? I told you to go back home!" I said in shock.

"Well, we were trying to before these buffoons trapped us and put us in chains!" Amelia said angrily as she went up and kicked a skinny bandit in front of her.

"OUCH! OW!" Winsley groaned as he rubbed his shin.

"Oh, you a wild one, ain't ya, Junglelady? Calic I wan' you to carry her, make sure she ain't cause no more trouble!" Wyatt said to the tall clueless giant behind all of them.

"Oh, okay, Wyatt," he said before carrying her.

"Put me down! Put me down now!" Amelia yelled.

"Hey, you leave my friends alone! They didn't do anything! Why are you even taking us?"

"*Why?* Are you really askin' me why? Its cuz' ya' screwed me, Jimmy! I trusted ya', an' ya' *screwed* me. That's why!"

"What are you talking about? He let you stay at his home!" Riley said flying around. She and Sal were the only ones not shackled up.

"Boy, I am about done lettin' you mess with me! Calic, Winsley, take this junglelady and her animals to the ship," he said after dumping everything out of my satchel. "Well, I'll be, if it ain't my very map right on in here!" At that moment, I shook my head and gave Sal one nasty glare. "Get a move on. We goin' back to yer house. That's where I bet ya' keepin' the Dream, ain't ya?"

"Wh-no! I have it with me, in my pocket!" I said, desperately shaking but unable to budge my hands out from the knot tied behind my back. The last thing

I wanted was my friends to be stuck on a ship with a bunch of rotten pirates. "If I give it to you, can you please just let us go! Please," I begged, but Wyatt didn't listen.

"You ain't in no position to negotiate," he said, reaching into my vest and pulling out the Dreamfruit. He stared at it closely for a second. "Is this 'nother trick, huh Jimmy? You tryna fool me again? Cus' I promise ya, it ain't gon end too well for ya'," Wyatt said, pushing me.

"No, I'm not. That's the real one. I switched them right before I gave it to you. That's what they wanted me to do. Please, just take it and let us go."

"'Fraid I can't do that, Jimmy. I really do need that ship, 'n Bacawly almos' threw 'way the deal once he foun' out it was a fake," he said after thinking to himself. "We'll have to see what he says firs'."

"Bacawly, Bacawly, Bacawly. That's all I ever hear from you. Looks like you managed to get that lil' fruit though. I jus' hope for yer sake that's the real one this time," a small kid said as he marched in with his large black hat. It was the same boy Wyatt was arguing with when I got caught sneaking onto the pirate ship.

"Oh, who invited Pickets out here?"

"You always talk the big talk, Wyatt. *'Oh, us bandits gon' take this ship, an' then we steal from all those corrupt governors an' free all the prisoners they lock up. Then we gon' travel the world fer more riches an' impress the ladies wit' all the ponies and houses they want.'* Always the same talk from you!" Kenny said, mocking him.

"'F you got a problem with how I lead the bandits, then leave! Ain't no time to start questioning ma' judgment on things, 'specially when we're this close. An' I don't need you startin' any riots neitha'!"

As they continued to argue, I slowly walked over to my friends and whispered to them.

"Psst, Sal, can you get the flute from my pocket? We need to call Seuss!"

"Jimmy, what's that crazy old man going to do to help us?"

"He's our only chance, Riley!" I said as Sal placed the flute in my mouth for me to blow. It only took a few seconds for an orange butterfly to come fluttering around us. "Please get Seuss! The pirates are still here, taking us to their ship right now!"

A few seconds went by before the same butterfly flew away gently. "Well? Did it work?" Riley asked as everyone leaned in.

"We'll have to wait and see," I said. It was our only shot at getting freed now, and the only chance at getting rid of these pirates once and for all. I only hoped he would come soon.

"-and you wanna screw this up, be my guest. But the bandits won' forget it! An' I'll tell you one thing, Wyatt, that Bacawly is a no-good liar! You really think he jus' gon give you this ship that he been sailin' on so long just caus' you shared ya' maps? You might just gone stupider than Calic! Tha's why I'm tellin' ya we-"

"Kenny, I don' wanna hear an'more 'bout yer-"

"Sneak attack! That's 'xactly what we need to take over the ship! You understan' me?"

"You think Bacawly and the crocs gon' be easy to fight off? Be my guest, jus' don't come cryin' to me when you get all caught up in ya' choices. An' I don' wanna hear anotha' word outta you 'bout this," he said before turning back to us. "Now all you quit standin 'round and let's go. Come on now, ain't got all day!"

"Oh whatever Wyatt, jus' don't expect none of the bandits to forgive you when we get screwed outta nothing!" Kenny said, standing his ground as we all walked away from him.

Turns out, we were not too far from the new site the pirates had decided to stay. How they kept a large ship moving and hidden from the rest of the Wazoo was still a wonder to me, but all my friends were in awe when they first saw it with dozens of pirates working around it.

"How could none of the patrols see this?" Damien asked.

"It's the Caecuweed. They can't see or even smell it, its how they've been getting away with all of this," I said looking at the tall hanging seaweed around the trees and over the ship.

"But how are they going to get this massive ship out? No way a few Wildlings can do this!" Damien asked, something I still hadn't figured out quite yet.

We walked up the steep old wooden board, and the dirty pirates chuckled as they saw us.

"Oh, cap'n gon' give it to these kids!"

"Now I see what we feedin' the crocs today."

Wyatt and his bandits walked us up to the old ship,

which was filled with barrels that had: WAZOO TRAD-ING COMPANY.

Most notably, however, I saw Peister and Hortley, trapped underneath a net, shaking in horror.

"Oh, Jimmy! Are you kids okay?" Peister said. "Help us! We have to get out of here!" he whispered.

"Why should we? This is all your fault! This is what you get for working with the pirates!" I yelled back.

"Hey, HEY! All of you shut it! Now Ima tell Bacawly I got his lil' ole fruit, an' then we'll be on our way. Got that? But I swear, Jimmy, if this ain't the real one, I am gonna help him crush your head with his metal boot," Wyatt said before walking to the cabin room I had snuck into before.

"We need to focus on getting out of here!" Amelia said before turning around and gasping. The doors barged open suddenly. Captain Bacawly pressed forward slowly, each step of his metal boot creaking against the wooden floors. Two long black crocodiles walked slowly, staring at us with their large red eyes and opening their jaws to show their long, jagged teeth.

"Are you sure Seuss is coming? I don't know how much more time we have!" Damien asked anxiously as the scar-faced captain walked in front of me.

"Nice to see ya again, boy," he said, smirking as he towered over me.

"I-I gave Wyatt the real one this time. I promise. Please just let us go."

"So, admittin' to cheatin' me before then huh? Think yer so clever, do ya?" He said right into my face before throwing me to the ground and kicking me in the stomach. "How's that feel boy? Hm? Tha's jus' the pain of the world makin' rounds to you this time," he said, kicking me and laughing as I curled up in a ball. I could feel my stomach caving inwards as my body ached.

"Uh, cap'n, the fruit. I got it here. It's the real one, see, take a look," Wyatt said, giving it to him. Bacawly closed his eyes as he took a whiff of the blue aroma.

"Ah, this one is a bit different. It gives me visions of all I ever wanted," he said smiling. "An' ya know what I see right now, boy? I see all the pirates who opposed me 'fore gettin' eatin' by me crocs. I see this whole island burnin' in flames," he said, laughing as the pirates around him cheered. "Men, get the catapults ready, we're going to have a show 'fore we leave."

"NO! PLEASE DON'T!" I yelled as the pirates lit their torches, poured oils over the cannon balls before placing their flames nearly on it.

RRRRAAAAAAWWWWRRRRR

We all turned to see Greygor Guildenhall and a half dozen or so Venali suddenly becoming visible as they jumped down from the trees and onto the boat. Immediately, the pirates pulled out their swords and backed up, looking nervous...

"CUT THE LINES, CUT 'EM ALL NOW!" Captain Bacawly yelled as he unsheathed his heavy sword. Every wooden block holding this ship upright collapsed as the ship sunk into the ground. But I was still confused. *How exactly was this ship going to get out of here?*

Slowly, the ship started to slide down the mountainside we were on, but it remained upright as we rode past the trees. I had no idea how until I looked off to the side and saw the thick brown lianas, the same ones I saw move us on the cart into the Twisted Caverns to find all the babaloos! It must have been something Hortley set up for them to come onto the island. And now, it was their only chance at escaping the wrath of the Venali tigers.

We were being carried through the air, zipping through the forest and making sharp twists and turns as the pirates and crocodiles were fighting the tigers who had managed to jump onto the ship. Others chased along, barely able to grab the edge.

"SNEAK ATTACK!" little Kenny Pickets said as he swung on a rope and kicked Bacawly to the ground.

"I always knew ye' kids were a bunch a' mutineers!" Bacawly said, getting back up and slashing his sword at Kenny, who had been spiraling around the air in circles.

"Don' you even think about touchin' my crew!" Wyatt said as he pulled out his sword. "Thornboot, Rus', Sammyboy, Grub, Jackie, and you too, Mickie! Get 'em!"

As Wyatt and his bandit friends took on the pirates, we were hidden against the side wall until a sword slid our way.

"Get that! We need to cut ourselves loose!" Peister said as I took the sword to cut him and Hortley free from the net.

"The hatch, hurry, open it!" Hortley said as they ran, running away from clashing swords around them. But I was too busy breaking the small chains off me and all my friends.

"Everyone, under here!" I said as I opened the hatch.

"Where are you going, Jimmy?" Amelia asked.

"I've got to get back the Dreamfruit - and the map! Stay here!" I said before dashing off with a sword that I barely knew how to use myself.

When I looked around, Greygor had now locked eyes with Bacawly and launched himself at the iron-fist pirate as Wyatt fell over onto the floor.

"Come on, I need to get the fruit back!" I said as I helped Wyatt up, seeing that he had the map clenched in his coat pocket. But before I could even grab it, we were all pushed sideways by the ship, still toiling through the jungle. Bacawly had managed to stay upright, walking towards the quarterdeck where the wheel of the ship was. Greygor had a few cuts on him and waited carefully before he finally charged and knocked Bacawly over. Pleaser Guildenhall leapt over, trying to wrap his teeth around the pirate's neck, but got bludgeoned in the head by Bacawly's metal boot and fell back, completely knocked out.

Wyatt and I quickly ran up to take down Bacawly. We threw our swords in the air, though I still had no idea what I was doing. I was trying for too long, barely helping Wyatt, until the idea hit me. "You wanna quit sittin' 'round an' help me Jimmy?" Wyatt said angrily as he was being pushed slowly towards the ledge. I quickly took the small piece of black twine from my pocket and let it wrap around my hand.

I threw my right hand in front of me and watched the vinewhip wrap around Bacawly before throwing him against the wheel and over the ledge.

"You done had that rope this whole time, Jimmy?" Wyatt asked in relief. I ran over to Greygor, trying to see if he was alright. He was opening his eyes again, slowly regaining consciousness.

"Greygor help, we have to get the fruit. Can you get up?" I asked, but he barely responded. Bacawly was still down, slow to get up, his sword a few feet away from him.

I ran down the stairs and looked through his jacket pocket before grabbing the Dreamfruit. But just as I was about to run away, he grabbed my arm and pulled me back, putting his metal fist around my neck. I tried to grab the vinewhip, but couldn't.

"Ye stupid little boy, give that back!" he said as I coughed, trying to grasp my breath. Greygor jumped down and dug his teeth into his arm, and I was able to push away, gasping for air. Bacawly punched Greygor with his iron fist before getting up and grabbing his sword.

"Argo, release all the crocs!" Bacawly said as the pirate pushed off the two bandits he was fighting and opened the captain's quarters. A few Venali came over to help the Pleaser, who was now gripping onto the captain's metal arm, before finally ripping it right off. The scarfaced pirate was enraged in pain, and lifted his sword to cut Greygor on his backside.

"NO!" I yelled from the upper deck. Bacawly looked at me and quickly marched towards us again. I grabbed my vinewhip, getting ready to throw him once again, until Wyatt nudged me.

"Jimmy, look behind!" he said as I turned to see the large blue sea coming up ahead. The ship launched high up from the jungle, and I didn't know if the boat would survive the impending splash. "Hold onto somethin' Jimmy!" Wyatt said as I grabbed the railing and ducked my head, making sure my body was scrunched tightly enough to not lose the Dream, now in my pocket.

A large wave of water flooded the boat and pulled everyone off to the side. Many of the bandits and tigers were now swimming in the water, while only the crocodiles, a few pirates, and Captain Bacawly remained. We got up, completely drenched in water, not even able to find our own swords.

"We've got to jump, there's no other way!" I said leaning off the ledge as Ironboot continued up towards us.

"Wh-NO! This my ship, Jimmy!" Wyatt said as Bacawly raised his sword above us.

But just when I thought we were done for, long green seaweed plants emerged from the sea and moved slowly up the sides of the ship.

"WHAT THE HELL IS THAT?" Wyatt yelled. At first, we both ducked until it slid past us and the few other bandits to grab every crocodile and pirate on board. My jaw dropped. *How was it only grabbing - unless it was - no, could it really be?* But it wasn't until I turned my head and looked on shore to see an old man in his white cloak staring at us that I finally knew. Seuss's connection with nature was something I never understood, something absolutely incredible to witness every time he used it at will.

The pirates continued to yell as they were all being thrown overboard, but when I turned around to look back at Wyatt, he was gone. I thought he might have been taken, but I looked to the main deck to see him

laughing as he walked towards Bacawly, who was slowly being pulled away.

"GET THIS STUPID WEED OFF ME!" Bacawly screamed as it slowly lifted him higher in the air. Suddenly, Wyatt came over and grabbed onto his metal boot.

"Well, guess there won' be any more orders from you, huh, *Captain*?" he said sarcastically before finally ripping off his metal boot. The seaweed then flung him into the air and threw him into the sea. Every pirate was now swimming in the water, and the crocodiles were plunged into the depths far below, drowning on the seabed.

"Lookie here lads, this be the remains of our ol' captain, who's off swimmin' with the fishes now," Wyatt said, standing on the upper deck and raising Bacawly's hollow, metal boot. The bandits all cheered loudly. "Many of you have question'd my authority to take us bandits from the good lands of Raleigh and sail with these dirty pirates so far 'ways. Well fellas, today we are due to none 'nymore. We are now free men of the sea as of this ver' moment, 'n all should know, there's a new captain of this ship! Let it be known, the Breakaway Bandits have rightfully claimed the Renegade free as ours!" he said as they all cheered. "Now get a move on, we're sett'n sail to Mondale! An' the whole worl' beknown, us bandits free at last, on the search for our due riches, here we come! But before we go, I must ask who do y'all swear yer loyalties to?"

"To Captain Picker!" a shoeless bandit said, raising his sword in the air.

"TO CAPTAIN PICKER!" said the rest of the bandits as they cheered, all raising their swords before getting ready to make way.

I walked over and lifted the hatch to let my hiding friends, along with Peister and Hortley, out. "Wh-they're all gone? How'd you do that?" Damien asked as he saw the pirates floating in the water, still wrapped in seaweed.

"Wow, even Bacawly's overboard!" Riley said as the Venali tigers began to swim over and drag the pirates back to shore.

"How did all this happen, Jimmy?" Sal asked, realizing my friends hadn't even seen the large wave and giant seaweed sweep the whole place clean.

"Seuss he-uh took care of everything," I said, walking back to Wyatt.

"WHAT! The old man? How'd he do that Jimmy?" Sal blurted out, all my friends were just as confused, but I didn't answer.

"Well, look who it is," Wyatt said smiling.

"Congratulations, *Captain* Picker," I said.

"Yeah, well - what the hell was all that? Seaweed flying through the air, I ne'er seen anything like it," he said.

"That's the Wazoo for ya," I said laughing. "Anyway, Wyatt, can I get the map back?" I asked, but Wyatt paused for a second before looking right back at me and smiling again.

"Sure thing, Jimmy, but lemme do *just* one more thing real quick," he said with his usual, half-hearted smirk. "ALRIGHT, BOYS, GATHER ROUND! My first order as yer captain is I wan' all them junglefolk thrown off ma' ship!" he said pointing at us.

"WHAT!" Riley said angrily before she flew around him and started to peck at his head.

"WHAT'S WRONG WITH YOU, WYATT?" Amelia yelled as two bandit boys shoved her into the water.

"Wh- Wyatt!" I said, marching up to him, but a group of his bandits grabbed and threw me into the water.

"Do you know who I am? Keep your dirty fingers off me!" Peister said as they lifted him up in the air.

"How dare you! We are business partners!" Hortley said to Calic, who gave up on lifting the fat pig and instead took a sword and began poking him with it as he oinked to the edge of the ship. "Uh- someone please, I don't think I can float! Help me Peister!" he said, splattering water everywhere.

"WYATT, YOU LIAR! GIVE ME BACK THE MAP. WE MADE A DEAL, REMEMBER?" I yelled from the sea.

"Well 'course I lied Jimmy, I'm a *scumbag*! And as fer the map, I'll be holdin' onto this a lil' while. How else am I s'ppose come back an' visit you?" Wyatt said, pulling out another ecotta from his pocket and taking a bite from it.

"YOU DIRTY PIRATE! COME BACK HERE! COME BACK HERE RIGHT NOW!" Amelia yelled.

"Aw, I'll miss you too, Junglelady! 'Til we meet next time, Jimmy!" Wyatt said, waving as the ship took off with the entire crew of young bandit boys.

We began to swim back to shore. All of the Venali were already back, dragging Bacawly's defeated crew through the sand and into the police cage cars.

When I looked past the circle of enraged Venali, some of whom were fighting each other at this point, I saw Greygor Guildenhall laying on the ground while being attended to by a group of nurses.

"Will he be okay?" I walked over and asked.

"We don't know. We're doing everything we can."

"Ji-jimmy," Greygor muttered, trying to open his eyes. "Th-thank you...for everything," he said before putting his head back down right before the medical staff lifted him into an ambulance and rushed away.

It was a heavy moment for me. I had spent so much of my time hating Greygor, fearing what he would do next. But in this moment, watching doctors try to stop the heavy bleeding as he ached in pain, while thinking about how he came and saved me not once, but twice. I had taken him for granted. I completely misjudged him this whole time and all I felt was shame.

"Well done, Mr. Jungles! You have managed to reprimand the pirates and protect this very island, not to mention myself," Peister said proudly, while Hortley was already walking to a carriage that had somehow arrived for him. "I must say, I do think I am in a great debt to you. Please, if there is-"

"OH, SHUT UP! THIS WAS ALL YOUR FAULT! THE PIRATES, YOUR FRAUD VICTORY, EVEN GREYGOR GOING TO THE HOSPITAL! ALL YOUR FAULT!" Riley said, unable to resist her anger.

"Excuse me?" Peister said, as a few Venali approached us.

"Sorry, so sorry, sir. It's been a stressful day for all of us!" Amelia said as she quickly grabbed her pet bird from sounding off even more. Peister looked back at us, before nodding and walking to the carriage. "You can't do that, he's the Pleaser now!"

"Ugh, I don't care, he's just an awful cheater who let all of this happen!" she said going on.

A few police officers finally walked up to us, wanting answers to everything that had happened, and for the most part, I was able to be honest, only leaving a few details out, like the Dreamfruit the pirates almost stole, the map to the island that the bandits managed to keep, and that I had become friends with one of them...

"Okay, young man, thank you. This helps a lot. Just one more question: How exactly were all the pirates thrown off the ship? We are getting many reports of this seaweed substance. Would you know anything about that?"

I really didn't want to explain that, mostly because I had no idea how Seuss pulled it off. I looked around, hoping he was still here and that maybe he could explain all of this to me, but he was nowhere in sight, gone almost as quickly as he had come.

Chapter 23

The Flying Fruits at Gideon's Rock

GREYGOR GUILDENHALL WAS SET TO make a full recovery as many of the restoration projects for new forestry and buildings (including Cross Rivers Middle School) finished up, and all lingering Balooza cases had been closed, most doctors saying there hadn't been a single infection in weeks. For the first time in a while, things were beginning to look better once again. So much so that the Elders had called for a wondrous celebration, *Chakula kwa' ah wotee*, or a feast for all in the old Wildlin language. More fruits were blooming and Wildlings were able to eat with no fear of getting sick.

But as great as everything was, I was beginning to think the Wild had forgotten about Peister's *technical* victory to become the next Pleaser of the Wazoo. He had broken nearly every rule and compromised his morals by working with Hortley Hasselback and his conniving ways, all for the sake of power. And that still did not sit well with me. But as Greygor himself had said, 'these were times of peace and reckoning, a time where we all can heal with an unwavering pursuit for unity and prosperity of our great future.' I just hoped he really meant it.

The following week was filled with news of the pirate trials, who were being prosecuted with too many crimes to count: illegal entry, robbery, vandalism, trespassing, extortion, slaughter, terrorism, invasion of sacred grounds, and abduction, just to name a few. I had no idea why any Wildling would provide them legal representation, if those savage buffoon pirates even knew what that meant. How Hortley's name was not mentioned even once in all of this though was beyond me at this point.

But the trials didn't last long. Anya Akahne, an energetic green Gahwa bird, and one of the hosts of *The Early Buzz,* was the first to break the news that the pirate Captain Rigwal Bacawly was found guilty on all twenty-eight counts and sentenced to a lifetime at Kyrokky, a far-away land rumored to somehow be more chaotic and dangerous than the Heloks. But it was strange how such an angry, tall, and metal-appendaged pirate lord with an army of men and crocodiles was now nothing more than a broken old man being strolled around in a wheelchair. To think, just a few weeks ago, he wanted to destroy the island and conquer the world.

A few more weeks had passed until we reached the Ascension Ceremony, a day Wildlings would all rise for the swearing in of the next Pleaser of the Wazoo at a sacred cliff known as Gideon's Rock, where Gaelor Gideon himself gave a speech as the first Pleaser of the island. Mom and Dad were off working, and Jackson, I think, was sleeping over at a friend's house. My friends and I had been sitting around in the living room, flipping through channels, a few of them trying desperately to find any excuse not to leave the house.

"Ughhhh why, *why* do we have to go to these events! He's a stinking liar, nobody even likes him!" Riley said.

"Yeah, I don't want to go to this; everyone is going to keep yelling and arguing the whole time," Barry said as he nervously played with his fingers.

"What? Everyone will be there! C'mon, it'll be fun and plus it's history, right, Damien? We have to go!" Sal said.

"Guys, let's just have fun alright, we deserve it don't we?" I asked as we got up and ready to go downstairs. We had pulled our bikes out, ready to go until suddenly, I saw a green butterfly with a few red dots flying around me. At first, I made nothing of it, and then it hit me. *Seuss? Was he really trying to call me? I hadn't seen him in weeks, or even talked to him in nearly a month.* "I'll uh, meet you guys there, I have to meet someone about my science project! Bye!" I said, riding off quickly, trying to catch up with the butterfly a few feet ahead of me.

"Wait, Jimmy, what science project?"

"Wh-seriously, Sal? I'm your partner! We were working on it yesterday!" Damien said as Sal scratched his head in confusion.

I followed the butterfly through the woods and up a hill until I reached a large rock on a cliff overlooking the waves coming down, crashing against the mountainside. I had never been to this edge of the Wazoo, and almost instantly it made me think of the day I saw the Renegade leave our island. And while I was glad to see all the pirates arrested and the Breakaway Bandits gone, I couldn't help but wonder where they were off to now. What it was like to be away from the Wazoo, even for a day, or longer. What would it be like to have no parents and just roam around with your friends, traveling the world, and seeing what was really out there? It was a life they all seemed so used to.

As I sat there, dwelling on my thoughts, a few dozen butterflies appeared and fluttered around me again.

"Ah, Jimmy, I see you got my call," Seuss laughed lightly as he walked over and sat next to me on the large rock.

"Yeah, I did! I was on my way to go to the Ascension Ceremony, but rushed over here as fast I could. I forgot to bring the Dreamfruit though," I said remembering that I left it back underneath a loose piece of wood in the room. I just hoped he wouldn't be mad at me for stealing it in the first place though.

"Ah, that's okay, you keep it," he said, throwing his hand in the air as he came down to sit by me.

"But isn't it going to rot or something?"

"Oh, a fruit like that won't ever rot, not the normal way at least."

"Doesn't it have incredible powers or something? You really want me to keep it?"

"Well, *yes,* it does, but I trust you to keep it safe. Who knows, maybe one day it might even come in handy. But I didn't call you here for that, Jimmy. I just wanted to catch up after the last couple of weeks, make sure you were still alright after everything," he said, lightly looking over at me.

"Yeah, after you helped the Wazoo catch those pirates, but how'd you do it? I've always wondered. How did you get the seaweed to spring out and grab the pirates like you did at the hospital?" I asked, but Seuss stayed silent as he looked down.

"This is a world of dreams Jimmy, and the Wazoo is always listening to us, whether we believe it or not," he said softly. I had almost too many questions in my head, I didn't know what to ask. "How have you been though? Everything else okay?"

"Uh, just a little off. Ever since the ship left our island, I've had this little bit of sadness in me. Like I wish I were leaving with them. Deep down, I think there's something out there. Something for me. And I hope I can go out and see it one day."

"Oh, don't worry about that, Jimmy. We all feel the need to explore, to grow ourselves. But I promise you this, everything you feel you ever need, anything you're looking for, it's right here at the Wazoo, where our dreams can never die. And I promise you no other place in the whole world can say that," Seuss said, reassuring me.

"Have you ever left the Wazoo, Seuss? Seen the outside world?"

"Uh, no, but I have heard stories, Jimmy, and believe me when I tell you we all are better off here, okay?" he said, patting me on the back before standing back up. "Go! Enjoy your day, Jimmy! Today, we are continuing one of our greatest traditions. It's no time to dwell on the past. Be grateful for what the present has brought, and what the future has in store for all of us."

I walked over to my bike and quickly got on, about to say goodbye and ride off, before a sudden thought came into my head. "Oh, Seuss, there was something else I wanted to tell you. I had another dream a few weeks ago, well, sort of. It was right before the pirates attacked the Assentory. I saw a stone passed to one of the candidates, and it gave me these visions, and I heard a voice."

Seuss looked at me and tilted his head, "And what did this voice say?"

"It was strange. They weren't talking to me, but I could still hear them as it was, well, tempting Aechus to side with Peister, which he did. But all it wanted was for Aechus to imagine a better life for himself, imagine how much better things could be. It was very odd. But then it all went away after a while, and the rock, well, it disappeared after that," I said as he looked away, scratching his head.

"Hm, that is...strange, Jimmy. I'll have to ask around. But do not dwell too much on it. Please, go enjoy yourself," he said.

"Ok, I'll see you soon, Seuss!" I said before riding

off, but Seuss was still looking down and away, as if somehow devastated by what I had told him. I just wish I knew what he was thinking.

I had been riding my bike for nearly twenty minutes, trying to make it to Gideon's Rock in a town called Gaantua, which meant great world in the old Wildlin language. I was about halfway there when I rode past three large trucks, each filled with barrels that had stamped onto them: WAZOO TRADING COMPANY. *What! Still? Wasn't this company bankrupt by now? How was Hortley still getting away with this?* I thought to myself angrily. I shouldn't have been surprised the trade route would still continue on, especially with Peister now becoming Pleaser, but just where was he storing all the fruits now? Maybe I could take some more for my friends, it would definitely help make this day less miserable for everyone. So, I followed them for a bit, but it didn't take long for something to go wrong.

"Oh no, no, no, no!" said a fat-nosed monkey in overalls as he got out of his truck and tried pushing off a tree that he crashed into.

"YOU IDIOT! WHY WERE YOU GOING SO FAST!" said a large rat with a large, stained shirt as he jumped to the driver's seat. Together, they were trying to get past a tree he had crashed into and was now sitting flat on his roof.

"I was just trying to get to the ceremony on time!"

"Yeah, great idea, go so fast you smash into a tree, that'll definitely help!" said the rat, throwing his hands up in the air.

"Well, why is the boss making us work during the inauguration! Most Wildlings get the day off! There's no way we'll be able to make the drop off at Aetertoki Port in time and go to Gideon's Rock!" said the monkey as he took off his hat and raised it in the air.

"Well, we could have if you slowed down! Now we're gonna get fired because you broke your truck!"

"Can you two get your act together!" said the beaver as he waddled over with a bag of his Skorrow's Sticky Nuts. "We're drawing too much attention! We're not supposed to be seen, remember? Now, hurry up and move this tree so we can get going!"

As the monkey's car was backing up, I ran over to the beavers and jumped into the back, leaving my bike hidden in a bush. I was just going to have to grab it later. I needed to see where their shippinig plant was. How Hortley's whole operation was still going on even after the pirates were gone.

"Alright, you're all clear! Now don't go too fast, we can't get caught up and waste any more time today!" The rat said as they all jumped back in their vehicles and went on their way.

I had been rolling around for nearly fifteen minutes, thrown back and forth against big barrels, each spilling more and more fruit onto the floor. The beaver was slurping on a Chugger's Wurple Purple Twist through a long bendy straw as he erratically steered through the steep hills. *Why weren't they going to the port? Was there more to pick up from Hortley's storage in this mountainous area?*

Eventually, we came to a stop, and they all walked

out of their vehicles to sit on the ledge. We were high on a mountain top, and at first, I was confused by all the cheering and noise until I walked towards the edge and saw for myself crowds gathered to see Peister Precarious become Pleaser. *The Ascension Ceremony? They really parked us on top of the mountain where this was taking place? Seriously? Were they really this stupid?*

As soon as Gleela Galees, one of the eloquent singing songbirds on the Wazoo finished, the elephants trumpeted their trunks and the beacons on Gideon's Rock were lit as the Royal Guard escorted the new Pleaser to the stand with the Chief Magistrate Roqin Rowdler, a large black hawk with red feathers and giant feet. He was wearing the typical black robe over himself with small glasses as he carried a small yellow book.

"All rise for the swearing in of our next Pleaser, Peister Precarious!" said the justice.

Peister raised his left wing as high as he could, put his right onto the book held by a familiar white monkey and repeated after the Magistrate.

"I, Peister Precarious, do solemnly swear to forgo all self-intention -and ensure that dreams will never die -in the presence of the great Ancients before us. -That I adamantly promise -to faithfully execute the branch of Pleaser of the Wazoo -and will preserve, protect, and defend the Grand Charter of the Wazoo.

"For the will of the Wild?" the Magistrate asked.

"For the will of the Wild!" Peister replied.

"Congratulations, Mr. Pleaser!" the bird said as Wildlings all around cheered for him. Aechus shook nervously behind him as Hortley clapped emphatically. Peister waved to the crowd before approaching the cliff to a podium stand, preparing to give his inaugural address.

"Thank you, thank you!" he said. The Venali tigers stood around him as he began his speech. But I quickly turned back to the trucks, not sure if he meant the words he had to say, or just to appease the Wild. *The games we all have to play.* I remembered how Greygor had described politics. All of which couldn't make a difference in a single Wildling's life. "Today, we celebrate the continuation of an ageless tradition of this beloved island. Many avons ago, the great Gaelor Gideon himself stood upon this rock to declare this lone island a land of dreams, and us the Wild as the rightful inheritors."

It didn't take long for me to get bored and start looking over at the three drivers sitting back over the mountain, eating away as they joked around with each other. This would be the perfect chance to pack a few berries. Heck, I could just drive away with one of the trucks. I had, after all, driven that ambulance from the hospital a few months ago. How hard could this be?

I crept up slowly to the driver's seat. The good news was that the keys were still in the ignition. The bad news was that the whole dashboard operating system was a lot more complicated with little buttons and switches all over the place, the descriptions smudged or missing. When I pulled the drive lever, the car wouldn't budge a pebble. I messed around with it, but after a while, I lost my patience, and was probably a little anxious too.

I began pushing random buttons and flicking any random switch, anything to get this truck to budge a foot. What happened next, well, I deserved every bit of it, but I couldn't quite call it out as the disaster others had made it seem.

I heard a click, and without even knowing, the back hatch opened. I tried to close it, reaching towards the high switch, but also accidentally taking my foot off the brake, causing the truck to jolt forward and smash into the other two trucks in front of us. But to make it all much, much worse, the trucks tipped over and let out large barrels of fruit from the uncovered tops.

MEEPERT MEEEEPERRRTTTT MEEEEPEEER-RRT!

The alarms went off as the three drivers quickly jumped up and ran towards me.

Meanwhile, the whole crowd was sitting patiently before the loud sirens blasted off from above the mountainside. Peister paused as he turned to see a barrage of tumbling barrels come crashing down. The Royal Guard pulled the newly named Pleaser back as bunches of fruits broke out and thumped onto many Wildlings in the crowd. At first, I thought they would all be terrified, and maybe they were, that is until they realized it was some of the freshest fruits our island had to offer. Almost immediately, herds rushed over to get as many as they could hold. Most Wildlings had waited months to try and eat them, but now it was practically raining fruits from the sky, truly a miracle if there ever was one.

Maybe Peister should have been happier with what was going on. Everyone else was, after all. But it was ruining his Ascension ceremony, a prized moment for every Pleaser to show the island how their leadership would go over the next six years. And for that, he sought vengeance.

"FIGURE THIS OUT! BRING ME WHOEVER IS RESPONSIBLE," Peister yelled at the Venali tigers before they went searching.

At this point, the truck engine was too mashed to even move. But to make matters worse, the drivers were pulling against the door knob, and screaming in fury. I had to figure a way out.

"WHO IN THE HELOKS ARE YOU? GET OUT OF MY TRUCK NOW!" said the beaver as he banged on the driver side window. The fat-nosed monkey then smashed the window with his fist and jumped in.

"YOU BLINKING IDIOT! WE'RE GOING TO GET FIRED BECAUSE OF YOU!" WHO ARE YOU? JUST WHO ARE YOU EXACTLY?" yelled the rat as he tried to grab me. I paused for just a second before I leapt up and dove to the back, shoving all the heavy barrels as I squeezed through. I ran down the side of the mountain, peeking down and gulping at all the havoc I created. And while every Wildling was enjoying themselves more than any other time the past few months, I was panicking. If there's anything I've learned in the past few weeks, it's that not all trouble is worth it, especially when you hadn't even planned on it to begin with.

Just when the coast looked clear and none of the drivers were running down after me anymore, I stopped dead in my tracks as two Venali tigers walked slowly in front of me.

"Well, if it isn't the master of disaster himself. Why am I not surprised? I should have known you were behind this mockery, Jimmy Jungles!" said the gray Venali tiger.

"I-it was an accident, I swear!"

"Greygor cannot protect you any longer!" said the other.

"Perhaps now we can prevent any of your problems from happening again. Magruh, alert the Pleaser that we have found the culprit," the tiger said, smiling. "And that the matter will be taken care of immediately." The other tiger walked away ,and I stood still as the large gray tiger with thick black stripes hunched over, just waiting for me to make a move. It had taken me a while, but I actually did recognize this tiger. It was the same one that tried to charge at me as I was being escorted out of the Palace after my meeting with Greygor. If he had wanted to kill me then, I had no idea what I could possibly do to stop him now.

I slowly reached into my pocket and clenched the vinewhip tightly before jumping off the side of the mountain, throwing my hand towards the nearest tree. The tiger was shocked, having never seen anything like this before in his life.

The whip latched and swung from branch to branch as I made my getaway from the Venali as fast I could. But the angry tiger persisted, taking long, risky jumps between tree branches that could barely hold its weight. He was determined to catch me and was willing to face death to do so.

I had made almost a full circle around the mountain,

most of the crowd had been too distracted by the fruit still tumbling down to even notice me, though Amelia did say they caught a glimpse of me zipping through the air.

"JIMMY JUNGLES! YOU GET BACK HERE THIS INSTANT!" Peister yelled at the top of his lungs. It was obvious by now. His inaugural day speech had been ruined. "GO! I WANT HIM NOW!" The new Pleaser said to a few more Venali.

It wasn't until I was about halfway down the mountain that I actually felt I had gotten away. The forest became much denser, so somewhere along the way, I was able to lose the tiger and hide. I stayed put for a while, looking around to make sure the coast was clear. This was the homestretch. I could feel it.

Just when I thought I had a clear opening, where I could make my escape and finally get off this mountain, I heard a few branches snap as a few others began to shake. I panicked, looking around nervously, but I couldn't tell if the invisible Venali had found me. I held the vinewhip ready, prepared to fly out of here, when suddenly the tiger appeared and tackled me. The tiger was crushing my body as its fangs hung right over my face. "I have you now, boy! And you are going to suffer for all you've done to me!" it said. But just when I thought this was the end, the branches slowly started to crackle until we fell, and we were sliding down the rigid mountainside, the jagged rocks ripping against my skin.

Eventually, the mountainside flattened onto a rocky plain. I hobbled past the large rocks, heavily bruised, as I searched for a tree. Behind me, the large gray tiger was getting back onto its feet, breathing heavily as it moved slowly. The beast was bleeding from its mouth and limping as it dragged its aching body.

GGGGRRRR RRRRAAAWWWRRRRR

I reached the edge of the mountain, and saw a large boulder hanging off the side. I had no idea if the vine-whip would grab it, but it was the closest chance I had of escaping. I threw my hand and swung into the air, swaying a few times before I was able to grab an edge of the rock.

RRRRAAAWWWRRRRRR

The tiger yelled angrily as it tried to grab onto the edge of the rock wall. I was baffled, having never seen a tiger climb a mountain. But this one was persistent, continuing to stare and roar at me. I looked around, trying to see if there was any way to escape as the tiger was now only a few feet away.

There was a small frail tree hanging off the wall beneath me, and it led to a flat plain off the side of the mountain. Beneath it, however, was nothing but a steep fall to an almost certain death. I didn't want to risk it. I was still too far so I began to push my weight back and forth against the rope, trying to swing further out to reach the rock wall.

As I slowly crept to the right, trying to get closer to the tree branch, the tiger jumped onto the large rock getting closer.

RRRRAAAWWWRRRRRR

It stared right at me with its red eyes. I tried to scale the mountainside faster, shaking as I moved my hands and feet, but the tiger took another large leap and landed right on top of me, pressing its body against me and the wall. I was stuck. There was nowhere I could go.

It grabbed my arm with its mouth and began to climb up, dragging me along. I was easily overpowered, and no amount of punching would let me loose, so I did the only thing I could think of. I bent my feet and pressed against the wall before pushing off.

We both fell back in free fall. I quickly lashed the vinewhip, and it was just barely able to wrap itself around the tree. I looked back. The large gray tiger who hated me for ruining its life and reputation was now roaring as it fell down thousands of feet deep. This whole time it only dreamed of getting revenge, seeing me suffer for what I had done to it, and now only getting death in return. And I could only wonder if all that anger was ever really worth it to begin with.

I climbed onto the tree and made it onto the flat plain, the last echoes of the roaring tiger beginning to die away. I walked down slowly, my leg severely scratched up as the rest of my body ached, but I was just glad to be alive.

As I walked the last few steps to reach the bottom, two tigers were sitting and waiting. Somehow, they had known I would come down this way, but I was too exhausted to even try to run at this point.

"What? What do you want from me? Are you going to try to kill me like that other tiger just tried to do? Huh? Well, go ahead! Kill me, I'm not afraid of any of you!" I said angrily, losing all patience at this point. But the tigers stayed still and silent.

"We do not wish to kill you like Hargaan did," he said

calmly. "But the Pleaser has given us orders to bring you to him. Come…". I walked between them, limping with each step until we reached the forest. Dozens of Venali tigers began to appear from their invisibility and looked directly at me with anger, growling silently as I walked closer to their leader, who was sitting on a large rock.

"Oh, you stupid boy. You stupid, *stupid* boy!" he finally said, looking at me in pure disgust. "You ruined everything! Today was supposed to be my big day. Mine! Where all the Wild would respect me and the leadership I would come to bring, but you just had to bamboozle it with your nonsense, didn't you? Flying fruits at Gideon's Rock! On the first day of my administration too! Oh, the history books won't ever forget it, and it's all thanks to YOU, Jimmy Jungles!" he said, continuing to stare down at me. But I stood in silence. Part of me wanted to say I didn't mean to, or that it wasn't even my fault, but Peister had lied to me all too long and all too well these past few months. From telling me he wanted to know if pirates were here when in fact he already knew, to convincing me to break into the Palace and spy on Greygor so he could win his nomination. Not to mention working with Hortley, who he knew was keeping the fruits away from the Wildlings. He allowed the reckless pirates to invade our lands, hurt Wildlings, steal from us, and yes, even spread the Balooza. It was *ALL* Peister's fault! Falling into Hortley's paws and doing everything he asked, all to get elected! And now he was blaming me because his celebration ceremony didn't go as well as planned? I wasn't having it. Not

after all he did. "Well, boy, what do you have to say for yourself?"

"Good."

"*Good?* Did you just say good? Do you know what you cost me today boy? Thyoor, Koswal, take him to Kyrokky, I don't want to see him ever again, do you understand? Never again!"

"Oh, are you going to lock me up? Go ahead. I've already told my friends everything you've done. Everything you've made *me* do. *Everything* you've been hiding. That's right, Greygor told me your lies, how you tricked me to break into the Palace! How you've had an alliance with Hortley the entire time. He explained everything to me! And I told my friends. We planned this together. That I was going to make it rain fruits at Gideon's Rock on your special day! And you know what? We're going to the press with it. I'm sick and tired of all your lies. It's time everyone knows *who* you are and how you *really* got elected!"

"Wh- you think anyone will believe you? I am the Pleaser!"

"I don't care. Lock me up. Come on, hurry up! My friends already know what to do anyway. And soon, everyone will know the truth!" I said, trying to control my sheer nervousness at that moment. I mean, I couldn't believe these words were coming out of my mouth. But I guess, these were the games we all must play. I just hoped he wouldn't call my bluff.

I was walking away, following the Venali as they guided me out, breathing heavily and feeling very, very nervous.

"WAIT! Bring him back here!" Peister said in a defeated tone before looking me dead in the eyes. "What do you want?" he asked. A little shock shook my whole body. "Come on boy, don't get so silent now! What is it you want? To keep this all a secret? Huh? And don't be ridiculous either, I won't have it!" he said sternly. A number of ideas were running in my mind. Right now, I could have anything in the whole Wazoo. So I thought for a few moments, rubbing my chin as I smirked. Peister stood up straight and gulped as he waited to hear me speak.

I walked out perfectly free that day, and best yet, Peister gave into the favor I requested. It was an immaculate day with even better days yet to come. The whole Wazoo was Balooza free. Wildlings were less angry and had almost completely forgotten about the pirates, the tension of the election, and their animosity towards each other. But above all else, more and more fruits were blooming each day and being given away to all the Wild, though I'm not sure how this would interfere with Hortley's trade route plan or if he was going to stir up another idea. Regardless though, things were looking up. These were times I had longed for and now they were finally here. Here for us all.

A few weeks had passed since the flying fruit on Gideon's Rock incident took place. School at Cross Rivers had finally resumed. The halls were pristine, the fields shining with green grass, and even the forest had a flurry of trees. Not a single piece of ash was in sight as my fellow Wildling students were all in awe at the restored school. It was almost as if the fire never really happened in the first place. But regardless, school continued on as usual. Class, lessons, and the bell in between with the same expectations of homework and tests as before. It was all as it used to be, well for the most part. There were a *few* changes, and let's just say, I found a great way to enjoy our return to Cross Rivers.

"AMELIA ATTAWAY, PLEASE REPORT TO THE PRINCIPAL'S OFFICE," Nurse Habada said over the intercom. She got up in surprise, as everyone stared and 'ooed' at her as she walked out the classroom door. She had always been a good student, and surely this was the last thing she ever expected.

I know Amelia. She was shaking all throughout the hallway, thinking about everything she could have done to break the rules, or, more likely, what I could have even done to get her in trouble. And believe me, there was plenty to go on. She must have been anxious, wondering how she let herself be friends with a delinquent like me for so long, and probably convinced herself never to talk to me again in that short walk to the principal's office. "Damien? Sal? What are you guys doing here? I thought only Amelia was called!" Riley said as she flew in.

"No, we got notes from an attendant to come down here," Sal said, scratching his head.

"Amelia, Amelia. I-I got this note to come to the principal's office. Am I in trouble? I don't even know what I did! Are we going to get detention? I don't want to make your dad mad," Barry said as he sobbed.

"Hey, it's okay, we'll be fine," Amelia said, carrying him. But she was shaking her head, already knowing this was my fault.

"Barry, you're here too? Oh, this *has* to be Jimmy's fault. It has his name written all over it. But what did he even do this time?" Riley wondered. They all walked up to the nurse, who was sitting at her desk typing away.

"Yes, Mrs. Habada?" Amelia asked.

"Ah, yes, the principal wanted to talk to you all about something you all did. I'm not sure what exactly, but he said you could go in now." My friends nervously opened the door and sat down on the cushiony seats as a tall leather chair had been turned around facing away from them.

"You five have quite some explaining to do. I am beginning to lose my patience," said the principal as he faced away from my friends.

"Mr. Fangoria, I-I'm so sorry."

"Well, you definitely should be!" I said as I turned the swivel chair around to face them.

"J-JIMMY?" Amelia blurted out, completely stunned.

"WHAT IN THE HELOKS ARE YOU DOING IN THE PRINCIPAL'S CHAIR? YOU'RE GOING TO GET EXPELLED IF HE SEES YOU LIKE THAT! GET OVER HERE, NOW!" Riley yelled. But I only laughed as I continued to suck on the lollipop in my mouth.

"You *are* talking to the principal!" I said as I leaned back in my chair and placed both my feet on Mr. Fangoria's desk.

"Wh- how are you principal, Jimmy? That makes no sense!" Damien asked, more confused than ever.

"Well let's just say I know a lot of things, a lot of things Peister Precarious wouldn't want the press to find out about."

"So you're principal now? What about Mr. Fangoria?"

"Oh, he's still here. I told him to finish photocopying worksheets for the elementary grades. Hila! Could you come in here, please?"

"Yes, Principal Jungles?" she said sweetly as my friends dropped their jaws.

"Could you check and see if Ferrallis has finished his work? I really need him to clean the cafeteria. I gave the janitors the day off today," I said with a smile. She nodded her head and quickly closed the door.

"Wh- I don't understand, how are you able to do all this? Riley blurted out. So, I told all my friends about the little deal I made with Peister. I'd stay quiet, and in return, he'd make me principal of Cross Rivers indefinitely.

"*Jimmy*, you can't do that to Mr. Fangoria!" Amelia said.

"Says who? Amelia, you know he's been trying to expel me for years now. I mean, look at what he did to me after I won that award. If he thinks he can just be angry and take it all out on me, well he can guess again! Besides, he was making everybody miserable, and I, for one, won't stand for it! Big changes are about to happen now that I'm in charge."

"Wow, Jimmy, you really stood up to them all! I love it! What've you got planned next? Oh, oh, can we play more games in class? A-and could you make sure we have no more tests?" Sal asked eagerly.

"WHAT! No more tests? What's even the point of coming to school then?" Damien asked angrily.

"You're right, we should just cancel school altogether!" Sal jumped up saying. "C'mon Jimmy, what do you say?"

"What! You can't cancel school, we all need to learn, you know! Jimmy, you're not seriously considering this are you?" Amelia asked anxiously.

"Eh, I'll think about it," I said as I jumped up from my seat and opened the window curtains to the backyard of the school. "Now take a look at this!" I showe my friends the large piles of fruits being poured onto by large trucks.

"What! How did you do this Jimmy? Where did you get all those fruits?" Riley asked.

"I didn't. I told Peister I wanted Hortley to deliver them from his company for all Cross Rivers students so we can enjoy them every day. Not sure how the fat pig felt about that one though, but that's what he gets for playing me as long as he did," I said, right before opening a drawer from the desk. It was filled with babaloos, and I threw one at each of my friends, who were each instantly delighted.

"Attention teachers, this is your school principal speaking. Please excuse all students from classes today so they may go out to the school yard and enjoy the freshly picked fruit donated to us by the *very* generous Wazoo Trading Company. We will be having recess for the rest of the day today as well. Thank you," I said, pressing a button and speaking into the microphone on the desk. There was a sudden burst of cheering and rumbling noise from the floors of the school as students ran out of class and out into the fields, every Wildling amazed at the sight before they stuffed their faces with pure joy. "Hurry up, before they're all gone!" I said to my friends as they all got up and ran out.

"Coming, Jimmy?" Amelia asked.

"Yeah, I'll be there in a second," I said as I continued to eat a babaloo and smiled as I looked out from the office window to the hundreds of students happily eating away. As I looked around, it was hard to believe we had been through any hard times at all. To me, it was just another day at the Wazoo. Another day in paradise.

The Breakaway Bandits

Wyatt Picker,
Head Rebel of the Breakaway Bandits

It's not very often you befriend a sassy and infamous thief, especially while he is in the middle of robbing your house. Anyone would tell you how angry they feel being bossed around by him all the time. But it seems to be the only way he knows how to talk to people. Still though, something tells me he means well. I can tell you all those schemes he plans aren't only for himself. In fact, he prides himself on sharing his earnings and loot from the rich with all the local poor. But deep down, he's never satisfied, as if he was always searching for something more than treasure and wealth. I only wish I knew what it was.

Winsley Shivers,
Savvyman of the Breakaway Bandits

Would probably not have even made it with the crew had he not somehow learned the incredible skill of reading and writing. A shy, frail fellow who is constantly shaking regardless of who he's talking with. It's a, real wonder where he'd end up if the bandits hadn't taken him in.

Calic the Knobhead,
Carrier of the
Breakaway Bandits

A simpleton goon who can barely put a sentence together. He follows orders and helps around whenever he can and, it also doesn't hurt that he can pick up a few barrels all by himself. Probably twice the age of Wyatt, but he only ever seems to be concerned about where he'll find his next meal.

Kenny Pickets,
Cabin boy of the
Breakaway Bandits

A no-good kid who's got a clever way of persuading almost everybody to do what he wants. But who really knows what his true intentions are? Known all around for his many plots and riots, it's no surprise he found himself with the bandits this young. I can say he's honest and truthful to any cause worth fighting for. Still, though, Wyatt's got a careful eye on him, and I don't blame him one bit.

Check out jimmyjungles.com
Our adventures have only begun!

www.ingramcontent.com/pod-product-compliance
Lightning Source LLC
Chambersburg PA
CBHW070601300726
48975CB00006B/1667